HONOR
THE
DEAD

T0033431

"A literary joyride."

—Louise Penny, *New York Times* bestselling
author of the *Chief Inspector Gamache* novels

"This is a gripping mystery novel. Cate Spencer, the lead character, is
a flawed individual who has to convince law-enforcement profession-
als as well as herself that she can bring down a murderer and solve
a crime. Everyone is either against her or lies to her, but just when
she sees no hope, she goes for one more try. I wanted to applaud and
fist-pump at the end."

—Ray Anderson,
author of the AWOL Thriller series

"Disgraced coroner Dr. Cate Spencer finds herself in a small town
divided by a longtime feud between two rival families over an outlaw's lost gold. When a double homicide occurs, Cate, unable to stand
by in the face of incompetence, rolls up her shirt sleeves and digs
in to solve the crimes. In the course of her investigation, Cate must
confront a town wracked with violence, crack sharp shooters, and
shocking revelations about her own family history. *Honor the Dead* is
a thrilling murder mystery that masterfully explores life's hopes and
disappointments, delving deep within the characters and keeping you
guessing until the end. Highly recommended!"

—Daco S. Auffenorde,
Award-winning author of *Cover Your Tracks*

"*Honor the Dead* is classic Amy Tector—an intriguing mystery peppered with fascinating historical tidbits and infused with a good dose of humor. Her cast of characters never disappoints and everyone is a suspect until the very last page. This book is too fun to put down. Don't be surprised if you finish it in one sitting."

—Kim Hooper, author of
People Who Knew Me and *No Hiding in Boise*

"Picking up from her previous book, *Speak For The Dead*, coroner Cate Spencer is still reeling from her brother's mysterious death. She is suspended from work, now having to pass the time as a country doctor in Quebec's Eastern Townships, an idyllic country setting masterfully obscuring many secrets and a sordid history. There, she can't help herself as she unofficially investigates a local murder. Layers of intrigue are uncovered with possible links to a legendary outlaw's lost gold, the drug trade, or an over-the-top family feud. However, it is Cate's hard-boiled and wasteland kind of life you will embrace. She exudes levels of empathy with crime victims which exacts a heavy toll on her. We care deeply for her and cheer her prowess as she unravels a textured plot of murder, tragedy and power. This is Tector's edgiest, grittiest and smartest work to date. One can't help but see hints of Wallander and V.I. Warshawski and wonder when this comes on the big screen."

—Wayne Ng,
author of *The Family Code*

"The heart of any truly fine mystery is the mystery at the heart of the detective. This new Dr. Cate Spencer story has to do with the world of hatred and lies behind the picturesque landscape of the Eastern Townships, but in the final analysis, it reveals more about Dr. Spencer herself than the world around her. Get your hands on this haunting tale and make friends with the prickly, determined Cate. By the end, you will be cheering for her with every breath!"

—Terry Roberts, author of
My Mistress' Eyes Are Raven Black and *The Sky Club*

HONOR
THE
DEAD

ALSO BY AMY TECTOR

The Honeybee Emeralds

THE DOMINION ARCHIVES MYSTERIES:

The Foulest Things
Speak for the Dead

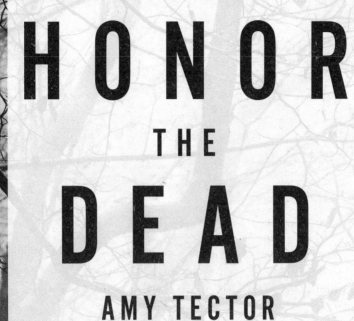

HONOR
THE
DEAD

AMY TECTOR

A DOMINION ARCHIVES MYSTERY

KEYLIGHT
BOOKS

KEYLIGHT BOOKS

AN IMPRINT OF TURNER PUBLISHING COMPANY

Nashville, Tennessee

www.turnerpublishing.com

Honor the Dead

This is a work of fiction. All the characters and events portrayed in this book are either products of the author's imagination or are used fictitiously.

Cover design by Emily Mahon

Book design by William Ruoto

Library of Congress Cataloging-in-Publication Data
Names: Tector, Amy, author.
Title: Honor the dead / Amy Tector.
Description: Nashville, Tennessee : Keylight Books, [2024] |
    Series: A Dominion Archives mystery ; [book 3]
Identifiers: LCCN 2022060432 (print) | LCCN 2022060433 (ebook) |
    ISBN 9781684428892 (hardcover) | ISBN 9781684428908 (paperback) |
    ISBN 9781684428915 (epub)
Subjects: LCGFT: Detective and mystery fiction. | Novels.
Classification: LCC PR9199.4.T393 H67 2024 (print) |
    LCC PR9199.4.T393 (ebook) | DDC 813/.6—dc23/eng/20230105
LC record available at https://lccn.loc.gov/2022060432
LC ebook record available at https://lccn.loc.gov/2022060433

Printed in the United States of America

FOR MY FATHER, Dr. David Tector—he loved ABBA, the Eastern Townships, fiddleheads, and, most of all, his family.

HONOR
THE
DEAD

MONDAY, AUGUST 10
KINSHASA, DEMOCRATIC REPUBLIC OF THE CONGO

ADJUSTING THE STRAP OF HER DRESS SO IT DIDN'T RUB DIRECTLY ON her sunburned shoulder, Cate Spencer took another sip of her merlot. With an effort, she returned her focus to her companion. Like many of the male expats she'd met in the Democratic Republic of the Congo, he wore a white linen suit with a bow tie. It must fit their conception of colonial glamour—*Out of Africa* for foreign affairs nerds.

"My wife doesn't think we need a pool boy, but what she fails to understand is that as expats, our large staff contributes to the economy. A pool boy is a moral imperative."

Politeness dictated that Cate pay attention, but she'd already asked this Canadian official about her brother, and he'd told her nothing new about Jason's death.

The terrace was perfumed by the surrounding gardenia shrubs, their white flowers emitting a spicy, sweet aroma on the twilight air. A flock of gray parrots landed in a nearby palm tree, calling to one another as they settled in to roost for the night. Uniformed embassy staff moved about, lighting tiki torches. By the pool, a group of Congolese musicians in traditional dress started playing a fast-moving rumba. Cate was underdressed for the swanky event, wearing the one thin sundress she'd thrown into her luggage as she hastily packed for Kinshasa. She wasn't bothered by her drab appearance, however; she had come to the Congo for facts, not fashion.

Her companion placed a sweaty hand on her arm. "My apologies, but I think they're serving crab cakes by the pool." He hurried off.

Cate finished her wine with a quick swallow. She scanned the party, looking for the final person on her list: Dr. Juanita Wayland, the other physician on her brother's mission in eastern Congo. She recognized the slim woman with a head of braids from her Instagram account and hurried over to introduce herself.

After exchanging pleasantries, Juanita touched her hand. "I'm so sorry about Jason. It's a devastating loss for us, but more so for you."

"Thank you."

"Your brother was wonderful, so committed. One of the best doctors I ever worked with." Juanita spoke in a light British accent. "I mean, you meet a lot of people here who take on a Medical Aid International mission for their ego, but not Jason."

Cate felt that familiar mixture of pride and frustration she'd experienced throughout this trip. Everyone loved Jason and praised his work ethic. They told her that he was special and a hero. She wanted to snap in response that *of course* he was special, but he was most special to her. These people would go on living their lives, doing their jobs, and thinking fondly of Jason, but Cate had lost her best, and possibly only, friend.

She cleared her throat and gave her well-practiced spiel about why she was in the Congo. She explained that for their peace of mind, she and her father wanted more details about how Jason had died. She didn't mention that she had been attacked and that her assailant had warned her off an investigation. The only clue to the attacker's identity was a Congolese bumper sticker on his car. That might point to a conspiracy to cover up something about Jason's death.

After ten days of meeting with officials, reading every report and newspaper account of the accident, and talking to investigators and forensics specialists, she now accepted that his passing was an accident. A horrible, shitty accident. While she was incredibly relieved to discover her brother hadn't been murdered, the question of why she'd been attacked remained unanswered.

Juanita dabbed a tear from her eye. "The plane crash was a shock, but not surprising, you know? I mean, the Democratic Republic of the Congo has the highest number of fatal civilian aircraft accidents in all of Africa."

Cate had been told that statistic many, many times during her stay in the DRC. As a coroner, she was charged with investigating and analyzing deaths and contributing to the gathering of similar statistics back in Ottawa. She realized now what poor comfort they were to the grieving. Every time someone told her that factoid, she wanted to scream, *"Then why did you let him get on a plane?"*

"Do you have any further information about the crash?" Cate didn't think Juanita would have much to add, but she had to investigate every avenue before tomorrow's flight home.

"Your brother was a literal saint," Juanita said, frustrating Cate by not answering her question immediately. "Most physicians take their leave and lie on a beach for two weeks or go on a gorilla safari. Not Jason. He used his vacation to volunteer with another charity—Rescue the Children. They're a major adoption agency in central Congo. He was flying from there when his plane crashed."

"I didn't know he was doing that." Cate couldn't keep the surprise from her voice. She'd assumed he was on the plane as part of his Medical Aid work. This was the first she'd heard of an orphanage.

Juanita shrugged. "That's Jason. He probably didn't want to toot his own horn."

Her brother was modest, but it was odd that he hadn't spoken of this trip. An orphanage seemed out of character. As far as she knew, Jason didn't even like kids. Cate bit her lip. She wanted to question the staff at the orphanage, but it would mean delaying her return to Ottawa. That wasn't possible. Two days from now she had a meeting with her boss—the acting regional chief supervising coroner for Eastern Ontario, Dr. Sylvester "Call Me Sly" Williams—to convince him to reinstate her. If she missed that meeting, her career was toast.

"It kind of comforts me, you know?" Juanita said.

"What does?"

"How Jason died."

Cate crossed her arms. "Nothing can make up for the fact that he's gone."

Juanita touched her arm. "No, of course not. That was clumsy. I meant he was a good man, and he died doing good things. Maybe I'm naive, but I do find solace in that."

Cate didn't tell Juanita that she would take a cowardly, unheroic alive Jason any day over this sainted dead one. Instead, they chatted a little longer before saying good night.

While waiting for her hired car to pick her up and take her to her guest house, she considered what Juanita had said. Cate came to the Congo looking for proof that something malevolent had harmed her brother. Instead, she found further evidence of Jason's sterling character. Juanita was right—there was comfort in that. The trip answered her questions and assuaged her doubts. She needed to accept that Jason was gone and let it go. In that moment, with the gardenia-tinged breeze cooling her face and the bright stars of an African sky shining above her, she honestly believed she could do just that.

CHAPTER 1

PEKEDA TOWNSHIP, QUÉBEC

CATE WAS IRRITATED BY THE SOFT PLUSHNESS OF THE WICKER LOVESEAT and wanted to silence the soothing chirp of the crickets. A russet leaf from a nearby maple floated to the ground, its slow descent further annoying her. She shifted in her seat and took a glug of wine. She missed the city's noise and distractions. The stillness offered too much room for reflection.

A low rumble interrupted her thoughts. As if summoned by her own dissatisfaction, a police car roared past the farmhouse, lights flashing. Crows startled from the trees, and the vehicle kicked up great swirls of dust along the dirt road. Cate jumped from her chair, spilling the last of her wine, and hurried to the edge of the porch in time to see the car skid through the gravel, barely slowing at the sharp curve by the big oak tree. It disappeared around the bend.

The MacGregor farm was the only house down that way. After that, Pelletier Road petered out into a dirt track leading to the Pekeda River. After staring in the direction of the car's path for a moment or two, Cate lit a cigarette. Whatever was happening at the farm was none of her business.

The dust settled in the late afternoon sun, and the siren faded. The crickets returned, and with them the peaceful, lazy vibe, but Cate wasn't fooled. Something was afoot. In the month she'd spent in Québec's sleepy Pekeda Township she'd never seen so much as a jaywalker, let alone heard a police siren. What was going on at MacGregor's?

To answer her question, a bright-yellow ambulance, its siren screaming through the afternoon quiet, now bellowed past, followed by a second cop car. She stubbed out her cigarette. The ambulance changed the equation. As a physician, she could be helpful at the scene. Thankfully, that merlot was only her first of the evening. She hurried to the living room, double-checking that her medical bag held the necessities for an emergency. Not bothering to lock the front door, she rushed down the creaky porch steps to her car.

The drive took a couple of minutes. The MacGregor house looked a lot like her own place: a neat wood-frame home with a wraparound porch. It even had the same hydrangea bushes blossoming pinky-white in the late September sun. Where it differed was the modern equipment shed behind the house and the rows and rows of apple trees stretching around it.

Cate parked beside the ambulance and hurried to the porch. A peek through the screen door told her the living room was empty. "Hello," she called. No answer. They weren't in the house.

She glanced around. Where had everyone gone? They could be in the shed, the fields leading to the river, or the orchards. Her Airbnb host had told her that Thomas MacGregor owned a huge swath of land, extending from her rental all the way to the river. A good portion of it was given over to apple orchards. Hundreds of mature fruit trees spread up the hill, drifting back toward her house; more rows of trees sloped downhill, almost to the water.

She jogged around the side yard noting that this house had the same view as hers: soft rolling hills ablaze with the golds and reds of an Eastern Townships autumn. It was getting close to five p.m. and the sun was getting low, but it was still warm. A rosy light suffused the surroundings.

Through the apple trees, Cate spotted the yellow flash of a medic's coat. She hurried toward it and was soon surrounded by the tall, gnarled trees, the blue sky obscured by the overhanging branches laden with bright-crimson fruit. A mellow, sweet smell filled the air: ripe apples. She stepped on a fallen fruit. The sensation was unsettling. The apple was still firm, and her ankle rolled, but at the same time she sank toward the ground, feeling the fruit's flesh break under her weight.

She strode toward a group of people: paramedics, two police officers, and a tall, older man with a mane of silver hair and an enormous beard in a reflective jacket. This was Thomas MacGregor. Over the past month, he'd often thundered past her place in his big pickup. They'd waved at one another but nothing more. Apparently, small-town friendliness didn't extend to people renting an Airbnb. Or maybe MacGregor was simply busy with the apple harvest. He ran a U-Pick through part of his orchard, and on weekends vehicles filled with families streamed past her split-rail fence en route to harvest apples and make Instagram memories.

The group stood over a man lying on the ground. The fact that the medics were standing rather than administering first aid told Cate everything she needed to know. No urgency. Nothing more to be done.

Her step quickened and her posture straightened. There was a dead body here, and this was her area of expertise. It was what she'd been missing while tending to the prosaic medical needs of the population of Pekeda Township. Filling a prescription or following a pregnancy was simply not as fulfilling as analyzing a death scene, searching for answers, and comforting families.

The policewoman spotted her first. "Halte," she said in French and stomped toward Cate. She was in her midtwenties, short, with curly hair and a prominent nose. She crossed her arms. "T'es qui, toi?"

Cate noted the belligerent use of the "tu" rather than the more polite "vous" form. "I'm a neighbor," she replied, speaking English in a calm voice. "I'm staying down the road, at the Tanguy place."

The officer glowered, and Cate wondered if she'd have to use French to be understood. Most people were bilingual out this way. "Je suis médecin," she said, before switching back to English. "I thought I could help."

"It's OK, Constable St. Onge." MacGregor stepped forward. Speaking English, his voice was deep and authoritative. "She's my neighbor all right." He inclined his head back toward the Airbnb, which was hidden from view by the apple trees. "The new doctor."

The other cop sauntered over. He was a bit older than his partner, with dirty-blond hair and a muscular physique. His moustache was so bushy Cate wasn't certain whether it was ironic. "Oh, she's the doc working at Canterbury." She didn't detect a French accent.

St. Onge looked dubious. "I did not hear of this." She shifted to deny Cate a view of the body.

"That's because you're not from around here," the male cop said. "Not plugged in to the gossip."

"You mean I don't still live with my mother," St. Onge countered.

The other police officer ignored her. "The regular doctor at Canterbury is on maternity leave, and those private-school kids can't wipe their noses without a personal medic."

Cate stiffened at the jibe. "Yes, the clinic is located at the Canterbury Day and Boarding School, but we serve every community member in Pekeda Township and follow all provincial guidelines." This was the line that Anya Patel, Canterbury's headmistress, gave her to say when this issue inevitably arose.

The officer rolled his eyes, and even MacGregor looked dubious. Cate wasn't surprised. The locals were annoyed at the closure of the old Manasoka Village Clinic and the consolidation of medical services on the grounds of one of Canada's most elite private schools. If they wanted to see a doctor in Manasoka, the townshippers had to humble themselves in Canterbury's hallowed halls, a school whose tuition was more than most people's annual income. Now that she was no longer a student at Canterbury, Cate could understand the locals' annoyance. "I'm Dr. Cate Spencer."

The male officer grunted, "Constable Douglass."

Her neighbor stepped forward. "I'm Thomas MacGregor. Should have said 'good day' when you moved in. Apologies."

"Not at all."

"Don't think we'll need your help, Doc," Douglass said with a little laugh. "This guy is as dead as a doornail."

Cate flinched. Over the years she had learned to honor the dead and to respect those who did the same.

One of the medics, a redhead with a French accent, agreed with Douglass. "Oui, there is no question. He is dead. No vitals, no pulse."

They opened a space around the body, and Cate approached the victim. He was about her age—late thirties. He wore jeans, a heavy plaid flannel shirt, and big work boots: the locals' uniform. He had salt-and-pepper hair and a couple of days' worth of stubble on his chin. A baseball hat with "Lachance Feed" written on the front lay on the ground nearby. His right eye was open, a piercing blue. The other was a bloody, pulpy mess. Despite the shocking sight, Cate noted how handsome he was, with high cheekbones and a strong jawline. She quickly surveyed his body but could see no other injury.

A strange metal instrument lay by his side. "What's that?"

"Looks like a metal detector," Douglass replied.

It was long, like a Weedwacker, but had a fancy digital reader and a white, space-age-looking ergonomic handle. She turned her attention to the body. Aside from the gruesome eye injury, there were no other visible signs of trauma. She felt the zing of curiosity she always got at the start of a new case. "Most likely a gunshot wound." She had learned to never assume cause until the autopsy results came back. "From here it looks like it went directly into the brain via his left eye." She wondered if the bullet exited or if it was still lodged in place. She turned to the friendlier Constable Douglass. "May I examine him?"

He hesitated. "Don't think so, Doc. We've called this into the provincial police force. The Sûreté du Québec will send out their forensics team. No one should touch anything until they get here and the coroner does his thing."

"I am a coroner," Cate argued. "I'm certified in Ontario. This is what I do." Well, it was what she did and would hopefully be doing again in two months, three weeks, and four days—not that she was counting.

Douglass wavered, but St. Onge stepped forward. "Non. Absoluement impossible. You do not have jurisdiction in Québec. We must follow the appropriate procedure."

Cate gritted her teeth, forcing herself to nod agreeably. She understood St. Onge's stance, even if it was frustrating.

"In any case, I don't think there will be too much question about cause of death." Douglass squatted down beside the body with an enviable effortlessness. Without touching the corpse, he pointed to the victim. "As Bon Jovi would say, 'Shot through the head and you're to blame.'"

Cate resisted the urge to tell him that was the wrong lyric.

Douglass spat on the ground. "No doubt," he said, unable to keep the excitement from his voice. "This is a good old-fashioned murder."

CHAPTER 2

"HOW CAN YOU BE SURE IT'S MURDER?" CATE KNEW THAT THINGS WORKED differently in the country, but it was rash to leap to such a conclusion. Firearms were the most common choice for male suicide, and though she didn't see a gun, the police might have already bagged it. A shot through the eye rather than the mouth was uncommon, but not impossible. What's more, people frequently killed themselves outdoors to minimize the burden of cleanup on those who discovered their bodies. Cate was often struck by the thoughtfulness of the suicidal for the people they left behind. Many put down towels to catch the mess, checked into hotels to prevent family from stumbling upon them, or wrote notes detailing everything from heartfelt goodbyes to their cat's feeding schedule. If only these desperate people could find the same care and attention for themselves that they lavished on others.

St. Onge pointed to the body. A small amount of blood was pooled on the grass, which was still green despite the lateness of the season. "Not suicide," she said. "One gunshot wound, straight to the brain. No weapon present on the scene."

"There's also the metal detector," Douglass chimed in. "People who are treasure hunting aren't there to kill themselves."

"Hunting accident?" Cate didn't think it was likely, but she wanted to remind the cops to consider all possibilities.

St. Onge spoke dismissively. "Look at the precision. You don't hit the bull's-eye by mistake. Besides, if this was an accident, where's the killer?"

"People panic," Cate argued. "They run when they shouldn't."

St. Onge shook her head in a decisive way that annoyed Cate.

"You've attended a lot of homicides then?"

St. Onge jutted out her chin. "This is my first."

"Mine too," Douglass said cheerfully. "Should be quite interesting."

They'd said that provincial authorities were on their way, which was a relief. The Sûreté du Québec would be more experienced. Still, it was obvious her skills could be useful. She looked at the body in frustration. Without being able to examine him, it was difficult to glean a lot of information. "When was the deceased discovered?"

"You're not investiga—" St. Onge began, but MacGregor jumped in with an answer.

"I heard the shot at four o'clock. It took me a couple of minutes to get out here, and I found him like that."

Cate nodded her thanks and clocked St. Onge's glower. She wanted to learn more, to contribute her expertise, but to do that she'd need to bring the police onside. Unfortunately, she wasn't very good at playing nice, especially with cops. "I've worked a lot of murders."

St. Onge crossed her arms.

Cate considered the gun deaths she'd attended. They were usually much messier than this single, perfect shot. "This kind of shooting would take a lot of skill." She glanced around. "Forensics will determine how far away the killer was from the victim. They'll analyze the wound to determine range of fire and look for gunpowder residue or for further clues. That kind of information could be vital in a case like this."

St. Onge appeared unconvinced, but Douglass listened avidly.

Cate would like to look at the preliminary autopsy report when it came in. She'd also love to see the forensic analysis. The wound must have been made with small-caliber ammunition. "The bullet might be from a twenty-two."

"Yeah, I bet you're right," Douglass said. He spat in the grass again, receiving an irritated look from St. Onge, but Cate was grateful for his support.

"Who could have done this to Marc?" MacGregor asked.

"Marc?" Cate asked.

St. Onge drew in her breath, about to speak, but Douglass piped up. "That's our victim, Marc Renaud. He worked at the feedstore."

Cate stared down at his face. She would have expected such an attractive man to be on a Hollywood screen or, at the very least, using those looks to sell real estate or cars.

"All right, everyone," St. Onge said, stepping forward. "This is a murder investigation." She turned to Cate and MacGregor. "You two need to clear the scene. Return to the house and wait for us there."

Not to be outdone by his younger, shorter, female partner, Douglass deepened his voice. "Yes, that's right." He put his hand on the small of Cate's back and pointed her toward the house. She stiffened, but short of punching him in the throat she had to be moved along. He wasn't nearly as handsy with Thomas MacGregor.

"Please try to return following the exact path you took to arrive here," St. Onge said. "We will gather evidence from this whole area." Her gaze swept down to the river, up the hill, and back toward the house.

Cate didn't want to leave. So much remained to be recorded and considered. "You'll want to determine which direction Renaud came from. If this is a homicide, which I think it is, you'll need to consider how his murderer approached. Maybe they arrived together, or maybe they met one another here."

St. Onge looked reproving. "Oui, oui. All this must be determined via physical evidence. Everything, every blade of grass, every gob of spit"—and here she glared at her partner—"will need to be analyzed. All must be done thoroughly and properly."

"You're a real by-the-book young lady, aren't you?" MacGregor said.

Cate couldn't tell if his tone was admiring or dismissive, but either way, St. Onge didn't appreciate the remark. "Get moving," she said to them both, pointing back to the house.

Douglass turned to the paramedics. "You two can clear out for now. We'll leave the body where it is until the coroner and the Sûreté arrive."

The redheaded paramedic looked irritated by Douglass's bossiness, but he tilted his head to his partner, and then they ambled to their vehicle.

Cate turned away reluctantly. She'd taken an oath to speak for the dead. She owed it to Marc Renaud to ensure his case was handled competently. "What exactly is the Sûreté du Québec's role here?" she asked MacGregor as they walked away from the river. Even though Ottawa bordered the province of Québec, in her former life—her "real" life—she mostly dealt with the municipal police force for Gatineau, Ottawa's sister city, rather than the provincial authorities. Still, she knew that just as small towns in the rest of Canada relied on the Mounties, rural Québec often depended on the SQ.

"Our local force manages small-time law enforcement, but as soon as there's a homicide, the SQ steps in. They're coming out from Sherbrooke." MacGregor scratched his beard. "They'll be here in their own time."

Cate paid careful attention to her footfalls, trying to remember exactly how she had arrived. MacGregor wasn't exercising the same care. The old man walked slowly, and Cate recognized the signs of arthritis in his jerky and disjointed movements.

Given his condition, he was unlikely to be the shooter. But then, who did it? The immediate aftermath of a crime was the best moment to gather evidence. Time of death, angle of shot, type of bullet—these were all things she liked to consider when she was called to a death. That kind of analysis wasn't strictly in her purview, but she'd found the cops could be surprisingly slack, and she enjoyed the investigation. If only they'd let her review the scene properly. She quelled the desire to turn around and demand the cops let her examine the body.

"Do the locals play nice with the SQ?" Cate gestured back to the constables. They were now cordoning off a wide perimeter around the body with yellow police tape. She could catch the tone, if not the words of their exchange. They were bickering.

"Well enough," MacGregor said. "The Pekeda force doesn't have the resources to investigate a homicide, and they know it."

"Are those the only two local police for the whole area?" Pekeda Township encompassed about sixty kilometers of farmland and several villages, the largest being Manasoka.

"There are two more, based at the other end of the township near Saint-Balthasar, but they don't come around here much. The SQ gets called in on the big stuff. It's not often homicides, usually drug busts."

"It's hard to imagine drug rings out here," she remarked. As a coroner for the city of Ottawa, which encompassed some rural villages, she had attended a fair few overdoses among farm fields and dairy pastures. Still, as the wind rustled in the trees and she caught the faintest smell of earthy cow manure drifting over from the Boisvert farm, it was difficult to reconcile.

MacGregor shrugged. "Human beings are human beings. We've got the same problems as anywhere else, only with more space to hide them."

Cate's impression of the area was entirely steeped in nostalgia, remembering it through the lens of happy student days at Canterbury Day and Boarding School, which she and Jason had attended. Her memories were of laughing with friends in the dormitories and playing hide-and-seek over the school's extensive grounds. They had only rare trips off campus—excursions to local landmarks, an annual visit to a sugar bush, and an occasional jaunt to Manasoka's Main Street to stock up on candy and Archie Comics. None of that clued her in to the reality of living in the region. "Are drugs really such an issue?"

Another shrug. "We're cheek by jowl with the American border, and you can bet there's skulduggery going on at the crossings."

The old-fashioned word made Cate smile.

"Mind you, we don't need the Americans to get into mischief," MacGregor continued. "We've got a flourishing homegrown marijuana business. Last year the SQ ripped up plants from behind the Bank of Montreal. That's right on Main Street." His voice conveyed outrage.

"Marijuana is legal now," Cate pointed out. In her teens she partook in a few illegal joints behind Canterbury's lacrosse fields.

"There's still plenty of money to be made on the unlicensed stuff, and where there's money, there's crime. The Hells Angels had a clubhouse in Lennoxville for many years. That's not too far from here. There was even a gangland massacre. Look it up."

They'd reached MacGregor's front porch.

"Do you think this death might be related to illegal drugs?"

MacGregor shrugged. "Drugs, guns, hanky-panky. Our winter nights are long, and people turn to a bit of illicit rumpy-pumpy to pass the time."

It took Cate a second to work out the euphemism and realize he was talking about sex.

"Course, that fool might have been killed for the gold."

"The gold?" Cate asked, startled.

MacGregor shrugged. "There's no accounting for stupid."

"No," she said, frustrated he'd misunderstood her question. "There's gold somewhere?"

MacGregor rolled his eyes. "We've got a local story in these parts, about a folk hero."

Something stirred in Cate's mind, a memory from a long-ago history class.

"You know, a real but larger-than-life historical figure? Like Billy the Kid in the States or Ned Kelly in Australia?"

"Sure," Cate said, uncertain where this was going.

"The Eastern Townships has the Megantic Outlaw," MacGregor continued. "Got into trouble with the law, went on the lam, and there's always been a rumor he squirreled away a cache of gold while in hiding."

Cate recalled the murder scene, the metal detector lying by the corpse. "So Marc Renaud was on your land . . ."

MacGregor snorted. "That idiot was looking for the Megantic Outlaw's treasure."

CHAPTER 3

"LOST GOLD?" CATE ASKED, ABSORBING THIS ODD TWIST.

MacGregor shrugged irritably. "It's balderdash. There's no hidden gold." He gestured to a wooden chair on his porch. "Have a seat. The constables will be a while. I need a drink. Want a whisky?"

Cate hesitated. She hadn't imbibed anything stronger than wine in a while. Some would say that drinking wine wasn't exactly abstinence, but the French considered it a food group, and who was she to argue? Besides, her current alcohol consumption was nothing compared to the volume of scotch she'd been pounding back in July. It was obvious to her now that she'd been trying to drink away her problems. That failed in a spectacular fashion. "I'll have water, thanks." There were a couple of bottles of merlot back at the Airbnb if she needed something when she got home.

"Suit yourself." MacGregor disappeared into the house.

She sat in the chair, letting the late September sun warm her skin. She would be glad when October arrived. Every day that passed was another X on the calendar, bringing her closer to a return to Ottawa and reinstatement. Her fingers tapped the chair arm.

She'd been infuriated when she returned from Kinshasa to find that Sylvester Williams—the self-satisfied, self-serving, self-important ass—had recommended her removal from the Ontario College of Coroners' roster, effectively ending her career. In the paperwork, Williams claimed Cate was too emotionally fragile after her brother's death to handle the job, though he conceded she was still able to practice regular medicine.

Williams had called her into his office to tell her of the decision with an ostentatious display of faux concern. She knew exactly what

Williams was up to: With her out of the way, there would be no obstacles to his own permanent promotion to the position of chief. This was a power grab, pure and simple. In response, she'd called him a "hypocritical shit." He'd raised an eyebrow and said, "Your strong reaction only confirms my suspicion about your fragile mental state." Then he'd smiled smugly and tented his fingers together like a goddamned Bond villain. She'd told him to go fuck himself and stormed out of his office. Not her most professional hour.

Despite her jet lag, Cate had rallied all the forces she could muster to prevent her dismissal. Ottawa detective Dominic Baker wrote a forceful letter about the assistance she'd provided in his homicide investigation, and forensic pathologist Naomi Gold penned an unemotional accounting of Cate's professional expertise. Cate suspected that their support prevented the College of Coroners from immediately ending her career. Instead, it approved a further three-month suspension while it considered her fate.

Now everything hinged on the College's decision. While her medical license wasn't in jeopardy, Cate didn't like contemplating what she would do if she couldn't be a coroner. Her time at the Canterbury Clinic only confirmed that she'd lost interest in practicing family medicine. Being a coroner was the career for her, and since her divorce from Matthew, and Jason's passing, her life was now her career. Grief unexpectedly hit her, filling her eyes with tears. Knowing Jason's death was truly an accident brought her peace but not solace. Losing herself in coroner work was one way of coping. If the College revoked her license, who would she be? She twisted her hands together, wishing she'd accepted MacGregor's drink.

He returned with two glasses—a tumbler of whisky for himself and a water for her. "Sorry it smells a bit sulphury," he said, handing her the glass. "Water table is low, and the well is drying out."

Like most houses in the region, Cate's rental was also on a well, so she was familiar with the unique odor of the water. She didn't mind. It felt like she was getting an extra dose of vitamins.

MacGregor sat and gazed out over the orchards. She caught the faintest whiff of woody, smoky whisky, and she shifted in her seat.

"So Marc might have been killed for the gold?" Cate asked. This was an opportunity to do a little digging, and she wasn't going to waste it.

MacGregor snorted. "There is no gold. People have traipsed over my property for years looking for it. Stuff and nonsense. I thought Marc was smarter than that."

"Still, there might be a connection. I mean, even if the gold isn't real, if someone believed it was, maybe they killed Marc to get it before he did?"

"Speculation and conjecture. I don't truck with gossip. You want to hear the town's dirty laundry, go get your hair set at Nicole's Salon and Spa. There's a gaggle of females there who will tell you all the news."

She wasn't offended by his brusque tone. She liked knowing where she stood with a person. "This isn't gossip," she protested. "Marc Renaud's been murdered, maybe over buried treasure."

MacGregor sucked his teeth. "The gold's a nonstarter. It doesn't exist, and no one would kill over it."

She tried a new tact. "What was Marc like?"

"A nice enough fellow. Low-key. I can't think of any enemies."

"No one with a grudge? No trouble with the law? No illicit affairs?"

"Now, I didn't say that." He paused. "Marc wasn't a blameless man."

There was a long silence. Cate waited for more, but MacGregor simply stared off into the distance. Finally, she couldn't stand it any longer. "What do you mean?"

MacGregor nodded his head. "He did a bit of drinking and driving. From what I hear, he had a few entanglements with ladies whose husbands might have objected—that rumpy-pumpy I mentioned."

Despite MacGregor's opposition to gossip, he knew a fair bit about Renaud.

"There was the feud between the Montaignes and the Renauds too, of course."

"*Feud*?" Cate echoed. The word reminded her of the Hatfields and McCoys or Alexander Hamilton and Aaron Burr. Something historical and old-timey.

MacGregor shrugged. "The Montaignes used to hate the Renauds, though I think it's settled down over the years. People have mellowed."

"What was it about?" Cate asked.

"Started out between their great-grandads. Before my time. Maybe a land deal that soured. Mostly the families avoid one another."

That didn't sound like much of a reason for murder. Cate could hear St. Onge and Douglass calling to one another as they moved about the property. The smell of whisky wafted over to her again. "You must have been startled by the gunshot so close to the house."

Another long silence. Was he simply going to ignore her? Cate regretted phrasing her statement as a sentence rather than a question.

The response came in a rumble. "I'd say I was angry more than startled. It was a single shot. Loud. Too close to the damn house. It's not quite deer hunting season yet, but you can bag small game. And, of course, bear hunting started last week."

"I didn't know there were bears out here," Cate said, uneasily. A little path from her front door to the top of the crest of the hill overlooked MacGregor's orchards and the river. She'd often wander up there with a bottle of wine at dusk. It was nice to watch the sunset. Maybe that wasn't such a good idea.

"We got black bear, but not too many. Anyway, I figured there was a hunter on my property. The gunshot sounded close. I grabbed my reflective jacket and my shotgun."

"Your shotgun?" Cate hadn't noticed him with one.

"Sure. I don't much like trespassers, and I've had words with a few idiots on my land. It's handy to have a weapon when I'm warning them off. Makes them more attentive."

MacGregor's hawklike face looked grim; anybody on the receiving end of his "words" would think twice before crossing him, or his property line, again.

MacGregor took another sip of whisky. Cate stared at the glass as he brought it to his lips. For a moment her mouth seemed to fill with its harsh, cleansing flavor.

He continued. "By the time I got there, it was just Renaud lying in the orchard. Didn't see anyone else, but I move pretty slow. The killer had plenty of time to run."

Cate nodded, remembering his careful, arthritic steps.

"Cops confiscated my damn shotgun, though it's obvious I couldn't have used that to kill Renaud. His face would have been ripped open."

Cate nodded again. The bullet wound was small. Had it not hit its target so accurately, it wouldn't have been fatal. It was a deliberate assassination.

"Clinic busy?" MacGregor changed the subject abruptly.

"It's OK," Cate said cautiously. It was actually pretty quiet, which explained her boredom. "We're not brimming with patients."

"Ha," MacGregor said in satisfaction. "Shouldn't have moved it to that highfalutin school." He shook his head and frowned ferociously.

Cate was about to ask him another question about the murder when he resumed speaking.

"Back in the day, the local kids would gather round to watch the Canterbury cricket matches. Cricket!" His eyes bulged with indignation. "We'd stand outside the fence. God forbid we step on their precious grass. After the game, the players would come up and throw pennies through the fence at us. They did it to humiliate us!"

He glared at her. Cate opened her mouth but had no reply. That kind of outdated elitism was gone now, but obviously its wounds lingered. Such deep-seated resentments might explain why the clinic had so few patients.

"Getting back to the murder—"

Cate was interrupted by the arrival of an enormous pickup pulling into the yard and parking next to a squad car. Big trucks were common in the Eastern Townships, but the sign on the side of this one was arresting: a cartoon of a bald man resembling Humpty Dumpty hugging an enormous white egg. Emblazoned above the cartoon were the words: "Je Suis L'Homme aux Oeufs" and, in smaller lettering, "I Am the Egg Man."

A short, plump, bald man (who did indeed look like an egg man) tumbled down from the truck. His shirt was stained and untucked, his pants were ripped in the knee, and his boots were unlaced. He stared up at them with a bemused expression.

"Hiya, Kevin," MacGregor called. "Body's by the river."

"OK." The new arrival turned to his truck to retrieve something.

"Who's this?" Cate whispered.

"Kevin Farnham. The coroner," MacGregor muttered.

Cate stared as the man withdrew a cloth grocery bag from the truck, stenciled with the words "Scratch and Peck Chicken Feed." Presumably it contained his laptop, paperwork, measuring tape, and other necessities of the job.

"He's the coroner?" Cate asked dubiously.

"Also a notary. And, obviously, his real job is the Egg Man Eggs business."

Cate knew that, unlike in Ontario, coroners in Québec weren't required to be physicians, but egg farming seemed a little too far. What on earth could this man bring to the case?

Kevin ambled over to them, smiling hello.

"This is Cate Spencer. She's renting the Tanguys' place," MacGregor said.

Cate inclined her head and said, "I'm like you—a coroner, back in Ottawa." She was unable to resist adding, "Only I'm a medical doctor."

"Is that so?" Kevin said with interest.

"I came to see if I could help, but Québec is out of my jurisdiction."

"Oh yeah. The police are very keen on protocol." He stared down to the river. "I hear we've got a murder on our hands."

"Marc Renaud," MacGregor said.

"Marc!" Kevin's mouth fell open.

"Did you know him?" Cate asked, although the answer was obvious.

"A bit." He shook his head. "You don't expect someone your own age to be murdered, you know?"

Cate wasn't sure how age related to a homicide, but she didn't pursue it. Kevin was processing a shocking piece of news. She gave him a moment and then said, "I'd love to give you an assist on the case. Help in any way I can. I have a lot of experience with murder investigations."

Kevin focused on her, and took a moment to respond. "Thank you very much. We don't get that many criminal deaths out this way and definitely not a lot of homicide. That's why coronering is a part-time gig."

Kevin was using her profession as a verb. Cate's doubts about him increased. Marc Renaud wasn't going to be well-served by the two bumbling constables and the Egg Man. The fact that she was professionally bored and desperate for a distracting challenge was also a factor. She tried to keep her voice casual as she pressed her offer. "We could discuss the facts of the case. I could answer any questions you might have."

Kevin met her eyes, and his gaze held a surprising intelligence. He knew her suggestion was coming from more than the goodness of her heart, but he smiled genially. "That sounds like a fine suggestion. Maybe we can talk it over later."

"I was hoping to accompany you back to the death scene." Cate pushed her luck.

"Well now, I think Constable St. Onge would lay an egg if we tried that." His tone was friendly but held a hint of steel. Despite his affable personality, Kevin wasn't going to be pushed around.

"Why don't I come by your office tomorrow and we can discuss?" Cate persisted.

Kevin caught MacGregor's eye, and they both chuckled. "My office is chicken hatchery, but you're surely welcome. Check out any carton of Egg Man Eggs, you'll find my address. Now, I'd better shake a tail feather and get to that murder scene before those constables start clucking."

Cate blinked at the barrage of poultry references, returning Kevin's wave as he ambled down the hill toward the body.

CHAPTER 4

THE EGG MAN NEVER REAPPEARED, BUT ST. ONGE AND DOUGLASS EVEN-
tually arrived at the house and took Cate's statement. She lingered as
they turned to question MacGregor. She wanted to hear the man's
official account, but St. Onge waved her to her car. "You can go."

"Mr. MacGregor said time of death was four o'clock, but it will be
important to establish that with certainty," Cate was unable to resist
contributing.

"Dr. Spencer," St. Onge said sternly. "You must leave now."

Cate wasn't used to being dismissed from a death scene, but she
walked away.

"Dr. Spencer," St. Onge called as she reached the car. Cate turned,
hoping the constable had had a change of heart. "You've given us your
official statement, but the Sûreté will want to interview you."

This rookie cop was treating her like an ordinary witness rather
than the asset she was. She gave a sarcastic salute. "Ten-four, Officer."
She grimaced. That was not the way to build a relationship with the
force.

St. Onge frowned. "Expect a visit from the Sûreté this evening."

Cate drove away. Maybe she'd gotten off on the wrong foot with
St. Onge, but that junior officer didn't run the show. The Sûreté was
where the power lay. Tonight, she would have to do something she'd
never attempted in her entire career: charm a police officer.

Cate hadn't left any lights on when she'd raced off, and now the
old farmhouse looked dark and unwelcoming. Clouds obscured the
early moon. She was struck by the feeling that the house actively didn't
want her. She felt scrutinized and vulnerable. She'd experienced a fair

amount of violence this past summer, but what lingered was the un-explained; she had no idea why she'd been attacked, shoved to the ground, choked, and threatened. Her trip to the Congo hadn't solved that mystery, and sometimes she felt poisoned by the randomness of the assault.

Nights like tonight, with the image of Renaud's body seeping blood into the cold grass, her feelings of terror and powerlessness from that attack rushed back. For a moment, she could feel the grip of her assailant's hands pressing against her throat. The house was out of earshot of any neighbors. Apart from Canterbury, where she had slept in a dorm room with three fellow students, Cate had always lived in cities. Given how much she liked being alone, she had assumed she'd love the calm and peaceful countryside. She mostly did, only every now and then—when she was on edge—she was reminded that this deep in the boonies, no one could hear her scream.

She limited herself to just two glasses of wine with her dinner of stale crackers and slightly newer cheese. For dessert she poured a third but vowed to sip it slowly. She didn't want to be tipsy for her Sûreté interview. The wine didn't dull her sense of unease. A couple of times she thought she heard noises—a thump, a low moan, almost a growl. She told herself it was the neighboring barn cats who roamed far and wide.

She made her regular call to her father. His live-in nurse answered, assuring her that all was well. His cognitive decline since learning of Jason's death seemed to have stabilized, and Cate allowed herself to hope that he wouldn't degenerate too quickly. While her relationship with Dr. Marcus Spencer—celebrated thoracic surgeon, cold and crit-ical father—was not easy, she preferred the sharp, angry figure of her childhood to the confused and slow-witted man he was becoming.

By nine o'clock, there had been lots of traffic along the road, but the Sûreté still hadn't come to interview her. Cate caved and poured herself a fourth glass. The automated song of FaceTime was a welcome distraction when Rose Li called her. Hiding the wine out of frame, Cate was pleased that her friendship with this younger woman was deepening beyond their shared summer trauma.

"Hiya, Doc." Rose's tone was cheery, which was a relief. She was still struggling with the psychological repercussions of the death of her colleague in July. The younger woman had insisted on helping Cate investigate Molly's murder, unwittingly placing herself in great danger.

Cate was responsible for the violence Rose had been exposed to. "Hey. How are you?"

"I'm OK." Her tone suggested a touch of surprise at that fact. "How are *you* doing?" Rose's emphasis reminded Cate that the younger woman had seen her at her most vulnerable.

"We had some excitement out here." Briefly she relayed the events of the afternoon. At least that was one positive of not being a coroner— she wasn't bound by any strict privacy rules.

"Whoa," Rose said. "That's heavy. A murder right next door. And hidden pirate treasure."

Cate laughed. "I said gold, not a pirate's hoard."

"Were you freaked out? I mean, after this summer . . ."

"I'm fine," she snapped, hating to be seen as weak. With a small effort she modulated her tone. "It was frustrating. The local police are in over their heads."

"Let me guess, you want to jump in and help?"

"I've got a lot of expertise. I mean, their coroner is a notary, but his main business is selling eggs. It's not exactly confidence inspiring."

"I'm sure you could bring a ton to the investigation," Rose said carefully, "but should you?"

"What do you mean?"

"You're waiting for the College of Coroners' decision. You don't want to do anything to jeopardize that."

"That's the thing," Cate said, verbalizing an idea she'd been pondering since leaving MacGregor's. "If I could offer substantial assistance, it might bolster my case. The College was impressed with Detective Baker and Dr. Gold's statements. If I could get the police here to make a similar attestation, it could help my reinstatement."

"Maybe," Rose said doubtfully. "On the other hand, it might bring back a lot of trauma."

Annoyed with Rose, Cate took a sip of wine, forgetting her friend could see. She flushed and defiantly deposited the glass in frame. She didn't have anything to be ashamed of. "I think it's a good plan. I can help them solve the case." Was the Egg Man going to look at all the relevant facts? Consider all the angles? "Maybe you could lend a hand when you come down."

Rose was scheduled to visit that weekend. Cate anticipated her arrival with a mixture of trepidation and excitement. She and Rose had spent a few intense weeks together, but they had nothing in common. Rose was a twentysomething archivist with a bright future. Cate was, well . . . Cate was divorced, pushing forty, holed up in an old farmhouse, and running out the clock until she could do "real" work again. What would they have to talk about? As morbid as it was, the murder would be a good focus of conversation.

"Maybe," Rose said slowly. "It could be interesting. If things get too heavy, though, I'm going to bow out. I'm only now coming to terms with everything from this summer."

"Of course, of course."

"I have news. It's not as exciting as hidden treasure, but I've transferred out of the photo unit."

"I thought you loved working there."

"I do, but it reminds me too much of Molly. Too much of everything."

A major part of Cate's job was comforting people in their grief, but she struggled to express empathy to people she cared about. She adopted a brisk, cheerful tone. "I'm sure your visit here will do you good. A change of scene can help."

"Thanks. But running away won't make a difference."

"I didn't run away," Cate said heatedly.

"No, of course not." Rose looked horrified by Cate's reaction.

Cate softened; the younger woman's tone held no malice. Cate was consciously working on being less defensive, but it was hard to

put the armor down. Their call soon ended, and she was left to pon-
der her friend's words. Did she run away? She'd come back from the
Congo, fought to regain her coroner job, and when that failed, she'd
been at a loss. Her old school friend Anya Patel's invitation to fill in
for Canterbury Clinic's doctor was a godsend. Instead of sinking into
a depression—and sinking into the bottle—Cate fled east. It was only
now, as she settled in to this new, temporary life, that she could see
that her abrupt move was more about escaping sadness and panic than
a sensible career choice.

When the Sûreté's knock came at ten o'clock, Cate was on edge
and cranky—not the best frame of mind for a police interview. Detective Inspector Vachon, a large-chinned man with enormous bags
under his watery eyes, swept in.

Manspreading on her sagging couch, Vachon asked her question
after question about her arrival on the murder scene. He pressed her
for an accounting of her afternoon, from the moment she saw the first
cop car all the way to her return to the farmhouse.

Despite the lateness of the hour, Cate was enjoying herself. She
could discern the traces of theories in the questions that Vachon
posed: Did she think there could have been more than one assailant? Could the victim have been fleeing when he was killed? In her
opinion, how difficult was it to make such an accurate shot? She was
pleased that Vachon treated her as an equal and acknowledged her
experience.

"So now," Vachon said with his slight French accent, "I think you
have told us everything there is to say about the murder, yes?"

Cate nodded with alacrity.

Vachon smiled. "Excellent, excellent. You are a very good witness.
You give all the details without embellishment or too much emotion.
You have expertise in criminal matters, which is a rare bonus indeed.
Undoubtedly your testimony will help us bring the investigation to a
swift conclusion."

Cate sat up a little straighter and bowed her head modestly. She
wished Constables St. Onge and Douglass could hear this; they

shouldn't have been so dismissive of her. Even better if the College knew of her helpfulness.

"It sounds like you've started thinking through possible suspects." She smiled sweetly and hoped her grin wasn't too sugary. This was new territory for her. Her relationship with Ottawa's Detective Baker was a kind of chummy antagonism that was confusing and prickly.

"Oh, already I am formulating theories. I trust my instincts, you know?" He tapped his large nose. "I can smell out the liars, the thieves, the murderers."

Cate stared at him, wondering if he was serious. He gazed back with no hint of humor in his eyes. "That's a handy talent, I guess."

"Indeed, indeed. We must move quickly. I do not have many re-sources to spare. The region, alas, is experiencing an explosion of crime due to drug gang activity. Do you know that right now they have seconded Sûreté officers from elsewhere in the province to assist us?" His voice rose. "As if we in Sherbrooke are not equipped to handle our own affairs. Headquarters keeps us in the dark. It's outrageous."

Cate shifted uneasily. Vachon seemed more concerned about vio-lations of his professional pride than about solving this murder. "That does sound challenging."

He smiled. "You understand."

This was her chance. "You know, I've probably investigated a dozen murders in my career. I'd be happy to help."

"Yes, my officers tell me you were involved in a double homicide this past summer."

Cate's neck stiffened. " 'Involved' implies I was somehow respon-sible," she snapped. She consciously relaxed her shoulders and spoke in a softer tone. "As the assigned coroner, I investigated a suspicious death. I helped solve the case." Cracked it wide open when the cops were clueless. "I'd like to offer my services to you. I could consult with Kevin Farnham, give him my advice, or even meet with your officers."

Vachon tilted his head. "Such vim might be useful. Help speed everything along. Yes, I'll inform Mr. Farnham that we do not object to you assisting him. While I don't think my SQ officers require your assistance, I'll drop a word with the local police, telling them you're available for consultation. Certainly, Douglass and St. Onge could use some help." He rolled his eyes.

Even though Cate wasn't impressed with them, she was irritated by Vachon. Leaders shouldn't undercut their subordinates.

"I'm sure it will not take up too much of your time," Vachon continued. "This case is certainly quite simple. Undoubtedly, it will be a dispute over a cow or an argument about whose snowmobile is faster."

Cate was appalled by his casual dismissal of homicide. She wanted to tell him that the victim deserved justice and his family deserved answers. Instead, she forced her mouth into a smile. "Happy to help." At the very least, her involvement would ensure that someone was fighting for Marc Renaud. "If you're pleased with my contribution to the case, perhaps you could write a letter to that effect to the Ontario College of Coroners?" She spoke hurriedly to gloss over her suspension. "I'm awaiting their decision on my reinstatement to duty."

Vachon met her eyes. "We have done our research on you, Doctor, and are aware of your current status."

Cate didn't like the idea of the cops looking into her background, but she pressed forward. "The review is a mere administrative hoop, but having an endorsement from an esteemed law enforcement officer such as yourself would undoubtedly help my case." Gag.

He smiled. "Yes, I'm sure my recommendation would be immensely useful, and as I trust you will be of assistance, I will have no objection to endorsing your work with us."

Cate smiled widely. This case would get her back to her Ottawa life.

CHAPTER 5

TOO HYPED TO SLEEP AFTER VACHON'S DEPARTURE, CATE LIT A BEDTIME cigarette on the porch. It occurred to her that she hadn't checked the voice mail on her Ottawa landline since coming to the Townships. She only used it for her coroner work, so she was surprised to find two messages.

She played the first. It dated from about a month ago, around the time she came here. She was startled to hear the voice of Matthew Tomkins, her ex-husband. She had blocked his number shortly after their very brief and very disastrous summer reconciliation, but he'd obviously tracked down her landline. "Cate, you keep avoiding me and you keep ignoring me, but we need to talk. Call me."

Cate took a puff of her smoke. That was standard Matthew. Direct, accusatory. The lawyer doing the cross-examination. The next message was from a week later, also from Matthew. Her heart rate increased as she heard his deep voice. Sure, they'd had a tempestuous relationship, but only Matthew had loved her for who she truly was, warts and all. "Cate, call me. I need to talk to you. You can't shut me out like this." His voice held a tinge of anger, or was it desperation? He was upset that he couldn't control the world in exactly the way he planned. Pissed at her for not doing as he wanted. One part of her wanted to appease him, but another was pleased that he was annoyed. They'd been divorced for five years, and she wasn't the same woman he'd married.

Their summer dalliance had certainly complicated things. She took a last pull of the cigarette and tried to calm her racing heart. For good or ill, Matthew excited and energized her. She knew her reaction to him was toxic, which is why she tried to minimize all contact. She considered Rose's comment about running away. Matthew was certainly a reason to leave Ottawa, especially because part of her was still so attracted to him. She was fiercely glad she'd come to Pekeda Township.

CATE'S SLEEP WAS RESTLESS, PUNCTUATED BY HER RECURRING NIGHT-mare: A plane in the sky circled, obviously in distress. A suffocating sadness overwhelmed her as she watched its death spiral to the ground, the machine whining in pain as it fell. Instead of exploding on impact, the plane morphed into her assailant from the summer, his hands choking the air from her lungs as thick flames roared around them.

She awoke in the morning drenched in sweat and twisted in her sheets. Shaking off the bad feeling, she got ready for work.

CATE SAID GOODBYE TO THE LAST PATIENT OF HER AFTERNOON PRAC-tice. It had been a quiet day. She'd seen a woman in the third month of her third pregnancy, a farmer with an injured back, a Canterbury algebra teacher who managed type 1 diabetes, a student suffering from anxiety, and more patients with other mundane ailments. She'd spoken in either French or English, depending on her patients' preference. While her French was rusty, she found that more was coming back every day. She'd executed the work competently—asking the right questions, not rushing her patients—but the whole time her mind kept drifting back to the orchard and Marc Renaud's shattered eye.

She finished up her paperwork and took a deep breath. There were the usual disinfectant medical odors of a clinic, but underneath was the warmer aroma of her childhood: floor wax, chalk, the dusty scent of a one-hundred-year-old building. As unchallenging as she might find her clinical work, the return to Canterbury, and the uncomplicated memories it represented, was a real pleasure. Private boarding schools got a bad rap in pop culture as sites of cruelty and abuse, but for Cate and Jason, Canterbury had provided a welcome escape for motherless children with a harsh and distant father. The siblings led their own lives at school. Jason was the golden boy, who was smart, kind, and athletic; she was quieter, snarkier, and not nearly as brilliant. Still, being Jason Spencer's little sister had eased her way at the school, as it did throughout her life. Now she was on her own.

After washing her hands, she locked up the clinic, which was on the ground floor of the massive neo-Gothic main school building. She could see why the locals resented their clinic being moved out here. It was a five-minute drive from town, the parking lot was on the far side of the playing fields, and after patients completed that trek, they passed through Canterbury's enormous and frankly intimidating main doors. It wasn't exactly welcoming. The clinic's receptionist said that community use had dropped off since the relocation. Patients preferred making the nearly hour-long drive to Sherbrooke.

This didn't bother Anya. On Cate's first day, the headmistress gave her a tour of the facilities, explaining how she campaigned to have the clinic moved to school grounds, waiving any rent charges, and even underwriting part of the doctor's salary.

"This was the only viable spot in the village," Anya had explained with the same confident authority she'd exuded as a skinny twelve-year-old, newly transferred to the boarding school and getting the grand tour from Cate herself, "and Canterbury has a tradition of altruism and service."

As students they'd recited the school motto at every assembly: "Canterbury students use our talents to make the world a better place." Cate was proud of that mantra; it was part of what had driven both her and Jason to pursue medicine. Judging by the number of posters in the halls exhorting students to participate in the Gay-Straight Alliance, the fundraising drive for refugees, the youth program for Yemen, and the orphanage volunteer opportunities, Anya was vigorously pursuing the school's founding vision of service.

"Plus," Anya had said crisply as she'd continued the tour, "the clinic is a real selling point to parents. They can rest assured that Archibald Bear's nut allergy will be monitored, and that little Elspeth Grace will have all the resources necessary to manage her eczema." She'd pointed out the clinic's locked drug cabinet, the examination room, and the waiting area as she went on. "We folded the clinic's extra costs into our latest tuition increase. Never underestimate the money a wealthy parent will spend to absolve their guilt at packing their little darlings off to boarding school."

Cate had been startled by the speech. She didn't remember teenage Anya being quite so biting. Cate worried that Anya's focus on the clinic's benefits to the school was doing a disservice to the bulk of its patients: the local community. As their doctor, she had a responsibility to them. She'd bring up her concerns at her next "coffee and a catch up" with Anya. Cate didn't love these slightly awkward get-togethers; she suspected the headmistress of instigating them out of concern for Cate's "grieving process," as she'd once put it. Still, she was trying to be more open to people and their attempts at connection. The new and improved Cate.

Driving out of Canterbury's high black gates, Cate felt the exhaustion of last night's poor sleep weighing upon her. She longed for the farmhouse's feather bed and heavy quilts, but instead of turning left toward home, she drove through Manasoka village, down the main street of red brick houses and businesses, golden ash trees, and bright-orange maples. Someone stood outside Fowler's Diner having a cigarette. Farther on, she saw Constable Douglass saunter out of the columned town hall.

About five kilometers past the village, she pulled into a long driveway, passing a couple of long, low sheds before coming to a big red brick house with a wraparound porch. She parked next to a large cube van with "Je Suis L'Homme aux Oeufs / I Am the Egg Man" emblazoned on the side. It sat next to the company truck she saw last night. A third vehicle, a black Range Rover, had no Egg Man marketing marring its sleek exterior.

Cate was deciding between the sheds and the house when a side door in the nearest outbuilding opened and the Egg Man emerged. He was wearing a long apron over a work shirt and jeans. As before, his boots were unlaced and the few strands of hair still on his head stood straight up.

"Bonjour," he said amiably. "How can I help?"

"It's Cate Spencer. I was out at the MacGregor farm yesterday."

Recognition dawned in his eyes. "Of course, you're Thomas's neighbor. The clinic's new doctor."

"That's right."

"What can I do you for? A dozen, two dozen?"

It took her a moment to realize what he was talking about. "No, no. I'm not here for eggs. I can help with the case. Remember, we discussed it yesterday? I said I'd come by." She held her breath. He was within his rights to tell her he'd changed his mind. She should have been more subtle. She should have at least bought some damn eggs. She cleared her throat. "I've spoken to Detective Inspector Vachon, and he doesn't object to my assisting."

An unreadable look passed over his face, and then he broke into a huge grin. "Of course! Vachon did mention that to me. I've been a little distracted lately. Come on in and have a cup of coffee. Let's hash the whole thing out. This is my first murder in a long while, you know, and I could use a hand."

Cate smiled. "Thanks, Mr. Farnham."

"Please, call me Kevin." He led her across the gravel driveway and up the steps to the porch, which was surprisingly inviting. It held a wicker love seat sporting an intertwined rose pattern of soft pink and a few deep chairs adorned with fluffy pillows that encouraged lounging. A big bouquet of late autumn flowers graced a glass table.

"It's a bit too chilly to sit out here." Kevin ushered her inside.

Large windows brightened a huge, gleaming kitchen overlooking the pastures beyond. Pristine white marble counters wrapped around a deep sink. An enormous six-burner range occupied one corner. Standing next to it was an equally large stainless steel refrigerator.

The cupboards were also white, and the floor was an intricate black-and-white tile pattern. Cate had never been in such a dazzling kitchen before. Another bouquet of flowers, like the one on the porch, dominated the far counter.

"Grab a seat." He indicated the ten-person harvest table at the far side of the room. A glass bowl filled with bright-yellow lemons decorated its surface.

"Do you want a fancy coffee?" He gestured to the large cappuccino machine, which wouldn't have looked out of place in Starbucks.

"No, thanks. Regular is great."

"Good," Kevin said with a grin. "I get nervous running that thing. Bunny is much better at it."

"Bunny" might explain the house's surprisingly good, and expensive, taste. Looking at Kevin's round, friendly face as he stood there in his stained apron, it was less credible that he could have pulled off the lemons in the glass bowl.

He handed her a mug of coffee and brought the milk and sugar to the table.

"Thanks," she said. She inhaled the scent, immediately feeling some of the ache of her nightmare-filled night dissipate.

"So, you want to talk about the case?"

"Absolutely." Her heart rate quickened.

"Wonderful. I don't usually have someone to chat things over with. My old man used to be the coroner." Kevin looked at her earnestly. "He also ran the funeral parlor. When he retired, my sister took over the undertaking business, but she didn't want to be called out at all hours for sudden strokes and hunting accidents. I didn't either." He chuckled. "I resisted for a year or so, but the region was desperate, so I took it up."

Cate sipped her coffee. Apparently, Kevin loved to talk; she didn't need to prompt him.

"Turns out, it's not so bad. I was used to being around dead bodies. I've probably been to more funerals than anyone in Pekeda Township—apart from my sister. The coroner gig was handy in those early days. I needed the extra income because the egg business didn't really get going until about five years ago."

"What changed?" This wasn't the direction Cate intended to steer the conversation, but Kevin was an engaging speaker, and she was interested.

"Bunny came up with the idea to make us organic and free-range. That's when we took flight."

He paused, waiting for Cate's appreciative chuckle, but she missed her cue. Her tired brain was not ready for chicken jokes.

Kevin continued undaunted. "Bunny said that all those fancy city folks who come out here with their lakeside cottages and ski chalets would gobble up our organic eggs and pay double. The only thing she got wrong was the price—they'll pay triple. She's an influencer, you know? On Instagram."

"Really," Cate said, another piece of the puzzle slotting into place.

"Yeah, she's got over 128,000 followers. We get free stuff some-times." He pointed to an enormous box of dog treats on the floor under the table. "She posted a bunch of photos with a neighbor's pup-pies, and some chemical-free organic dog food company in Seattle sent her this whole crate. We don't even like dogs—they can harass the chickens." He shook his head. "She's amazing."

"So, about the case." Cate decided it was time to get down to business.

"Oh yeah." Kevin sipped the coffee, making the faintest slurping sound that was the more off-putting for being so quiet.

"Cause of death is awful straightforward. Gunshot wound to the eye."

CHAPTER 6

CATE WAS UNSURPRISED AT THE NEWS OF MARC'S CAUSE OF DEATH. Still, it was good to confirm the method. "Has the type of weapon been ascertained?"

"Not my bailiwick," Kevin said. "The folks at the Sherbrooke lab will figure that out."

Cate was annoyed by his readiness to shrug off any responsibility, but reminded herself that even in Ottawa she relied on forensic analysis and pathologist examinations to confirm the facts of the death. Still, she'd studied enough gunshot wounds to make educated guesses. She pushed Kevin a little further. "Presumably the killer would need something sophisticated for that level of accuracy. A high-tech gun, or at least one with an excellent scope to make a kill shot. That should be simple enough to trace."

"Maybe," Kevin said, sipping his coffee and adding another scoop of sugar. "But maybe not." He paused.

Cate wanted to bark at him to spit out his idea but reminded herself that she was here on Kevin's terms. She smiled encouragingly. "What do you mean?"

"We're not far from the border with the United States of America. They've got a fair few weapons down that way. That makes it pretty easy to get one."

As a student, Cate had never really considered Pekeda Township's border with Vermont. Few of her classmates were from the States, and the American drinking age was twenty-one whereas Québec's was eighteen, basically removing the entire country from her teenage sphere of interest.

"You're saying there are gun smugglers?" MacGregor had mentioned a surprising level of criminal activity occurring in these bucolic hills.

"That or if you wanted a gun, say a specific type they don't sell in Canada, you could nip across the border and buy one."

"Are they allowed to sell guns to Canadians?"

Kevin shrugged, a deliberate movement that irritated Cate with its slowness. "Depends on the state and their laws. You've got Vermont of course, but also New Hampshire, New York, Maine, and even Massachusetts all within a few hours' drive. Worst case, you get a friend or a relative in the US to buy it for you and then smuggle it home."

"Isn't that risky?"

"Pekeda Township is a border community. All the locals have friends or relatives who live across the line. We are back and forth every week. I get my gas in the States because it's cheaper. My cousin in St. Albans comes across every month to visit our grandmother and stock up on Cadbury's chocolate."

Cate was not interested in Kevin's cousin or his grandmother, but she painted an attentive look on her face as he continued.

"Most of the time the guards on both sides know you and you get a nod and a wave. It would be easy as pie to smuggle a gun across."

Cate bit her lip. Tracing the weapon was an important line of inquiry in a murder investigation. The police were going to have a hard time with this one. Vachon's presumption of an open-and-shut case might not be warranted.

"We've been smuggling for centuries," Kevin continued. "You can head over to the Pekeda Museum on Main Street and see a rocking chair with a false bottom they used to sneak tobacco in. They'd set old granny up in the chair and pull her across in a horse-drawn cart, with the customs fellows never looking at her twice."

She was anxious to get back to the topic at hand. "Did the forensic pathologist have anything to say about the wound?"

"It was caused by a .22-caliber bullet, which is lodged in the skull. The doctor will remove it and complete the autopsy."

Cate leaned back, pleased with herself. She wasn't a ballistics expert, but her guess had been on the money. "Any idea how close the killer was standing to get the shot?"

Kevin shrugged. "I don't know. The forensic specialists with the police will be able to tell us after their analysis."

"It would depend on the skill level of the shooter," Cate said, thinking out loud. "That will be significant in terms of who our killer is."

Keith's eyes widened. "I hadn't thought about that. It likely requires a sophisticated weapon and a highly, highly skilled marksman. I can see I've got to put my thinking cap on for this case."

Cate appreciated Kevin's willingness to admit his limitations. "A murder demands a different approach. You need to document thoroughly and analyze all the angles. I find it helpful to cast as wide a net as possible to make sure I don't miss anything."

"A wide net," Kevin repeated. "I like that."

Cate sipped her coffee. "All right, who possessed the skill to make the shot?"

"Hunting's big around here. The Duponts out near Saint-Evodus are a family of skilled hunters. Terry Larkin is also excellent. Then there's Guy Montaigne."

Cate recalled what MacGregor said about the Montaigne–Renaud feud. "Tell me about him."

"Guy is a crack shot, no doubt. Probably one of the best in the township."

"And there's some kind of feud between his family and Renaud's?"

Kevin shrugged. "Yep. I don't know the cause, but the animosity between the Montaignes and the Renauds goes back generations."

"Anyone else in that family as good a hunter as Guy?"

Kevin considered. "I'd imagine that most of the Montaignes can hunt, but none in the same league as Guy. A bunch of them live at the south end of Manasoka. Some folks call it 'Cornflake Village' because all the houses are as cheap and flimsy as cereal boxes. They're a rough lot—violence, jail time, rumors of drug running, domestic abuse, the whole gamut."

"And they'd hate Marc Renaud, simply for being a Renaud?"

Kevin stroked his chin. "Hate him, sure, but kill him?" He shrugged. "Maybe not. Like I said, I don't even know what the feud was about."

"That's kind of vague as far as motives go."

Kevin read her disappointment. "The feud isn't our only motive. For instance, we should also look into the gold angle."

She recalled MacGregor's words. "That's to do with the Megantic Outlaw, right?" She now remembered discussing the story in her ninth-grade history class, but was sure her teacher never mentioned any lost gold.

Kevin spoke enthusiastically. "Donald Morrison was a settler in the 1800s. He got into trouble with the law and went on the run. The local population was on his side and hid him for months and months. The police search for him is still the longest manhunt in Canadian history."

"I remember learning that," Cate said, more of the story filtering back.

"I'm sure they would have covered it, even at Canterbury," Kevin said. "It's a big deal around here."

Cate was surprised Kevin knew she had attended the boarding school. Word got around fast. "We did a bit of local history but tended to focus more on global issues."

"Sure, sure," Kevin said. "The school is always being featured in the newspaper—students heading off to some far-flung corner of the world to do good." His tone held a slight edge, and Cate wondered what it would be like for the locals to coexist with the elite school, with its clutch of wealthy globe-trotting students descending on them every September. You never heard about the muggles surrounding Hogwarts and how they felt about wizard trains blowing through town in the dead of night or errant wand blasts disturbing the peace.

"Anyway," Kevin said and then cleared his throat. "Rumor was that Donald Morrison came into possession of some ill-gotten gold."

"Surely that's only a tall tale," Cate protested.

Kevin shook his head. "It's not that outlandish. A lot of gold floated around back then. Look at Butch Cassidy and the Sundance Kid. They were real outlaws who died protecting a cache of gold and silver coins stolen from a bank in Montpelier, Idaho."

Cate had no idea if this was true or not, but she wanted Kevin to get to his point.

"Stories have persisted that right before he was arrested, the Megantic Outlaw buried this gold along the Pekeda River. A lot of people think it's on MacGregor's land. The Outlaw died before he could retrieve it."

"If that's true—" Cate said slowly.

Kevin interjected, "Then we've got an awful good motive for murder."

CHAPTER 7

BEFORE CATE COULD QUESTION KEVIN FURTHER ABOUT DONALD MORRI-son's lost gold, the swing door by the table opened, and a tall blonde woman strolled into the kitchen.

About the same age as Cate, she looked much better. Where Cate had started to notice the slow sink of her chin into her neck and the dismaying deepening of a furrow in her forehead, this woman's skin was taut and suspiciously unlined. Her hair was dyed a beautiful warm blonde, and while she wasn't exactly pretty—her eyes were set slightly too close, her chin was a bit too prominent—she was nonetheless striking. She wore leggings and a wraparound shirt that emphasized her small breasts and the jutting bones of her clavicles.

Kevin stood. "This is my wife," he said with pride. "Bunny."

"It's actually Bethany," she corrected. "Kevin is the only one who calls me Bunny."

He grinned. "My nickname from when we first started dating. My fluffy Bunny. Her hair was so soft."

"Kevin," Bethany exclaimed, her face hardening. "He likes to remind everyone that we were high school sweethearts. It was kind of cute in our twenties, but now it feels weird." She laughed in a forced way.

Cate didn't want to join in, so instead she introduced herself.

"Oh yeah, I heard about you," Bethany said. "Is everything OK?"

Keith cleared his throat. "Cate was asking about Marc's murder."

Bethany nodded without expression and opened the fridge to retrieve something.

"Cate's a coroner in Ottawa," Kevin said to his wife's back.

"Uh-huh," she murmured while rummaging. She pulled out what looked like a small ice cream container. "It's a smoothie," she said to Cate. "Do you want one? I get them from Home Chefs Direct. They're totally healthy. Purest ingredients. Wild blueberries, organic strawberries, oat milk, a touch of kale, hemp seed, and fish oil for the omega-3s."

Kevin made a disgusted face.

Bethany spotted the look and frowned. "Ignore my husband. He thinks it's cool to eat toxins and make jokes about bacon being the food of the gods."

Cate was embarrassed by the disdain in Bethany's voice, but Kevin calmly put his coffee mug down. "I'm fine," she said.

"You sure? They're like nine dollars apiece retail. I get them free. Home Chefs is one of my sponsors. It's no big deal."

"All good," Cate reassured her. Between the coffee she'd been mainlining all day and her lack of sleep, she doubted her system could handle hemp seed and fish oils.

Bethany popped the smoothie into a large glass and whizzed it with an immersion blender. The mixture was an appealing, frothy pink, which Bethany topped with a sprig of mint she plucked from a healthy plant growing in a cute pot on the windowsill and a couple of fresh blueberries and raspberries she pulled from the fridge. It looked so perfect that Cate regretted her decision to forego one.

"Anyway," Kevin said, once the noise of the blender died away, "like I said, we know the bullet was a .22."

Bethany brought the smoothie to the table and sat a few chairs away from her husband. Cate glanced at Kevin, tempted to suggest they go somewhere more private, but then again, he wasn't really supposed to share this information with her, either.

"I assume that type of bullet wouldn't be unusual around here?" Cate said.

Kevin shrugged. "Twenty-twos are everywhere because they're a good caliber for small animals. Squirrels, grouse, rabbits."

"Would a serious hunter use them?"

"Oh sure," Kevin said. "I'd say most people who hunt use .22s and have a bigger rifle for the larger game like deer."

"We've got a box of bullets here," Bethany said and disappeared into the other room.

"I don't think Cate needs a show-and-tell," Kevin called after his wife, but she'd already returned, carrying a bullet in her hand. It looked small and inconsequential, but shooting it directly into some-one's eye would make it deadly.

"I have a gun to keep the coyotes at bay," Kevin explained. "There's nothing they like more than a chicken dinner."

"You couldn't hit a coyote with a .308," Bethany scoffed. See-ing Cate's blank expression, she said, "That's what you need to bag a moose."

Kevin chuckled. "Bunny's right. Most of the time if the coyotes or a stray dog prowl around, I shoot in the sky. Scatter those varmints."

"God, Kevin," Bethany said, rolling her eyes and looking apolo-getically at Cate. "He's making us sound like absolute hillbillies."

"Not at all," Cate said. She did not want to be drawn into what-ever marital spat this was.

"Constables Douglass and St. Onge came by this morning and took our gun for testing," Kevin offered. "They said they were ordered to do that across the region. Eliminating possible murder weapons."

Cate was glad Vachon was investigating that angle. "I imagine we've got an accurate time of death, given that MacGregor heard the shot?"

"Yup," Kevin agreed. "Four p.m., MacGregor was in his kitchen. He heard the gun, put on his safety vest, and ran down to the river."

Kevin didn't mention MacGregor's shotgun. An oversight on his part, or was he not aware of a second weapon on the scene?

"MacGregor's arthritic, so he couldn't move very fast," he con-tinued. "He spotted Marc's body and checked to see if he was still breathing. According to MacGregor, he wasn't. Then he went back to his place to call the cops. Cell reception is iffy out that way. All the mountains cause interference."

"If the killer hadn't fled by the time MacGregor got out to the body, they could have easily hidden among the trees in the orchard and waited for him to go back to make the phone call before escaping," Cate observed.

"Exactly," agreed Kevin. "MacGregor didn't return until the emergency services arrived, which took a good twenty minutes. The cops are searching the whole orchard and the riverbank for footprints and any DNA."

"That might be hard to find," Cate said.

"What do you mean?"

"For the past couple of weekends, MacGregor hosted an apple U-Pick. There were droves of people headed into that orchard all Saturday and Sunday. That place will be covered in DNA."

"Dang it," he said. "I forgot about the U-Pick. It's going to come down to tracing the gun."

Cate wasn't sure that that was their only lead. She'd like to know how far the shooter was from the victim, any hints about blood spatter, the presence of physical evidence around the body, and precisely what type of gun was used. Those questions all relied on forensic analysis, which would take a while. Meanwhile, there was the issue of motive.

"I dated him, you know," Bethany said.

"What?" Cate asked.

"I dated Marc Renaud, back in high school. Didn't Kevin tell you?" Her voice held a faintly malicious note. "We went to high school with him."

Kevin blushed. "It wasn't really the same school. Marc was on the French side."

Cate looked quizzical, and Kevin explained.

"We're sparsely populated, so there aren't enough kids to make up both an English and French high school. The kids share the same building, and the powers that be divided it down the middle. The eastern half is for the frogs, the western half is for the 'tête carrés.'"

Bethany nodded. "Yeah, Marc was French, so he wasn't in any of my classes. We met at our church."

Kevin looked pained. "Bunny, I don't think any of this matters to Cate."

She ignored him. "My parents were big into the Holy Adventists."

Her tone implied Cate should understand the significance. When she didn't respond, Bethany explained, sounding impatient. "A fundamentalist church. We switched over from the English Catholics. Members came from everywhere—the English Protestants and both the French and English Catholics."

"What about French Protestants?" Cate asked.

Kevin scoffed. "I don't think I've ever met a French Protestant out this way. If you're French and religious, you're Catholic. It's a funny thing about religion—"

"Unless they joined the Holy Adventists," Bethany corrected. "Lots of French people at that church. We were taught to dress modestly, obey our parents—especially our fathers—go to Bible study. Not drink. All that sort of thing. My family did it for about three years until even my mum was sick of the bullshit. Then we quit, but we didn't go back to the Catholic church either. I guess by then we were done with God."

"What about Marc Renaud?" Cate asked.

"Oh yeah. He was cute."

Kevin winced.

Cate remembered Renaud's handsome face. He was more than cute.

"His mother joined the church at about the same time as us. We were in a Bible study class together. The church really wanted all the kids in that group to couple off—chastely of course." She rolled her eyes and continued. "We probably dated for about a year when I was fifteen. We never did anything that wasn't church-related." Bethany directed a stare at Cate. "Well, we did manage a few steamy nights in the back of his mother's Impala."

Kevin shifted in his seat.

Bethany obviously enjoyed needling her husband. Cate was sympathetic to Kevin, but she was more interested in getting information from his wife. "What was Marc like?"

Bethany shrugged and looked away. "I don't know, a fifteen-year-old boy? He was into Pink Floyd—super retro and was always trying to cop a feel. Your standard hormonal teen."

"Did you have much to do with him since?" Cate asked.

"I'd see him around sometimes. I'd bump into his mother more. Poor Mrs. Renaud," Bethany said. "I liked her. She hadn't yet remarried when Marc and I were dating. She was a widow raising Marc and Geneviève all alone."

"Geneviève?" Cate inquired. Pieces of Marc's life were being revealed.

"Marc's little sister." Bethany's voice softened a little. "That family has had a rough go. Marc's dad died when the kids were young, and they struggled for a long while. Eventually Mrs. Renaud remarried, so I guess it worked out."

A pained look crossed Kevin's face. "I've got to go over to her place tomorrow to discuss Marc's death with her and Marc's stepfather."

"I could come with you," Cate offered. "I have a lot of experience talking to victims' families." In fact, it was one of the most rewarding aspects of her job.

"Really?" Kevin's face lit up. "That would be great. Those conversations are so tough."

"Happy to help," Cate said. Discussing a loved one's death was hard enough, but when something as horrible as homicide entered the picture, it was even more difficult. God knows she'd ridden a roller coaster when she had thought Jason was murdered.

"Perfect, you can be my 'wing woman.'" He stared at Cate expectantly, but she wasn't sure what he wanted.

"Like with chickens?"

Cate chuckled, but Bethany rolled her eyes. "No one finds your fucking poultry jokes funny, Kevin."

Cate stared at her hands while Kevin ignored the remark.

Bethany stood and walked to the sink, where she rinsed her glass. "I'm going to do my workout." She said goodbye to Cate and then disappeared down a set of stairs in the corner.

"Home gym in the basement—fully kitted out. Peloton, elliptical, the whole bit."

Between the home gym and the expensive kitchen, either the egg business, the notary business, or the coroner business was making bank. Cate doubted they paid for their beautiful home with dog treats and fish oil smoothies. "What was Marc like in adulthood?"

Kevin added more sugar to his coffee. "I didn't know him well. He worked part-time at the feedstore, so I'd see him there sometimes. He was a jack-of-all-trades. There are lots of people like him in the area, picking up seasonal work. Snow clearing and plowing in the winter, landscaping in the summer. They can fix an electrical problem or do basic plumbing and carpentry."

There was silence for a moment, and then Kevin blurted, "Marc was a nobody."

Cate looked at him, surprised by this unexpected harshness.

Kevin blushed. "I mean, I think he was a nice guy, but he couldn't get his life together. He wasn't going anywhere, you know? He was never going to be successful. No ambition."

Cate thought about the metal detector found by Marc's side. "Maybe that's what he was looking for at MacGregor's . . . The gold was his shot at fortune."

Kevin grimaced. "His shot certainly found him."

CHAPTER 8

CATE FINISHED HER CIGARETTE AND GROUND IT INTO THE EARTH WITH the toe of her boot before she bent and picked up the butt. She didn't want to leave a trace of her nasty habit in this peaceful spot. The sun had set, but the path by her house still yielded a dim view of MacGregor's orchards and the Pekeda River below.

Cate pondered what she knew about the case. She didn't have much info on either the pathology or forensics fronts—her usual areas of expertise. Without that data, there was little she could offer, unless she started to explore other avenues. Her conversation with Kevin produced some insights. First, like MacGregor, the coroner mentioned the porousness of the border. Smuggling was afoot, whether it was drugs or guns. That likely meant violence. The story of the lost gold might yield results. Bethany's high school relationship with Marc made Cate wonder who the victim had been dating recently. Romantic relationships gone wrong were often a motive. The Montaigne–Renaud feud was also worth exploring. Kevin had mentioned Marc's workplace; it might be worthwhile to go to the store and talk to the victim's colleagues. Yes, she had ways she could contribute to the case, and she would exploit them.

The wind picked up, blowing in gusts from the west. Clouds rolled across the sky. A storm was coming. Cate turned to the farmhouse and, remembering MacGregor's warning about bears, deliberately jangled her keys as she walked back.

Rose's arrival on Friday meant she couldn't put off this chore any longer. A hockey bag containing Jason's belongings from Kinshasa sat on the guest bed and it needed to be cleared away. There wasn't much.

Her brother had prided himself on being a "digital nomad" before the term even existed. Prior to leaving for Africa, she'd gone through his sparsely furnished Ottawa condo in a fruitless quest to "prove" something about his death. Sorting out the detritus of his Congolese life was the last thing she had to do. A final farewell she didn't want to face.

Unzipping the bag, the first thing she pulled out was a T-shirt with Vimy Brewing Company emblazoned on it. She had bought it for her brother after a glorious afternoon of beer and fried foods at the brewpub. They'd talked and laughed, Jason regaling her with stories of his previous missions, including a misunderstanding with a confused sheep farmer in northern Syria and a disgusting tale about rotten mangoes in Darfur. Cate brought the shirt up to her nose and sniffed; it smelled like Jason. She stood abruptly. She'd need a glass of wine to manage this.

She spent another half hour pulling items from the bag, fortified by some mellow merlot. Jason's clothes, malaria medication, documents related to his medical work (containing an Ebola outbreak), pamphlets concerning other charitable causes and projects—that was everything. His cell phone, wallet, and other personal effects were destroyed in the crash that killed him.

She noticed a piece of paper stuck to the bottom of the bag. It was an information sheet about Rescue the Children, the charity Jason volunteered with on his leave. She recalled Juanita's words at the embassy party so many weeks ago—most doctors opted for R&R, but not Jason.

Cate had emailed the charity after returning to Ottawa to ask about her brother's final days, but they never responded. She tapped out a follow-up message on her phone. If they didn't get back to her, she would reach out to Brilliant Aduba, her brother's boss in Ottawa. He'd been helpful in repatriating Jason's remains to Canada and might be able to connect her to the charity.

Cate was calmer after finishing with the bag. Accepting that Jason's death was an accident gave her some peace. While she rebelled against such touchy-feely concepts of closure, she had been a coroner long enough to know that answers to the "why" of death were often the first step in moving forward.

She went downstairs and made herself a peanut butter sandwich. Checking her phone, she saw a thunderstorm warning. Next, she scrolled to Instagram; she had an account, "KitKat123," where she occasionally lurked. Bethany's Instagram held lots of selfies: a posed shot of her prepping garden produce for a salad as her waterfall of warm-blonde hair flowed around her shoulders (rather unhygienically in Cate's opinion); a reel of her feeding a couple of brightly colored chickens, the ugly hatchery buildings hidden out of frame; a pretty photo of her in front of a dirty window, the light filtering in just perfectly; a snapshot of her lifting weights in her home gym, a "Home Foods Direct" smoothie discreetly featured in the corner. The feed portrayed an enviable life of country simplicity and fashionable chic. If Cate hadn't witnessed Bethany's apparent bitterness, she might have been envious.

Thunder crashed overhead. The storm had arrived. The lights flickered and, with an ominous swoosh, went out. Damn it. After seeing the forecast, she should have prepared—located the candles and made sure the flashlight's batteries worked. She found the flashlight, breathing a sigh of relief when it flickered on. She checked her cell phone. No service, but reception was weak at the best of times. She switched to low-battery mode.

Moving around the dark room, she listened to the rumble of thunder, counting the seconds until the crack of lightning. Ottawa had frequent summer thunderstorms, especially in August. When she and Jason were home on vacation, she'd get scared in their cavernous house. "Don't worry, Kit Kat," Jason would say in a calm voice. "The lightning is far away. We're safe." They would count the seconds together, and Jason's confidence soothed her even more than the words he spoke.

She recalled a storm kit under the sink and pulled it out: a large battery-operated lantern, a dozen candles, two boxes of matches, a high-visibility vest, and a large bottle of water. Damn. The pump for the well didn't work when the power went out. She checked the tap in the kitchen. There were a few drips and then nothing. Her Airbnb hosts had shown her the deep hole, about twelve inches wide, by the side of the house that was covered by a heavy metal lid. They'd carefully explained the pump mechanism that drew the water up and what to do in a power failure. Unfortunately, she couldn't remember a single thing. In the short term, she'd need water to run the toilet. She pulled out the big mop bucket and ventured outside.

The rain was pounding down, thick, fat drops drenching the earth. The tops of the large spruce trees lining her driveway waved in the wind, and the sky was a strange dark purple, beautiful and odd. Lightning cracked, briefly illuminating the whole front yard. She blinked. Did she see a shape on the bare hill? All was blackness again. The storm made her jumpy. She placed the bucket at the bottom of the porch steps and scurried back. Her hair was soaked from her brief foray. It was a relief to close her door on the violence outside. Remembering the dim shadow, she locked the front door as a precaution.

The storm raged on, and Cate kept vigil by the flickering light of a few candles. By hour three, the farmhouse was chilly, and she pulled an old quilt out of the cedar chest, wrapping it around herself. She blew out all of the candles in case she drifted off and settled back into the armchair, closing her eyes.

A clatter outside snapped her eyes open. She reached for the flashlight, listening intently. She might have dreamed it. She sat tense. The noise again. She peered through the window. The rain continued, though the thunderstorm had passed. Nothing out there. Then the shed door flapped in the wind. It had slipped its latch and was caught by the wind. It banged back and forth, repeating the noise she'd heard. If she left it like that it might blow right off.

Braving the rain, Cate ran out and grabbed the heavy wooden door. She was pulling it closed when she heard a low whimper. The hairs on the back of her neck stood up. It was the whining noise from last night's nightmare. She stumbled back, her fists clenched, her breathing shallow. Then she heard it again, different this time. Lower, guttural.

Someone was in pain. "Hello?" she called. "Who's in there?" The sounds stopped. "I'm a doctor," Cate said. "I'm here to help."

Silence again, a listening silence.

"I'm going to come in. OK?"

No answer.

"J'entre maintenant," she repeated in French. Cate pulled the door open, securing it on the hook at the side of the shed. She wanted a clear escape route. The flashlight's heavy metal weight was reassuring. She breathed deeply. A dry, woodsy smell of dust and logs greeted her, underlaid with another scent she couldn't place right away. Her throat tightened, but she remembered the moan. "I'm going to shine my flashlight in here to help me find you. Don't be startled."

She swept the shed with the light. Three rows of logs were stacked to the left. A few broken wooden chairs and some odds and ends cluttered the remaining space. A long wooden saw and an axe hung on the far wall. Cate wished the axe was in her hands right now. She could see no one.

She stepped farther inside. A movement by the woodpile. She turned the light toward it.

A large furry shape was curled up in a tight ball. Too small to be a bear, thank God. Coyote? Wolf? Dog? Cate took a step back and placed her hand on the door frame, ready to bolt if it lunged.

"You OK, big guy?"

The animal turned its long, shaggy face toward her, its eyes pleading. Not a wolf or a coyote, but a dog. A big one. Relief unknotted her shoulders, followed by worry. Cate didn't know the first thing about dogs. They'd never had one growing up, and when she was married to Matthew they'd been far too busy to think about pets. She couldn't help this creature. She'd lock up the shed and phone animal control—or whoever you called—in the morning. The dog would be cared for by the proper authorities.

It whimpered again and shifted. Its huge brown eyes met hers. This animal needed her. She took a cautious step forward. "I'm coming to examine you," she said in a soothing voice. "I'm going to come to your side." She realized it was nonsensical to talk to it, but she couldn't help slipping into doctor–patient mode.

The animal didn't respond. Cate edged across the small space separating them and knelt by its head. She didn't know anything about breeds, only that this one was large and hairy. It didn't get up or move away from her. Mud—and other things—matted its long fur. There was a cut across its snout. Its ears were crusted in muck. "Hey there," she cooed. "Are you OK?"

A soft thump: its tail wagging. Cate took courage.

"What's going on with you?"

She could see only its head and neck in the glow cast by the flashlight. It had scooted the rest of its body between the woodpile and the shed wall and didn't seem inclined to move. "I'm going to touch you now." She used the same tone she would with a toddler fearing a needle. "This might hurt, but it's to help you, OK?"

Those eyes stared at her, and Cate touched its back. The dog stiffened, but as she continued to stroke its fur, it relaxed, shifting its head a bit, allowing her to continue. It wore no collar. After years of being both a coroner and a general practitioner, she had a strong tolerance for bodily grotesqueries. Still, running her hand down the dog's smelly, matted back, uncertain whether its fur contained ticks, burrs, mud, or other unpleasantness, was testing her limits.

At last, when she thought the dog was calm enough, she began examining rather than patting. This led to the discovery that he—for he was male—had a nasty slash across his nose. But she didn't think the cut on his snout was the main source of his distress. Instead, she palpated slowly down his shanks, unsure what she was looking for, but confident she would know when she found it. She was surprised to catch herself singing a long-forgotten song, half-crooning to the wounded animal that it was safe to close his eyes and reassuring him that he could stay as long as he liked.

She found the wound eventually, a deep gash in his left hindquarter. Whether it was from an encounter with barbed wire or an attack from another animal, she couldn't tell. She pressed gently on the area, and the dog's head whipped around, teeth bared. She snatched her hand away and put it up in a peaceful gesture.

"It's OK. I won't hurt you."

She wouldn't be able to suture the wound, not without drugging him. Could she give him Ativan? She didn't know enough about canine physiology to risk it. She checked her phone, which was down to 10 percent battery. Still no signal. She'd clean the wound as best she could. If she could coax him into the car, she'd take him to the vet in the morning. No chance of carrying him. She stood slowly. "I'm going to get my medical bag. I'll be right back."

She ran across the yard. The rain had ended. It must be past midnight. The moon was out and high overhead. Ridiculously, she waved to it as she ran up the porch stairs. It felt like an old friend.

Returning to the shed with her bag and a bowl of water, Cate did her best, but the work was challenging. She could not clean too close to the injury without getting a warning snarl from the dog. At last, she had done all she could and stopped.

The dog seemed to realize she was finished with the unpleasant stuff and dropped his head, his exhausted body falling into sleep. Cate sat beside him and began working the burrs out of his fur, watching him sleep. Minutes or hours passed. Eventually she heard the first cheeps of the earliest early birds.

Before she stood, she checked his paws. He lifted his head when she got to the right front one. A long thorn was embedded there, the wound black and oozing. She had built up a certain rapport with the creature. Did she dare remove it? The infection was nasty, and it would be painful to the touch. Unlike suturing, however, if she was decisive and skilled, the thorn would be out in a second. She took her medical tweezers and gently lifted his paw. The dog was watching her, but his teeth were not bared. She clasped the end of the thorn in the tweezers and tugged with one clean pull. It came out easily, but the dog was surprised. His teeth snapped toward her, making contact before she could move her arm away.

The animal was weak, so the bite wasn't deep. She stood up in case he wanted another chomp. "That is called biting the hand that feeds you." She grabbed her medical bag. He paid no attention, licking the paw that had held the thorn. She would like to disinfect his wound, but she wasn't getting near it again.

Back in the house, the power had returned. With the TV news on and the joys of toasters and Wi-Fi restored, Cate was cheerful. She examined the bite. It was superficial and hadn't broken the skin. She'd updated all her shots and vaccines before she'd gone to the Congo, and she didn't think the injury warranted a rabies shot, so no worries there.

She glanced out the window at the shed. She'd closed the door but had forgotten to latch it. It should be fine; the wind had died down, and the dog was in no shape to move. The sky was lightening in the east. Homer's "rosy-fingered dawn" approached. Funny how more memories from her school days—snatches of poetry, bits of geography, half-recalled history lessons—were coming back to her here in Pekeda Township. It was as if the proximity to the place where she learned those facts was reconnecting circuits in her brain.

No time to sleep; she was due at the clinic soon. She took a long shower and threw on her work clothes. She googled what to feed a sick dog and then cooked up a bit of rice, chopping up some deli chicken and mixing it in and then putting the whole bowl into the fridge to cool. It was nice to cook for someone, even if they weren't human.

She found herself humming the song she had sung to the dog. It was a lullaby, she realized, one her mother used to sing. A Joni Mitchell and James Taylor duet about leaving and loss. She could almost hear her mother, dead when Cate was only five years old, singing the old tune. Her eyes filled with tears.

"Fuck me, I'm sad," she said out loud, startling herself with the words and the sentiment. She allowed herself to feel it all for a second. Jason's death, the violence of the summer, her father's mental decline, even her mother's long-ago passing. It hurt, but it didn't take her breath away. She took a swig of coffee. She had an animal to tend to.

Despite her tiredness, Cate's step was springing as she carried the bowl of food. She opened the shed door and peered into the gloom, wishing she'd brought the flashlight. She stepped all the way into the empty room. The sadness returned like a blow to the chest. The dog was gone.

CHAPTER 9

"THANKS FOR LETTING ME TAG ALONG," CATE SAID TO KEVIN. THEY stood in Marc's mother's driveway, leaning on her car and staring at the small house. Kevin's large, gleaming "Egg Man" truck dwarfed the rusty sedan and dark blue SUV beside it. Kevin had described this as Manasoka's suburbs. Given that the tree-lined area was only two streets wide and two streets long, "suburb"—singular—might be more appropriate.

Kevin bowed his head. "I should be thanking you. I appreciate the backup."

Cate had spent her entire morning clinic shift distracted by the disappearance of the dog and was happy to have something new to focus on.

A moment after ringing the doorbell, Cate heard the unlatching of a security chain and the slide of a dead bolt. A tiny, thin woman with short brown hair and sunken, reddened eyes opened the door. "Jacques," she called out in French. "They are here."

Kevin and Cate were ushered into a modest living room containing a small couch and two La-Z-Boys. All the seating was positioned to view the large television. It took Kevin and the bearded Jacques a few moments to pull it into a more conversational arrangement. Jacques and Mireille sank into the recliners with long-practiced ease. Cate and Kevin sat on the couch.

Kevin took the lead, speaking careful French that sounded fluent to Cate's ear. She appreciated his unhurried enunciation. She sometimes missed a few words of Jacques's and Mireille's responses, but they were subdued and spoke slowly, so she was able to follow the conversation. Kevin explained that Cate was a fellow coroner and a medical doctor, and they accepted her presence without question.

He discussed the facts of Marc's death as they were understood: For reasons unknown, Marc was in Thomas MacGregor's orchard by the river. He was shot through the eye with a .22-caliber bullet. The weapon was still to be ascertained and located. The shot was heard by Thomas MacGregor at four p.m., so the time of death was definitively established. When MacGregor arrived on the scene, Marc no longer had a pulse. The farmer called the authorities.

"What you say is not quite true," Mireille interrupted, speaking in a husky voice. Cate wasn't sure if that was her natural tone or if grief had lowered her register. "We do know why he was at the MacGregor farm."

Jacques nodded. "Yes, he was looking for the gold. The Outlaw's treasure."

"Marc really believed it was there?" Cate asked.

"Yes," his mother replied. "Lately he was very interested in the old stories. He was convinced the gold was somewhere by the river."

"When did this interest start?" Cate asked in her slow French. Any change in behavior was worth investigating. The gold angle had a bonus: She doubted Detective Inspector Vachon considered buried treasure a likely motive for murder, which meant she'd have unique insight to offer, if it proved viable.

Mireille thought about it. "Right around the time he moved in with Gen."

"Marc was living with his sister?" Kevin asked, surprised. "When did that start?" His tone was aggressive, and Cate was annoyed by his clumsiness. These people were managing terrible grief; they must be treated gently.

"At the end of August," Jacques answered. "For many years he lived in an apartment above the drugstore, but his landlord evicted him. They turned his place into a 'shared workspace.' Do you know what that is?" His tone was aggrieved.

Before Cate or Kevin could reply, he answered his own question. "It's simply a room with some desks. These city people move here for the beautiful countryside because now they can work from anywhere. Only they miss having people to talk to, so they invent these offices and re-create the city again. It's nonsense."

Mireille put her hand on Jacques's arm, and her touch calmed him. "Marc was evicted. He was living with Gen for a month or so while he looked for something else. They were both miserable with the situation." Mireille chuckled without mirth. "They love each other but fight like cats and dogs."

"And that's when he became interested in the Megantic Outlaw?" Cate confirmed. "About a month ago?"

"Yes. Within a couple of weeks, he was obsessed, talking about the gold, saying he was sure it was simply waiting to be found."

"Did he have a new clue or something?" Cate asked.

"Who knows what Marc thought." Jacques said. "He was a dreamer. A little lazy, a little foolish."

"You're not being fair, Jacques," Mireille said and then turned to them. "Marc was a good boy. Not a slacker. He worked two days a week at the feedstore and had started a big job at the Blakeney Inn. He was willing to work. He could have been more than a laborer, a house painter, but he struggled in school."

Cate stole a glance at Kevin, remembering his harsh assessment of Marc. His face was impassive.

"He didn't have a chance . . ." Mireille's voice quavered, and Cate thought she might cry, but she carried on speaking in a rush. "His childhood—his father poisons everything."

Cate furrowed her brow, wondering if she had misunderstood Mireille's French. Kevin caught the verb tense too. "I'm sorry," he interrupted. "Is Marc's biological father still alive?"

"No, no. He died decades ago." Mireille's hands gripped one another.

Cate could see she wanted to talk but was struggling. "That must have been very difficult for you. I'm so sorry."

"I'm not," Mireille said with surprising vehemence. "He was eaten alive by cancer, and I'm glad."

A startled pause, and Jacques rushed in. "Chérie, you don't have to talk about this."

Mireille's mouth twisted and she hesitated.

Kevin leaned forward to ask a question, but Cate shot him a look. Mireille was contending with a lot of big emotions. Sometimes it was best to give people a moment to compose themselves.

Cate's instincts paid off, and Mireille continued. "Jean-Michel was abusive. He spent years beating me." She pointed to a jagged scar on her chin. "The last time he hit me was with an iron. Smashed my face again and again. He broke my jaw and then threw the iron at me. He told me to be grateful he hadn't turned it on. Then he drove off with the car."

She paused and continued in a detached voice. "Marc and Geneviève called the ambulance and rode with me to the hospital. Gen held my hand and cried the whole way. Marc couldn't even look at me. That was my breaking point. I took the kids and moved to my grandmother's in the Gaspé for a couple of years. I didn't come back until after the cancer killed him."

"I'm so sorry," Kevin said. "I had no idea."

Cate still struggled to understand how news traveled out here. Everyone seemed to know one another's daily business, but some deeper secrets remained buried.

Mireille gave a shaky laugh. "It happened decades ago, and I kept it quiet. I was ashamed, you see."

"Did you report him to the police?" Cate asked. "Was he charged?"

Mireille scoffed. "Even though Jean-Michel was known to the police, they were useless. I called them a few times, but they gave me no protection. Eventually I stopped trying because it only made him more violent."

Anger bloomed in Cate's chest. Abusers were some of the most dangerous men in society, responsible for far more deaths than terrorists, but police attitudes toward domestic violence were only now starting to change.

"No, I never filed charges. Instead, I ran. Like a coward." Mireille's eyes filled with tears, and her thin frame shook with sobs.

Jacques rubbed her back. "There there, chérie. It's OK."

When Mireille composed herself, Cate leaned forward, speaking with authority. "You did what you needed to do. You were the victim of intimate-partner violence, a terrible form of torture. You got yourself out and saved your children. You should be proud."

Mireille sniffed, and Kevin handed her a tissue, which she twisted in her hands. "I tell myself this, but I wonder what kind of an example I set for my kids. I should have pressed charges. I should have shown them and the world that I wasn't afraid of him."

Cate shook her head emphatically. "You were right to be afraid. You did the best thing."

"I wish I could believe that." Sobs engulfed her again, and Cate's heart broke for this woman. It was horrible enough that she and her children had been terrorized, but now she was flattened by guilt.

When Mireille stopped crying, Cate resumed her questioning. "You said Jean-Michel was known to the police? For what?"

"He was involved with one of the gangs around here. Low-level stuff—a bit of theft, smuggling. He got into fights. Kicked one of the Montaignes in the head on the steps of the Thirsty Bucket. Gave him permanent brain damage. I thought he'd be sent to the Cowansville Institution for that one, but no one pressed charges. Jean-Michel could be charming." She paused and spoke with deep satisfaction, "But even he couldn't charm his way out of pancreatic cancer."

Was Marc following in his father's criminal footsteps? Was he influenced, even subconsciously, by the kind of decisions Jean-Michel Renaud had made? Cate knew she must proceed delicately with her next question. "That must have been hard on Marc. Did you ever worry he might take after his father?"

"Absolutely not," Mireille's response was vehement—a righteous mother defending her son, or a woman who had harbored those exact concerns? "We moved back here because my parents live nearby, but we started a new life. Turned a page. Marc rejected everything his father stood for."

"That's probably why he wanted the gold," Jacques interjected. "He wished to prove to himself he wasn't a failure like his bastard of a father."

"He didn't need gold for that," Mireille said. "He didn't need gold." Her eyes again filled with tears, and Kevin handed her another tissue. "Thank you," she sniffed. "I can't believe he's really gone."

They were all quiet for a moment.

"Marc escaped his father's influence," Jacques said. "We can take comfort in that."

"Yes, but what about Gen?" Mireille asked. "This is what I mean when I say I failed them. If I had set a better example for Gen, she would have avoided my mistakes."

"She was in an abusive relationship?" Cate asked.

"Years ago," Mireille said quickly. "He was a real piece of work. They lived together in Montreal. When we realized what was going on, Jacques and Marc went to the city, put the fear of God into the bastard, and brought our girl home. He never bothered her again. She was safe."

Mireille's sobs started again, and this time she stood shakily. "I'm sorry, I can't continue. I must lie down."

"Of course," Kevin said solicitously.

Jacques stood and offered Mireille a hand, and they disappeared into the back of the house.

CHAPTER 10

JACQUES RETURNED. "I'M SORRY ABOUT MIREILLE. SHE'S SO fragile." He glared out the window, obviously trying to rein in his own emotions. Concern creased his face. "She can't sit still. She's so anxious."

"She suffered great trauma as a result of her first marriage," Cate pointed out gently. "Now her son has been murdered. I think her anxiety is understandable."

"This reaction is normal?" Jacques asked eagerly.

"Absolutely," Cate confirmed. While she'd never faced this precise scenario, she had seen enough families ripped apart by tragedy to accept any reaction as "normal."

"Thank you. It is a relief to hear that from a doctor."

Cate bowed her head, glad she'd inveigled this invitation from Kevin. He looked relieved as well.

"I couldn't manage if something were to happen to Mireille on top of everything else. She hasn't slept you know, not since news came about Marc."

"I could prescribe her a sleeping pill," Cate offered. "That might help."

Jacques shook his head. "She won't take anything. She says it's because she wants to remain 'alert,' but I know it's because of Geneviève."

"What do you mean?" Cate asked.

Jacques sighed. "We've already told the police. Gen is in rehab for opioid addiction."

"What?" Kevin asked, surprised. "I didn't know she used drugs."

Jacques shrugged. "Neither did we," his voice wavered. "May God forgive me; I didn't know my own stepdaughter was struggling."

"That can be the way with addiction," Cate said. This whole family was mired in guilt. "You can't blame yourself. People with dependence become very good at hiding things, even from themselves." The words lingered in the air. Cate flashed to her own struggles with alcohol in the summer. Thank God that was behind her.

Kevin cleared his throat. "May I ask what kind of drugs she's struggling with?"

"What's everywhere out here? Fentanyl." Jacques looked down. "She was such a good girl. A real perfectionist like her mother. For the past few years, she's led the youth group at the Holy Adventists. She was a role model to them. It was very important to her." He punched the armrest of his chair in anger. "How does a girl like that get mixed up in drugs? It's as unbelievable as Marc's murder."

Cate had seen the reach of opioid addiction, from Ottawa's unhoused populations to the city's wealthiest mansions. Its tentacles reached everywhere.

"It took Marc moving in with her for him to notice her behavior. He became worried. He's always been very protective."

Cate's heart squeezed. Marc had been a concerned brother, just like Jason. While she didn't grow up with the violence that Marc and Geneviève had endured, her father was a tough, unyielding man. That experience had bonded her and Jason, and it seemed to have done something similar to the Renaud siblings.

Jacques was still talking. "Marc confronted Gen, and she admitted everything. She went into treatment on Saturday."

Two days before Marc's murder. "Has she been informed about her brother's death?" Cate asked.

"No," Jacques exhaled heavily. "Marc organized everything and didn't tell us what facility she's in. Mireille has been calling around, but they are incredibly protective of patient privacy. Even the police need a special warrant for that type of inquiry. We've asked them to get it so we can find Gen and inform her but . . ." Jacques shrugged.

"Detective Inspector Vachon doesn't seem to think it's a priority. For now, Geneviève is ignorant of her brother's death."

Cate leaned back, filled with sadness. This murder had devastated a family already deeply harmed by violence. Geneviève Renaud was battling her own demons at rehab and would be faced with shocking news when she was released.

"I think Geneviève is where she needs to be," Kevin said with forced cheer. "She's getting better, and she'll be clean and sober when she learns this news."

His words rallied Jacques. "That is how I comfort Mireille. Gen is surrounded by therapists and support. She will kick the drugs and come home stronger. We will manage this with God's good grace."

There was a pause, and they could hear the recorded sounds of a choir coming from the back of the house. Mireille must be listening to hymns. "We've pushed Marc's funeral off a little, while we wait for Gen to come home," Jacques said. "I don't want to wait too long, though. Our church believes in burial as quickly as possible after death."

Cate nodded. The forensic pathologist would release the body for burial or cremation as soon as the autopsy was complete. While the lab analysis and test results could take days, weeks, or even months, the authorities made it a priority to release bodies to grieving families as soon as possible. Ritual was so important in honoring the dead. The silence lengthened.

Jacques stared at them with red-rimmed eyes. Cate wondered how much sleep he was getting.

"I'm very tired," he said, as if reading her thoughts. "Could we finish this interview another time?"

Cate wanted to press on, knowing that with every passing moment the events of the past few days became further shrouded by the march of time and the dulling effects of grief.

"Of course," Kevin said. "We'll come back another day if we have more questions."

Cate forced a smile. This was Kevin's show, and she was here out of the goodness of his heart.

The three walked to the door, where Jacques unchained the security lock and released the dead bolt.

"I trust you're in regular contact with the police about the case?" Cate asked.

"Yes, Vachon was here with Douglass and the lady cop. They asked a lot of questions about Marc's work. His friends. If he did drugs. His girlfriend. That kind of thing."

"What did you say?" Cate asked.

"I told them Marc didn't do drugs." He paused. "Mind you, I didn't know Gen was using." He stared into the distance for a moment, blinking back tears, and then rallied. "Marc might have had a girlfriend. He kept his love life on the QT. No enemies, that's for sure. Everyone loved him."

Cate thought of his lifeless body. Not everyone.

They said their goodbyes, and then Kevin and Cate conferred by her car.

"That was some intense coronering," he said.

"Yeah," Cate said thoughtfully. She stared at the stand of maples across the street. Marc Renaud was a simple man living in the same small town he'd grown up in. He was recently evicted and had a newly awakened interest in local history. His sister was abusing drugs. He was discreet about his love life. Somehow, that added up to his murder.

"I never knew Marc's biological dad was such a bastard," Kevin remarked.

Jean-Michel Renaud beat a man—a Montaigne no less—severely enough to cause brain damage. Such violence was bound to create enemies. "Did you interview Guy Montaigne?"

"What?" he asked. "No." He sounded worried. "Should I have?"

"It's something we do in Ottawa," she said. "Talk to people involved in the case." That was definitely not true in a homicide, where the police, rather than coroners, were the lead investigators. Still, that nuance never stopped Cate.

Kevin shot her a sharp look. "They let you get away with that?"

She laughed. He wasn't stupid. "Not really, but I've done it, and it's been helpful."

"Yeah," Kevin said. "I googled you. You cracked a double homicide."

"Only because I didn't follow all the rules."

Kevin rubbed his face for a moment, considering. "I don't know," he said. "That might be taking things too far. It's not my purview."

Cate was disappointed. "I understand. I can do a little digging without you. I might work the gold angle. Why was Marc suddenly so interested in it? I also want to learn more about him. Did he have a girlfriend? A boyfriend? Was he into drugs like his sister?"

Kevin stared at her in surprise. "I thought you'd stick to analyzing the pathologist's evidence or the forensic results."

Cate shrugged. "We're at a standstill until we get that analysis. I might as well try to learn a bit more about Marc."

"Darn it. I'll kick myself if I don't lend a hand. I can organize a meeting with Montaigne—maybe tomorrow or the next day."

Cate grinned, delighted to have Kevin's help. "Perfect." She hesitated. "Could I take the lead in the interview?"

"Sure," he said affably. "I'm not used to any of this, so I figure I'll learn from the expert."

Cate stood a little straighter. "Thanks." Most of the men in her life had too much ego to stand aside like that. Her father didn't tolerate any kind of dissent. Her ex, Matthew, always needed to be right. In Ottawa, Detective Baker didn't like her questioning his methods, and lord knows Sylvester Williams would never admit to imperfection in the coroner field. Only Jason was more easygoing. It was a welcome relief to work with a man with so little ego.

CHAPTER 11

CATE SAT IN HER CAR IN MIREILLE'S DRIVEWAY, SUMMONING THE EN-
ergy to get home. The interview had been emotionally draining, and
her two nights of sleeplessness were catching up to her. Her phone
pinged. A text from Anya Patel: "Wylie and the kids are at a soccer
tournament. Come by for tea and a chat?"

Cate was surprised by the invitation. Anya was a busy woman, not
known for spontaneity. Their get-togethers were usually scheduled far
in advance. She texted back, declining the offer. She'd head home,
see if the dog had returned, and fall into bed. She checked her email,
but there was no response from Rescue the Children. She was about
to drive away when her phone pinged again. Cate had forgotten how
persistent Anya could be. She was now sweetening her invite by promising that Dr. Lionel Keene, Canterbury's former headmaster, would
also join them.

Cate relented. While she didn't have the energy to navigate Anya's
sharp intellect and sharper edges alone, having Dr. K as a buffer made a
visit more appealing. What's more, Anya and Dr. K might have insight
into Marc Renaud's murder. Cate drove back onto the Canterbury campus and into the circular driveway in front of the large home that was a
stone's throw from the main school building. This was the headmaster's
house, one of the many perks of running an exclusive private school.

Anya welcomed her into the spare, modern living room—
completely redesigned when she took over as headmistress—and
served her a heavenly piece of baklava. The flaky, sweet pastry melted
on Cate's tongue, and the sugar was a welcome boost to her flagging
energy.

"I'm so glad we're doing this." Anya tucked a strand of glossy black hair behind her ear and took a sip from her cup. "This is exactly what I wanted to happen when you came out here—rekindling our friendship."

Despite her exhaustion, Cate couldn't help smiling. Anya was the type of person who always got exactly what she wanted. At school that made her seem kind of ruthless, intense, and frankly a pain in the ass, but the older Cate got, the more she appreciated this attribute in women. It was rare and, though Anya could be abrasive, it was admirable.

"This is nice," she agreed, stifling a yawn. After her divorce from Matthew, Cate let most of her friendships wither away. It meant a lot that people like Anya reached out after Jason died. In the first few weeks she was too numb to notice the emails, texts, and phone calls, but now she was opening herself up, looking around and seeing the support that was being offered.

"So how is everything?" Cate asked. She and Anya had been in the same grade at Canterbury but moved in different crowds. Anya, the daughter of an extremely wealthy Indian businessman and his Canadian wife, was from a much more privileged strata of the Canterbury pecking order than Cate, whose father was "only" a thoracic surgeon. Like so many alumni, Anya entered a helping profession, studying humanitarian development, then going to teachers college. She'd worked for a United Nations agency in the Central African Republic for years before being handpicked by Canterbury's board of governors upon Dr. K's retirement. She was the perfect candidate: an alumna with a teaching degree and a background in international development.

"Fine," Anya said crisply. "Wylie is going on sabbatical next year, which will be good."

Anya's husband was a professor at Bishop's University, a small liberal arts college in nearby Lennoxville.

"And the kids?" Cate asked. Sophia was a twelve-year-old with a bright smile. Ten-year-old Emmerson was more intense. Anya and Wylie had adopted them both before leaving Africa for Manasoka.

"Sophia is trying out for the Canterbury swim team this year, and Emmerson will continue with his harp lessons."

"Sounds great," Cate said.

"Yes. It's all absolutely perfect."

Cate hesitated. Despite the brightness of Anya's smile, she heard a dark note in her friend's tone.

Anya didn't allow any room for follow-up, however. "How's our clinic doing?"

Cate noted the "our." Anya recruited her and Canterbury paid part of her salary, but Cate was an independent contractor, and the clinic was under the purview of the provincial health ministry, not the school. "It's good. Top-tier facilities. The students are great. The locals are lovely." Cate paused, remembering her resolution to have a discussion with Anya.

Anya picked up on the hesitation. "But?"

"I think some locals stay away because of the clinic's location. It's not serving the community as well as it could be."

Anya waved a hand. "That's the conservative old farmers who don't like change. Once they get used to it, they'll come around. This is better for them."

Cate thought of MacGregor's deep-seated anger. "I'm not sure they agree."

"It's a good clinic," Anya's voice rose. "You know it is."

Even as a teenager, Anya didn't like to be challenged. Luckily, Cate had never backed down from an argument. She spoke firmly. "It can be the best clinic in the world, but if the locals don't like it, it's worth considering whether it serves them."

"Just because folks in Manasoka are annoyed, doesn't mean everyone is. People who live on the farms around the school are delighted to have nearby healthcare, and my students and their parents are thrilled. The voices of a few can't drown out the needs of the many." Anya's voice took on a self-righteous ring. "You know the school motto, Cate: 'Canterbury students use our talents to make the world a better place.'"

"I don't see what that has to do with any—"

Cate was interrupted by a deep voice a little cracked with age. "Anya, did I hear you quoting our motto? Be still my old headmaster heart."

Cate's annoyance dissipated at the sight of the slim, elderly man in Anya's entryway. His hair was thinner and entirely silver now and he walked with a cane, but he was still the kindly headmaster who had welcomed seven-year-old Cate to Canterbury Day and Boarding School. She remembered clutching Jason's hand, terrified, until Dr. K knelt down to eye level and asked her very seriously if she liked books about mice detectives, because the library had stacks of them.

After everyone greeted one another and Dr. K was settled, he turned to Cate. "How are you, my dear?"

One of the real pleasures of her time in the Eastern Townships was reconnecting with her former headmaster. Occasionally, she'd stop in at Dr. K's century-old stone cottage up the hill from Manasoka. They would sit in his cozy den, or "snuggery" as he called it in his faint Welsh lilt. He would pour her strong tea and offer up buttery, crumbly Welsh cakes.

"I'm doing great," she said. "The clinical work is good." Another yawn threatened to split her face in two, but she continued. "I'm even helping with the Renaud investigation."

"I heard you were assisting Kevin Farnham," Anya said.

"You did?" Cate asked. "How?"

Anya shrugged. "Bethany was checking on the egg delivery to the grocery store and told everyone Kevin was consulting with you on the case."

Cate pressed her lips together. Murder investigations usually demanded extreme discretion.

Dr. K cleared his throat. "Are you sure getting involved is the best idea, Catherine?" He searched her face, undoubtedly noting the dark circles under her eyes and the gray pallor of her skin.

"The Sûreté has recognized that I can be of service. They asked me to consult with the police, assist the coroner, that sort of thing."

Fine, she was stretching the truth, but she couldn't stand anyone's pity, especially Dr. K's.

Anya clapped her hands together. "That's wonderful, Cate. You are such an asset to them."

Cate was surprised by Anya's enthusiasm; if anything, she'd have thought her friend would disapprove of any distraction from her duties at the clinic.

Dr. K cleared his throat. "Jason's death is still fresh. Perhaps a bit more time away from this type of investigation would be beneficial to you."

Cate's stomach twisted. This was the argument Sylvester Williams made to keep her from her job, and it was a betrayal to hear Dr. K express the same sentiment. "I'm up for it. Jason's accident was terrible, but I've made my peace. I'm moving on."

"Of course you are," Anya said, pouring more tea. "I think it's very healthy. You're not letting Jason's death flatten you."

Cate smiled, grateful for the support.

Dr. K quirked an eyebrow but let his objections go. "Jason was such a bright boy. So full of conviction and courage."

His voice held a note of pride. The old man deserved to feel a sense of ownership in Jason's life choices; Dr. K was instrumental in getting Jason hired at Medical Aid International.

"Yes," Cate said. "Jason lived to help others." Her voice soured. "And it killed him."

"Tut-tut," Dr. K said mildly. "Would you have preferred Jason live a conventional life? No, his work and his death held meaning and purpose. That is something to take pride in, not regret."

Cate's chest tightened. Easy for the old man to say. He hadn't lost a brother.

She couldn't respond, but the headmistress chimed in. "Jason was a superstar here at Canterbury. We're going to put his photo on the cover of the next issue of the alumni magazine." Anya's eyes welled up, and a few tears spilled out. The other woman had barely known Jason. A hateful, cynical part of Cate wondered if such a cover would help Anya's next fundraising drive for the endowment.

"It's true," Dr. K agreed. "Jason was beloved. I remember I shared the stage with him at Old Home Week. After he'd finished his speech, no one had any interest in hearing mine." He chuckled.

"Jason spoke here? When was that?" It surprised her to learn that he had returned to their old school without telling her.

Anya seemed disconcerted by the intensity of Cate's question and stammered an answer. "It was a couple of years ago. He talked about Medical Aid International. It was very inspiring."

Of course it was fine that Jason hadn't told her about the event, but his silence niggled. Like the work he'd been doing at the orphanage before he died, it was a reminder that everyone had their secrets. For instance, Jacques and Mireille were oblivious to Geneviève's addiction.

She changed the subject. "I wonder what you both know about Marc Renaud."

Dr. K scratched his chin. "I'm surprised you want to gossip, Catherine. You know, Plato once said, 'Strong minds discuss ideas, average minds discuss events, weak minds discuss people.'"

Anya coughed. "Actually, I think that was Socrates."

There was an awkward pause. Cate admired Anya. She would never have dared correct Dr. K.

He broke the silence with a chuckle. "You're quite right, Anya, my dear. At any rate, I can't tell you much about Marc Renaud. I didn't know him. Frederick said he'd chatted with him at the feedstore a few times."

Frederick Blanchette was Dr. K's long-term partner. They'd married about ten years earlier. Cate, along with many other alums, had been invited to the springtime event, apple blossoms scenting the air. She and Matthew had shared a table with Jason, Anya, and her husband, Wylie.

Dr. K turned to Anya. "I think Renaud worked at the school, didn't he?"

Anya shrugged. "He did occasional handyman jobs. He was efficient and reliable. Kind of cute. He had a good laugh. Very throaty."

Cate wasn't surprised Anya had noticed Marc's good looks. Her friend had been boy crazy in their school days.

"Were you satisfied with his work? Any problems?" Cate asked.

Anya considered and then shook her head. "Nothing springs to mind, but Beatrice deals with all the staffing issues."

Dr. K laughed. "Is she still the faculty and staff manager? I assumed she'd be retired by now."

Anya rolled her eyes. "She's hanging on, possibly to drive me insane."

"Now, now, Anya. Simply because someone has old-fashioned methods doesn't mean you should discount them."

Anya smiled tightly, and Cate considered how difficult it must be for her to fill Dr. K's shoes. He was a beloved headmaster who had served the school for almost fifty years. Anya must find it irksome to listen to his opinions on how the school should be run.

Anya turned to Cate. "Beatrice is a Canterbury stalwart. She's in charge of all the school's hiring. It might be worth chatting with her about Marc's employment."

"Actually," Dr. K cut in, "I don't think those details should be shared. There are some serious privacy concerns at play, and Cate isn't law enforcement."

Anya flushed. "Of course, I wasn't thinking." She cleared her throat and moved on from the moment of disharmony. "Sometimes I wonder if Beatrice might be losing her edge."

"Oh?" Dr. K asked.

"Now I'm gossiping, but she's made a few decisions about short-term hires that I've found puzzling." Anya shrugged. "It's not important."

"Do either of you know any other member of Marc's family?"

"I think the sister does a bit of catering and cleaning. Mostly off the books. The mother worked as a secretary for a construction company. I don't know what the stepfather does," Anya said.

No mention of Geneviève's drug addiction or stint at rehab. That gossip hadn't spread.

"Do you know anything about Marc's biological father?"

"I understand he died when Marc and Geneviève were children," Dr. K said.

It appeared the story of Jean-Michel Renaud's abuse wasn't widely known either. Mireille was right: Some secrets were possible in a small town. Although, Anya and Dr. K's knowledge of the Renauds might not be a great barometer of what was known and by whom; Cate doubted there was a lot of social overlap between the administrators of Canterbury Day and Boarding School and a part-time handyman.

They moved on to Dr. K's retirement project: a complete history of Canterbury's founding. Anya had allocated him a small office at the school to work from, and he was delightedly ferreting out every detail of Canterbury's first years.

Unfortunately for Cate, her sleepless night, Anya's comfortable sofa, and Dr. K's melodious accent combined to make her drowsy. She drifted off and then started forward in her seat with an undignified snort. She forced herself to spend another punitive half hour asking Dr. K attentive questions about the intricacies of Canterbury's bylaws to make up for her accidental nap.

CHAPTER 12

THERE WAS NO SIGN OF THE DOG WHEN CATE PULLED INTO HER DRIVE-way, and the bowl of food she'd left was untouched. She checked the shed, but he wasn't there. She called to him until dusk and then sat in the rocking chair, pulling out her cigarettes. She inhaled and felt as much as saw the darkness descend around her. The world stilled and dimmed. The birds quieted, and the shadows deepened.

The dog was gone. Tears filled her eyes, and she let them fall without trying to stop them. It was one more abrupt departure without a goodbye. She should be used to those, but it still hurt. She had just finished her smoke and stood to go in when a noise in the darkness caught her attention. A scuffling near the shed. It could be a racoon, a skunk, or even the rumored black bear. She walked toward the sound, her heart thudding. Her eyes adjusted to the night, and the food bowl gleamed silver. There was a movement to the left of the shed. She spotted the tip of an ear, a long nose.

"Hey, boy," she said softly.

A shadow moved. A tail wagged. "Hey," she crooned. He appeared from the gloom. She hadn't seen him standing until now. He was a bigger version of a German shepherd, all hues of brown and black, with alert ears. She held out her hand, dimly remembering the instructions for feeding goats at a petting zoo on some field trip. All digits needed to be flat. Surely the same principle applied to an enormous, half-wild dog? He didn't come any nearer to her hand, but he extended his nose, giving her a good sniff.

Did she imagine he winced? She must stink of cigarettes. "Sorry."

The dog made no further effort to approach. She edged her hand slowly, so slowly, toward his head to give it a pat, but he backed away. His hackles didn't rise, however; he was simply removing himself from her sphere of influence.

She put her hand down. "That's OK," she said in the singsong voice she adopted around him. "Boundaries are good." She thought of all the boundaries she had erected around her own life. "You're looking after your own emotional well-being." The tail wagged again. She smiled. They understood one another.

The next morning he was gone, but she didn't lose heart. Instead, she refilled his food and water bowls and propped the shed door open. With luck she could lure him into trusting her and get him to the vet.

CATE AND KEVIN BUMPED ALONG THE RUTTED ROAD TO GUY MONTAIGNE'S home, passing a house with a car up on blocks in the yard and a cracked clawfoot bathtub leaning against a tumbledown shed. Another house was missing several shingles from a moss-covered roof, and wild animals had knocked over a garbage can, strewing trash across the yard.

Guy's house was at the end of the lane, surrounded by a little wood. A modest but well-kept bungalow, its carefully trimmed grass rebuked its disheveled neighbors. Kevin rang the doorbell, and they heard a pretty tune ring through the house. No answer, so Kevin pushed it again. Cate hummed along; she knew the song.

No one came to the door, but they heard noises in the backyard. As they approached, the sound became clearer: grunts and something dragging. Rounding the corner, they saw two figures hunched over a blue tarpaulin. The closest man—about forty, tall, and thickly muscled—turned toward them. He was covered in blood and held a sharp, slim knife in his right hand. "Quoi?" he snarled.

Cate took a startled step back before spotting the carcass on the tarp behind the men. A deer with a small rack of antlers lay on its side.

Its soft brown eyes were open and staring. It was sliced open from neck to tail.

The other man, speckled with blood and about the same age as the first, asked. "Qu'est-ce que vous voulez?"

"Bonjour, M. Montaigne," Kevin said to him in French. He continued in that language, introducing himself and Cate and mentioning their appointment to discuss Marc Renaud's death.

The blood-soaked companion, who still held his knife, unleashed a torrent of French in the accent particular to the Eastern Townships. Cate struggled to follow. Every now and then she'd catch a word: *médecin*—doctor; *meurtre*—murder.

At last, his speech slowed, and Kevin turned to translate. "This is Thierry Montaigne, Guy's cousin. He doesn't like the Canterbury Clinic and nosy doctors. He says his cousin has already told the police everything and we should leave."

Guy Montaigne stepped forward, speaking in good, almost unaccented English. "Please forgive my cousin, he is protective of me, of our family name. I am happy to answer your questions. I had nothing to do with Marc's murder."

Thierry Montaigne spat on the ground and said, "J'l'aurais étripé, l'osti d'trou d'cul, si j'avais eu du temps à perdre."

The French was too fast for Cate. She turned to Kevin. "What did he say?"

Kevin hesitated. "Thierry said that he certainly didn't kill Renaud."

Cate raised an eyebrow. "Is that exactly what he said?"

Kevin blushed. "Actually it was 'I would have killed the motherfucker, but he wasn't worth my time.'"

Guy scowled at his cousin, who shrugged.

"T'would be a waste of a good bullet," Thierry said in thickly accented English.

"I'm so sorry for Thierry," Guy said again. He stepped away from the deer, obviously hoping to lead them away from his cousin. "It's no secret that the Montaignes and the Renauds have a long history." He laughed. "Thierry takes the feud more seriously than I do."

"I 'ate that cafard," Thierry called, putting the knife down and lumbering toward them.

"'Cafard' is cockroach," Kevin interpreted for Cate. Thierry glared at him.

"Why did you hate him so much?" Cate asked. She'd come to talk to known marksman Guy Montaigne, but Thierry was proving more interesting.

"He's one of the Renaud scum. They think they are better than us."

"What about that fight at the Thirsty Bucket?"

Thierry laughed, revealing a missing tooth. "Two years ago? I smashed Marc's pretty face in. Gave him a black eye."

"No," Cate said, though she was interested to learn there had been more recent violence. "The one from many years ago—Jean-Michel Renaud beat someone up."

Thierry's face turned purple, and he spit out, "He sucker punched my papa. Knocked him down and kicked him in the head before my uncles could pull him off. Jean-Michel was a motherfucking—"

Guy put a calming hand on his cousin's shoulder, but his voice held a thread of anger as he addressed Cate and Kevin. "Uncle Henri was never the same after that. Lost the use of his left hand. Got fired. Started drinking. Died two years later."

"I'm glad that cockroach got cancer. If not, I would have killed him myself." Thierry's eyes bulged, and he glared at Cate.

She squared her shoulders and resumed questioning. "What did you say about a fight two years ago?"

Guy laughed. "That was nothing. A little scuffle after too much to drink. We all got into it."

"What started it?"

Guy scratched his chin. "If I remember correctly, Marc was hitting on a lady who wasn't interested. We taught him some manners."

Cate had a hard time imagining Cousin Thierry knowing anything about manners, but the tidbit about Marc was interesting. "Who was he hitting on?"

Guy shrugged. "Who knows, one of those sluts who hangs out at the Bucket. Next thing I knew, half the bar was brawling." He shook his head. "It was stupid."

"Don't be a tapette," Thierry said to him, making his wrist go limp. "Marc Renaud is a cockroach, just like his cockroach uncles and his cockroach father. Jean-Michel Renaud drove into your father's truck and totaled it."

"Marc's father did that?" Cate asked.

Guy put up a placating hand. "We don't know if he did that on purpose. He was drunk . . . or maybe high."

"You hate them as much as I do, Guy, you're just too much of a moumoune to admit it."

Guy cleared his throat. "I think the feud is stupid, but that doesn't mean I liked Marc Renaud much. He was a villain."

Cate's attention was caught by his odd choice of words. "What do you mean?"

Guy shrugged. "He was selling drugs. Maybe he pissed off some bad men. Got killed."

"Interesting." Kevin shot Cate an excited look. He obviously believed they'd landed a major lead. Cate was less certain. The Montaignes weren't exactly impartial when it came to Marc Renaud.

"Why do you say that?" Cate asked.

"Everyone knows Marc was pushing," Guy said.

"What kind of drugs? Where did he get them?"

"Opioids, mostly. I don't know where he got them. Probably one of the gangs."

Kevin piped up, "The Sûreté busted a major ring last night. There's a provincial push to rout out the trade."

Vachon had said something similar. Geneviève was in rehab somewhere, fighting an addiction to opioids. Did Marc sell his sister the drugs? That didn't square with him as a protective sibling who scared off her abusive boyfriend, but addiction could destroy familial bonds.

"You see," Guy said, as if that proved his point. "Marc Renaud was involved in drugs. 'Violent delights have violent ends.'"

Cate blinked at the unexpected quotation. "That's a theory." She didn't like being shoved in one direction.

"It's the only theory," Guy said.

"Why's that?" Cate asked.

"I heard about the wound. Through the eye? It was an assassination. That was done by a professional hit man."

"Or a great hunter," Cate countered, nodding to the dead deer. "From what I hear, Guy, you could have made that shot."

He opened his mouth to respond, but Thierry butted in. "He already told the cops he didn't do it. Those fuckers took away all his hunting rifles. They confiscated mine, too, and demanded I show them the licenses for the other guns. Fucking government." His eyes bulged, and a vein in his neck pulsed.

As doubtful as she was of the police's abilities, she was impressed with their nerve. Removing weapons from Thierry Montaigne was not for the faint of heart.

"How did you kill that, then?" Cate asked, pointing to the animal.

"I used this." Guy picked up a complicated piece of metal equipment with levers, gears, and stabilizers.

"Is that a bow?" Cate made out the arced shape through all the mechanisms.

"But of course," Guy said. "Very effective. It's a compound bow. These are the arrows."

Guy turned from the dead deer and marched to the side of the house. He picked up a long bag—a quiver, Cate supposed. Carrying it over, he pulled out an arrow. He handed one to Cate and one to Kevin.

It was lightweight, with a vicious-looking tip, so sharp it gleamed in the light. "Bloodsport" was written on the shaft. Cate quelled a shiver, grateful not to be the deer hunted with this.

"I didn't even realize people hunted with bows," she said. "I guess it's similar to regular hunting?"

"Not really," Kevin surprised her by interjecting. "It's an entirely different skill set. Totally different movement."

She looked at him inquiringly.

He shrugged. "Bunny and I do a little archery in the town league."

Guy cleared his throat, obviously annoyed by Kevin's interruption. "That is not correct. In any hunting, whether with bow or gun, patience is the most important ability. Your prey is frightened, aware of danger. Wisely and slowly you must take your shot, because those who move too fast stumble." His voice lowered. "An archer or a marksman uses these same skills." Guy's words had a fairy-tale cast. "You must be quieter than a little mouse. As quiet as death itself, because that is what you bring."

Cate shivered.

"When the moment is right and your prey is within your sights, you empty your head of all thought and take careful aim," Guy continued. "That ability to zero in on your target, without any distraction, that is the most important element, whether you are hunting with a bow or a rifle. You want accuracy. Precision."

Guy's words hung in the air. Even Thierry was subdued by his cousin's expertise. The dead deer behind them was an obvious example of his skill.

"That's enough talking," Thierry said, abruptly breaking the silence. "You both need to leave." He gestured toward the driveway.

"Wait," Cate said. "We have more questions."

"We answered everything to the police."

Cate wasn't going to leave without getting more information. "Where were you both on the day of the murder?"

"I was working," Guy said.

"M. Montaigne is an orderly at the regional hospital," Kevin chimed in.

Cate blinked. Given his speech about the terror of the prey, it was hard to imagine Guy in a caregiving profession. "What time did your shift end on Monday?"

He waved his hand. "I went to Thierry's after I got home. We drank some beers and watched the hockey game."

Thierry nodded. "I'm not working right now. I'm on disability for my back." He stared at Cate, as if challenging her to question this.

Guy hadn't answered her question, but before she could ask again, Thierry stepped forward. "We've talked enough. Go now."

"You agreed to meet with us, Guy, to answer our questions," Kevin insisted.

"What about the Megantic Outlaw's gold?" Cate asked.

Thierry scoffed. "Renaud dreamed of a magical pot of gold. Like a woman." It was clear from his tone that there was no greater insult. He walked toward them, herding them to the car.

"You don't believe that there is treasure hidden on MacGregor's land?" Cate glanced over to see a crafty look in Guy's eye.

"Maybe there is. Maybe there isn't."

Thierry interjected, "Renaud was too much of a loser to find it." He invaded their space as he urged them toward their vehicles.

Cate turned back but tripped over something and landed painfully on her knees. She'd stumbled over Guy's well, its metal cover askew.

"Be careful." Thierry yanked her upward. His hand tightened like a vice around her arm, and he held on for a second too long.

Her bicep radiated pain. She choked back a whimper. She shook her arm, and at last he released her.

Cate met Guy's glance. Something flickered in his eye, and he looked away. She resisted the urge to rub her arm, not wanting to give Thierry the satisfaction.

They reached their cars, and the two Montaignes turned. "We must dress the kill," Guy said apologetically, before striding back toward the deer.

She and Kevin waited to confer until after the two disappeared around the house.

"That was interesting," he said quietly.

"You're telling me. Thierry is a piece of work." She touched her arm. She got the distinct impression he had enjoyed hurting her. "Is he a good shot?"

Kevin rubbed his neck. "I've never heard that Thierry was particularly skilled, but he does a lot of hunting. Maybe with the right gun and with luck by his side, he could have made the shot that killed Marc."

Cate considered. "He doesn't hide his feelings about Renaud."

"Yeah. It's a real Hatfield and McCoy thing in his mind—a blood feud. You hit a nerve with that question about his father and Jean-Michel."

Cate pulled up the sleeve of her shirt. Sure enough, a ring of dark bruises was already beginning to form. Thierry was rough and strong and capable of violence. "I think we got some good info."

"Yes," Kevin said enthusiastically. "We confirmed that Guy is a skilled hunter. He brought that deer down with nothing more than an arrow."

She thought of that razor-sharp tip. "It's a surprisingly formidable weapon. Guy was dismissive of the gold angle."

"Remember what Jacques said, that Marc believed that the gold was real. That's why he trespassed on MacGregor's land. We shouldn't abandon that on Guy's say-so."

"Fair enough." Cate was heartened by Kevin's "we" and she felt a surge of friendship toward him. "Do you think the autopsy report and preliminary forensics results will be back by Monday?"

"Maybe. That drug bust I mentioned was some province-wide thing with Guns and Gangs. They were using tactical units and dog teams. I imagine the Sherbrooke Sûreté is going to be busy with that."

"Homicide trumps a drug bust." Cate's voice held outrage.

"Of course, of course. But there are limited resources, so it might slow things down on the Renaud case."

"Can you let me know as soon as you hear?"

"Absolutely."

"Guy didn't answer the question about what time he left work," Cate said.

"That's right. Good catch." Kevin paused. "Still, it's easy enough to check. Presumably the police will establish that."

Kevin had more faith in the cops than she did. "I was thinking of visiting the Blakeney Inn tomorrow. Marc was working there before his death. I want to follow up on Montaigne's accusation of drug dealing. Maybe it connects with this bigger provincial initiative."

Kevin scratched his chin. "I've got some notary business to attend to." He hesitated. "You know what, though, this is a homicide. I'll reschedule."

"Fantastic," Cate said. "I can pick you up."

"Great. Now, I'd better fly home. Bunny really starts clucking when I'm late to dinner."

Cate forced a laugh. No matter how friendly he was, or how helpful his endorsement, she didn't think she'd ever reach a point when she would enjoy Kevin's chicken puns.

CHAPTER 13

THE BLAKENEY INN WAS IN QUIET EAST SKYE, A MUCH SMALLER VILLAGE than Manasoka, about twenty minutes away. The village consisted of a general store, a white painted church, and the hotel. From the inn's parking lot, she and Kevin stared at the building. Wooden and rambling, a deep veranda skirted the ground floor, and an equally large balcony encircled the second story. Half the building was painted a soft, pretty blue, while the other was a weather-beaten whitish gray. A sign out front written in French and in smaller English lettering read "Coming Soon: Pub Paint Night! Enjoy a pint of organic microbrew while discovering your inner artist. Saturday: Ukulele jam!"

Kevin snorted. "My granddad would turn in his grave if he knew this place now hosted ukulele jams."

They approached the main doors. The windows of the inn were sparkling clean, but here and there a faded old handbill was plastered over the glass. Someone had obviously tried to peel them off, but it was still possible to read a few: "Gilman's Corners' Danseuses Nues"—with a cartoon of a busty woman sliding down a stripper pole. Another sign advertised Molson Export, its bright red faded to pink.

They found themselves in a surprisingly clean and pleasant hotel lobby. Kevin whistled. "They're really fixing the old girl up. I'll have to tell Bunny. This is right up her alley."

It was indeed aesthetically pleasing. In front of them stood a gleaming front desk. To their left were comfortable armchairs and sofas clustered around a cozy fireplace. A large modern chandelier brightened the whole space. A tall man with a nose ring and a sleeve tattoo waved a greeting from behind the front desk. Cate was still processing the cognitive dissonance of the well-appointed lobby and the inn's confusing external appearance when Kevin tugged on her arm and pointed. "Let's check out the bar."

They walked through a set of double doors at the far side of the room, above which the word *Taverne* was written in faded gold lettering.

This space had not received the same makeover. A long, scratched wood bar dominated the room. Mismatched tables and chairs—some wood, others plastic—were scattered around. Cate's and Kevin's shoes clung to the sticky, cheap vinyl flooring. High booths lined the far wall. A chubby young man in jeans and a waistcoat scrubbed a table.

"Hi," Cate said.

"Hello hello," he said and smiled. "What can I get you?"

They sat on two tall stools at the bar. Cate's wobbled; Kevin's was missing a couple of spindles, making it impossible for him to lean back. He sat up straight, like a boiled egg in a cup. "I'll have a beer," Cate said. They needed to buy something to curry favor with this guy, but she was mindful of her afternoon shift.

"Sure, take a look at our local microbrews while I get you a snack." He handed them a long, laminated menu listing dozens and dozens of beers and disappeared behind a set of swinging doors. He returned a minute later with a small bowl of chips and another of olives. "The chips are house-made—Dead Sea salt and aged balsamic vinegar. The olives are brine-soaked Castelvetranos."

"Great," Cate said. "I'll take a half-pint of your lightest lager."

Kevin bobbed his head in agreement. "Me too."

The man looked disappointed at their unimaginative order but set to work drawing the pints.

"You guys are undergoing renos," Cate remarked.

He brightened. "Yeah, it's a total rebrand. We're putting the Blakeney back on the map. Last year we concentrated on the hotel portion. We spiffed up three of our ten rooms and are working on the others. You saw the lobby?"

"It's really nice," Kevin said.

The bartender beamed and handed them the beers. "It turned out great. We'll keep redoing the rooms, but now I'm turning my attention to this place." He gestured around him. "I want to make this pub the cultural and artistic hub for the whole region."

"Are you from around here?" Cate asked. She wasn't sure how locals like Constable Douglass or Thierry Montaigne would feel about "artistic hubs," although Bethany would undoubtedly be on board.

"Oh sure. Sixth generation. My mum's a McDougall. Her family came over from the Isle of Lewis back in the day. Mum and Dad retired to Florida two years ago. I moved back from Toronto. They handed me the keys and walked out."

"Carol McDougall?" Kevin asked. "She used to babysit me. Never let me watch *Unsolved Mysteries* because she said it was too scary."

The barkeep laughed. "Sounds like Mum. Anyway, the place was a total dump. The kitchen is a mess. All they served were hot dogs and poutine. I'm going to gut it as soon as I get a bit more capital."

"Nothing wrong with pickled tongue and a good Scotch egg," came a thin voice from a booth concealing the speaker from view.

The young man waved a hand. "That's over now, Grandma," he called. He rolled his eyes at Cate and Kevin and whispered, "I wish Mum and Dad took her with them when they went south."

"I heard that, Timmy, you little turd."

Cate met Kevin's eyes and looked away. She would not laugh.

The young man cleared his throat and spoke more loudly, obviously addressing his remarks to his unseen grandmother. "The area is changing. The drunks and poker machines used to keep us in business, but dart tournaments and cribbage nights don't cut it anymore." He raised his voice even louder. "We have to move with the times."

"Bullshit" was the riposte.

He closed his eyes and seemed to be counting to ten. When he spoke, he directed his attention to Cate and Kevin. "They've ripped up the railroad tracks behind us." He gestured with his thumb. "First we served the stagecoach, then when they put in tracks we pivoted to train passengers. Now the province turned the tracks into a multi-use pathway. We're getting cyclists and hikers looking for a beer and a snack. They even come in winter because it's groomed for cross-country skiing."

"We used to get the Ski-dooers," came the voice. "Those mother-fuckers could drink. None of this hoppy beer crap. A pint of Molson and whisky chaser."

"That might have been true in the glory days, Grandma," Timmy yelled back, his face getting red, "but there haven't been snowmobilers in years. They can't drink and drive anymore."

They heard a muttered "Bullshit."

"She has no vision," he whispered.

"Watch it, Turdy," came the voice again.

"It sounds like a really exciting project," Cate said.

"Thanks. It's a work in progress." Timmy slipped back into suave bartender mode. "The exterior is a mess because the guy I hired to paint the building died last week."

"Was that Marc Renaud?" Kevin asked.

"Yeah," Timmy said glumly. "You heard about it? He was shot. Very sad."

"Fucking tragic," came the voice again, with a hint of melancholy.

"Did you know Marc well?" Kevin asked.

Timmy shrugged. "I didn't, but he and Grandma hit it off when he was working here. They ate lunch together most days. She'd cook him a Pogo or a poutine and they'd yak away."

"He loved my pickled eggs." Now the voice sounded downright mournful.

Kevin and Cate exchanged looks. Cate stood and walked over to the booth. A tiny, hunched figure with a cloud of snowy-white curls sat knitting. She wore a pale-blue cardigan over a flower-print dress.

"Ma'am, do you mind if I ask you a few questions about Marc? I'm a coroner."

The older woman met Cate's eye. "You're *a* coroner but not *the* coroner." She turned to Kevin, who had followed. "That would be you, Kevin Farnham. I knew your grandfather. Horny bugger." She closed her eyes in recollection. "Always trying to cop a feel behind the cigarette machine. One night I finally let him have a good grope and then walloped him across the face with a serving tray." She chuckled and opened her eyes. "I would have let him keep going if he'd had a hope in hell of making my knickers damp, but I was as dry as a bone."

Cate gaped. Kevin's mouth dropped open for a long moment until he said, "Oh."

The old woman grunted. "It probably wasn't his fault. I think I'm a lesbo, but I missed my chance. Too old now to learn what to do with someone's fanny."

"Grandma!" came a shout from the bar.

"Oh, grow up, Timmy."

At that moment, a couple in full spandex walked into the tavern, bicycle helmets under their arms. "Avez-vous de la bière en fut?" the man asked.

Timmy turned to serve them, and Cate and Kevin slid into the booth opposite his grandmother.

"I'm Dr. Cate Spencer, and you know Kevin."

"I'm Marjorie Taylor. My friends called me Madge, but they're all dead. You can call me Mrs. Taylor."

"You knew Marc? Spent time with him?"

"Oh sure, good-looking lad. Loved to talk. We'd gab away when he was on break from painting."

"What did you talk about?" Cate asked.

"Life, mostly."

"Any specifics?" Cate asked. "Did he mention any worries? Any romances? What was on his mind in the days leading up to his death?"

Madge shrugged and then winced, as if the gesture hurt her shoulder. "He was a cagey little dickens. From what he let slip, I knew he had a girl on the scene. He wanted to leave town with her."

Cate glanced at Kevin in excitement. Here was confirmation of a serious girlfriend.

"What did he say exactly?" Kevin asked. "When were they leaving?"

Madge shrugged and winced again. "He didn't give specifics, but I picked up on hints. He mentioned a 'her' but then shut up right quick."

Cate hoped Madge might have more. One mention of a mysterious "her" wasn't going to crack this case. "Was that everything?"

"No. Like I said, he wanted to leave town, and he wanted to go soon. I was surprised. Marc didn't strike me as an adventurer. For some people, home is rooted in their bones."

The poetry of those words caught Cate's attention. Where was "home" for her? It wasn't Pekeda Township, where she was unable to do the work she loved, and it wasn't the house she grew up in, a cold, loveless collection of bricks. She thought she'd built a home in her marriage with Matthew, but that was an illusion. Her house in Ottawa was serviceable but not homey. Maybe the last time—the only time—she'd ever felt at home was at Canterbury, where she had been welcomed and nurtured. Dr. K built that sense of community and safety. She owed him so much.

"Anyway," Madge continued, "he asked me what I knew about living in Toronto or Vancouver. He wanted to know how much money he'd need to get set up and start over. I had no fucking idea, but I told him moving would be real expensive. It was clear he needed cash for his big adventure. He was always begging Timmy for more hours."

Marc hustling for painting jobs didn't square with him being a well-known drug dealer, as Montaigne claimed.

"I was joking with him one day, and I told him that if he really wanted to hit the jackpot, he should do what no man in this township has had the smarts to do—finally find the Outlaw's gold."

Cate leaned in closer. Here, potentially, was some valuable information she could contribute to the investigation. Madge's encouragement might explain Marc's sudden interest in local history.

"He was my great-granduncle, you know," Madge said.

"Who?" Cate asked.

"Donald Morrison, the Megantic Outlaw," Madge said impatiently. "My granddad remembered when they brought Donald's body back from Montreal. Every Scotsman in the Eastern Townships showed up for the funeral cortege."

Kevin nodded. "I've heard about that. It must have been something."

"What did Marc say when you suggested he look for the gold?" Cate asked.

"He scoffed. Told me he didn't believe in fairy tales. That's when I looked him right in the eye"—here the old lady fixed her rheumy gaze on Cate—"and I told him that I knew for a dead certainty that the gold was real. I even proved it to him."

"And how did you do that?" Cate asked.

The old lady's eyes flashed. "Wouldn't you like to know."

There was a silence, and Cate realized the old woman wasn't going to reveal her secret. "Marc was murdered, and his actions, especially in the weeks leading up to his death, are extremely pertinent. Who knows, he might have been killed for the gold. If that's the case, your life might be in danger. You should tell us what you know so that we can protect you."

The old lady burst into a wheezing cackle. "Dearie, I'm ninety-three years old. I was born in the Great Depression and lived through the Second World War, the FLQ, the Cold War, and that fucking pandemic. I'm not worried for my safety."

Cate tried another angle: "You convinced Marc that the gold was real, and he started scouting for it on MacGregor's property. Why didn't you tell him where it was buried?"

The old woman looked at her like she was an idiot. "If I knew where the fucking gold was, I would have fucking well dug it up sixty years ago when I could have flown to Miami Beach to drink mai tais in a bikini while my tits were still good."

"Right," Cate said. "You convinced Marc the gold was there but couldn't actually tell him where it was."

The older woman tilted her head. "That's right. I told him he should check the old records. I know one of my cousins recently donated his father's papers to the Regional Archives. I thought they might contain some clues, but Cousin Joey was a bugger and never let me take a look."

Cate's heart rate quickened. Rose was an archivist and could help with that research. Luckily, she was arriving that very night.

"Have you told the police about the origins of Marc Renaud's interest in the gold?" Cate asked.

Madge sniffed dismissively. "Haven't seen hide nor hair of the buggers." There was a pause, and when the older woman spoke again, her voice betrayed uncertainty for the first time. "Do you really think Marc might have been killed because he was looking for the gold?"

Cate shrugged. "I'm honestly not sure, but I'm trying to keep an open mind. If you would tell me what you told Marc, I'm sure that would help."

Madge's jaw tightened. "That secret will follow me to the grave."

"Mrs. Taylor—" Cate began.

"That's enough. I'm tired. Stop badgering a defenseless old woman. Timmy!" she called. "Take me up to my room. I need a break from these two morons."

Timmy emerged from the bar and smiled apologetically at Cate and Kevin. "Sorry, but she gets crankier in the afternoons. She's overdue for her daily infusion of the blood of newborn babies."

"Shut up," the old lady swatted at his head, which he easily sidestepped. He offered his grandmother his arm and helped her to her feet with surprising gentleness. The pair disappeared up a side staircase next to the bar.

CHAPTER 14

CATE'S AFTERNOON SHIFT WAS WINDING DOWN. THE GOOD THING ABOUT managing the most unpopular medical clinic this side of Sherbrooke was that the workload was reasonable, giving her time to think over Madge's revelations. She hummed a snatch of a song that had been stuck in her head as she finished up her paperwork and pondered the case. Marc was looking for the gold because he needed money, possibly to leave town. The older woman believed it was because he'd met a woman, but if Marc was embroiled in the drug trade, he might have required money to pay a debt or fund an escape. Cate needed to get a handle on what Marc was up to.

The receptionist interrupted her ruminations. "I'm leaving for the day, but do you have time to squeeze in one more patient? He's a Canterbury student."

Logan Pierce was a senior, taller than Cate and broad like a man. He didn't walk so much as strut, and Cate struggled to quell a surge of unprofessional antipathy. She didn't like his bro-ish vibe.

Such an attitude was rare here. Unlike most expensive boarding schools, Canterbury didn't exist to churn out titans of finance or high-powered lawyers. Dr. K still boasted about the number of former students who were heads of international nonprofits, high-ranking officials at the United Nations, and even members of parliament. Humanitarianism was his legacy. She recalled how he spoke of Jason. Her martyred brother was now part of that narrative. A poster child for do-goodery. It made her stomach clench to think of it. He was so much more than that.

"Good afternoon, Dr. Spencer," Logan said politely. The kids at Canterbury had excellent manners. They called everyone "ma'am" or "sir." They knew how to make small talk and how to stand up straight. Their parents paid top dollar for a world-class education, and part of that excellence—perhaps even more important than the museum trips or foreign-policy discussions—was the transformation of their children from seething, surly, complicated teenagers into polite, neatly dressed youngsters with perfect posture. Cate was once one of those earnest kids, but no more. She'd learned that being "good" and doing everything right didn't guarantee your happiness. Look at Jason—the best there was and still dead too early.

"What brings you here today, Logan?"

He shrugged.

Cate quashed her impatience. "Are you feeling OK?"

"No, ma'am."

She waited but he didn't say anything more.

"Why don't you sit down?" She gestured to the chair.

He folded his long frame into the seat, and Cate took the stool opposite him. "Let's talk."

"I guess I've got a sore back."

Cate kept her eyebrows from rising. While back problems were the world's most common injury, they were rare among young people who hadn't yet been beaten down by life and gravity.

"Where is the pain?"

He gestured to the small of his back and said, "It's kind of here and down my leg."

"Do you have any idea when it started?"

"Oh yeah. Gordo Mueller tackled me in football six months ago. It's been hurting ever since."

It sounded like a damaged disc. "There are some exercises you can do—"

"It really hurts," Logan interrupted. "My doc back home prescribed some pills. They helped."

Cate was loath to prescribe the kind of painkillers that often got ordered for back pain, at least for a child. "I'll order some tests. An ultrasound and an X-ray. Meanwhile, icing and heat can help."

"I've tried all that," Logan said, an edge to his voice. "I need something stronger."

"How old are you?"

"Eighteen."

OK, so not a minor. "I'll give you some extra-strength ibuprofen."

"No," he said loudly. He modulated his tone and continued. "With all due respect, ma'am, that stuff doesn't work on me. It makes me sick."

Cate paused. An intolerance to ibuprofen, a nonaddictive anti-inflammatory, wasn't uncommon. "Have you tried eating something with your pill?"

"Yes, ma'am, but I'm allergic to that medicine."

"What happens when you take it?"

"I break out in hives and have trouble breathing," he said promptly.

Too promptly. It sounded like the response of someone who had looked up symptoms of the allergy and memorized them. This was typical of drug-seeking behavior. What other behavior was he exhibiting? He wasn't taking her diagnosis to heart. He was also, within the parameters of well-behaved Canterbury students, being a bit aggressive. She glanced through his chart and saw that his doctor back home had prescribed one hundred tablets of Percocet. That was entirely too high. It was clear that she couldn't prescribe him anything. "I'm going to review your file."

"My doctor in Calgary fills my prescription."

"That may be, but I'll need your test results to determine a course of treatment," Cate said firmly. "The drugs you want are highly addictive, and I'm hesitant to prescribe them to someone as young as you."

"Come on, ma'am," Logan pleaded. "I need the prescription."

Cate shook her head, ushering him to the door. "Not today."

"Please," he begged.

Cate said no again and walked him to the hallway. He was saun-tering away when an idea occurred to her. She called his name. He turned eagerly, obviously hoping she'd had a change of heart.

"Do you know Marc Renaud?" If Renaud had been selling drugs, maybe that's why Logan needed to fake an injury—his dealer was dead.

"Never heard of him." His answer was quick and confident.

A well-practiced lie or innocence? "He worked here. He did odd jobs sometimes."

"Like a handyman?" Logan's lip curled ever so slightly at the word, leaving her in no doubt of his opinion on the working class. So much for Canterbury's egalitarian ethos.

"He was murdered on Monday."

"Whoa, really?" Logan's voice betrayed amazement and a prurient interest.

Cate wasn't surprised that he hadn't heard about Marc's death. Canterbury students lived in their own bubble, generally insulated from local affairs. His shock was legitimate, which killed her theory of Marc as the campus drug dealer.

She turned back to the office to finish her paperwork. Logan's behavior was troubling. She couldn't violate his confidentiality to dis-cuss her concerns with his parents or Anya, but she could keep an eye on it. She took a few moments to type an extensive note into his file. She was here for only another two months, but she wanted to leave a record of the issue. She'd have a word with Anya, not mentioning any names, to see if drug abuse was a concern at Canterbury.

Entering her notes, she paused. Despite its unpopularity, a lot of people still used the Canterbury Clinic. Could Marc Renaud have been a patient? Ethically she should not examine his file without a medical reason; however, legally, as the doctor in charge of the clinic, she was within her rights to access it.

Acting quickly so she wouldn't second-guess herself, she typed Marc's name into the patient database. Nothing. After a pause, she did the same for the rest of the Renaud family. Nothing.

She'd come up empty, but that didn't mean there weren't records. The clinic converted to digital only recently. The old paper-based patient files were stored in a secure space within the school's records room. The receptionist usually pulled the relevant dockets for the patients before Cate saw them; the keys to the record room hung behind her desk.

Cate had about an hour before she needed to pick up Rose from the bus station. She descended to the basement, which was mostly used for storage. The school records were held at the far end of the building. She unlocked the door and stood in a large, open room filled with shelves. Some held boxes of paper records. The deeper into the room Cate ventured, the older the records became. At the back were bookcases crammed with leather-bound ledgers, presumably documenting the school's founding back in the 1860s. This is what Dr. K was using to write his history project.

Back here were two smaller locked rooms. One, Anya had informed her while giving her the tour, contained the school's most sensitive records, consisting mainly of financial accounts, including the details of Canterbury's substantial endowment fund, and employee personnel files. The other stored the Canterbury Clinic health records.

Unlocking that door and closing it behind her, Cate scanned the shelves. There was nothing on either of Marc's parents or his stepfather, but she found a file for Marc himself. Sitting next to it was his sister's. She grabbed both and opened Marc's dossier. It was thin, recording childhood checkups and vaccinations until age ten, when all visits stopped. The date probably coincided with the family's departure from the township, when Mireille had fled her first husband.

Nothing in the dry notation of infant measurements and inoculation dates hinted that Marc was being abused. If Marc's father was beating his son, he wasn't leaving any physical signs. Even without bruises or broken bones, Cate knew that the violence Marc had witnessed left emotional scars. The record resumed a few years later, presumably when the family returned to the Eastern Townships after Jean-Michel's death. Marc's file ended at age eighteen. Cate wasn't surprised to see nothing in his file after childhood. Men, especially single men, were notoriously bad at managing their own health. In any event, there were no clues as to why he ended up dead in that orchard.

Geneviève's file was more fulsome. Again, she'd had childhood appointments and standard vaccinations up until age eight, when the records stopped, resuming at age fourteen for a visit about bad menstrual cramps. Things got busier for Geneviève at twenty-eight. Her family doctor recorded a referral to a physical therapist because every finger on her right hand had been broken. Furthermore, her jaw had been cracked, and she'd required dental surgery. Geneviève had had an abortion at this time. She'd been issued prescriptions for Zoloft for depression and Wellbutrin for anxiety. The doctor's notes discussed trouble sleeping, panic attacks, and a "general feeling of fear and despair."

The words *violence conjugale* attracted Cate's attention. Mireille had said Geneviève was in an abusive relationship eight years ago. The clinical notes corroborated its mental and physical toll. After that, Geneviève's chart held nothing much for years beyond a regularly renewed prescription for birth control and decreasing dosages of the anxiety and antidepression medication. By the time she was in her midthirties, according to her chart at least, Geneviève Renaud was fully recovered.

Cate turned to the last two pages. Here things became busier again. This past winter, Geneviève slipped and fell on some ice, breaking her arm and shattering her collarbone. She went to the local hospital, where she had surgery and was monitored for signs of concussion. Cate laboriously deciphered the doctor's French handwriting to make sure she didn't miss anything but found no mention in the chart of intimate-partner violence.

It appeared that Geneviève's accident really had been just that. She'd been released from the hospital after two days and prescribed Dilaudid for pain management, which in the case of a broken collarbone, could be severe. Dilaudid was in the opioid class of drugs.

Cate grimaced. Opioids were incredibly effective pain relievers, but if not carefully managed and controlled, they could sink their claws into those taking them. Here was the possible root of Geneviève's addiction.

Cate was locking up the patient records room when she paused. Staffing files were kept in the other secure room. If the extra key on the receptionist's key ring fit, it would be an easy matter to slip inside and peek at Marc Renaud's employment records. She moved quickly, aware that she'd have no excuse for being in there if she were caught.

It took a few moments of opening filing cabinets filled with the school's financial affairs before she found the employee records. Marc Renaud's file was thin: He'd worked sporadically at the school over the past five or so years. He'd rebuilt a fence near the playing fields, did some carpentry work, painted the gym walls, built an archery range. There were no comments about his character or his performance. Just standard administrative information. This was a waste of time.

She had just slipped the file back in the drawer when she saw the doorknob turn. Cate was about to be caught. Her breath quickened. She took a step back, her mouth dry. Memories of the July attack swarmed back, and her vision tunneled for a moment. The door flung open, and a short man with a head of jet-black, perfectly gelled curls stepped into the room, starting in surprise when he saw her. His eyes shifted to the side, but he broke out in a wide grin, revealing a gleaming set of white teeth.

Fear made her voice harsh. "Who are you?" She put her hands on her hips.

He spoke in smooth, accented English. "I'm Yannick Poitou, the new physical education assistant. You are, I think, Dr. Catherine Spencer?"

"Yes," Cate said, wrong-footed. Only two people called her "Catherine": Dr. K and her father—when he could remember who she was.

"We have not yet had the pleasure of an introduction." He looked at her with bright, friendly eyes, but Cate could see him assessing her. "I arrived at the school only two weeks ago."

"Nice to meet you," she said, but it wasn't. Despite his smile, there was something sharp in his gaze.

"What are you doing down here?" he asked pleasantly.

"I needed to review some patient files."

"But they are next door, are they not?"

"I got confused and came in here by accident." Cate realized she sounded defensive and was annoyed with herself. "What are you doing here?"

He shrugged. "I was meant to receive my first paycheck today, but it did not arrive. The staff and faculty manager said that because I was hired so quickly my paperwork might not be in order. She told me to double-check."

He saw her next question and forestalled her. "Of course, she would have come down herself, but alas, she has a toothache and has gone to the dentist."

He pronounced it "toot" and touched his cheek, grimacing in sympathetic pain.

Cate didn't trust this guy. "I didn't see an announcement about your arrival." Usually, a notice went around to Canterbury faculty and staff welcoming new hires. Cate, though not a school employee, was included in the list.

Yannick shrugged. "'Twas a last-minute arrangement, and I am not here long term. I am, as they say, a temp."

Cate recalled Anya saying that the faculty manager had made some questionable hires lately.

She left the room, and Poitou watched as she unlocked the patient records area. He closed the door to the secure room with a soft click. Cate waited for five minutes before exiting. She didn't hear him leave; as far as she knew, he was still in there. He hadn't believed her reason for being in the secure records room, which was funny, because she didn't believe his, either.

CHAPTER 15

THE DÉPANNEUR JAUNE WAS PEKEDA TOWNSHIP'S BEATING HEART. CON-
venience store, gas station, post office, and bus depot, it was where locals filled up their tanks, perused the community bulletin board, and
gossiped in Canada's two official languages. Rose's bus from Ottawa
was due in about fifteen minutes.

Cate had some time to kill. Against her better judgment, she dialed
into the voice mail on her Ottawa landline. Two more messages. In
the first—left at eleven p.m. on Tuesday—Matthew was drunk. Slur-
ring, and less insistent than in the others, it was self-pitying.

The tone changed in the next message. His voice now held an
edge. It sounded almost desperate. "Listen. I don't know what your
game is, but I want to talk to you. I need to check on you. See if you're
OK. You almost died, for Christ's sake." His voice broke on the final
word, and he hung up. Cate stared at the phone. Was he crying? As
with all the others, she deleted the message.

The "dép" contained a small coffee counter that attracted a con-
tingent of locals, chatting about the day's events. Thomas MacGregor
had a regular nine a.m. date there, where one could find him seated at
the corner table, talking with a group of fellow farmers and orchard-
ists about the price of feed, new grafting techniques, and, of course,
the latest gossip. It was too late for MacGregor's coffee klatch, but a
couple of older men were at the counter discussing Renaud's murder. Edging closer, Cate tried to keep a low profile as she shamelessly
eavesdropped.

"Money, revenge, or sex," said a man, whose white suspenders
strained over a prodigious stomach. "Those are always the motives."

His companion—a short, ferret-faced man—shook his head, speaking with a French accent. "You forget jealousy, terror . . . those are reasons to kill also. These days, though, I think it is most likely to be drugs. C'est toujours les drogues."

Cate stared at the display case, pretending to consider which pastry to buy.

"I never heard Renaud was involved with any of that," suspenders said.

His companion shrugged. "You just can't know who is a user. Who is a pusher."

"He *did* sometimes work at the school."

This was interesting. Was Canterbury known as a source for drugs? If the school was the site of dealing, did that bolster Montaigne's claim that Renaud was selling? Logan exhibited drug-seeking behavior but didn't know Marc. According to his employment file, Marc wasn't at the school on a regular basis. A dealer needed a consistent spot from which to sell, otherwise his clients couldn't find him.

As if responding to her unvoiced thoughts, the ferret-faced man dismissed the insinuation. "That's only a rumor. This village likes nothing more than to blame Canterbury for all its troubles."

Suspenders persisted. "You're telling me all those rich kids don't have big-city connections? I heard one student was from a mob family in Montreal."

Cate would have been surprised if Canterbury, with its liberal do-gooder reputation, was the first choice for the children of Canada's mafia, but then again, Meadow Soprano had attended Columbia.

The smaller man waved a dismissive hand. "Who knows. I try to steer clear of the whole place."

His friend grunted in assent. "If it wasn't drugs, I bet Marc was killed for the gold."

The ferrety man guffawed. "Don't tell me you believe that horse shite? If there were gold on MacGregor's land, that wily old bastard would have found it long ago."

Suspenders considered and then shrugged his shoulders in seeming agreement. "That rain we got yesterday isn't enough to make a difference to the water table." The topic of murder appeared to be dropped.

"You're telling me. My son says his well's seventy meters deep and almost dry. He's got sixty-five head of cattle to water every day. Town council has to do something."

"The mayor of Manasoka isn't in charge of the rain."

"He could try saying no to a developer every now and then. All this new housing is using up our water—"

Just then the bus from Ottawa pulled into the parking lot, and Cate left to meet her friend.

After a warm welcome and a slightly awkward hug, they drove back to Cate's place. En route she stole a glance at her Rose. The younger woman looked exhausted. Her hair was scraped into a thin bun, and her face was pale and devoid of makeup. A youthful twenty-four, Rose looked even younger thanks to her pallor and weight loss.

"How are you doing?" Cate asked gently.

"I'm OK," Rose said, staring ahead of her. "It's good to get away. The stuff from the summer still lingers, you know?"

Cate thought of her nightmares and her unresolved questions about the attack. "I do."

Rose smiled. "It's nice to hang out with someone who gets what I've been through."

Cate's heart lifted. She felt the same way. Shared trauma was a powerful bond.

"You know, I've connected with someone like that at work too," Rose said. "My new boss, Jess Novak, was a witness to that murder in the archives back in 2010."

Cate remembered the homicide, though not the details. It happened before she became a coroner. Something about a body trapped in the stacks. "What a coincidence that you two should end up working together."

"Not really. She reached out after everything, and we've been going for coffee. She's got wild stories about what went down with that murder. The police detective was a total character, and she uncovered some dark stuff about the archives. It's been good to talk to her."

Cate couldn't quash a twinge of envy. She didn't have a Jess to talk to about this past summer; she relied entirely on Rose. She knew that there was enough friendship to go around, but she had so few close relationships that she was possessive of this one.

"Jess is the manager of the Political and Cultural Affairs section," Rose continued, "so when a spot opened up, I thought it would be nice to work there."

Cate said nothing, battling a bigger wave of jealousy. Jess was obviously a cool, fun-loving woman with a million friends and a vibrant future, not a grumpy, abrasive loner who might not even have a career come December.

They turned onto the dirt road leading to Cate's place, and Rose said, "Tell me about this murder."

Cate hesitated. "Are you sure? I know you're struggling. Do you really want to—"

"I'm not fragile."

Cate knew how frustrating it was to be worried about. Sylvester Williams and even Dr. K had questioned her emotional strength. She sometimes wondered if Anya had offered her the Canterbury Clinic job out of concern for her mental health. The idea of people fussing over her was stifling. She owed it to Rose to give her the same respect she herself yearned for. "OK. I'm still working things out, but this is what we know so far. Marc Renaud was a local handyman and feedstore employee who was recently evicted and living with his younger sister. His body was found by Thomas MacGregor after being shot through the eye with incredible accuracy. A metal detector lay by his side. According to his parents, he was searching for buried gold."

"Right, you mentioned the gold before. What's the story with that?"

Cate told her about the Megantic Outlaw.

"A hidden fortune would make an excellent motive for murder," Rose mused. "We might be able to get more information about it at the local museum or library."

Cate smiled. Trust the archivist to latch on to the historical element.

Before Cate could mention Madge's tip about the archives, Rose continued, "Actually, I think I know someone at the local historical center." The younger woman was already looking at her phone. "Yup," she said triumphantly. "Reggie Patterson is the archivist at the Pekeda Township Regional Archives."

"How can you possibly know someone who works there?"

Rose shrugged. "Reggie was my teaching assistant back in archives' school. He was older—finishing up his PhD. He drove an ancient, battered Mercedes convertible, which we thought was the coolest, and had a fling with one of his students. He was dreamy."

Neither fact appeared particularly appealing to Cate, but what did she know? "That's still a pretty big coincidence."

"Not really. There aren't many archives' schools in Canada, and there's only one big conference every year, so we all get to know each other. If you haven't met someone at grad school, you've played against them at the conference's softball game. I bet he'll know all about the Megantic Outlaw."

Cate was excited. Madge had mentioned that Marc was doing archival research. This could be a meaningful clue for the police.

"Great," Cate said. "I think it's a long shot that the gold exists, but the fact that Marc was so interested makes it worth pursuing. Who knows," she said with a laugh. "Maybe it's real and Farmer MacGregor killed Marc to keep it all to himself."

Rose took her seriously. "Definitely. If the gold exists, that gives your farmer a motive."

Cate shook her head. "Thomas MacGregor is arthritic. He'd never be able to make that shot."

"Maybe's he's faking."

Cate hadn't even considered the possibility. Given MacGregor's age and movements it was unlikely; still, she shouldn't rule out possibilities. Her heart lifted. It was one thing to question people with Kevin, but the pleasure of this kind of investigation was in having someone to share the brainstorming.

Rose asked more questions, and Cate went over everything she knew about the case. She concluded by saying, "In terms of motive, the Montaigne family is high on our list. Thierry Montaigne hated Renaud and is very hostile." The bruise he'd given her had darkened to a nasty black. She recalled her interview with the two men. Something about that encounter niggled. She went over the conversation but couldn't place her elusive thought.

"But is a family grudge enough to murder someone? And why now?" Rose asked.

"I've wondered the same thing. There's another possibility. Pekeda Township has an opioid problem. Guy Montaigne said that Marc Renaud was dealing. Marc's sister, Geneviève, is in rehab right now for an opioid addiction, so there's some family involvement in the drug trade. From what I know of their relationship, I doubt Marc was selling to his sister, and I've found no one to corroborate Montaigne's accusation, but it's interesting. According to Madge, Marc needed money, so he had a motive to sell drugs."

Rose spoke thoughtfully. "You think there are criminal gangs out here? Mafia?"

"Maybe not mob," Cate said, "but there is organized crime. A couple of people have mentioned it as an issue. There was even a big Hells Angels killing spree years ago. They call it the Lennoxville Massacre— five people murdered in an internal struggle. The violence disrupted power dynamics and led to the eight-year-long Québec Biker War. More than one hundred people were killed across the province."

"Whoa."

"Another avenue," Cate said, "is Marc's mystery girlfriend. According to Madge, he was so wildly in love that he was ready to run away. That's why he was after the gold, to fund a new life."

"There's also the Renaud family," Rose said. "Most murders happen incredibly close to home."

"I can't imagine Mireille or Jacques killing Marc. They were shattered by his death." Cate paused and told Rose the story of Jean-Michel Renaud.

"He was a criminal with a proven record of violence," the younger woman said, her voice thoughtful.

"None of that is hereditary." But Cate wondered how that history had shaped Marc and Geneviève. No one escaped their upbringing unscathed.

They pulled into her driveway, and Cate was happy to see the dog poke his nose from the shed. With Rose still in the car, Cate approached him slowly. His tail wagged, and Cate beamed with pride, turning to see if Rose was watching. The younger woman opened her car door, and the dog bolted from the shed along the path up the hill. Cate wasn't disappointed at his sudden disappearance. This would take time. She walked toward the shed to pick up the water and food bowls.

"What's with your new pony?"

Cate laughed. "He's big, isn't he? He's a stray. I'm waiting until he's less skittish so that I can get him into my car and take him to the vet. He's got some injuries, and he probably needs vaccinations. Then I'll see about getting him adopted. I'm not keeping him."

Rose glanced at the bowls Cate held. "Uh-huh. Sure."

"I can't. I'm moving back to Ottawa. He'd hate the city."

"Maybe so," Rose said, "but I've known you for months and I've never seen you smile like that. Brace yourself, Cate Spencer—you might be a dog owner."

"What?" Cate gaped at her, but Rose climbed the porch steps without waiting for a response.

CHAPTER 16

THE NEXT DAY, ROSE AND CATE WALKED THROUGH THE WIDE DOORS OF Marc Renaud's only regular employer, Lachance Feed. The dry animal odor reminded Cate of the time she and Matthew watched the Royal Canadian Mounted Police Musical Ride. It was early in their marriage, and they'd been delighted by the beauty of the horses and the shining sun. Their lives were as perfectly planned as the show's careful choreography.

Lachance's was the size of a small grocery store and laid out like one, with aisle signs advertising their contents. Only, instead of cookies and olive oil, the shelves contained things like "feeding pellets" and "parasite control." There was a large area devoted to water drums and another spot displaying corral gates. Different sections focused on horses, cattle, poultry, pigs, sheep, and pets. Incongruously, there was also a section selling pool equipment.

"I guess they diversified," Rose said, pointing to a waterslide.

Cate smiled but was distracted by a counter marked "Hunting" at the back of the store. The small section contained knives, scopes, camouflage clothing, and boxes of bullets behind a locked glass cabinet.

"Excusez-moi," Cate said to a passing woman in an employee vest. "Do you speak English?" Rose didn't understand French.

The woman smiled. "Yes," she said with a thick accent. "'ow can I 'elp?"

"I wanted to talk to someone about what's involved in buying a firearm."

The woman smiled apologetically. "Désolée, we have a policy. Only our licensed staff can sell bullets or firearms. No one is on duty until after lunch. Come back then for help."

"That's fine." Cate's attention was caught by a display she noticed above the counter. Written in French and English, it said "Lachance Feed: Proud Sponsor of the Pekeda 4-H Sharpshooters Award since 1965." She approached to take a closer look. A wall of photographs exhibited grinning children of about twelve, each proudly holding a ribbon in one hand and some type of rifle in the other.

Cate read the names, a mixture of French and English, like the township's population. Guy Montaigne was the winning boy from 1991 to 1997, when presumably he aged out. The name of the female winner for 1996 stopped her: Bethany Robinson. She peered more closely at the smiling girl with close-set eyes and dirty-blonde hair. It was her. At age twelve, Bethany "Bunny" Farnham was an award-winning markswoman. She pointed the photo out to Rose. "I had a whole conversation with Kevin and Bethany about what a terrible shot he was, but neither mentioned that she was so skilled."

"Maybe she gave up shooting. It was over twenty-five years ago."

Cate recalled what Guy Montaigne said about hunting, that patience and a ferocious dedication to the shot were of utmost importance. Cate didn't think you simply forgot those. Bethany and Kevin had kept quiet deliberately. The question was, why?

They moved on, and Cate caught sight of the woman who helped them earlier. She approached. "I was wondering if you sold metal detectors."

The woman looked puzzled. "You know," Cate said, mimicking the sweeping movement of someone surveying the ground, "looking for treasure. For gold."

The clerk's face cleared. "Oh, I see. Détecteur de métaux. No. We do not sell those."

"Is there somewhere local I can buy one?" Cate persisted. She'd been reading up on the machines. They weren't as easy to use as TV made them out to be. Marc would have needed some instruction for the one he had purchased. True, there were hundreds of YouTube videos available, but if he'd bought locally, the seller might have given him lessons. They might have discussed his plans.

The woman shook her head. "No, I don't think so. Try Amazon." She turned back to stocking the shelf, but Cate didn't want to waste this opportunity. She paused, searching for a delicate way to bring up the murder.

Rose beat Cate to the punch. "I heard a metal detector was found next to Marc Renaud's body."

The woman turned back, her mouth set in a tight line, her eyes welling with tears. "I will answer your questions about the store, but I will not gossip about Marc. It is too troubling."

Cate backed away. "We're so sorry."

They hurried to another aisle. "Apologies," Rose said when they were out of earshot. "I flubbed that."

"It's fine," Cate said, unable to keep the annoyance from her voice. Undoubtedly Rose's new BFF, Jess Novak, would be a better friend and forgive Rose with more grace. They moved farther up the aisle, and Cate took a calming breath. There was still more they could discover here.

"Avez-vous besoin d'aide?" asked a voice behind them. It was a man with sandy-blond hair in an employee vest.

"Yes," Cate replied. "I'm looking for some things for a dog." She might as well stock up on a few essentials.

The employee switched to English, without a trace of a French accent. "Pet supplies are this way. What do you need?"

"Definitely some food." She couldn't keep feeding him rice and chicken, even though when she'd cook a meal for the dog, she'd make some for herself, meaning she was eating better than usual. They arrived at an aisle filled with a bewildering array of products, from bags of dog food to every manner of toy and chew bone. "I guess I need a leash and a collar," Cate added. "I've found this dog, and I'm not quite sure what to do with him."

"You're feeding a stray?" An old man who was perusing invisible fencing—and evidently eavesdropping—glared at her.

"Yes," she stammered, startled by his belligerent tone.

"I've got a wild dog harassing my sheep," he said. "You shouldn't feed strays. You should shoot 'em."

"That's terrible," Rose gasped.

The old man shrugged. "What's terrible is that some creature is wearing out my stock. Causing panic. One of my ewes will break a leg."

He glared at both Cate and Rose, appraising their appearance. "You from the city?"

Rose nodded.

"Figures." He stomped away.

Cate gazed after him, unnerved by the idea of someone shooting the dog.

"Sorry about him," the employee said. "Now, in terms of food, I advise getting a small bag to start, to see if the dog likes it. For collars, you want something that is easy to put on and not too constraining. If he's a stray, I don't imagine he'd react well to a halter."

Cate examined the wares, and they moved to a discussion of leashes. She hadn't realized there were so many choices, many of them hinging on her "dog-parenting philosophy."

They had settled on a simple four-foot-long red lead when Rose interrupted. "I think you should get this stuff too." Her arms were filled with a dog bed, various toys, and what looked like a winter coat.

"Rose!" Cate laughed at her friend's enthusiasm. "I'm not buying all that."

"Come on. He's had a hard life. He deserves some spoiling."

Cate's heart softened, the last of her annoyance with the girl dissipating. "Fine, everything but that coat. There's no way he'd let me put it on him."

"Here," the clerk said. "I'll carry it for you." He gathered up their items and led them to the front. They passed a section with dog treats, and Cate was reminded of the free box that Bethany had received. She wondered if the influencer would be willing to part with them. Rose was right, the dog deserved the best organic, sustainably sourced dog treats Instagram could provide.

"I guess there must have been a lot of excitement around here lately," Cate said as they walked. After their last interview, she was treading carefully. "With the Marc Renaud murder."

"Oh yeah," the man said. "Tragic. I hope they catch the asshole who did it. The police questioned everyone who worked here. Some of us had to come in on our day off."

"You must have known Marc," Rose chimed in.

"A little bit, but I only started in August, and he was part-time. For the past month or so he didn't have many shifts. Renata, our day manager, was pals with him, so he got the pick of the schedule." He sounded bitter, but flushed, as if remembering he was speaking of a dead man. "I didn't mind. I mean I'm new, so I don't have seniority."

The clerk dropped the goods down in front of the cash register. Seeing no one around, he scooted behind the counter and scanned their purchases.

"You were saying that Marc Renaud wasn't working here much?" Cate returned to the conversation.

"He'd landed a big painting job at the Blakeney Inn. He spent most of his time out that way."

"What was Marc like?" Rose asked.

The clerk shrugged. "Fine. Nice. Very low-key. I think he was a separatist."

This was new information. "Why do you think that?"

"I don't know. He could speak English, but he didn't like to. His truck was plastered with fleur-de-lis decals. Nothing major. Like I said, he was a low-key guy."

"Did he have a girlfriend?" Rose's voice was eager, and Cate wanted to tell her to play it a bit cooler.

Echoing Cate's worry, the clerk raised an eyebrow. "Why all the questions? Are you guys reporters or something?"

"No, no," Cate said, putting her hands up. "We're only curious. It's so shocking."

The clerk tilted his head. "Yeah, I get that. It's all anyone's talking about. Makes a change from the usual topics—the state of the roads, the low water table, and the town council's latest screwup."

"So," Rose said, pushing her luck, "*did* Marc have a girlfriend?"

Cate shot Rose a look, but the other woman didn't notice. If Rose continued like this, the clerk would shut down completely. Indeed, rather than answer, he asked them whether they had any coupons, effectively ending the conversation about Marc Renaud.

Cate was frustrated. She cleared her throat. "I actually need to talk to the manager." If Renata was friendly with Marc, she might provide insight into his character.

The clerk shifted his weight. "She's out of town, but I can find an assistant manager."

"No, it needs to be Renata," Cate said. "If you give me her number, I can text her."

The clerk lowered his voice. "Actually, she's at the Sherbrooke Treatment Center."

"Oh?" Cate said.

"Yeah, she was stoned on fentanyl and crashed her car. Judge sent her to rehab. She's been gone a few weeks. Apparently, she's doing real good. Getting out soon."

Opioids again. The men at the Dépanneur Jaune were right—everything came back to drugs. The township was swimming in them. Could Marc have been supplying drugs out of the feedstore? Lots of people came through the store, so it would provide a good opportunity from that perspective. Problem was, he didn't have regular shifts here, either.

"Wait, isn't Geneviève in treatment too?" Rose blurted.

Shit. The Renaud family was keeping that quiet. Before she could think of a way to deflect, the clerk interjected. "Geneviève Renaud in drug treatment? No way."

Cate forced a laugh, hoping to quash the gossip before it spread. "My friend's from out of town." She glared at Rose. "She's talking about someone in Ottawa. Different person."

Rose bit her lip and looked down.

The clerk looked at their faces. "Makes sense. Geneviève is super straitlaced. Mega Christian. She wouldn't mess with hillbilly heroin. Neither would Marc."

A common story: a carefully masked addiction revealing itself only when the person hit rock bottom. Geneviève's own parents were fooled.

Thanking the clerk, they grabbed their purchases.

"That could have been smoother," Cate remarked quietly as they headed to the door.

"I know, sorry." Rose bit her lip. "I get too eager, and I blurt."

Cate softened. God knows she herself didn't always make the right move. "It's fine. That clerk didn't know much anyway. Let's forget about this murder and enjoy the weekend."

CATE AND ROSE SPENT THE REST OF THE WEEKEND VISITING THE AREA'S antique shops, pottery studios, cafés, and vineyards. They didn't talk of murder or shared trauma. Instead, the conversation was easy and lighthearted. At one point Cate joked that they were behaving like the teenage girls in *The Sisterhood of the Traveling Pants*, and Rose stared at her blankly, reminding her of their fifteen-year age gap.

Monday morning dawned, and Cate woke from a restless sleep marred by the return of her nightmares. Although they were happening less frequently, the visions of Jason's aircraft plunging to earth were still terrifying. She now got them only when she was upset. She knew what was bothering her: Rose was leaving today. Over the space of a weekend, she'd grown used to the younger woman's company, and her absence would leave a void.

Cate crept down the stairs to get the coffee going and then popped outside to feed the dog. The air was chilly, and a slight mist rose from the earth, softening harsh edges and mellowing the morning. She put out the kibble she'd bought at the feedstore. She was slowly moving the dog's bowl toward the house, hoping to one day lure him inside. They were about halfway there.

The dog padded out from the shed, blinking in the soft light. His big tail wagged twice at the sight of her. His limp was gone, and he'd lost his gaunt, wolfish look. His coat gleamed. After he ate, he came up to her, allowing her to pet him. She ran her hand lightly along his wounded flank. No swelling, and the gash was healing. She'd still like to get him to the vet, but it was no longer urgent. She'd rather build up some trust with him before getting him his shots. She'd managed to put his collar on, but her attempts at walking him with a leash had frustrated both of them.

Back in the house, she scrambled some eggs and toasted some bread. Humming that same snatch of a song that had eluded her for the last few days, she placed the food and two mugs of coffee on a tray and carried everything to the dining table. Rose came down, and they ate their breakfast at the pine table overlooking the yard. The logs in the woodburning stove scared off the morning chill as they chatted about their plans for Rose's last day. Her bus didn't leave until the afternoon, so they'd organized a morning visit to the archives.

On their drive over, Cate thought about the case. Marc Renaud's lab results still weren't in, and a week had passed since his murder. She flipped on the radio to catch the hourly news. She wanted to hear if there were further developments in the Sherbrooke drug busts. She didn't want more reasons for delay on the pathology and forensics. There was no reporting on anything relevant to the Renaud murder, but Cate's ears perked up at the mention of the Congo. "UNICEF has released a damning report from Kinshasa, accusing a major French charity of child trafficking, kidnapping, and child endangerment. Rescue the Children officials have been arrested in Paris, and further arrests are expected at the Canadian headquarters in Ottawa."

That was the charity Jason volunteered for right before his death.

"Hey, are you OK?" Rose asked, seeing her face. "The Congo— does this have something to do with your brother?"

Cate found her voice. "I'm not sure." She concentrated on the road, thinking rapidly. "He worked for Medical Aid International but did some volunteering for Rescue. I emailed them a few times to inquire about his work." She'd meant to follow up but had been distracted by the Renaud murder. "I guess I know why they never got back to me . . . they were busy covering up international crimes."

CHAPTER 17

THE REGIONAL ARCHIVES WERE LOCATED ON THE CANTERBURY CAMPUS, not far from the school's main entrance. Apart from being its landlord, Canterbury had no affiliation with the institution. Instead, the archives were part of the County Museum and run by a board of governors. The small brick building had once been a groundskeeper's cottage but was converted to the archives back in the 1930s. Cate remembered one dull trip to do research there during a Canterbury history class, but otherwise she'd never paid the building any attention.

She and Rose walked into a large room filled with tables. It was like a smaller version of the Reading Room at the Dominion Archives. A gray-haired woman sat at a far corner, an open box in front of her. She was reading from a file folder and taking notes on a laptop. A younger woman in a bright yellow headscarf sat at a service desk at the front of the room, casting the occasional glance at the researcher. Four big windows opened on a vista of pine forests and rolling hills. The spires of Canterbury's main building could be glimpsed over the trees.

An attractive man of about thirty with curly brown hair approached.

"Reggie," Rose said with pleasure. "It's so good to see you." They hugged, and she introduced Cate.

"What a stunning view." Cate gestured to the window.

"Yes. I hate it."

"What?" Cate asked with a laugh.

"It isn't good for the documents. Fades the ink and encourages aging."

"Just like us worrying about sun damage to our skin," Cate said.

"Exactly," Reggie agreed with a smile. Cate found herself grinning back at him. "Come along to the back," he said. "We can talk in my office." He ushered them through another door to a series of small rooms, pointing to one marked with his name.

When they were seated, Reggie said, "Rose mentioned you're looking into Marc Renaud and his interest in Donald Morrison—the Megantic Outlaw." He raised an eyebrow in a way that made Cate feel like they were in on a secret together.

"That's right. I'm assisting the coroner, Kevin Farnham, in investigating certain aspects of the murder. From what Mr. Renaud's parents said, he was actively looking for the Outlaw's gold when he was killed. We'd like to learn more about his interest in the treasure. I know he was doing some research here."

"How do you know that?" Reggie asked.

Cate didn't want to reveal Madge as her source. "It's not a secret, is it?"

"No, of course not, but we consider our researchers' privacy to be very important."

He looked to Rose, who nodded in agreement. "Yes, sorry, Cate. I thought you were interested in the general history of the Megantic Outlaw. I didn't realize you wanted specific information about Marc's research. Most libraries and archives are ferocious about guarding their patrons' privacy, especially their research interests. It's one of our core values. It ensures our clients can look at what they want without any fear of censorship or restriction."

"It's a central tenet of our code of ethics," Reggie chimed in.

Cate shrugged, unreasonably irritated with Rose, Reggie, and their professional values. "I take it that means you won't confirm what Marc was researching?"

Reggie shook his head.

"You'd tell the police, though, wouldn't you? Archivists haven't taken an oath like a psychiatrist or a priest, right?"

He laughed, his eyes crinkling in the corners. "Yeah, of course I would, but I haven't heard from them on this matter. I don't know if they knew Marc had been coming here."

Cate would tell the constables about Marc's research interest. Maybe they'd be so grateful for the tip that they'd let her tag along to their interview. She thought of Constable St. Onge's scowl. Fat chance.

Rose cleared her throat. "We were hoping to get some background on Donald Morrison, you know, learn more about who he was."

Cate leaned forward slightly. It was important to learn what Marc knew about the gold. It might help them understand his frame of mind.

"That, I can give you," Reggie said with enthusiasm. "First thing to know is that he was a real person. Sometimes people think he's a tall tale, like Robin Hood or the Lone Ranger, but we've got his baptismal attestation, death certificate, and tons of newspaper clippings about his exploits." Reggie spoke with calm confidence. Cate noted he wasn't wearing a wedding ring.

"In his twenties, Morrison heads out west, where he becomes a bona fide cowboy. He's this tough, capable guy and a great shot. He returns to the Townships, and he's just swaggering. Only he finds out his father has been swindled out of the family farm."

Cate liked the way Reggie's expression opened up as he talked about history.

He continued, "Morrison's dad's first language was Gaelic, and he didn't speak much English, so he got conned by a better-educated neighbor. The Scottish community was outraged by this trickery and sided with Morrison."

"It does seem unfair," Rose agreed.

"In reaction to this," Reggie continued, "Donald allegedly burns down a barn and then evades arrest for about ten months. They deputize this quasi-criminal American whisky smuggler, Lucius "Jack" Warren, to catch him, but Morrison keeps hiding. Then, at noon on June 22, 1888, Warren has Morrison cornered."

"Whoa. Confrontation in the streets at high noon? That's right out of a Western," Rose said.

Reggie resumed, "In the middle of the deserted main street in the village of Megantic, the Outlaw shoots Warren straight through the base of his brain, tearing the carotid artery."

Cate considered. That was a well-placed bullet, bringing instant death. Morrison must have indeed been a crack shot . . . much like the person who killed Marc Renaud.

"With murder added to his charge sheet, the manhunt intensifies," Reggie continued. "They bring in a task force from Montreal, but the Scottish settlers feed the police false information, pretend not to speak English, and generally cause chaos. The English authorities shouldn't have been surprised—the Scots used the same playbook their ancestors deployed when they shielded Rob Roy, William Wallace, Robert the Bruce, and Bonnie Prince Charlie."

"Then what happened?" Cate asked.

"They caught him eventually," Reggie said. "Betrayed and ambushed at his parents' home. He's sentenced to eighteen years of hard labor. He goes on a hunger strike, and his health wanes. He dies not long after. He's been a local hero ever since."

"And where does the treasure come in?" Cate asked. She wanted the answer, but she was also enjoying Reggie's storytelling. His eyes glinted with excitement as he told the tale. She was drawn into his charisma.

"There are lots of stories about that. Some say it was a community collection to support Donald. If that was the case, it couldn't be that much. The Scottish settlers weren't wealthy and wouldn't have had a lot of extra to contribute. There are also accounts about the spoils of bank or train robberies, although there's no evidence for that. The best tale, and the most likely if the gold exists, is that Morrison stole some gold bars from the area's whisky runners."

Cate recalled Kevin's stories about the region's long history with contraband. The gun that killed Marc Renaud may have been smuggled in from the United States.

"There was a flourishing illicit trade happening along the border. Morrison spent ten months hiding in the hills, woods, and swamps. He could have figured out where the 'bank' for the trade was and stolen from the smugglers to fund his escape when he made a break for it."

"Do you think there's really any truth to the idea?" Cate asked. Purloined treasure still seemed far-fetched to her.

"Paper currency was certainly more common, but gold wasn't unheard of. From my research, criminal trade was often conducted with gold because it was untraceable."

"So it's really out there, hidden and waiting to be found?" Rose's voice was awestruck.

"Who knows?" Reggie shrugged. "There's nothing in the official record about stolen gold, but if it was illicit there wouldn't be, would there? Just because it wasn't written down doesn't mean it didn't happen. There is oral tradition supporting the treasure's existence. Morrison's family swore the gold was real. It certainly caused enough feuding in the region over the years."

His use of the word *feuding* caught Cate's attention. "What do you mean?"

Reggie chuckled. "There are two families who've hated each other for generations. I think half of them don't even know the root cause, but it all goes back to the gold."

"Is that the Renauds and the Montaignes?" Cate asked.

"Indeed," Reggie said. "I've come across a couple of newspaper articles from the turn of the last century. In 1901, Alphonse Montaigne and Marcel Renaud were best friends, determined to find the gold. They thought they'd figured out a sure thing and were set to dig it up. Only, Montaigne got paranoid or greedy and accused his best friend of cheating him. They got into an altercation, and Renaud shot Montaigne. Blew his lower leg right off."

"Wow," Rose said.

Reggie nodded. "By some miracle, Montaigne survived, but he couldn't work in the sawmill anymore. Renaud was arrested and went to jail. Both families fell on hard times as a result and have hated each other ever since."

"All over the Outlaw's gold," Cate said thoughtfully. She wondered if Thierry's and Guy's ignorance about the origin of the feud was real or if the story of this violence was family lore, a burning ember of hatred carefully passed down through the generations.

"What a wild story," Rose said.

"Yeah, they taught us about the Megantic Outlaw in school but never mentioned the gold or the feud," Reggie said. "I found out about it doing my own research."

"You're from Pekeda Township?" Cate asked. Reggie gave off an urban, intellectual aura that was hard to reconcile with the pickup trucks and gun racks she saw on Manasoka's Main Street.

Reggie smiled. "Born and raised. I went to university in Ottawa"—he gestured to Rose—"but ended up back in my hometown. I studied history because of what I had learned in school about the Megantic Outlaw. It captures the imagination."

They chatted for a little while longer, and Reggie walked them back to the researcher room, introducing them to the younger woman at the reference desk. "This is Ilyana. She's a student at Bishop's University who works here part-time."

"We're interested in Marc Renaud's research," Cate said. "Did you assist him when he came here?" Rose shot her a look; she knew Cate was fishing for the specifics of Marc's research.

"It was so terrible what happened to him," Ilyana's eyes filled with tears. "I didn't usually have a shift when he was on-site."

Cate wondered about the tears. Did Ilyana have a small crush on Marc, or was there more to it? Before she could broach the subject, the younger woman continued. "I helped him once, though. He needed a locker for his research notes, all his maps and stuff. We got to talking. He was sweet."

"Marc Renaud took notes? He drew maps?" Cate turned to Reggie.

He looked uncomfortable. "I can't show them to you," he said. "Researcher privacy."

"That material might be germane to a murder investigation," Cate said sharply.

Ilyana's eyes widened.

Cate was annoyed with Reggie's reticence; he was taking his professional ethics a little far. "You should inform the local police about Marc's notes and keep them safe until they can review them."

Ilyana nodded seriously. "Absolutely. They're all locked up, but I'll inventory everything now and keep the key close by so no one can get access." She looked fierce as she said it, and Cate was confident that the girl would do what she could to protect this potential evidence.

CHAPTER 18

CATE AND ROSE DROVE INTO THE PARKING LOT AT THE DÉPANNEUR Jaune. The bus to Ottawa was idling. "Thanks so much for visiting, Rose."

The younger woman smiled. "It was a nice break for me. Thank you." She glanced out the car window. The Dépanneur was perched atop a small hill that rolled down to the Pekeda River. They watched as a heron swooped over the water. "It's such a peaceful spot. I'm glad for you. I mean, I know you were struggling this summer."

Cate stiffened, ready to deny any weakness. Then she considered. "I think things are better. Going to the Congo was helpful. It brought me acceptance." That was true, at least until she heard that item on the radio. Now some of the old questions were resurfacing. What was Jason doing at Rescue the Children? She didn't want to share her worry with Rose, however. She spoke briskly. "Now I need to get reinstated to my duties and return to Ottawa. Restart my life."

"I'll be glad when you're back in the city." Rose's smile wavered, and her eyes filled with tears. "I'm still processing, you know? I'm doing OK, going to work, getting through the day, seeing my therapist, but . . ." Her voice choked with emotion. "I'm so isolated carrying those memories. I'm so fucking lonely." The younger woman turned her head to stare back out the window, her shoulders shaking.

Cate was startled by Rose's reaction, but even more by the honest expression of such a vulnerable emotion. She had been so fucking lonely for huge chunks of her life. She'd carried grief and sadness in her long before her brother died, never admitting it to anyone, not even Jason. She hadn't realized that such a confession was allowed. Rose's words were a revelation.

"I'm sorry," Cate said. Utterly ineffectual.

Rose stopped crying and forced a watery smile. "Thanks. According to my therapist, these 'feeling waves' only last ninety seconds, so I just have to surf it until it's over. I'm sad about leaving. You've been a good friend to me."

Cate wasn't used to hearing that kind of sentiment. "I'm glad." She swallowed a lump in her throat. "You know, I don't have a lot of friends. It's hard for me to be vulnerable."

"No kidding," Rose said with a sniff and a laugh. "You're not exactly warm and welcoming."

Cate laughed. "Hey, I think I'm softening."

Rose cocked her head to the side. "Maybe," she said. "I've been here for a full weekend, and you didn't tell a single person to fuck off."

"See," Cate said, getting out of the car. "Softening."

They walked to the bus, and Rose gave her a fierce hug.

Cate welcomed the contact, this literal and figurative connection.

"Remember," Rose said as she pulled away, "don't soften too much. There's a murderer out there, and we need some Cate Spencer steel to catch him."

Marc Renaud's wounded gaze, staring at the autumn skies, flashed before Cate's eyes. "I won't," she promised.

SITTING ON THE PORCH WITH HER LAPTOP AND A CIGARETTE, CATE googled Rescue the Children. She clicked on a link to a video segment.

A blonde news anchor spoke: "We turn now to legal expert and child advocate Mercy Mwangi for further analysis."

A Black woman appeared on the screen.

"Disturbing allegations about the charity, Dr. Mwangi," the news anchor said.

"Indeed, we have long suspected this adoption agency of criminal practices, especially in the Congo and neighboring Burundi. The UNICEF investigation has established irrefutable proof."

"What is the organization accused of?"

"Knowingly allowing children with living parents to be adopted, mostly to France, Canada, and the United States. Furthermore, the charity violated norms around fees and costs, profiting from the sale of African children to the West."

"If the children had parents, why were they in orphanages?"

"This is not uncommon in poor countries. Parents—often single mothers—become overwhelmed and send their children to an orphanage for a time. They are not giving up their parental rights, however."

"For additional perspective, we've also invited Terrence Bauerly, a lawyer and author of *Adoption for Dummies*."

"Thank you, Melissa," said a portly white man in a book-lined study. "I think the key word here is *adoption*. While Ms. Mwangi"—he stumbled over her name—"uses inflammatory rhetoric, what we're discussing are perfectly legal and appropriate adoptions. These children go to good homes where they have access to medical care, education, and material comfort."

"Some have been stolen from their parents," Mwangi insisted.

"Obviously, there were some irregularities in how this particular charity operated—"

"These are not irregularities. UNICEF did a full-scale yearlong investigation, canvasing child advocates and working with local and international experts to establish its case. It proved without a doubt that Rescue the Children deliberately thwarted the law."

"It might have bent some rules, but African rules are easily twisted. Rescue's basic mission was a noble one. They were giving these children a better future than their parents could provide."

"This is nonsense," Dr. Mwangi replied. "Material wealth is not a guarantor of happiness, security, or education. It is wrong to remove children without parental consent. This so-called charity is an example of deep-seated racist and colonial assumptions."

"Thanks very much, you two," the anchor's smooth voice cut in. "That's all we have time for."

Cate turned uneasily from her computer. Jason was volunteering for this charity while it was under investigation. He couldn't have known about the accusations, or he would never have helped such an organization. Still, she couldn't shake the feeling that there was something more to her brother's time with the charity. Using the end of one cigarette, she ignited another. It wouldn't hurt to ask a few questions.

She picked up the phone and called Jason's boss, Brilliant Aduba. He was plugged in to the world of international development and might have additional insight about the scandal. His voice mail informed her that he was away from the office at a refugee camp at the Thai-Myanmar border. He would be unreachable for several days. She left a message asking him to call her back.

Next, she dialed her voice mail. It was fucked up, but it comforted her to hear from Matthew. To know he was still thinking about her. To know that the man she'd spent so many years with, some of them even happy, still cared. There was only one message. It started abruptly. "The thing is, I've left Tansy. After the night we spent together, I knew I couldn't stay with her. I'm free now, and I love you. I've always loved you. I want us to try again." A ragged sigh. "I guess that's not what you want, though. I'll stop calling you. I'll leave you alone. You're grieving Jason, and I understand." Matthew's tone deepened, and Cate recalled how much she had enjoyed laying her head on his chest on lazy Saturday mornings. They'd talk about their weekend schedules, and she would feel the resonant rumble of his voice as they planned out their days, their lives, together.

The message continued. "Know this, Cate—I'm here. I love you, and I want us to try. I will wait."

She stared at the phone. She wasn't going to call him. She hesitated. Instead of hitting "Delete," as she had for all the other messages, she hit "Save."

CHAPTER 19

MANASOKA'S TOWN HALL SAT AT THE CENTRAL INTERSECTION OF THE village. It was an imposing red-brick edifice, its grand columned portico a sign of the village and township's former prosperity. The railroad used to run through the far side of the village, bringing the region's agricultural bounty to Sherbrooke, Montreal, and points beyond. The wealth of those years dissipated, but its legacy was reflected by the number of substantial homes in the town's core and the grandeur of its municipal buildings.

Now new money was arriving: Montrealers and people from farther afield who liked the hilly landscape and proximity to ski slopes, golf courses, deep lakes, and untraveled roads. Thanks to producers like Kevin and Bethany, they could even expect city luxuries like organic eggs and fine cheeses. The gourmet pastries that Cate carried in a white box from the Gratitude Café were an example of the small indulgences now available in Pekeda Township.

The police station was in the town hall's basement. Constable Douglass sat behind a desk. Cate was pleased. He was easier to handle than St. Onge. "Morning, Officer."

He looked surprised. "Doctor."

"I thought this would be a homicide command center," she said, looking around the empty space. Filing cabinets lined a back wall, and desks were scattered here and there, holding computers and other electronic equipment.

He shrugged. "Inspector Vachon and the SQ are running the investigation out of Sherbrooke."

"Looks like you've been sidelined," Cate said without thinking. Damn it, that sounded snarky when she wanted to appear friendly and helpful.

Constable St. Onge entered the room from a side door, holding a coffee cup. "We're setting up the interviews, providing vital local information. We're integral to this whole operation." She tilted her head defensively.

Recalling Vachon's assessment of the local force, Cate wasn't so certain, but she wasn't going to quibble. "I'm sure you're doing great work."

"We've confiscated every suspected firearm in the entire township." Douglass gestured to a locked metal cage, which contained many labeled weapons. "We've pissed off half the region."

"I bet that's quite a flash point." Cate grimaced, recalling Thierry's rage at the removal of his rifle.

"It hasn't been too bad," Douglass said. "When we explain that it's to catch Renaud's killer, most people come around. It's kind of surprising when you look at how many gun owners are out there. Heck, we took eight from Canterbury's firing range. Even Bethany and Kevin had to hand over their little rifle."

Kevin had mentioned that, but the fact took on a more suspicious angle now that she knew Bethany was a crack shot. "They'll all be tested to see if they match the bullet that killed Marc Renaud?" Cate asked.

"Yes, of course, in due time," St. Onge said.

"In due time? This is a homicide investigation. Ascertaining the murder weapon should be the highest priority."

"You'd think," Douglass said. "Only something big is brewing in Sherbrooke. They're tracking a major drug—"

"Dougie," St. Onge said sharply. "That information is classified." She turned to Cate. "Why are you here, Doctor?"

Cate was here to offer material assistance in order to impress their boss and get a glowing letter of recommendation from him. She didn't want to share the blatantly self-serving part, so she said, "Kevin Farnham asked me to join him in a few interviews related to the Renaud murder, and Detective Inspector Vachon agreed that I could help with the investigation. I wanted to know if there was anything I could do for you guys."

"No," St. Onge said before Douglass could speak.

She had to respect St. Onge's bloody-mindedness, but Cate herself could be stubborn. "I brought pastries." She opened the box to reveal two flaky croissants, a chocolatine, and a cinnamon bun. This was a step above the usual donuts.

Douglass's eyes lit up and he grabbed the cinnamon bun. St. Onge crossed her arms over her chest and repeated her "No."

Cate needed to push. "Whenever I assist police in Ottawa on their investigations"—how her sometimes ally, sometimes enemy Detective Baker would laugh at that one—"they value my contribution. That's a central tenet of police work: Use all the resources available to you."

"That makes sense," Douglass said, receiving a glare from St. Onge. "Have you worked a lot of homicides?"

Cate shrugged. "Probably about fifteen as coroner." She didn't tell them that almost every one was an open-and-shut case: either domestic violence with the male partner the obvious guilty party or gangland retribution that was untangled by the Guns and Gangs squad.

Douglass whistled. "That's more than Inspector Vachon has overseen, for sure." He took an enormous bite of the cinnamon bun.

"We're not interested in working with civilians," St. Onge said repressively. "We'll follow standard protocol."

"OK," Cate said, before playing her trump card. "It's only that I was thinking about the gunshot wound and what it might mean for the investigation. I guess I can wait and tell Detective Inspector Vachon."

"No, no," Douglass interrupted. "You can tell us. We'll take it to Vachon."

Cate smiled. "Great. I was thinking about the forensic implications of the precision of the wound, directly through the eye."

A pause, and Cate assumed that the two officers were recalling the murder site as she was. The crisp autumnal air, the burble of the river splashing over rocks, the neat bullet hole.

St. Onge furrowed her brow. "So what?"

"A direct shot to the brain immediately stops the heart from pumping, resulting in very little blood loss. Even if the killer was within a couple of meters of their target, it would be unlikely that the victim's DNA would be on their clothes."

"Interesting," Douglass said, polishing off the bun.

"Kevin probably explained all that to you already, though," Cate added.

Douglass wiped crumbs from his mouth. "I'm not so sure he'd know those finer medical details."

Cate regretted casting doubts on Kevin's abilities, but she needed to prove she had knowledge and skills that the Egg Man couldn't bring to the table. "I wonder if the forensic pathologist has made the same conclusion," she said, all but batting her eyes.

"We have access to the case file," Douglass said. "The Sûreté haven't completely excluded us."

St. Onge opened her mouth, presumably to protest, but Douglass turned to his desktop, tapping in a few key words. He read the results. "Autopsy isn't back yet."

It was eight days since the murder. Forensic analysis in Ottawa moved faster than that, but there were probably fewer resources out here in the country. "Will you get the results soon?"

Douglass avoided her eye. "It might not be until next week."

"That long?"

Douglass shrugged. "With what's going down in Sherbrooke"— St. Onge glared at him, and he moved on—"I mean, it takes a while to get labs back. When we had that overdose, we didn't get the prelim report for quite a while."

"Is that right?"

"Nope, nothing for two weeks. The forensic pathology lab is understaffed and overwhelmed. Kevin was on me like a rash because he wanted to talk to Fred Leduc's wife and give her the confirmation of cause of death." He grimaced at the memory. "Fentanyl."

Cate flinched. Opioids again. "When you get Renaud's autopsy report, pay attention to the results, bearing in mind what I said about the amount of blood."

Douglass took out a pen. "Can you repeat that, Doc?"

"You could call me when the results come in," Cate said casually. "I can help you interpret them. Tell you what they mean."

St. Onge hesitated, but Douglass nodded enthusiastically and eyed the pastry box again. "That would be great. Kevin doesn't have the medical know-how, you know?"

Cate abstained from making an egg joke. "Who are the Sûreté's main suspects?"

"We shouldn't really discuss that kind of—" St. Onge began.

Douglass waved her into silence, a move that outraged Cate's feminist principles while delighting her curiosity.

"The doc is on our side," Douglass said. "Vachon said it was OK to discuss the case. She might be able to help."

The younger cop rolled her eyes.

Douglass gave Cate his attention. "Given the family's animosity toward the Renauds, Guy Montaigne and his cousin Thierry are on the list. They've been brought in for questioning, and we've got their rifles. They're a priority for testing."

"What are their alibis?" Cate asked.

"They've vouched for each other. Guy finished his shift at the hospital at one p.m. Thierry says that they hung out after that. Their story is basically worthless. Everyone knows the Montaignes stick together. That family has a history of lying to the police. I wouldn't be surprised if Thierry is protecting Guy."

"Maybe you're looking at this all wrong. Maybe Guy is providing an alibi for Thierry." The cousin was certainly menacing enough.

Douglass scoffed. "Thierry doesn't have the skills to make that shot. The way I see it, Guy learned Marc was sneaking around Mac-Gregor's and saw his opportunity to settle a family score." Douglass brought an imaginary rifle up to his eye. "Bang," he said. "Renaud drops dead, and Guy runs. Only he's made a fatal mistake. Driven by his own pride, he's fired too perfect a shot, giving the game away." Douglass leaned back in his chair, glancing from Cate to St. Onge with complacency.

Cate hesitated. "Sure, that's feasible—"

"An old family feud is pretty thin, as motives go," St. Onge interrupted.

Douglass looked annoyed. "You're just fired up about your pet theory."

"What's that?" Cate asked with too much eagerness.

St. Onge set her mouth in a tight line, but Douglass supplied the details. "She thinks Marc was having an affair."

"Oh?"

St. Onge glowered. "Shut up, Douglass."

The other cop ignored her request. "We've got a coworker at the feedstore claiming that in the past few weeks he was paying more attention to his appearance and that he had a spring in his step."

Cate wondered if their witness was the woman she and Rose first talked to. She had seemed close to Marc.

"St. Onge thinks that means he has a mystery girlfriend."

The constable jutted out her chin. "Sounds like a guy getting laid to me."

It sounded like that to Cate too. That jibed with what Madge had said. "So who is the lover?"

Douglass chuckled. "That's the thing, we can't find a trace of a girlfriend." He glanced over at his partner. "Typical woman, looking for the romance angle."

St. Onge's hand curled into a fist. "At least I'm in a relationship, not some lonely loser who can't find a partner."

Douglass's face darkened, while Cate tried not to apply the constable's insult to herself. "There might be other motives. Drugs. All the fentanyl floating around."

"That's what they're looking into in Sher—" Douglass saw St. Onge's glare, and his voice stopped abruptly.

"Maybe the Sherbrooke stuff is connected to Marc's death," Cate said.

"We've been working that angle," Douglass said eagerly. "We figure Vachon would pay more attention to this case if we could tie it to the criminal gangs. That might get us more resources."

St. Onge snapped. "Detective Inspector Vachon is following all procedures and implementing every appropriate protocol to identify and arrest the murderer. There is no evidence that Marc Renaud has any connections to gangs."

Cate considered. She was more and more doubtful of Montaigne's assertion about Marc's drug dealing. Her interactions with Madge and Logan didn't support the theory. What's more, Farmer Mac-Gregor had confirmed that drugs were a problem in the area but didn't mention Renaud as a source. No one she had talked to since— Bethany, Kevin, Anya, Madge, the feedstore employees—mentioned drug dealing in connection with Marc.

Still, it was important to investigate all angles. "There's Marc's sister, though," Cate insisted. "Geneviève's in rehab for opioid addiction. That's a link."

"As soon as we locate her, we'll—"

Cate interrupted Douglass. "You still haven't found her? It's been over a week. She hasn't been informed her brother died? You haven't interviewed her? What about the funeral?"

St. Onge shifted uncomfortably, and Cate could tell she'd struck a nerve.

"It appears that only Marc knew which facility his sister checked in to. We've found no documentation indicating her location. Furthermore, we've encountered some delays in obtaining the necessary paperwork permitting the facilities to divulge patient information and confirm or deny her presence."

"In other words, the Sûreté can't be bothered?" Cate interrupted.

St. Onge flushed but said nothing.

"I don't think it's a big deal," Douglass said. "Marc drove Geneviève to the facility on Saturday. She was locked up tight in rehab well before the murder took place." He coughed. "As for the funeral, the family has decided to go ahead this week. It's happening Thursday."

"Without Geneviève?"

Douglass's face reddened. "Their church is very particular about performing the death rites quickly."

"So they're going to have a funeral without one of the chief mourners, all because the Sûreté can't prioritize the case." Cate's voice shook with anger. This was not how grief should be handled.

St. Onge and Douglass both looked down at their feet. At least they realized how shameful the police's failures were here.

Cate returned to the question of the murder. "What about Geneviève's abusive ex-boyfriend? Violent exes can be incredibly volatile."

"When was that relationship?" St. Onge asked with an edge to her voice. She was annoyed that Cate had the jump on her.

"It was about eight years ago," Cate said. "Apparently Marc and his stepfather went to Montreal and intimidated the guy, so he stopped hassling her. Still, the ex's anger might have been festering. Abusers are controlling, violent. He could harbor long-term resentment."

St. Onge didn't look convinced, but Douglass took notes on a pad in front of him. "What else have you got?" he asked.

"I assume you know about Marc's biological father and his criminal history?"

St. Onge's face remained impassive, but Douglass blurted, "Yeah, someone pulled his arrest sheet, but it's from thirty years ago. There was nothing there."

"Anything else?" St. Onge looked bored.

"Marc was researching the location of gold belonging to the Megantic Outlaw. According to Madge Taylor at the Blakeney Inn, he was passionate about it."

"Oh sure," Douglass said enthusiastically. "You know, Donald Morrison was my great-great-great-granduncle. Grandpa owns his

Colt .45. He's got it in a display case in his living room. Keeps it in primo condition and fires it any chance he gets—anniversary of the Outlaw's capture, day of his sentencing, and the anniversary of his death. Also St. Jean Baptiste Day, Canada Day, and New Year's Eve. It's Grandpa's prized possession."

"I was at the archives yesterday," Cate said. "It turns out Marc was very serious about researching the gold. He made tons of notes. The archivist won't share them with me, but maybe you—"

St. Onge interrupted. "We received a call from Reggie Patterson yesterday afternoon. I will go over and review these notes."

Good, the archivist was being proactive about working with the police. "Can I come with you?"

"That would be inappropriate."

Cate could see from St. Onge's face that the officer wasn't open to persuasion. She'd have to find another way to tag along.

CHAPTER 20

CATE AND ANYA SCANNED THE PEWS FOR A PLACE TO SIT. THEY HAD arrived early to Marc Renaud's funeral, but still the church was almost full. Cate's gaze swept the room, stopping at a blonde head. Was that Bethany? The woman turned to her companion, a tall Black man with excellent posture. No. This woman's features were more angular, and she moved in a controlled, precise way, like a ballerina. Cate continued examining the mourners, spotting MacGregor toward the middle, a few rows over from Constables Douglass and St. Onge.

She didn't see Vachon anywhere. Would the Sherbrooke cop even bother to come, or were all his resources concentrated on that big drug case? Kevin wore a dark suit and looked suitably somber. Bethany sat beside him, her hand moving nervously to her hair. Bracelets glittered in the light of the stained glass window, and Cate identified the jewelry as Bethany's favorite set of Mejuri wishbone stacked wristlets; the influencer's Instagram account was oddly addictive.

"I'm grateful you let me tag along," Cate said as she and Anya found seats. When she had learned the headmistress was going to the funeral, she'd asked to accompany her. Anya knew lots of townsfolk and could offer useful insight. "Though I didn't think you knew Marc well."

Anya shrugged. "I didn't, but he worked at Canterbury, so it's expected I put in an appearance." Anya was acutely conscious of societal expectations. Even in high school, she made sure to always move in the right circles, always wear the correct sneakers, always like the cool bands.

"You're not the only one here from the school." Cate nodded in the direction of Mr. McNeilly, the head of physical education. Yannick Poitou sat beside him. "Why are they here?"

"Marc's family was involved with the Holy Adventist Church, and Mr. McNeilly's one of the faithful. I have no idea Poitou's connection. He's only recently moved here from Gatineau. I can't imagine he knew Marc." As if sensing their stares, the small man turned and gave them both a wave.

They waved back, and he turned away.

"What's his deal? I bumped into him the other day. He seems—"

"Smarmy? I agree. He's charming, but in a desperate way."

The phrasing caught her attention. Jason said something similar once about a colleague in the Congo. Jason . . . The funeral was bound to bring up memories of her brother. Her throat tightened. She closed her eyes. The grief was like a physical weight pushing on her chest.

She breathed deeply a couple of times, turning to Anya only once she was calm. "I've been wanting to mention something to you." Speaking in a low whisper, and without revealing any identifying facts about Logan, she recounted the student's drug-seeking behavior. "I've requested his medical file from his Calgary doctor, and I've made a note in his records. All is in order from the Canterbury point of view, but I found his demeanor troubling."

"I'm glad you told me all this, Cate. Possible misuse of opioids by one of our students is quite concerning, of course."

"It might be more than that. I've heard a rumor about Canterbury being a source for illegal drug trade."

"What?" Anya raised her voice in an uncharacteristic break from decorum. She immediately lowered it again, nearly hissing. "That's preposterous. We're an elite academic institution, not some dodgy back-alley crack house. Listen, I encouraged you to investigate Marc Renaud's death, but if all you're doing is digging up scurrilous gossip about Canterbury, I might have to reconsider."

Anya's high-handedness irked Cate, and she spoke without think-ing. "You may have recruited me, but you're not my boss. You don't get to tell me what to do."

Anya opened her mouth, as if to argue further, but closed it again. She inhaled deeply and spoke in a low tone. "You're right. I'm sorry. I was out of line. I get defensive when protecting the school. We endure so much criticism."

Cate had a hard time thinking of Canterbury, a wealthy bastion of privilege, as victimized, but that's probably why she wasn't headmis-tress. "It's no problem." She and Anya shuffled down the pew to make room for more arrivals. The funeral was packed.

Cate spotted the clerk she'd talked to at the feedstore. Madge Morrison, supported by the long-suffering Timmy, tottered in. Reggie Patterson, accompanied by Ilyana, the archival clerk, grabbed a seat at the back. He looked very handsome in his dark suit, his curls brushed back from his face. Ilyana's eyes were red from crying.

"The whole town is here," Cate said. Well, not Guy or Thierry Montaigne, but given their family's long-standing animosity toward the Renauds, that was probably for the best.

"It's the murder factor. Everyone is curious."

Marc's mother and stepfather entered the church surrounded by extended family. Mireille looked even more wan and haggard. Jacques exuded a weary exhaustion. A round-faced woman in a dark suit guided them to the first couple of pews. Given the re-semblance to Kevin, Cate assumed she was his sister, the town undertaker.

"No Geneviève," Anya murmured. "That's odd."

"I heard she was out of town and couldn't get back in time," Cate was pleased that the rumor mill hadn't leaked Geneviève's where-abouts. At least the Renauds were spared that gossip.

"Oh, how sad she's missing her brother's funeral, but I know the Adventists have rules about the timing of funeral rites."

The family was seated, but there was another delay as the minister consulted with Mireille.

"Who are they?" Cate jutted her chin toward the blonde she'd mistaken for Bethany and her companion.

"That's Joseph Ngoma and his wife. He's a businessman." Anya anticipated Cate's next question. "He probably knew Marc through archery. Joseph was an Olympic archer. He coaches the local league. We let the townsfolk use Canterbury's range most weeknights. Marc practiced there."

"Archery," Cate said in surprise. That hadn't been offered when she attended school.

"I introduced it three years ago," Anya said with a self-satisfied smile. "Very successful. Trains students' bodies and their minds."

"And the woman is his wife?" Cate confirmed.

"Diane Doucette." Anya paused as if expecting a reaction from Cate. When none was forthcoming, she added, "Former Olympic gold medalist."

"Wow, does she do archery too?" Cate asked.

"You've really never heard of her?" Anya asked in disbelief. "The whole country celebrated when she won two golds in Beijing. She's a biathlete."

"I don't even know what that is." The Olympics, with all their hope and possibility, were never her bag.

"It's a cross-country skiing event combined with sharpshooting. You ski for miles and then drop to the ground and hit a tiny target. Very intense."

"You're telling me that woman is an Olympic-level sharpshooter?"

"Uh-huh," Anya said. "Why?" Then realization dawned. "Cate, you can't possibly think she murdered Marc Renaud. She's a national icon. Also, I don't even think she knew him."

Cate stared at the woman. One of the important things about this case was the skill required to complete the kill shot. Diane Doucette literally won gold medals doing exactly that.

CHAPTER 21

CATE STOOD ALONE IN THE CHURCH BASEMENT. MOURNERS MILLED around, talking in subdued voices. Anya was engaged in an animated conversation with Manasoka's mayor. Bethany and Kevin spoke to Mireille and Jacques. The constables were conferring together by the door. Still no sign of Vachon. Cate wanted to speak to Diane Doucette and her husband, but she couldn't see the Olympians anywhere. Yannick Poitou talked to Ilyana, the archival clerk. Reggie Patterson seemed to have left. She spotted the gym teacher, a tall, muscular man of about fifty-five, standing alone. "Hi, Mr. McNeilly," she said, approaching him.

"Yes?" he said abruptly.

"I'm Cate Spencer. The doctor at Canterbury Clinic."

They'd nodded hello a few times in the hallway. "Oh yes," his gaze was trained on a group of younger people, perhaps feedstore employees, who hovered over the buffet table, stuffing crustless egg salad sandwiches into their mouths and talking loudly. He tsked disapprovingly. "What can I do for you, Doc . . ."—his gaze sharpened—"Spencer. Did you attend Canterbury in the nineties?"

"Yes," she said, surprised.

"I remember you and your brother. Wonderful athlete."

"Really?" Cate cast her mind back but couldn't recall Mr. McNeilly.

"I was a student teacher in those days. I spent six months shadowing old Mr. Castle."

"I remember him," Cate said with a smile. She recalled a red baseball cap perched atop a large head and white knee socks pulled up to knees as knobby as rock formations. "His belly was so big he couldn't bend down. Not exactly an inspiring physical specimen."

"I loved that man like a father. God rest his soul."

"Oh," Cate said, scrambling. "He was a great teacher, very passionate." She remembered him as being a jerk: screaming at the weak kids, mocking those without a lot of athletic ability.

"Like a father," Mr. McNeilly repeated, staring at her balefully.

"Yes," she said quickly. "A wonderful man."

"He died two years ago," the gym teacher continued.

Cate sighed inwardly. She was not escaping this reminiscence. "What did he die of?" It was the question she always asked. Professional curiosity.

"Kidney stones," Mr. McNeely said, his eyes carefully following the group by the sandwiches. They were now cracking open cans of soda and talking about last night's hockey game.

"Kidney stones aren't usually lethal."

"One got infected. He swelled up like a blowfish. He was vomiting blood by the end and pissing it out too. Was in complete agony. It was a mercy when he finally went toward the light."

"That's horrible." Kidney stones were an extremely painful ailment, comparable to childbirth. That would be an agonizing death.

"It took a long time too," Mr. McNeilly said, pausing. "He lingered."

Much like poor Mr. Castle, the silence now lingered. Cate wasn't quite sure how to break it.

"Anyway, how can I help you?" Mr. McNeilly asked. The loud group was now lounging by the back wall. They were quieter, which appeared to satisfy Mr. McNeilly's vigilance. He was obviously a teacher who believed in policing people's behavior, even when off the clock.

"I wanted to find out more about the Canterbury archery program." She recalled what Guy Montaigne had said—that shooting a bow and shooting a gun shared some skills. If that was the case, it would expand her pool of suspects.

"What do you want to know?"

Cate had been prepared to explain her interest, but apparently Mr. McNeilly wasn't a curious person. "Have you been the coach since the program started?"

"Yes, three years now."

"You must be a good shot."

He shrugged. "Average. You don't have to excel at something to teach it. I'm good enough to hit the target. I coached the junior girls to the provincial championships two years ago."

"Sounds like there are lots of skilled students." She doubted that a Canterbury student killed Marc Renaud, but she wanted to be open to possibilities.

"You considering taking it up?" He tore his eyes away from his surveillance and assessed her as a butcher would evaluate a piece of poor-grade meat. He cocked his head to one side. "You're tall enough for it, but your shoulders look weak."

Cate tried not to be upset about having her nonexistent archery ambitions thwarted by a high school gym teacher. Before she could formulate another question, they were joined by Yannick Poitou.

"Good day, Dr. Spencer," he said in his smooth voice. "How are you?"

"As well as can be expected on this sad occasion."

"You did not, I don't think, have a personal connection with the deceased."

It was an odd phrasing, and Cate wasn't sure what he was implying. "No, but I happened to be at the scene shortly after his death. I don't think you have a connection either, do you?"

He put his hands up, and Cate noticed his beautiful cuticles, much more manicured than her own fingernails.

"No, surely I do not. I came to lend support to my friend Garth here." He pronounced it "Gart," and he patted Mr. McNeilly warmly on the arm. The gym teacher looked pained by the contact. "He knew M. Renaud through his attendance at this wonderful church."

"Yes, Marc and his family are stalwart members of the Holy Adventists. Stalwart," McNeilly confirmed. "It's sad that Geneviève, Marc's sister, couldn't make it, but I understand she's hiking in quite a remote location. Of course, she's trying to get back as quickly as possible."

"What location is that?" Poitou asked with interest.

"I, er, don't know," McNeilly responded.

"Surely you have an idea. Northern Canada? Out west? Perhaps out of the country? Mexico? The United States? Where is Miss Renaud?"

Cate winced at this guy's pushiness. The family didn't need him stirring up questions about Geneviève's absence. "I don't think it matters," she said firmly.

"You are quite right, of course, Doctor," Poitou said. He glanced at the door. "Forgive me, please, but I must make my excuses and depart."

Cate turned to see Detective Inspector Vachon entering the basement reception area. So the cop had deigned to come after all.

"What's his story?" Cate asked Mr. McNeilly, jutting her chin toward Poitou's back.

He shrugged. "Funny fellow. I didn't even ask for an assistant— they foisted him on me. I'll tell you one thing about him, though . . ."

Cate leaned in closer, ready to learn some valuable information about the assistant gym teacher.

"He's got a terrible hitch when he shoots a basketball," Mr. McNeilly said sorrowfully. "I've told him to lead with his legs so he's got enough power to get to the rim, but I haven't seen any improvement. I don't know what they're teaching coaches these days."

Cate leaned back in disappointment. Yannick Poitou was acting suspiciously, but the only insight Coach McNeilly could offer concerned his shooting stance.

CHAPTER 22

THE FUNERAL CROWD HAD THINNED A BIT, AND CATE SPOTTED DIANE
Doucette standing by herself. She hurried over and introduced herself. "I'm Dr. Cate Spencer. I'm a coroner assisting Kevin Farnham in the investigation of Marc Renaud's death."

Diane was tall, with strong features and a proud posture. "Let me guess—you want to ask about my biathlete career?" Her English carried a faint French accent.

Cate was planning to finesse things a little, so she was caught off guard by Diane's bluntness. "Yes," she stuttered.

"I'm glad to help. I want this killer caught. I don't like the idea of a murderer on the loose. I was happy to be interviewed by the police."

"They were interested in your skills?"

"They couched it like they wanted my expertise, but I think the fact that I can hit a bull's-eye at fifty meters makes me a person of interest."

"The police told you that?" Vachon wasn't conducting a very discreet investigation.

Diane laughed. "Not in so many words, but they confiscated my two very expensive rifles and I've spent more time talking about my Olympic abilities in the past week than I have since Beijing 2022."

Cate enjoyed this woman's candor. She was—and Cate hated herself for even thinking it—a straight shooter. "Did they describe the wound to you?"

"Directly through Marc's left eye."

"And could you make that shot?"

"Absolutely."

"Even if he had been moving? Even in dimming light?"

Diane crossed her arms. "A person's eye socket is the size of a golf ball, right?"

"Yes, about that."

She spoke in a quiet voice. "As I told the police, for my event I cross-country ski fifteen kilometers in arctic temperatures, racing against some of the fastest athletes in the world. I stop, drop to my stomach, and regulate my breathing and heart rate to such an extent that from fifty meters away, I accurately hit a target four and a half centimeters across." She held out her fingers to indicate less than two inches. "I have done all of this to compete for a gold medal with the weight of an entire country's expectations on my shoulders while literally the entire world watches." She paused. "If I wanted to, I could certainly hit a slow-moving man ambling by a river."

The silence between them pulsed for a moment, and then Diane laughed. "Luckily I had absolutely no reason to kill Marc."

Cate wasn't sure what to make of Diane's statement. The woman spoke with blithe confidence about her expertise, but everyone knew what she was capable of, so she couldn't very well pretend to be unskilled. If she had murdered Renaud, she'd be smart to brazen it out rather than act like she couldn't have done it. Cate decided to move on. "How did you know him?"

"His sister used to clean for us. Marc picked her up a few times."

"What did you think of him?"

"Seemed nice."

Cate waited. Every heterosexual woman she'd asked about Marc mentioned his good looks. Diane surprised her by highlighting something different.

"He was kind to Geneviève. Years ago, she was having troubles with her partner. That jerk beat the hell out of her, but Marc and his stepfather dealt with it."

"What did they do?"

"Threatened the boyfriend. Told him to leave her alone or they'd rough him up. The way Geneviève tells it, Marc was fierce. He was protecting her."

"You know a lot about Geneviève's life, about her troubles."

"This is a small town. We take care of each other. We gave Geneviève a big raise when things were volatile. She's part of our family now. She comes to my son's baseball games. We even had Geneviève and her parents over for Christmas dinner that first year, right after things with the ex unraveled."

"Did Marc come to that Christmas?"

Diane flushed. "I can't remember."

Before Cate could press her, a tall Black man arrived at their side, carrying a plate of desserts. Nanaimo bars, lemon squares, and brownies were piled high. Not exactly the fuel of elite athletes. "Voilà, ma belle," he said to Diane. He nodded politely to Cate. Joseph Ngoma was a couple of inches taller than his wife, with shoulders broad enough to meet even Coach McNeilly's exacting standards.

"Dr. Spencer," Diane said, "this is my husband, Joseph."

"Nice to meet you."

"Likewise," he responded in lightly accented English. "I heard you were replacing the doctor at Canterbury."

Cate was now used to her reputation proceeding her.

"The doctor was asking about Marc Renaud's death. She's a coroner in Ottawa."

His eyes were wary. "Is this part of the police investigation? This is the second time you've been questioned, Di. Maybe we should have a lawyer present."

"No, no," Cate rushed to placate him. "I'm concerned with the medical aspect of the death. I'm helping Kevin Farnham."

"Joe, we want to assist," Diane chided him. "We need to catch Marc's killer."

"OK," he said, relaxing. "I get defensive when police are involved."

"With good reason," Diane said, patting her husband's arm. "Until I started dating Joseph, I never realized how often police do 'routine traffic stops' or how terrifying they can be."

He looked grim. "It's better out here. The nice thing about a small town is that people are forced to get to know you as a person, rather than a skin color. How can I help, Doctor?"

"I was explaining how good Marc was to his sister," Diane said.

Joseph nodded sadly. "Yeah, great guy."

"Your wife mentioned you invited Geneviève over for Christmas one year but couldn't recall if Marc came too."

"Of course, Di, don't you remember? The kids were tiny, but he took them sledding at the village hill. They loved it."

"Oh, you're right. Stupid of me to forget that." She took a big bite of brownie and closed her eyes at the taste. "So good," she murmured.

"Did you have much more to do with Marc after that?"

"I'd see him in town," Joseph said. "We'd shoot the shit. I was so sad to hear of his death."

Diane leaned into Joseph, and he squeezed her arm.

Watching the two interact, Cate felt a twinge of envy. It had been a long time since she had someone to lean on. It took her a moment to phrase her next question. "I understand you're teaching at the community archery course?"

"Yes, indeed," Joseph said, smiling for the first time in their conversation. "I love the sport. I was on the Olympic team twice—London and Rio. I never medaled. Now it's fun to teach it. Canterbury has great facilities."

"Would archery skills correlate to marksmanship?" She was talking to an expert, so might as well get his opinion.

"No," Joseph said. "Shooting a gun and shooting an arrow are entirely different."

He spoke confidently, but remembering Guy Montaigne's words, Cate pushed. "What about someone who was skilled with a hunting bow rather than an archery bow?"

Diane chimed in. "Joe is right. The only shared skill is that ability to aim."

"But that's the hardest part, isn't it? That capacity to calm the mind and focus?"

Diane shrugged. "Perhaps, but an archer would have to practice long and hard before they had facility with a gun. Joe and I have tried one another's sports, but despite his tremendous skill, there's no way he could do what I can with a gun, and I can't match him with a bow."

Cate recalled Diane's confident recitation of her own abilities. "How talented a marksman would someone need to be to make the shot that killed Marc Renaud?"

Diane and Joe exchanged glances; it was obvious they'd already considered this question. "The shot was difficult, but not impossible," Diane said. "Much easier than anything I accomplish in a race."

"Oh really?" Cate asked.

"Yes," Joseph said with certainty. Here a trace of his belligerence returned. "It doesn't require an Olympian, only a decent hunter possessing a good gun with an excellent scope. Find that gun, and you'll find your killer."

CATE SAT IN THE DARKNESS. THE DOG WAS CURLED UP ON THE BOTTOM step of the porch. She was heartened by his willingness to come nearer. Hopefully he would eventually trust her enough to enter the house. The arrival of the cold weather might help with that. Her heart lifted. It would be nice to sit on the couch, the dog by her side as the wood stove crackled.

A rustle in the shrubs. A night creature, nosing the earth. She finished her glass of wine. The animal was too small to be a bear, but the dog was interested. His nose twitched in the direction of the sound. She puffed her cigarette and poured another glass. After the first bottle, she'd realized it was more efficient to bring the second outside to the porch with her.

She had planned to write up her latest thinking about the case—compile what she knew, create a list of next steps. Instead, she found herself musing about death. Remembering the scattering of Jason's ashes, only she and her father witnessing the wind carry her brother over the Ottawa River. Now it felt like a stingy gesture. Jason had been a popular guy with lots of friends; why hadn't she hosted a celebration of his life? She knew why—she didn't want to be confronted by the abundance of love in Jason's life and the lack in her own. She wanted to keep Jason's death all to herself. She'd been selfish, hoarding her brother to herself.

She had only dim memories of her mother's funeral. Some relative, an aunt or a second cousin, wore a dress with black lace trim along the bottom, and five-year-old Cate thought it looked like cobwebs. It was only she and her father left now, and even he, as problematic as he was, wouldn't be around forever. Indeed, his mind was no longer the sharp, snapping rubber band she used to fear. Sadness pressed against her chest. She was all alone in the world. She took another sip of wine and reached for her phone. As she had for the fifth time that night, she called the voice mail and listened to Matthew's last message. She finished the glass of wine, and without allowing herself to think any more about it she dialed his number.

CHAPTER 23

"WHAT ARE WE DOING TODAY?" THE HAIRDRESSER, VIVIENNE, WAS A
friendly thirtysomething with long blonde hair, an orangey tan, and
a tight dress. She spun Cate's chair and stared at her in the mirror.

Cate looked at her own reflection, something she generally
avoided. Wrinkles, a few gray hairs, and a nose that was starting to
resemble—she realized with some alarm—her father's. She was getting old, and what did she have to show for her life? This is why she
avoided her reflection. Who needed an existential crisis every time
they passed a mirror?

"Just a trim." She'd come to Nicole's Salon and Spa after her morning
shift and before she was due to meet Dr. K. She booked the appointment
with a specific purpose: The day Renaud was murdered, Farmer MacGregor grumbled about the salon being a hotbed of gossip. Now she wanted to
find out exactly what the village was talking about. She and Vivienne were
alone, which Cate hoped would lead to unimpeded chitchat.

"Really?" Vivienne asked. "Only a trim?" She picked up a strand
of Cate's hair that held more than a little gray. "Want me to dye it?
Honey gold is a very popular color. Half the women in town have it."

"I think my natural color is fine."

"That's exactly what Bethany Farnham said three years ago. We
took the plunge, and look at her now—an influencer." Vivienne said
the word with the same awe you'd reserve for "Nobel Prize winner."

"Is she a honey gold?" Bethany's hair was a very pretty shade of
warm blonde.

"Oh totally. She's the one who started the trend—influencing. I
think it would look great on you."

"I'll stick with a trim," Cate said firmly. She recalled mistaking Diane Doucette for Bethany at the funeral. The Olympian must also be a honey gold aficionado.

Vivienne shrugged and got to work. "You're the doc up at Canterbury, huh?"

"Yes," she said. Normally Cate shut down hairdressers' attempts to chat, finding the burden of small talk stressful, but this time she wanted the dish. "Only temporarily."

"That's good," Vivienne said with an edge.

"Do you not like the school?" Cate asked, playing innocent.

"The clinic had to go somewhere, I guess, but I wish it wasn't there. All my clients—the old ladies—complain about the walk and how hard it is in the winter, how intimidated they feel going in. That school has a long history of being assholes to the local community. People remember."

Cate considered her own time there. She was cocooned in privilege and wealth and gave little thought to the locals. They were only townies, after all. Her South African friend referred to them as "louts." She recalled MacGregor's story about having pennies thrown at them from the cricket field. While the school focussed on rescuing the "third" world, Canterbury had run roughshod over its own community. She could see now there was more than a hint of white saviorism in the attitude. "That was a long time ago," Cate said. Anya wouldn't allow that kind of behavior anymore. Things must be better today. "The school is a positive force—"

"Baloney," Vivienne interrupted. "The older students, the seniors, slum it at the Thirsty Bucket every now and then. Rich pricks who have no respect." Vivienne's eyes were wounded, and Cate wondered what kind of encounter she might have once had with a wealthy Canterbury student.

"I'm sorry," Cate said, uncertain what she was apologizing for.

"Oh, it's not your fault," Vivienne laughed. "You're only the doctor."

Obviously, the stylist hadn't heard she was also an alumna. Cate cleared her throat. "That's right. I'll be going back to Ottawa in December. I'm a coroner there."

"A coroner!" Vivienne said with interest. "That's so cool."

Cate's profession was rarely greeted with such enthusiasm, and she didn't hesitate to capitalize on it. "Yeah, I'm taking an interest in the Marc Renaud murder."

"It was so sad," Vivienne said. "Mireille, his mother, came in yesterday to get her hair done for the funeral. Didn't say a peep, poor lady, but she looked haunted, you know?"

"Is she a regular client? What's she like?"

Vivienne stopped cutting hair to consider. "Normal. Both she and Geneviève get their hair done here. Geneviève gets honey gold too. She's a real looker, like her brother. Marc was really hot. It's so tragic."

Cate was unsure if the tragedy was that Marc was dead or specifically that someone attractive was gone. "Did you know him?"

"Enough to say hi to. My oldest brother went to school with him, and I always had a little crush. But it's not like he came in to use the salon services. We get lots of men now who want manicures, pedicures, even facials, but they're mostly from the city."

"Spa treatments weren't Marc's bag?"

"No way," Vivienne laughed. "He was a local local, you know? Drove a truck, worked at the feedstore, maybe went to Florida for a week over the winter. He wouldn't have given a thought to his cuticles. He wasn't sophisticated."

Cate wasn't sure if tending to your nail beds was a sign of civilization, but she took Vivienne's point. Montaigne had said that Marc was a small-town guy, and even Kevin had described him that way. Madge had claimed he specifically wanted the gold to move to a city, but that didn't track. "I heard he was thinking of leaving town."

"Marc?" Vivienne scoffed. "No way. He'd die in Pekeda Township." She put down her scissors again, and her eyes softened. "I guess he did." Vivienne shook away her melancholy, trimming a piece of hair. "What's your professional opinion on the murder? Who do you think did it?"

"Who do *you* think did it?" Cate countered. She was here to gather information, not spread it.

"I heard that Guy Montaigne is a suspect cuz he's such a crack shot."

"Is that likely?"

Vivienne shrugged. "I don't know. He's real quiet, but kind of intense. Seething."

That hadn't been Cate's impression, but then again, Thierry's unabashed aggression took up a lot of space.

"I do know that Guy is bonkers good with a gun," Vivienne said. "My dad went to a turkey shoot once and wouldn't shut up about how amazing Guy was. Apparently, he killed twice as many birds as anyone else." She snipped a lock of hair. "According to my dad, the man could bag a bird."

Cate remained quiet, assuming Vivienne would fill the silence. Her hunch paid off.

"I saw him a few nights ago, you know? At the Thirsty Bucket."

"Really?" Cate asked. Guy didn't strike her as a big drinker.

"Oh sure. Tuesday is ladies' night, and my girlfriend and I always go—two for one from the bar rail. Guy and his Neanderthal cousin Thierry were there, belly up to the bar, pounding back beer. I introduced myself."

"You hadn't met them before?"

Vivienne stopped cutting again. "I mean, I knew who the Montaignes were. You kind of know everyone in this goddamn place, but I'd never talked to either of them." She wrinkled her nose. "They're like, forty or something."

"He's the same age as Marc," Cate pointed out.

Vivienne shrugged. "Guy's got an older, watchful vibe. His cousin also seems old but like in an Incredible Hulk way—all rage and smashing, you know?"

Cate recalled Thierry's tight grip on her arm. She did know.

"What made you interested in them the other night?"

The stylist stared at her, wide-eyed. "You serious? They're suspects in a murder case. That's literally the first exciting thing to happen in Manasoka. I wanted to hear all about it."

"Weren't you nervous to talk to them?"

Vivienne waved an unconcerned hand. "As if those two would murder Marc. What could be their motive?"

"What about the feud?"

Vivienne laughed. "That stupid thing? It's an excuse for teenagers to TP each other's houses on Halloween."

Vivienne's dismissal echoed what a few others had said, but Thierry Montaigne still cared about it. "Wasn't Marc attacked because of it?"

"That fight at the Thirsty Bucket like a hundred years ago? My brother was there. It wasn't over the feud. Guy was getting obnoxious with some girl, and Marc intervened. Everyone had been drinking and things got a little physical."

"Did you learn anything about Marc or the murder from talking to the cousins?"

Vivienne shook her head. "Nah. Thierry was hammered and obsessed with showing us GoPro footage of his dirt bike practice in the woods by his house. He thinks he can make the Hare Scramble one day, but he's too old. My brother says he has no clutch control." Vivienne's voice dripped with disdain.

"What about Guy?"

The hairdresser brightened. "I had a decent conversation with him, although he did say he thought Marc Renaud was a pussy, but like, not in a mean way. Just like stating a fact."

"Did he mention anything else?"

"Like a confession to murder?" Vivienne tilted her head wryly. "Do you think if he'd admitted to killing someone, I would have kept quiet? I liked Marc. I would report that."

"Of course, of course. I'm sorry. I meant did you glean any other insights."

Vivienne shrugged. "Not really. Guy was pretty wasted. He told me I had pretty hair." She twirled a lock with a laugh. "Like I said, honey gold never fails. He called me his beautiful Juliet. That bugged me because I thought he'd forgotten my name." She leveled a stare at

Cate. "You know how they do that—try to butter you up with over-the-top romantic bullshit so that you'll suck their dick or they can screw you without a condom."

In fact, Cate did not know how they do that. She'd had only a couple of sexual partners before marrying Matthew, and after the divorce there had been no one else.

"Anyway," Vivienne continued, "I was annoyed with the Juliet crap and told him to stop, but he explained that I looked exactly like her."

"Like Juliet?" Cate asked, trying to understand where this was going.

"Yeah, like the girl from the movie. The one with Leonardo DiCaprio? We watched it in grade eleven English class."

Cate remembered that film—*Romeo + Juliet*, a remake starring Leo and Claire Danes. It was set in the modern day, with guns instead of swords and a contemporary music soundtrack. Cate loved that movie when it came out, thinking she was very sophisticated for swooning over Paul Rudd's portrayal of Dave Paris rather than the more obvious Leonardo. Cate considered Vivienne. She was blonde and pretty, but there the resemblance to Claire Danes ended.

The stylist looked impatient. "Now, I've told you what I know. You've got to give me something in exchange. Tit for tat."

Cate wanted to test out Guy's accusation, which she found increasingly hard to credit. "I heard Marc was dealing drugs."

"Absolutely not," Vivienne said flatly. "I've known Marc Renaud my whole life, Geneviève too. That family is straitlaced." Vivienne lowered her voice. "Not many people remember this, but their dad, their bio dad, was a real piece of work. Total asshole and a big cokehead. I heard Marc telling my older brother he'd never do drugs because he didn't want to end up like his old man."

Vivienne's story squared with what others had told Cate. It was unlikely Marc was dealing drugs. That begged the question, why had Guy claimed he was? Was it to besmirch the name of a man and a family he despised, or was there a more nefarious motive?

"What else have you got?" Vivienne asked.

Cate considered. Whatever she said would be all over Pekeda Township by tomorrow. It wouldn't hurt to throw out some fresh possibilities. "There's a rumor that Marc had a secret girlfriend." Both Madge and St. Onge suspected as much.

"Really?" Once again, the scissors went down. At this rate, Cate's trim would take hours. "It could be. Marc Renaud was real discreet. So handsome, but you never heard about girlfriends." Vivienne mused, "You know, sometimes I wondered if he might be gay."

Cate raised an eyebrow.

"It would make sense." Vivienne expounded on her theory. "He was such a small-town guy; he'd never have been able to come out. I mean, if he was too insecure to get a manicure, there's no way he'd have told his buddies he liked men. I bet that's what it is." Her voice now rang with conviction.

"I haven't heard anything to that effect," Cate cautioned.

Vivienne wasn't listening. "No, it all fits together. I spotted him at the drugstore a couple of weeks back. He had a big box of condoms in his basket. He was awkward when he saw me looking at them. Like, more awkward than running into your buddy's little sister with a gi-ant box of rubbers. He had something to hide."

"Surely, if he'd had a boyfriend or a girlfriend"—Cate wasn't ready to jump on the secretly gay bandwagon—"that person would come forward. Talk to the police. Let people know they were dating. As it stands, the cops have no information about Marc's romantic life."

"That's what I'm saying," Vivienne said excitedly. "He must have been gay. That explains why no one has spoken up. There's still a lot of bigotry out here. I bet Marc's secret gay lover shot him through the eye."

Cate blanched. She could see how the rumor would spread. Vivi-enne would advance this piece of speculation to her next client, per-haps saying that "the new doc at Canterbury was wondering if Marc was gay." She needed to distract the hairdresser from her theory. "You say you get a lot of men in for treatments?" She recalled Yannick Poitou's beautifully manicured hands. "Is the new assistant gym teacher at Canterbury one of your clients?"

Bingo. Vivienne's eyes lit up. "Oh yeah, big-time. He's been in town only a few weeks, and he's already come in for two manicures, a facial, and he's booked for a back wax later today."

"What's his story?"

Vivienne leaned in closer. "Have you heard something?"

"No," Cate protested, but she remembered his intrusive questions about Geneviève's whereabouts. "Only, I don't buy that he's an assistant gym teacher."

Vivienne considered. "You might be right. I tried to talk baseball with him, but the only sport he knew about was hockey. He's also come all the way from Gatineau, which is like eight hours away, for some shitty assistant job."

"Only four," Cate corrected. "It's near where I'm from. It neighbors Ottawa."

Vivienne wasn't interested in a geography lesson. "Come to think of it, he did ask me a lot of questions about the village, about Marc Renaud, about Canterbury." She paused. "You know, he really wanted to know about the archery club. Like, who was part of the town league, how often they met. That kind of thing."

Cate's excitement rose. What was this guy up to? Was he looking into Renaud's death? Did he think there might be a crossover between archery and marksmanship? Or was he Renaud's murderer, looking for ways to widen the pool of suspects so suspicion wouldn't fall on him? "What did you tell him about the league?"

Vivienne shrugged. "Not much. Half the town does it. My mother even goes, though she says her boobs get in the way. I told her she should cut one off like those Amazons. She didn't find that funny."

The trim was finished, and Vivienne pulled out the blow-dryer. The noise from the machine meant they could no longer chat. Cate leaned back and relaxed, humming a snatch of a song she'd heard recently. It was the tune that had been haunting her for days now. Where had she heard it before?

Cate pulled out her phone. As she had many times over the past few days, she found herself clicking over to Bethany's Instagram. The shots of bright-green smoothies, artistic arrangements of gray and black pebbles, and filtered images of vintage albums leaning against a record player were extremely soothing.

Bethany presented a curated, calm life filled with the certainties of macronutrients, organic cleansers, and expensive charm bracelets. Idly, Cate scrolled farther back into Bethany's feed, reviewing images from the previous month.

One shot brought her up short. She'd seen it before, but this time it grabbed her attention. It was a selfie of Bethany in the beautiful warm glow of afternoon sunshine streaming into a room through a window. Bethany's expression was pouty, almost seductive—more sexually charged than the brisk, professional perfection she usually projected.

The filtering of the light was also arresting. Cate studied the image, trying to figure it out, and realized that the window itself was quite dirty. This was interesting. Such a filthy window would not be found in the pristine environs of the Farnham home.

Cate studied the image. Bethany wore an oversize man's plaid shirt, which was also very different from the cool white linens or bright athleisure wear she usually posed in. Cate zoomed in on the image, looking for clues. Yes, the windowsill was grimy, and it held a screw, a bunch of thumbtacks, and a stick, like the kind you used to stir paint.

Where was Bethany posing? Cate could make out a man's work boot lying discarded behind her. It was almost cropped out. She clicked back to the windowsill, staring at the paint stirrer. Its tip was covered in a soft, pretty blue. Cate knew where she'd seen that color before, and then she knew who she needed to talk to.

CHAPTER 24

CATE DROVE UP TO THE EGG MAN'S HOUSE AND WAS RELIEVED TO SEE that Kevin's truck was gone. The trunk of Bethany's Range Rover was popped open and packed to the brim with belongings. Cate got out, noting three suitcases, a set of weights, boxes marked "dishes," and two laptops. The front passenger seat was covered in green houseplants.

Bethany Farnham hurried down the steps, carrying a box filled with crystals.

"You going on a big trip?" Cate pointed to the packed car.

"I'm divorcing the Egg Man," Bethany said in a clipped voice. "I am the walrus. Goo goo ga joob."

"You're leaving Kevin?" Cate hadn't been expecting this.

"Don't look so stunned," Bethany snapped. "It was a long time coming." She blew out a noisy breath. "Kevin knew it, as much as he tried to pretend it wasn't happening."

"I'm sorry."

Bethany's eyes filled with tears. "I didn't want it to go down like this. I thought I could tough it out, make things work. I know Kevin. I know he's a good man." She broke out into noisy sobs, and the crystals wobbled dangerously. Cate took the box before they smashed down.

"Do you want to talk about it?" As much as she liked Kevin, her heart went out to Bethany. A divorce brought out the worst in people.

Bethany stared at her. "Thank you. Everyone in this goddamn town thinks I glommed on to Kevin in high school and landed myself a rich guy. Only he wasn't rich in high school. He wasn't much of anything. Imagine Kevin now, but with acne. He was always an Egg Man, and I loved him." This last came out as a long wail.

"Hey, hey," Cate said in a panic. "Let's get you inside. I'm not sure you're in a fit state to drive." Cate was used to dealing with the excesses of grief, but messy, complicated emotional turmoil for any other reason was not her forte.

Bethany allowed herself to be led inside and took a seat at the harvest table. "Do you want coffee?" Cate asked, pointing to the pot.

"No, I can't drink Kevin's garbage." Bethany sniffed. "There're a couple of bottles of Voss water in the fridge."

Cate grabbed the waters and brought them to the table. "Want to tell me what happened?"

"I can't take it anymore." Bethany's eyes crinkled up at the corners. She looked like she was about to wail again.

"Shh," Cate soothed, patting the other woman's hand. It was very soft. The Aesop Resurrection Aromatique Hand Balm she was constantly shilling really did work wonders. "Take a sip." She pointed to the water bottle.

"Things have been going downhill with Kevin for years," Bethany confessed. "He's happy living here. I want more. I can be more. He doesn't see it."

Bethany paused, staring at Cate with a sense of wounded pain. Her makeup wasn't smeared. What a testament to the Glossier mascara and eyeliner Cate knew she loved. "Are you telling me everything?"

Bethany hesitated, and Cate stated the suspicion that brought her here. "You were sleeping with Marc Renaud."

"How did you know?" Bethany gasped.

"I figured it out today. I was talking to Vivienne at the salon. She said she thought that Marc was seeing someone on the down-low. Then I saw your Instagram post from about a month ago . . ."

"Was it the one by the window?" Bethany asked. "I knew it was risky to post it, but I couldn't resist. The lighting was so perfect. I mean, it was the golden hour."

It seemed appropriate that Bethany's affair was exposed thanks to her dedication to Instagram.

"So you and Marc were having an affair?" Cate confirmed.

"Only a little one," Bethany said defensively.

"How do you have a 'little' affair?"

Bethany shrugged impatiently. "It was a casual thing. It started up when I bumped into Marc at the feedstore with Kevin. We were buying pine shavings for chicken bedding." She shot Cate a look, telling her exactly what she thought of that particular outing. "Anyway, Kevin wandered off, and Marc was there. Of course I'd seen him hundreds of times before, but this time he was more focused. We got to talking about different cities in Canada and where would be a nice place to live. I thought he might actually be considering leaving Pekeda Township. He never had a lot of ambition, but that day he was different. More appealing. I started to sense this real charge between us, you know? A kind of zing of attraction. He felt it too, I could tell."

Bethany smiled at the memory, and Cate could picture the fizzing chemistry between these two attractive people. For someone who valued aesthetics as much as Bethany, handsome Marc Renaud would have held a lot more appeal than schlubby Kevin.

"Kevin came back and was kind of gruff. He basically shooed Marc away, and we had another big fight. Kevin wants kids; I don't. He wants to expand the egg business. I want us to sell up and move on. I can't stay in this hinterland forever. I need to go to the city. Maybe Toronto. Maybe New York or LA."

"So, after this fight, you started seeing Marc?" Cate asked.

Bethany's eyes filled with tears. "Yup. Marc was staying at his sister's place, but she was hardly there—out most nights. That's where that photo was taken. Anyway, we'd meet up at her house and, well, get reconnected . . . Like connected in ways that we hadn't before . . . Like we had sex."

"Right," Cate said. "I get it." Marc wasn't gay; he was having an affair, hence the secrecy. This was a major revelation in the murder investigation—and made Bethany a prime suspect. Cate's heart rate quickened. Was she in danger? She looked around the room. Did they keep their gun nearby? No, the police had confiscated their weapon . . . . Unless crack-shot Bethany kept a second gun stashed somewhere.

Bethany didn't notice Cate's concerns. Instead, she was lost in reminiscence. "Hooking up with Marc was fantastic. I mean, I've been with Kevin for twenty years, and he's, you know . . . the Egg Man. It's not the sexiest thing. Sleeping with Marc confirmed that I needed more and that I should take it. Our affair showed me that I am still hot, still interesting. I am more than the goddamn Egg Wife."

Bethany didn't seem intent on murder, and Cate's anxiety abated somewhat. "You wanted to be with Marc."

"God no," Bethany sputtered. "Despite that first conversation, Marc was even more stuck in this stupid town than Kevin. He was obsessed with that ridiculous Megantic Outlaw story. He really believed gold was buried somewhere on MacGregor's farm. He was never going to leave Pekeda Township."

Cate considered. That didn't jibe with Madge's story. The older woman had said Marc was desperate to get out of town with his secret lover, which was why he became interested in the Outlaw's gold in the first place. Bethany implied that Marc was already interested in the gold when they got together.

"If you knew it wasn't going anywhere, did you dump Marc?" She watched Bethany carefully, looking for signs of turmoil or jealousy. Her face was serene.

"*Dump* is a strong word. I mean, he was a good-looking guy. There were lots of women interested in him. I think what we had was more of a nostalgia thing."

"You sure?" Cate asked. None of this squared with Madge's version of events. Could Marc have masked his deeper feelings from Bethany, or was she lying right now to make it appear that Marc was less in love with her?

"Yeah. I mean, he was more focused on the stupid Outlaw than anything else."

"You and Marc ended things amicably?" If Marc dumped Bethany and sent her into a murderous rage, she was masking her feelings very well.

"Yes. I told him it was over, and he was fine with that. He wasn't looking for anything long term."

"Then what happened?" Cate asked.

"I'm not a bitch, despite what everyone thinks. I love Kevin. I'm just not in love with him. I respect him. I had to be honest. I told him what happened."

"You confessed the affair with Marc?" This was major. Kevin now had a very compelling motive for murder. Cate's stomach twisted. She didn't want to believe the pun-loving Egg Man could be a killer.

"Yeah," Bethany shrugged. "I owed him that."

"When did you tell him this?"

Bethany closed her eyes, thinking back. "The whole thing happened so fast. Marc and I were together for only a few weeks. I told Kevin two Thursdays ago. I remember because that's delivery day. Always kind of hectic."

That was four days before Marc was murdered. Lots of time for Kevin to build up a head of jealous rage. "How did he take the news?" Given how deeply he loved his "Bunny," Cate could imagine his heartbreak. She was amazed that he hadn't revealed any of this pain in their interactions. She'd known the Farnham marriage wasn't happy, but she'd missed those undercurrents completely. It turned out Kevin was a good actor. The discovery was not comforting.

Bethany shrugged. "I can't say he was surprised. He'd known our relationship was in trouble."

"Wasn't he angry about Marc?"

"He didn't like it." Bethany laughed, a harsh sound. "But I think he saw it for what it was. The affair was the catalyst, but our marriage is dead. I told him I'm leaving him, but not for Marc. I am getting out of town." She saw Cate's face and said defensively, "Don't look at me like that. Everyone loves Kevin. They think he's a sweetie pie, but he's no saint. He's capable of some dark shit."

"Are you implying he killed Marc?"

"What? No, of course not. I mean, when I heard that Marc had been killed, I did think for a second that maybe Kevin did it, but as soon as I heard about the accuracy of the shot, I knew it couldn't be him. Kevin's hopeless with a gun, completely inept. I'm a much better shot."

"Right," Cate said. "You got the 4-H Sharpshooters Award."

"How did you know that?"

"You're on a plaque at Lachance Feed."

Bethany sighed. "See? I can't escape my past here. Everyone has an idea of who I am, and no one will let me forget it. I'm done with this town. I'm making my break."

"Where are you headed?" This was important information Cate was going to need to relay to the cops.

"First, I need to collect a couple of things I've left here and there. Then I'm going to Montreal. One of my followers has a place she's subletting. It's on the Plateau. Very trendy."

Good, it didn't sound like Bethany was moving out of province right away. "You'd better let the police know your new address."

"Why?" Bethany asked.

Cate stared at her. Bethany honestly didn't understand that her affair with Marc made her a suspect in his death. In her mind, they were completely disconnected. Cate didn't think this was an act. Bethany could have left town without revealing any of this. Didn't her frankness point to her innocence? "They will want to question you about Marc's death."

"Kevin has my contact details," she said breezily. "We're going to meet up in the city early next week. We've got a lot of business to sort out. He's worried I'll go for the egg business, but I don't want anything to do with his goddamn hens."

Cate recalled the pain and confusion of her own divorce. She and Matthew both earned about the same and split their assets without acrimony—one of the easier aspects of their breakup. "You're entitled to some of the egg money. After all, the business grew over the marriage. Kevin even credits you with making the decision to go organic."

Bethany shrugged. "Despite what this town thinks, I'm not a gold digger. I want the cash from half the house. I poured all my creative talents into this place, and I deserve to reap the rewards. Kevin can keep the chicken sheds and hatchery and sell off the home. That will give me plenty of start-up money."

"Start-up?" Cate asked.

"Yeah, I'm going to follow my bliss."

"What's that?" Cate asked.

"Candles," Bethany said with confidence. "I'm going to sell fancy-as-fuck candles, and I'm going to make a fortune doing it."

Cate nodded. If anyone could make it work, it was Bethany.

CHAPTER 25

CATE HELPED BETHANY LOAD THE LAST OF THE BOXES INTO THE RANGE Rover. As soon as the other woman drove off, she called Detective Inspector Vachon and left a detailed message about Bethany and Marc's affair. The officer was undoubtedly busy, but given that she'd discovered a major piece of information about the homicide, she assumed she'd hear back quickly.

She could do nothing more until he returned her call, and she was late for her date with Dr. K. He and Frederick were doing some shopping and suggested they meet at the Gratitude Café. Dr. K's partner was a slim, clean-shaven man of about sixty. A painter, originally from Montreal, he'd moved to the Townships many years ago, lured by the vaguely artsy scene and cheap cost of living.

Still processing Bethany's revelations and waiting for Vachon's phone call, Cate kept the conversation light. They were finishing up their coffees when Cate checked her phone once again. No response from Vachon. Bethany's affair with Marc changed the whole thrust of the investigation. The Farnhams were now prime suspects. "Everything OK, Catherine?" Dr. K asked. "You're distracted."

He stared pointedly at her phone, and she flushed, shoving it in her bag. She hated to appear rude in front of her former headmaster. "It's something to do with Marc Renaud's murder." Hopefully that was a weighty enough subject to excuse her discourtesy.

"So macabre." Frederick shivered. "He was shot right through the eye, you know."

"'Eyes, look your last! Arms, take your last embrace!'" Dr. K looked pleased with the aptness of his quote. There was nothing her former headmaster liked more than shoving Shakespeare or a classical quotation into everyday conversation.

"I was at the Regional Archives the other day," she said. Given Dr. K's current history project, she thought he would be interested in her visit.

"How wonderful. Did you see Reginald Patterson? A former Canterbury student, of course."

"What?" Cate asked, surprised. "Isn't he a local?"

"Oh yes, he's from Manasoka," Dr. K said. "Every year the school offers a couple of scholarships to promising children from the community. A small way we can give back." He smiled complacently.

Cate remembered those scholarship kids. They showed up for only the last two years of high school and were looked down on for not being "real" Canterbury students. Cate bit her lip, remembering they had a horrible name for them—not "townies" but "brownies" for their supposed overeagerness and brownnosing. Cate never participated in the bullying, but she hadn't stopped it either. Reggie was about eight years younger than she was, and she was relieved that she didn't remember him. She'd hate to think she might have treated him with the casual cruelty of entitled youth. "I was learning about the Megantic Outlaw and his treasure."

Frederick looked at her blankly, but Dr. K smiled. "Don't tell me you believe that poppycock about the gold, Catherine."

"What poppycock?" Frederick asked.

Cate explained what she knew. "So you see," she concluded, "Donald Morrison hid the gold he'd stolen from the whisky smugglers, burying it, according to local legend, on MacGregor's land."

"It's utter tripe," Dr. K said. "Go and look through the records. There was never any robbery. The whole thing is a sensational story, designed to boost tourism to the area."

"I'm not sure," Cate said. "Reggie thinks there might be some truth to it."

Dr. K scoffed. "Not a shred of evidence."

"You are awfully definite, Lionel," Frederick chided.

"I investigated it myself decades ago, when I first moved here. MacGregor's father was alive then and wasn't so territorial. He encouraged the locals to have a look around, only making us swear to split the find. In fact, that's the law."

"You went searching for a pot of gold," Frederick teased.

Cate was amused to see her old professor redden.

"I was a young man. Interested in history."

"Who would have thought my romantic partner was so, well, romantic."

Dr. K looked stern for a moment and then chuckled.

"Sorry," Cate said. "Did you say that you legally have to split the gold with whoever owns the land?"

"That depends. When I investigated many years ago, anything found on private property belonged to the landowner. A detectorist—that's the name for someone using a metal detector—could have an agreement with them to split the find."

"So, anyone searching for gold on MacGregor's property without his permission—"

"Would have to be prepared to steal it, otherwise it would all belong to the farmer," Dr. K finished.

Marc hadn't had permission, so he must have planned on stealing the gold. That would have angered MacGregor. She didn't doubt the old man would vigorously defend his property. Recalling Rose's speculation, she vowed to take a closer look at the orchardist.

"Of course, I never really considered those issues when I was looking," Dr. K said with a laugh. "I was in it for the thrill of the hunt. I even bought myself a metal detector," he said. "It's ancient, but I've still got it."

"Is that the thing in the shed?" Frederick asked. "You told me it was a Weedwacker."

Dr. K shrugged. "I knew you'd tease me."

"Could I borrow it?" Cate asked impulsively.

"Why in the world would you want to do that?" Dr. K asked.

For a moment Cate was quelled, the way she had been as a young girl when the fearsome, admirable Dr. K would stop her in the hall and ask her to name the capital of Manitoba or multiply six by seven. Cate was no longer a child, however. "I don't know. Retracing Marc's final movements might give me some insight into his death. It would help to have a metal detector so I could put myself in his shoes."

"I think that's a terrific idea," Frederick said. "While away a Saturday afternoon seeking out a hidden treasure. What could be more fun?"

"There's no harm, I suppose," Dr. K said. "You must ask MacGregor's permission, of course," he said sternly. "If you find anything, it will belong to him."

"Absolutely," Cate said. "I don't need a pot of gold." They finished their coffee and stood. Cate took the opportunity for a quick phone check. Nothing from Vachon.

"Shall we head home?" Frederick suggested. "We can dig out the detector for Cate."

They moved toward the door, but Frederick stopped by the cash register. "I'll meet you outside. I'm going to pick us up a few things for dinners this week."

"Get a tourtière," Dr. K said. "And those baked beans in maple syrup. Also, grab a pâté chinois."

Frederick laughed and met Cate's eye. She grinned back. Dr. K had a weakness for a good meal. She remembered a night at the start of Easter break. Most of the boarders traveled back to their families, but she and Jason, along with the international students who were too far from home to make a short trip practical, stayed behind.

The bulk of the staff were gone, but Dr. K worked to make the holiday special for them all. He introduced them to Welsh rarebit, raiding the school's kitchen for old cheddar, fresh sourdough, and strong mustard. He'd made them giggle by putting on one of the school cook's aprons and chef's hat and firing up the gas stove. He'd licked his fingers, winked, and said, "'Tis an ill cook who cannot lick his own fingers—*Romeo and Juliet*." The result was a late-night feast of gooey, melted cheesy bread. Cate felt comforted and included instead of abandoned by their father, who couldn't be bothered to collect them.

She and Dr. K walked toward the car. "Frederick is wonderful," Cate said, immediately aghast at her boldness. She couldn't believe she dared comment on her headmaster's private life. Jason would have gaped at her presumption and laughed at her panic.

"He is, isn't he?" Dr. K agreed. "I've been a lucky man and lived a lucky life." He hesitated. "You know, you could find someone to share your life with, Catherine. Companionship is a wonderful thing."

"I don't know about that." She recalled Bethany's tear-streaked face and could imagine Kevin's heartbreak. She thought of Mireille and her daughter, both survivors of abusive relationships. Her own marriage had ended in sorrow. "I think it's OK to be alone. Society wants to pair everyone off as if that's the only way to live."

"Yes, of course," Dr. K agreed. "Only, don't wall yourself away completely. Friendship is as important as romantic love."

He was right. She had lost Jason, but that didn't mean she was friendless. Her visit with Rose solidified their relationship. Back in Ottawa, Detective Dominick Baker had awkwardly called himself a friend. Her bond with Anya was deepening. Until this afternoon, she might have put Kevin on the list, though now she wasn't so sure. It was tricky to know who to trust. She thought of the dog, and her heart softened. She didn't have a vast pool of friends—and one of them was her quasi-boss, one of them was a possible murderer, and one of them was a dog—but still it was something.

She and Dr. K watched the afternoon crowd bustle past. A group of cyclists sped their way to Fowler's Diner, about to undo their hard work by consuming poutines and grilled cheese. A young mother pushing an expensive stroller came out of Brie et Cie, the fine cheese shop that had replaced the shoe repair business. Next to it was a store specializing in linen clothing. The breezy, light outfits on display appealed to Cate, and she realized she was entering her "loose linens" phase of life.

Eventually Frederick returned, and Cate followed the couple to their cozy home on the outskirts of town. Dr. K left her in the living room. "I'll pop out to the shed and dig out the metal detector for you."

She gave him five minutes, and when he didn't return, she ventured outside to help. The shed was at the end of the backyard, which was planted with an English garden. Even this late in the season, it was filled with tall flowers that Cate couldn't identify.

Dr. K was in the midst of emptying the small building. An old mechanical lawn mower, a wood-handled rake, and a big bag of fertilizer were chucked on the lawn. She heard clattering, and Dr. K emerged, pulling out croquet mallets, a large rubber archery target, and a very tangled volleyball net. "I don't know how we accumulated all this junk." He sounded disappointed in himself.

She poked her head into the dark, cobwebby space. It took a moment for her eyes to adjust to the dimness. She saw a pile of snow tires, ready to be put on before the first flurries. There were fishing nets hanging on the wall and flowerpots stacked in the corner. "I don't see anything that looks like a metal detector."

"No," he agreed. "It's the most blasted thing. I was sure I had it."

Frederick chimed in from where he stood in the doorway. "Lionel, you're right. It was there. I tripped over it the last time I was looking for something. It was by the door." He pointed to an empty spot.

"It's been stolen," Cate stated.

Dr. K looked surprised. "Why, I guess it has."

"Is the shed usually locked?"

Frederick shook his head. "Never. It's at the end of our yard. You'd have to come through the side gate to get to it."

"Whoever took the metal detector must have known you owned one."

"Who would that be? *I* didn't even know," Frederick said.

Dr. K considered. "Even though MacGregor put a stop to our gold hunting when his father died, he certainly knew I had one. All the people I used to treasure hunt with would know—the machines were hard to come by back then, and mine was the only one in the region."

"Can you recall any names?" Cate asked.

Dr. K tugged on his beard. "Lots of locals. Paul Montaigne, Guy's father. Madge Taylor and her husband. Kevin Farnham's father, Joseph. Philippa Patterson, Reginald's mother, was also quite keen. They all tried their luck at one point or another."

For a moment Cate wondered if Marc could have stolen the metal detector; perhaps it was sitting in police evidence right now. Recalling the sleek machine with the digital reader she'd glimpsed at the murder scene, she ruled that out. His was not a thirty-year-old metal detector.

Cate's phone rang. It was Constable Douglass. Vachon must have told him to follow up on her information about Bethany.

"Hello?"

"Dr. Spencer?" His voice quavered.

"What's wrong?"

"Uh. There's been a death. We're at Geneviève Renaud's house. Seventy-one Milton."

"Right," she said. She was concerned, of course, but also pleased that the police were including her. "I'll come right away. Will Kevin be meeting us?" Much as she'd like to lead the investigation, she did not have jurisdiction.

"That's the thing," Douglass said, his words coming out in a rush. "The victim is Kevin's wife. Bethany Farnham has been murdered."

CHAPTER 26

CATE STOOD IN THE DOORWAY, TAKING IN THE SCUFFED COUNTERS AND dull white cupboards of the small kitchen. It was a banal space, except, of course, for the jarring sight of Bethany Farnham's body sprawled across the table, her expression contorted in pain and her blonde hair spilling around her face. Constable St. Onge stood next to the table, her arms folded across her chest. She stared down at Bethany with an inscrutable look.

"Jesus," Cate breathed. She'd seen Bethany only a few hours ago.

St. Onge's head reared up. "Halte." She walked toward Cate. "Do not take another step. You are not authorized to be here."

"Douglass called and asked me to come." Cate was anxious to examine Bethany.

"Câlice," St. Onge hissed under her breath. "That is not the protocol."

Cate stared past St. Onge. Bethany appeared to have a head wound. It was hard to see more with the constable in the way.

Bethany's phone lay cracked on the kitchen floor, below her outstretched hand. She had probably been holding it when she was shot. One shoe had fallen off, and her bare foot dangled an inch above the ground. She wouldn't appreciate looking sloppy in death, but Cate quelled the desire to slide the high heel back on.

Douglass appeared behind Cate. He'd been talking to the ambulance driver when she'd pulled in beside Bethany's Range Rover and Geneviève's more modest sedan. His skin was sweaty with a greenish cast. "I sent the paramedics away," he said with bluster, but undid his bravado by wiping a speck of vomit from the corner of his mouth.

"What the hell, Dougie?" St. Onge gestured to Cate.

"I asked Dr. Spencer to come," he said. "I'm the senior officer. It was my call."

St. Onge rolled her eyes. "You don't outrank me," she said. "You've just been on the job six months longer."

Douglass ignored that. "We can't call Kevin, and it will take the Sûreté a while to find a coroner to bring with them. We needed professional eyes on this right away."

St. Onge didn't reply, but neither did she insist on Cate's departure.

Douglass's phone rang. He checked the call display and ignored it. He moved to step through the door, but St. Onge raised a hand. "No. You both stay out. I want to do this properly."

The emphasis she placed on the word *properly* made Cate wonder if they had been reprimanded for failing to secure the scene correctly at Renaud's death.

"I've already been in there," Douglass said. "I was the one to find her."

"Yeah, and the sight made you spew," St. Onge scoffed. "We're not going to throw a party like we did for Renaud." She glared at Douglass. "No one but me is coming into this house until forensics has been through."

"St. Onge, stop being a dick. Dr. Spencer needs to examine the body."

Cate raised both hands. She didn't want St. Onge to dismiss her from the scene entirely. "It's OK. I can see a lot from here."

The three of them turned to the corpse, and St. Onge moved out of the way. Cate quelled a gasp. The head injury looked like a perfectly aimed bullet to the left eye. The same MO as Marc Renaud. No, not quite the same. Cate peered at Bethany's injury. This time the wound was messier—greater soft-tissue injury, and the orbital floor was exposed. Bethany's one remaining eye stared up at the ceiling fan. Was that black powder around the wound? She sniffed. An acrid, burned smell filled the air. Could be gunpowder. "Has Kevin been informed?"

Douglass cleared his throat. "Not yet. We wanted to wait for the Sûreté."

St. Onge squared her shoulders. "We'll be the ones to break it to him, though. Not them."

Douglass looked unhappy at the prospect, and Cate didn't envy him that visit. "He'll be a suspect."

They both nodded.

"Did Vachon tell you what I learned this morning?"

They looked at her blankly, and Cate's heart sank. "I saw Bethany earlier today. She had packed up all her stuff. She was leaving Kevin."

Douglass's and St. Onge's mouths dropped open. Cate wished she had called them as well as Vachon when she had learned the news. They might not be any more competent than the senior officer, but at least they cared about finding the killer. "I figured out that she'd had an affair with Marc."

"What?" St. Onge sputtered. Her voice rose. "And you didn't bring this to us?" Her eyes narrowed, and a frown thundered across her brow.

"I left a message with Vachon as soon as Bethany confirmed it." Quickly, she relayed her conversation with the dead woman.

"She was sleeping with Marc," Douglass repeated. He shook his head. "You figured that out. Good job."

Cate was pleased by his acknowledgment.

"It is absolutely unacceptable that you didn't inform us immediately," St. Onge said.

"I told Vachon," Cate said, raising her voice. She was irritated by the officer's officiousness. "It's not my fault the Sûreté didn't keep you in the loop. Anyway, isn't it more important to figure out what happened?"

"This really doesn't look good for Kevin Farnham," Douglass said grimly.

The obvious conclusion was that Kevin discovered the affair, murdered Marc Renaud, and killed his cheating wife. It was such a common story that a whole genre of country music was devoted to the very theme. Only Bethany wasn't scared of Kevin. She claimed that he didn't blame Marc and that he accepted their marriage was over.

Kevin could have been faking it, of course. Cate knew firsthand that murderers could lurk behind the most benign facades. She didn't want to believe it was Kevin because she liked him, but she couldn't let her feelings cloud her analysis. She adopted a professional tone: "Was the body warm when you arrived?"

"Yeah. We got a report of a gunshot from the neighbor." Douglass jerked his head to the left. "I arrived about twenty minutes later. St. Onge was right behind me, followed by the ambulance."

"Report of the shot came in at four p.m.," St. Onge added grudgingly.

That was the same time as Marc's death. It was now 4:45 p.m. Cate stared at Bethany. Her limbs appeared loose, with none of the typical tightening of rigor mortis, though it was impossible to be certain without physically examining her. "A four p.m. death is consistent with the victim's appearance." How depressing that vibrant, confident Bethany was reduced to two shitty, powerless words: *the victim.*

St. Onge circled the body. "The deceased is exhibiting a traumatic injury to the head." Ostensibly she was talking to Douglass, but Cate caught the other woman shooting her a glance. She was pleased the cop was including her in her thinking. St. Onge continued the review. "Wound appears to be a firearm injury to the brain through the left eye."

The silence was heavy as they absorbed the implications. The same injury as Renaud.

"Any other wounds besides the head trauma?" Cate asked.

St. Onge shook her head. "I don't think so."

"Surely to God that hole in her head is enough of a cause of death," Douglass said with a nervous laugh. "What more do you need? Decapitation?"

Cate shot him a withering look. "When the coroner arrives, they will examine the victim and make sure we're not being blinded to other causes."

Douglass bowed his head, and Cate regretted being so biting. He advocated for her to be here, after all. Still, he needed to learn to honor the dead.

"She might have been standing at the sink," St. Onge pointed to the corner of the kitchen closest to the door. "She heard the murderer, turned, and was shot, falling back onto the table."

Douglass's phone rang again. He glanced at the caller ID and blew out an exasperated breath. "Sorry," he said. "I'll turn the ringer off."

"This is Marc's sister's house," St. Onge said, glancing around. "Marc was staying here. Bethany and Geneviève Renaud look quite similar—same age, same build. Same blonde hair."

"Honey gold," Cate said abruptly.

"What?" St. Onge asked.

"They have the exact same hair color." She recalled her conversation with Vivienne. "Apparently, it's very popular. Diane Doucette has it too. Could the killer have mistaken Bethany for Geneviève?"

Douglass looked surprised at the idea, and St. Onge considered the possibility.

"If so, Geneviève's in danger," Cate said.

"She's at that rehab facility," Douglass said. "She should be safe there."

"Do you know which one?"

St. Onge shook her head in frustration. "No, we've made no progress. We still don't have the paperwork. The facilities won't talk to us."

"If Vachon is smart, he'll make that a priority now," Cate said.

St. Onge met her gaze, and she saw the doubt in the other woman's eyes. Despite her dedication to protocol, the constable wasn't blindly loyal to the Detective Inspector.

"I wonder what Bethany was doing here at Geneviève's house," Douglass said.

"I have an idea," Cate said. "Bethany told me earlier that she needed to pick up a few items before she left town." She pointed to the large cotton tote bag she had noticed on the floor. It was a rich cream color and bore the logo for Drunk Elephant, which, thanks to her new habit of Instagram-lurking, Cate knew was a high-end skincare company. The odds of the bag belonging to Bethany were high. "Maybe that will offer us a clue."

St. Onge was already wearing blue crime scene gloves, but she snapped one at the wrist, as if to emphasize it. She bent over the bag and opened it, concealing the contents from the doorway.

"Well?" Douglass asked.

"A blow-dryer, a bottle of fancy-looking shampoo, and maybe a weird . . ." St. Onge hesitated. "Maybe a sex toy?"

"Really?" Douglass asked with interest.

St. Onge held a small, white, cylindrical object up by its plug.

Cate stared at it for a moment before laughing. "That's a portable air humidifier. Bethany went everywhere with it. It kept her skin hydrated."

"How do you know that?" St. Onge asked.

"I started following her on Instagram."

St. Onge raised an eyebrow and turned from the bag. "There's nothing else in there."

Cate paused. Earlier that day Bethany said something about Geneviève's house that had struck her as odd. She tried to remember, but the thought slipped away and she didn't have time to chase it. She needed to keep asserting her usefulness, or St. Onge would force her to leave. "I think this injury could have been caused by an antique weapon."

"What?" St. Onge asked.

"Look," Cate pointed at Bethany's face. "You can see black marks. That might indicate powder burn. Most modern weapons wouldn't leave that kind of residue."

St. Onge peered at the wound. "Maybe," she said reluctantly.

"OK, we have the same method—a shot through the left eye—but a different firearm. Why would the killer switch?" Douglass asked.

"Maybe they wanted to confuse the police." St. Onge was drawn in despite herself.

"Or he was caught off guard and hadn't planned to kill Bethany, so he grabbed whatever gun was available," Douglass said.

"Maybe the killer had no choice," Cate said.

This stopped St. Onge. "What do you mean?"

"You've been confiscating rifles, right?"

"Yup," Douglass agreed.

"What if you already impounded the killer's usual gun, so they were forced to use another firearm that they had at hand?"

St. Onge opened her mouth to respond.

Douglass's phone vibrated loudly. He looked down, exasperated. "I'm sorry. My grandpa keeps calling. I'll answer this and tell him to stop." He punched the button to respond. "Hi, Gramps, I'm working right now." He listened, his face blanching. "Are you sure?" Another pause. Douglass promised to call him back and hung up. He looked at St. Onge and Cate.

"My grandpa got home from bingo at the Odd Fellows Hall . . ."

"Et puis," St. Onge said impatiently.

"And his door was broken in, and he had been robbed."

"That's too bad," Cate said. She was irritated that Douglass's family troubles were interrupting their investigation.

"The only thing they took," Douglass continued, "was his prized possession—Donald Morrison's revolver."

CHAPTER 27

NO LONGER A SLEEPY, EMPTY ROOM, THE MANASOKA POLICE DEPART-
ment was the command center for a double homicide investigation.
Cops bustled around, shouting orders, bringing in equipment, connecting computers. Cate was directed to a chair and handed a pad
of paper to write her statement. Moments later she caught sight of
Kevin's bald head bobbing toward a small interview room. She was relieved to see a short, competent-looking woman walking beside him,
presumably his lawyer.

Two hours later, Cate was still waiting to be questioned by Detective Inspector Vachon. Her written statement outlined everything she
knew: the region's apparent troubles with drugs, Montaigne's accusation that Marc was a dealer, Bethany and Marc's affair, Marc's interest
in the Megantic Outlaw's gold, the stolen metal detector, even Diane
Doucette's skill with a firearm.

At last, the interview door opened and Kevin, Vachon, and the
woman exited.

"You can go home now," Vachon boomed to Kevin, "but stick
around Manasoka. We're going to want to question you again."

The lawyer shook Kevin's hand and walked away. Vachon was approached by two officers from Sherbrooke and was quickly immersed
in conversation. Kevin stood alone, seeming exhausted and defeated.

"Hey," Cate said, hurrying up to him. "How are you doing?"

He looked more rumpled than ever. He turned to her with dull
eyes, recognition slowly setting in. "Cate," he said. Then his face
crumpled. "Bunny is dead."

"I know. I'm so sorry."

He rocked slightly forward, and Cate had no choice but to envelop him in a hug. He sagged against her, sobs wracking his body. She held him up as his emotion flowed. She had cried like this after Jason's death, though it had taken her longer than Kevin to plumb the depth of her grief. At last, he stopped crying.

"I'm sorry," he sniffed. "I haven't been able to cry. The police rolled up and told me what happened. Before I knew it, I was here at the station answering their questions." His voice was bewildered.

Cate was used to seeing people in the first flush of terrible, unexpected grief. Kevin's reaction seemed authentic. "You had a lawyer with you, right?" In this state, Kevin would probably confess to a crime he hadn't committed.

"Yes, I've got a firm I deal with as a notary. She was from their criminal arm. I don't know if it was a good idea to have her here though. She told me not to answer certain questions. I couldn't be as helpful as I would have liked."

"It's OK," she soothed. "I'm sure you were very helpful."

"I want them to find whoever did this. Whoever killed my Bunny." His voice broke on her name, and he started crying again. Cate glanced toward Vachon; he was still in discussions with various officers. She probably had some time before she'd be called for questioning. She led Kevin upstairs, to a bench in the main corridor of the town hall. The employees had gone home. They were alone.

"What happened, Kevin?"

He shook his head. "She was shot. Murdered."

"Do you know why she was at Geneviève Renaud's house?" Cate asked gently.

Keith sunk his head. "Yes. She was leaving me, and she needed to collect a few things from where Marc had been staying."

Cate wanted to believe Kevin, but she'd been fooled by the seemingly innocent before. She spoke in a stern voice. "Why didn't you tell anyone she was having an affair with Marc? This doesn't look good for you."

His head sank lower, and he spoke in a mumble. "I was ashamed, and I was devastated. I couldn't talk about it. I thought if we pretended the affair hadn't happened, maybe she would stay with me and we could put it behind us."

"Did you kill Marc, Kevin? Did you kill Bethany?"

"No!" he said passionately. "No," he repeated. "I wouldn't do that. I was mad at Marc, but I'm not a killer. As for Bunny, I forgave her. She knew that. She knew I wanted what was best for her. She knew I understood."

"You lied to me about the affair."

"No, I didn't," he said quickly. "I just didn't volunteer that information."

Cate leveled him with her stare, and his shoulders drooped.

"I kept my mouth shut, but only because I knew it had no bearing on the murder. Bunny didn't kill him. She left him. It was only a fling."

"You can see why the police are suspicious, though, can't you?"

"They think I hated Marc or was jealous or possessive. I've never felt that way," he said earnestly. "I've always been so proud that Bunny loved me. I can't believe I was lucky enough to have her for as long as I did. I understood I couldn't give her what she needed. I mean, look at me." He gestured to his face, torn with grief, and Cate felt immense sadness for him.

He spoke in a shaky voice. "I was shocked when I showed up at MacGregor's farm and learned that Marc was the victim."

Cate recalled that day. He had seemed stunned by the news. True, he could have been acting, but she thought it unlikely.

"I knew we needed to keep the affair quiet. The cops might think Bunny had a motive!"

The affair gave Kevin an even stronger motive to kill Marc, but Cate didn't want to push him on that for now. Instead, a new idea occurred to her. "Is that why you let me help with the investigation?"

"Yes, I wanted to find out who really killed Marc, so Bunny could avoid suspicion."

Cate recalled their discussions about the case. "You pushed the Megantic Outlaw angle—the lost gold. You encouraged me to follow up with the Blakeney Inn. You were keen when I suggested we talk to Guy Montaigne. You were diverting attention away from the fact that Marc and Bethany were having an affair."

"No!" Kevin exclaimed. He reddened. "Well, yes, I did do that, but not to cover anything up. I wanted us to follow leads I knew would bring us closer to the killer. The affair was irrelevant."

Cate's mouth thinned. Kevin was cloaking his actions under a veil of righteousness, but there was no doubt he had actively pushed her into investigating angles that pointed away from Bethany's secret. Cate didn't like to be used; anger bloomed in her chest. "What you did was shitty and cowardly, Kevin. You lied to me. You lied to the cops. What's more, by not giving everyone the full story, it's possible you've led to Bethany's death."

"What?" Kevin's breathing quickened, and he started to hyper-ventilate.

"Head between your knees," she barked. "Deep breaths, in and out."

When he could breathe normally, he looked up, wan and shaky. "Do you think that's true?" he whispered. "Could I have prevented Bunny's death by coming forward about the affair?"

Cate regretted her harshness, but she couldn't soften the truth. "I don't know. I will say that secrets are harmful in a murder investigation. Maybe if the police had known the full story they could have prevented this."

Kevin gulped, but something hardened in him. "You're right. I've been selfish and scared."

"Do you have alibis for the two deaths?"

"I went over this with the police. I was working in the hatcheries all afternoon the day Marc died. Bunny would have vouched for me. We ate lunch together, and I stopped when I got the call about the death. As for today, I was doing notary business. I sent some emails, that kind of thing. I told them they could check my computer, review my email. They'd see I was working all afternoon." He closed his eyes. "The cops didn't find that very convincing. They said I could have scheduled the emails to be sent to give myself an alibi. As if I deliberately planned to kill my little Bunny."

Cate recalled his shock at Marc's death, thought about Bethany's attitude this morning and considered Kevin's obvious distress now. Maybe she was a naive fool, but she took his hand. "I don't think you killed her."

He looked at her with a grateful, tearstained face. "Thank you."

"You've got a tough road ahead. I need you to go home tonight and rest. Tomorrow I want you to sit down and think about anyone, anyone at all, who would want to hurt Bunny. I'll drop by and we'll go over your list. We'll figure this out together, OK?"

He nodded like a small boy.

"Do you have someone coming to pick you up?"

"I called my sister. She's bringing me home."

She squeezed his hand. "This is horrible, Kevin, but you will get through this."

"Really?"

"Absolutely. I have seen people devastated by loss, and I've seen them survive it. You are a fighter, Kevin." She paused. "I have high egg-spectations of you."

It took a moment, but a small, wan smile crept across his face. "Thank you, Cate."

Kevin left, and Cate returned to the police station, where Vachon waited. He was gruffer than at their last meeting, but still courteous. St. Onge sat beside him, taking notes.

"Thank you for your immediate assistance at the crime scene. I've reviewed your statement, and it is most helpful." Cate's heart lifted. Such praise boded well for that letter of recommendation.

"This second homicide, while extremely unfortunate, has at least clarified things for us."

"Oh?" Cate asked, though she had a sinking feeling she knew to what he referred.

"The sequence of events is obvious. Jealous husband discovers affair, murders lover, kills his own wife."

Cate was irked by his complacency but kept her tone light. "Don't you think the timing is off? According to what Bethany told me, she had already broken up with Marc and confessed the affair to Kevin on the Thursday four days before Marc's murder. If Kevin was filled with jealous rage, wouldn't he have killed Marc that very night?"

Vachon tilted his head. "Sometimes these things fester, stew, and build. That must be the case here." Cate saw St. Onge's pen falter and resume. The constable's head was down, so Cate couldn't read her expression, but she hoped she was as shocked as Cate by Vachon's narrow focus.

"Nothing *must* be the case," she said, her tenuous forbearance slipping. "It's less than six hours since the body was discovered. You should be keeping an open mind about the whole thing. There is no solid evidence that the two cases are even connected."

Vachon narrowed his eyes but was unruffled. "The deceased were having an affair, and they were both shot through the left eye."

"One was outside," Cate countered, "the other in a home. One was done using a modern firearm, the other probably with a stolen antique. One a man, one a woman. One a francophone, one an anglophone."

"Dr. Spencer, do you know how many homicides there were in Pekeda Township last year?"

She stared at him.

"Zero. Do you know how many there were the year before that, and the year before that?" He waited for her response. "Also zero. In fact, there hasn't been a murder in Pekeda Township in over eight years. Do you honestly expect me to believe that two deaths, happening twelve days apart, are not connected? When the victims shared an intimate relationship? When the wound is the same? Come now, you're an intelligent woman. You can see that it cannot be."

"It doesn't mean that Kevin Farnham did it."

"He is the only person with a motive for both deaths."

"He's terrible with a firearm."

"Incompetence is easy enough to fake."

"If that was the case, he'd have to have been planning to kill Marc for years to establish what a bad shot he was."

Vachon shrugged. "You said it."

"But that doesn't connect with your theory of an explosive rage."

"As you said," Vachon spoke blandly, "we're at the very early stages of this investigation. Undoubtedly M. Farnham's thinking will be clarified as we progress."

"That's the thing, though," Cate said heatedly, "you're focused on Kevin when there are alternatives!"

"Oh?" Vachon raised an eyebrow.

"The metal detector," Cate said. "Marc Renaud was looking for the Outlaw's gold."

"Irrelevant folktale."

"What about all the drugs?"

This caught Vachon's attention. "What do you know about that?"

"Everywhere I turn, I come up against stories of drug abuse and opioid overdose. Pekeda Township is swimming in the stuff."

"Yes," he said curtly. "There is much drug activity. New sources, possibly over the American border. There is a great deal of investigation happening. You read about the bust in Sherbrooke recently? They seconded some of my officers to work on it."

"Couldn't Renaud have been involved in that?" Cate asked.

"There is no evidence. Not a scrap to indicate such things." That disproved Montaigne's assertion.

"What about Geneviève? She's in rehab. Her brother was murdered, and now Bethany was killed in her house. Have you found her?"

He shifted in his seat. "We've put in an emergency request that will compel the treatment centers in Québec to divulge whether she's a patient. We'll locate her in the next twenty-four hours."

He should have made that request weeks ago. "Mistaken identity is a possibility in this case," Cate said. "Bethany and Geneviève looked alike. Marc's sister might be in danger. Don't dawdle."

"Dawdle?" His cheeks turned pink. "I've always treated this investigation as a priority."

Damn it. She had pissed him off. She'd been trying hard, but she found it so difficult to give the police the diffidence they craved. "If Geneviève was the intended target, maybe there is a vendetta against the Renaud family. Maybe that's your motive."

Vachon smiled at her kindly. "You are obviously an imaginative person. You've offered many possible theories about these two deaths, but in my experience the most obvious answer is the correct one."

"You can't simply railroad Kevin for a quick solve," she blurted in frustration.

Vachon's nostrils flared, and he uttered a distinct harrumph.

She had worsened his anger. St. Onge stopped her note-taking and looked up.

"I can assure you we are building a careful case. We will not railroad anyone but will conduct an examination of all the facts and evidence and proceed accordingly. Justice will be served. Now, I thank you for your time and your service. Your work"—he gestured to her statement—"has been most helpful. I am pleased with your cooperation, and as we discussed last time, I am happy to provide you with written documentation to that effect, which you require to be reinstated as a coroner in Ontario, since you are currently suspended."

St. Onge blinked and looked down again. Cate fought back a surge of anger. Vachon brought up her suspension deliberately to embarrass her in front of the young constable. He wasn't done. "I will provide that necessary letter as long as you do nothing to jeopardize our ongoing investigation or complicate a straightforward case. I would hate to have to write a different type of letter to the Ontario College of Coroners, one that complains of your interference."

There was the threat. Support Vachon's approach and get his recommendation or continue to advocate for alternate lines of inquiry and have him slam her, scuttling her chances of reinstatement.

She stood up silently. She had no choice, really. "I'll support the police investigation to the best of my abilities," she said. Vachon smiled. St. Onge kept her eyes trained on her notepad.

If Cate shut up now and walked away, she would secure Vachon's support and guarantee her return to the career she loved. She straightened her shoulders. She couldn't allow Vachon to railroad Kevin. "And I'll do so," Cate continued, "by making sure you look at every possible angle to find justice for the victims."

Vachon's face darkened. She might have quailed under his scowl but for the small smile that snuck across St. Onge's downturned face. Cate was doing the right thing.

CHAPTER 28

SHE MET KEVIN ON HIS PORCH THE NEXT DAY. HE LOOKED LIKE HE'D LOST ten pounds overnight. "Have you eaten anything?" she asked in concern. He seemed frail and bewildered. She was a bit disoriented herself. Only yesterday she'd stood on this same porch, talking to Bethany.

He hung his head. "I can't go into the kitchen. It reminds me too much of Bunny. She loved that room." His lower lip quivered.

If Cate was going to protect Kevin, she needed his help, not his tears. She guided him to a seat. "I need you to think." She'd been considering a plan of attack on the way over. As improbable as it was, it was possible the two murders weren't connected. She wanted to make sure they weren't leaping to conclusions. "Would anyone want to hurt Bethany?"

"No," he said. "She was wonderful. The sweetest, most gentle woman in the world."

Those were not the adjectives Cate would have used, but she let it slide. "What about her business. Did she have any enemies?"

He shook his head. "No. Everyone loved her. She had almost 128,000 followers, you know." He blanched. "I'll have to tell them she's gone."

"Don't worry about that right now. What about the egg business? Was there anything untoward there?"

"There used to be another organic outfit near Magog. Thanks to Bunny's savvy, we cornered the market pretty quickly. That business went under, and we were able to buy some of their hens at very low rates. The owners weren't happy. We ruffled their feathers."

"I'm sure you did," Cate said, heartened by his joke. "Can you give me their names?" She jotted down the information in her notebook. She paused. Her next question was delicate. "What about Marc?"

"I didn't kill him," Kevin said. "Neither did Bunny!"

"I believe you," Cate said. She laid out a theory she'd been considering. "What if Bethany wasn't Marc's only girlfriend? Or he had a jilted lover who was jealous of his new relationship with Bethany?" Several people remarked about how discreet Marc was with his love life, and Bethany categorized their relationship as a fling. Perhaps he was juggling two different women. That would explain the discrepancy between Madge's claim that Marc wanted the Megantic Outlaw's gold to leave town with a girlfriend, versus what Bethany said, that Marc was already obsessed with the treasure when they started their affair and had no intention of leaving Manasoka.

"I guess he could have been seeing someone else," Kevin said slowly. "He was certainly very popular with the ladies in high school."

This was an avenue to pursue. "Any idea who might have been the other woman?" Again, a niggling thought, something Bethany herself had said, tried to swim up from her subconscious. What was it?

Kevin was thinking about her question. "I don't have a clue."

"Whoever it is must want to keep quiet about the relationship, so maybe she's married."

Kevin's jaw tightened. "That would certainly prove Marc had a type."

It was cruel to pursue such a line of inquiry with him. She'd do this brainstorming on her own. "What about drugs?" She didn't think Guy's accusation of dealing was correct, but Geneviève was an addict, and the words of the old men at the Dépanneur Jaune came back to her: it was always drugs.

"As far as I know, Marc didn't take any."

"What about Geneviève Renaud? Could her addiction have involved her brother in something shady?"

"Maybe Geneviève owed money over drugs, and her dealer learned that Marc took her to rehab and shot him in revenge." Kevin's voice grew excited. "Then he could have mistaken my Bunny for Geneviève and shot her!"

Cate considered; it wasn't totally outlandish. If they were talking about a professional hit, it would explain the accuracy of the shots. Guy Montaigne had suggested something similar. She hoped Vachon was looking at known criminals who used a bullet through the eye as their execution method.

The police were finally following up on Geneviève's whereabouts, so they'd be able to talk to her soon enough. Cate jotted down all the ideas and chatted with Kevin for another half hour about possibilities. She left only when his sister arrived to check on him.

It was Saturday, so she spent a little while following up on Kevin's leads and running errands. When her phone rang in the late afternoon, she was hoping it was the Magog egg rival returning her call. She was surprised to hear Constable St. Onge informing her that she'd organized an off-hours visit to the archives and wanted Cate to join her.

She didn't need to be asked twice. When Cate pulled up to the archives' main doors, St. Onge was already there.

"I wouldn't think reviewing Marc's research notes was a top priority in light of Bethany's death," Cate said as they waited for Reggie Patterson to unlock the door. He'd instructed them to come by after closing so they wouldn't disturb the researchers.

"It is a lead that must be pursued. I leave no stone unturned."

Cate looked at her to see if she was joking, but the other woman's face was serious.

"I'm surprised you included me," Cate said.

St. Onge glanced down. "You impressed me."

"Pardon me?" Cate asked, though she had heard the officer perfectly well.

"Last night, with Vachon. He's desperate to wrap this up because he's worried about the Guns and Gangs cops muscling him out on the drug task force. He doesn't see this case as important. You stood up to him." St. Onge met her eyes, and Cate could see the fierceness there.

For all her youth and inexperience, St. Onge believed in the job, and she wanted justice. Before Cate could say anything further, Reggie swung the glass door open.

"Welcome, welcome." A grin broke over his face. He really was attractive with his curly hair and easy smile. He flicked on the lights in the reading room, disappearing into the back to fetch the material from Marc's locker. An awkward silence descended. "Any luck finding the weapon that killed Bethany?" Cate asked St. Onge.

The constable leveled her with a stare. "Despite what Douglass thinks, it's inappropriate to discuss these issues with you."

Cate knew she shouldn't push her luck, but she couldn't resist. "Are you working with the theory that it's Grandpa Douglass's antique revolver?"

The police officer glanced at her nails. Cate wasn't going to get anything out of her about the gun.

"What about Kevin's alibi? Can your computer experts tell if he'd scheduled those emails to send at the time of death?"

St. Onge's lips thinned. Cate got irritated. "I don't think Kevin killed Bethany."

"Our job is not to exonerate the innocent but to incarcerate the guilty." St. Onge looked quite pleased with herself, and Cate wondered if she'd rehearsed the line.

No point in prodding St. Onge further about their investigation, so she tried another tack. "I learned that Canterbury has an archery team and there's a town league that also practices out here."

"So?" St. Onge said.

"People who are good at archery might have skills that translate to marksmanship. It could be a new angle Vachon hasn't looked at." That caught St. Onge's attention.

"Archery?" Reggie said, emerging from the back, pushing a cart bearing the contents of Renaud's locker. "Are you talking about the Manasoka town league?"

"You know it?" Cate asked.

"Uh-huh. Joseph Ngoma coaches the townies. The evening classes are quite popular. A goodwill gesture from Canterbury that has actually succeeded."

"Manasokans use Canterbury's facilities?" St. Onge asked.

"Every second person in the village does it these days. It's very inclusive. We had grandmas hitting the bull's-eye and twelve-year-old girls trying to be Katniss Everdeen."

Cate noted the *we*. "Sounds like you're quite involved."

Reggie shrugged. "When I read that Canterbury was embracing the sport, I approached Anya Patel and encouraged her to set up a community program. I advertise the program around town, encourage people to come. I try to get to a couple of sessions a week. I'm still working on my string grip."

"That's very community minded of you," St. Onge said.

He grinned. "I had an ulterior motive—every time a townsperson drives to the archery range, they pass the archives and see our sign, reminding them that we exist. You'd be surprised at how often people forget about us."

Cate didn't think she would be surprised, but she smiled at Reggie.

St. Onge cleared her throat. "Can we get to the matter at hand?" Her tone suggested the matter at hand was on par with a bad date or a colonoscopy. "What was Marc Renaud doing here?"

Reggie hesitated, glancing at Cate.

"Dr. Spencer is assisting with the investigation," St. Onge said evenly.

Cate fought down a grin.

Reggie cleared his throat. "Marc was looking for information on the Megantic Outlaw."

"When did he start coming?" St. Onge asked.

"A few weeks ago, and it took up a lot of my time."

"How's that?" St. Onge asked.

"He's not our usual type of client. We mostly get historians and genealogists. Occasionally, we'll get a third- or fourth-year history student from Bishop's. Marc was different. He'd never been to university. He didn't know the first thing about archival research. I really needed to help him."

"How?" St. Onge asked.

Reggie pointed to some wall shelving. "I showed him everything we have."

Four boxes sat there. "That's it?" Cate asked.

He shrugged. "It's our Megantic Outlaw Collection. It was mostly amassed in the 1940s by Morrison's relatives, though we've had a few small accruals over the years."

St. Onge spoke up, retaking control of the interview. "Renaud reviewed this stuff?" She gestured to the boxes.

"Yes. For a guy unused to working in an archive, he was very patient. I got the sense that he was committed." Reggie's voice had a nice, deep timbre, and Cate liked how seriously he took his job.

"This wasn't idle curiosity for him." Cate mused, recalling her conversation with Madge. Something that woman said inspired Marc, convincing him that the gold was out there. What was that clue, and did Renaud's research lead to his and Bethany's murders? "He was on a mission."

"Definitely. He wanted to see everything." Reggie pulled a box from the bookcase, opening it on a table. Cate and St. Onge peered at the labeled folders.

"It's a standard collection from that time. There's family stuff, a couple of old Bibles, some letters between relatives and even a few from the Megantic Outlaw himself." Reggie paused. "There are also maps of the local area."

"Maps?" St. Onge asked.

Cate's heart rate increased. These could be what Marc was using to track down the gold.

"Yup." He reached behind her for another box. He smelled of smoky cedarwood; Cate, who didn't normally like men who wore cologne, didn't object.

He placed the flat horizontal box on the table, easing off the lid. A stack of large maps were layered in tissue paper. "These are county maps drawn during Morrison's lifetime. They cover the whole of Pekeda Township and include farmsteads and village. Marc pored over them with a magnifying glass, examining every centimeter. He was cross-referencing the archival letters and documents with locations on the maps."

"Not surprising," St. Onge said impatiently. "We know he was looking for the gold. We didn't come here for a history lesson, but to see Renaud's notes. You can vouch that they haven't been tampered with?"

"Absolutely," Reggie said. "They've been sitting in that locker since the day Marc died. Ilyana made sure they were locked up tight."

"Excellent," the young woman spoke ponderously. "The chain of custody is very important."

"Right, right." Reggie turned to the cart and spread its contents on a long table: a dozen rough maps hand drawn by Renaud, a stack of information printed up from the internet, and a sheaf of loose-leaf papers covered in handwriting. Marc was not a methodical researcher, and the sheets were undated, written in a messy hand, and filled with crossed-out words and doodles.

Cate sat and pulled some material toward her. St. Onge and Reggie followed suit. They leafed through pages in silence. Cate looked at Marc's maps. "Are these all the same place? It looks like MacGregor's property."

Reggie glanced over. "Yes. The rumor was that Morrison bunked down with the MacGregors. The family was sympathetic to his cause."

"Wait. MacGregor? Like Thomas MacGregor who lives there now? The same family from Morrison's time?" Cate asked.

"Yup. The MacGregors are one of the oldest families in the township. They've farmed that land for nearly two centuries. As I understand it, Mr. MacGregor is the last of the line. The only one left."

"That house has been standing for two hundred years?" It didn't strike Cate as that old.

"Oh no," Reggie said. "There've been many dwellings on the property over the generations. There's an original cabin, which would have been in ruins even by Morrison's time, and a series of houses and barns that were put up and replaced over the years. At one point, three different branches of MacGregors lived there, each with their own house, barn, and outbuildings, spread all over the acreage. They had a gristmill and even a blacksmith's forge."

He stood and went to the box of official maps he'd opened earlier, carefully placing a document on the table. "This is a survey. You can see the ruins of the original homestead." He gestured to a small square. "They built by the river because there weren't even roads then. The thick brush was impenetrable, so the rivers were the highways. They'd bring everything in by canoe. Then over here, here, and here"—he pointed to a scattering of larger shapes all over the property, including one on the spot where the current house stood—"are other houses built later."

Cate counted fourteen different buildings across the MacGregor land. That was a lot of places to hide a fugitive . . . and his gold.

St. Onge was flipping through Marc's notes. "Look at this," she said, gesturing to a page.

Cate was delighted that something had captured the officer's interest.

"It's a poem he's copied out." St. Onge read aloud:

Flow gently, sweet Afton, among thy green braes,
Flow gently, sweet river, the theme of my lays;
My Mary's asleep by thy murmuring stream,
Flow gently, sweet Afton, disturb not her dream.

"That's by Robert Burns," Reggie said.

"The Scottish poet." Cate remembered Mrs. Marquis standing in front of them in English class, affecting a terrible accent to make them laugh. "He wrote 'Auld Lang Syne.'"

"Why has Renaud copied this out?" St. Onge asked. The officer was interested despite herself.

"It's a good question," Cate said. "His notes are all in French, except for this, and I doubt he was a poetry lover. It must have significance for the location of the gold."

"I did some research when I came across it," Reggie said. "Afton is a river in Scotland. The poem is about the poet's love for Mary, who is sleeping by the river. Sleeping might be a metaphor for death."

St. Onge stared at him, as if waiting for more.

He shrugged. "That's all I know."

The constable stood abruptly. "Marc Renaud's notes are potential evidence." Her tone was clipped and urgent.

Cate was startled by St. Onge's change in demeanor, but she'd obviously come around to the gold angle as a decent avenue for investigation.

"I'll take them to the station immediately," St Onge addressed Reggie. "Please assemble them now, ensuring that I have every single item that Marc Renaud reviewed."

Reggie stood as well. "Certainly, Officer." He gathered Renaud's papers while St. Onge pulled out a notepad and wrote him a receipt for the goods being taken into evidence. The transaction was over in a couple of minutes. "There's nothing else?" she confirmed.

"Not another scrap of paper from Renaud, I promise."

St. Onge narrowed her eyes, and Cate winced in secondhand embarrassment at the cop's posturing.

Her domineering attitude had its effect on Reggie, who spoke almost apologetically. "Marc spent an afternoon going over microfilm reels. If you wanted, we could review what he looked at. It might give us further insight."

St. Onge curled her lip impatiently. "I'm not interested in this imaginary gold. I'm interested in the victim's thought process. I won't find that in microfilm reels. His notes," she said, and gestured to the box now in her arms, "are all that I need at present. Good day."

St. Onge left. Cate and Reggie were alone.

CHAPTER 29

CATE WAITED UNTIL THEY HEARD THE OUTER DOOR CLOSE AND THEN turned to Reggie. "I'll admit, I'm curious. Could I look at those microfilm?"

Reggie grinned. "Of course. Marc only reviewed newspaper accounts from the period. There was lots of coverage of the Megantic Outlaw. Donald Morrison was the Kardashian of his time."

Cate raised an eyebrow at this.

Two old machines sat in the microfilm room. Reggie showed her how to load the reels and scroll through the black-and-white images. He stretched before joining her at the other reader. His shoulders were broad, and his jeans fit him well. Because she and Reggie sat so close, occasionally their hands would touch or their knees brush.

Cate enjoyed reading the antique typeface, sinking into a time before cars or phones. She read about convoluted local politics, robberies, and buggy accidents. She learned about cows dying of mysterious diseases, farmers planting apple trees, and plans for the railroad. The Megantic Outlaw was threaded through it all.

According to the published accounts, he had a fulsome moustache, a ready wit, and a saintly devotion to his own dear parents. He paid his respects at a funeral and danced at a ceilidh, all while thumbing his nose at the authorities. The premier of Québec angrily vowed to bring him to justice. Article after article detailed the Outlaw's exploits. He really was a Kardashian—if not a Kim or a Kylie, at least a Khloé.

"Listen to this," Reggie said. "It's from *The Montreal Star.* 'People will keep close watch on the Montreal Police as they try to catch the

Canadian Rob Roy. Donald Morrison is of Highland descent, so it is peculiarly appropriate that Sergeant Clarke took his bagpipes with him. If Donald Morrison cannot be wooed by Sergeant Clarke's piping, he must be utterly devoid of the finest feelings of a Scotchman. There's no more impressive sight than the Montreal Police Department scattered over the hills behind trees and stumps while the sergeant strides boldly forward, pipes under arm, playing "Come Under My Plaidie" in the hopes that Donald Morrison will put in an appearance.'"

Cate laughed. "The papers were having fun with the story." As she read more about the Outlaw's adventures, she found herself foolishly rooting for him, hoping he would evade captivity and escape to the safety of the United States.

They located several newspaper accounts of his death, many varying in detail, but the majority were clear: After years in prison, Donald Morrison was pardoned but a few hours later died of consumption at Montreal's Royal Victoria Hospital on June 16, 1894. His brother was by his bedside and reported in a later interview with the *Sherbrooke Daily Record* that Donald said a touching goodbye, hoped to be forgiven in heaven, gripped his hand tightly, and spoke the final lines of a beloved Robert Burns poem.

"Oh wow," Cate said. "This might be the poem Marc copied out. Somehow, he figured out which Burns poem Morrison quoted." Maybe Madge Taylor gave him that hint.

"I read an account of Donald's death that said he was surrounded by officials and doctors," Reggie said excitedly. "He wouldn't have been able to tell his brother directly where the gold was, so maybe the poem was a clue. Let's take another look at that survey I showed you."

Back in the reading room, they pored over the map. Reggie pointed to a wiggly line. "That's the Pekeda River east of the present-day house." He had long fingers and a scattering of dark freckles on the back of his hands. "It's too bad we don't still have Marc's notes to check where he was looking."

Cate read the poem from her phone. "'My Mary' could have been Donald's gold," she speculated. "His Mary is asleep, meaning it's buried."

Reggie nodded enthusiastically. "That's a good theory."

"Murmuring stream," Cate said. "A river runs quietly, but if there are rocks or a drop, it makes more noise. That area might be shallower."

"There's a spot on the Pekeda called 'Barton's Crossing' that was a popular river ford for travelers. It's on MacGregor's property." Reggie pointed on the map. "Right about here."

Cate thought the area was near where Marc's body was found, but she couldn't be sure. "It's hard to tell."

Reggie agreed. "We need to see the site with our own eyes."

"What would that do?"

"We could search, see if the gold was actually there." Reggie's voice was surprised, as if the answer was obvious.

Cate laughed. "I'm not sure how digging up the gold helps us solve these murders."

"It would," Reggie said. "If that gold really exists, and Marc knew about it, that's a huge motive. A stash of gold would be worth a lot of money. It's likely to be bullion—meaning over ninety-nine percent pure. In bar or coin form, it would be untraceable."

"You seem to know a lot about the subject," she teased.

He chuckled. "I told you, I learned all about it in school, and it sparked my imagination."

"According to Madge, Marc needed money."

"Madge?" Reggie asked.

Cate waved a hand. "Old Mrs. Taylor at the Blakeney Inn. She was talking to Marc about the Outlaw's gold. She's the one who inspired him to do this archival research."

"I wondered what had brought him here. I think her cousin donated some of our later material."

Reggie put everything back in the archival boxes and placed them on the shelf. Their research was winding down. "We've done good work tonight," he said. "Want to grab dinner?"

It was a casual invite, and Cate accepted before she could over-think it.

Reggie no longer drove a convertible Mercedes, but instead had a slick, low-slung Audi. He brought them to a small bistro on a dirt road off the highway. Tucked behind a stone fence, the little cottage was covered in late autumn roses. The building looked enchanted, and for a moment Cate hesitated. It was almost too romantic.

The interior was quiet, with only one other couple sitting at one of the half dozen candlelit tables. They snagged a spot by a window over-looking the Pekeda River and chatted about inconsequential things until the waitress took their order. Though nervous now that she most definitely found herself on a date, Cate limited herself to beer rather than wine or the double scotch she really wanted.

"I heard through the grapevine that you're actually a Canterbury grad," she said.

Reggie smiled. "Let me guess? Dr. K?"

"He can't resist bragging about former students. I hadn't realized we shared a school." Reggie's involvement with the archery town league made even more sense; as a born and bred local, he was a nat-ural bridge between the community and the school.

Reggie smiled, a slightly twisted grin. "I only went to Canterbury for my last two years of high school."

That's right, Reggie was a scholarship student. The kind the other kids teased.

Reggie was watching her face, and his twisted grin deepened. "Yup," he said, reading her thoughts correctly: "I was a 'brownie.'"

"Did you like Canterbury?" Cate asked.

"Sure. It was a different universe from Manasoka High. Such bright students from around the world." He cleared his throat. "The caliber of teaching was incredible. We went to the Met and the Gug-genheim on one class trip, and to Boston for the Symphony Orchestra and a tour of MIT on another."

Cate remembered similar trips.

"My mother was delighted," Reggie continued. "She knew I'd meet a 'better' class of students. Make connections that would set me up for life."

"Did it work?"

Reggie laughed. "I'm an archivist, not exactly a mover and shaker. I made some great friends though. Finn Stackhorn is a good buddy. We went skiing in Switzerland last year."

Seeing Cate's blank face, he explained, "His father was the under-secretary for the United Nations."

Cate shook her head.

Reggie's chest puffed up. "I'm also close with Thomas Whitford. You must know the Whitfords? His older brother would have been at Canterbury the same time as you."

Cate dimly remembered an arrogant little shit who was a couple of years younger. "William Whitford?"

Reggie's smile widened. "Yeah, that's right. He's an investment banker in Toronto now. His little brother is my buddy. Tommy's the vice chair of a major philanthropic organization in Australia. *Major.*"

"Did the Whitfords breed polo ponies?" Cate asked, wondering if that memory could possibly be correct.

"That's right. They owned a place in Australia and a huge spread in Argentina. I was invited to their sister's wedding a couple of years ago. It was at the Alvear Palace Hotel in Buenos Aires. Totally amazing. Four days of partying. I brought three different types of dinner jacket."

It was an odd thing to brag about, but this glimpse of Reggie's insecurity made Cate feel for him. It must have been difficult to be the perpetual poor one among the fabulously wealthy. Cate and Jason were certainly not in the top tiers of Canterbury wealth, but her father came from some family money and living in Ottawa's Rockcliffe neighborhood gave her a certain cachet. What would it be like for a kid from Manasoka to be thrust into that world?

"Now, what's happening with this murder investigation?" Reggie asked after the waitress delivered their drinks.

"I'm only a civilian," Cate demurred.

"Oh, come on. I assume you're using your coroner mojo to get the details."

Cate smiled. "My mojo?"

Reggie cocked an eyebrow. "Don't tell me you don't have any."

She laughed. "Oh, I've got mojo." She couldn't believe the flirtatious words tripping from her mouth. Reggie chuckled, so he mustn't think she was a total dork. Her stomach fluttered. She took a long sip of the pint of golden, triple-blonde La Fin du Monde in front of her. "It's the end of the world," she said, and pointed to the label on her bottle, "the name of this beer."

He smiled. "Yeah. It's a tribute to what the first explorers supposedly thought when they arrived here—they'd reached the end of civilization."

"Pretty Eurocentric," Cate said. "Indigenous people might object."

"Oh yeah, most definitely! Rampant colonial conquest."

Their meals arrived, a delicately flavored risotto for Cate and a locally sourced Brome Lake duck for Reggie.

"Speaking of colonialism, I was recently in the Congo," Cate said. "It's an incredibly resource-rich country, but there is corruption and tribal hatred and greed. So much of the mess can be traced right back to the horrific things that colonial Belgium did there for decades."

"What were you doing in the Congo?"

Cate hesitated but then told him about Jason and the plane crash that took his life. "I was there for almost two weeks, but thankfully, I didn't turn up anything suspicious about his death." Rescue the Children hadn't been in the news for the past couple of days, or at least not that she'd seen. She'd follow up with Brilliant again. He should be back in Ottawa by now.

"Why did you think his death might have been more than an accident?" Reggie asked.

Cate's hands twisted together. "I was, uh, attacked this summer." Only Rose, Detective Baker, and Matthew knew about how she had been shoved to the ground and threatened. Now she found herself recounting the event to Reggie. "I was terrified," she concluded. "The worst thing about it is that I still don't know why it happened. What that guy wanted . . ." Her voice quavered, and Cate wondered if she'd ever be free of that acidic fear.

"Wow," Reggie said. "After facing something like that, most people would have run away, not flown to another continent for answers."

Cate grimaced. She usually managed to forget about the attack.

His hand shot out and covered hers. "You've been through a lot."

"Yeah," she answered in a quiet voice. She looked at his hand holding hers. His thumb brushed lightly against her skin. "Want to get out of here?" she asked.

He looked pleased. "Uh-huh."

Reggie paid for the meal, and they drove back to the Canterbury campus. Cate was surprised when he passed the archives' parking lot where she'd left her car, instead turning down a little lane she'd never noticed before. They pulled up in front of a small red-brick two-story house, its design matching that of the archives' building. He unlocked the door and ushered her inside. There was a momentary awkwardness. Did they rip each other's clothes off now, or did they have to chitchat first?

"Want a drink?" he asked.

"Please." A quadruple scotch. "A glass of wine would be great."

He disappeared into the kitchen. She looked around. The living room was dominated by a huge bookcase. She wandered over and perused the shelves. Mostly history books, covering everything from Medieval Europe to local events. They appeared to be arranged by subject and then alphabetically. Very methodical.

Many plants thrived in the windowsills; their glossy green leaves turned toward the light. Not a brown leaf or a dead stem to be seen. Very conscientious.

The furniture was mismatched but well-made and in good condition. The sofa was no frat boy curbside find. The pieces were selected with care. A bright round rug picked up the room's color and hadn't been purchased at Ikea. Very tasteful.

He came back with the wine, and their fingers brushed as she took the glass from him.

"You don't have a girlfriend or a partner, do you?" she asked.

He didn't meet her eye. "It's complicated."

Cate took a sip of the wine and considered. Did she care if he had a wife tucked away somewhere? That was his decision to wrestle with. "This wine is excellent."

"Cabernet sauvignon," he said, taking her comment as willingness to continue. "A friend of mine owns the vineyard in Napa. I try to get down there as often as possible. I helped with the harvest one year. Absolutely magical."

She cleared her throat. "This is a nice place."

"This?" He looked around. "It wouldn't be my first choice, but it's part of the salary package with the job at the archives. I can't say no to free rent."

Reggie's hair curled at the nape of his neck. One faint dimple appeared when he smiled. She wanted to kiss that little indent.

They made eye contact, and her heart rate increased.

"Should we sit?" he gestured to the couch.

She sank into the sofa, and he sat beside her, their knees touching. "Cate, I—"

She didn't want to talk about what was about to happen; she just wanted to do it. She put her hand on his thigh.

He leaned toward her, and his lips found hers. Her stomach tightened and she deepened the kiss. His breath was warm and tasted of the wine. Her hand touched his shoulder, her fingers tightening. He broke the kiss to nibble down her neck. "You're so pretty," he said. "I like your eyes."

She didn't want to talk, so she kissed him harder. He gripped her neck, pulling her closer. His hand brushed her breast, and her whole body tightened with desire. She needed to feel more of him, so she straddled him. He moaned. She could feel the hard bulge in his pants, and her lips parted. She ran her hands down his shoulders, which were more muscled than she had anticipated.

"Bedroom?" he asked.

Cate stood and Reggie grabbed her hand, leading her up a narrow set of stairs.

They fell onto his bed, suddenly able to touch each other with ease. Reggie started unbuttoning her shirt. She kissed him and gasped when his hands found her breasts.

"Do you have a condom?" she remembered to ask.

"Yes," he said, pointing to the nightstand. "No problem."

There was a framed photo by the bed. It was Reggie, holding a younger blonde woman in a loose embrace. They stood beside a lighthouse. Cate closed her eyes and turned away from the image, concentrating on the man in front of her.

CATE WOKE THE NEXT MORNING AND LOOKED FOR HER CLOTHES. SHE HAD slipped on her jeans and wriggled into her bra when Reggie awoke.

"I thought I'd make breakfast," he said.

Cate shook her head, picking up her shirt. "I've got to get going."

"Hey, what's that?" he asked, frowning.

Cate looked at her arm. A dark bracelet of bruises still encircled the spot where Thierry Montaigne had grabbed her. It was no longer tender but remained a reminder of the man's aggression. She shivered, pulling on her shirt. "It's nothing."

"You really can't stay?"

Cate stiffened. Last night was the satisfaction of an attraction. She didn't want or need a Reggie in her life. She pointed to the framed photo on the bedside table, now face down. He must have turned it over at some point in the evening. "I'm not sure we want this to continue, do we?"

He flushed. "It's not what you think. Like I said, it's complicated—"

She put up a hand. "It's simple for me. This was a onetime

thing. Thanks for your help with the research. I really do appreciate it."

Reggie looked surprised, and Cate felt an ungenerous surge of satisfaction. He was an attractive man, and probably unused to rejection. It was nice to be in control.

CHAPTER 30

CATE SPENT SUNDAY WORKING ON VARIOUS LEADS TO CLEAR KEVIN'S name. She had a long and unfruitful conversation with the embittered organic egg rivals, researched criminal gang activity in the Eastern Townships, and booked an appointment for a manicure for later in the week. She wanted to question Vivienne about Marc Renaud's old girlfriends and find out if any were the jealous type. She was energized by these possible leads, which almost drowned out worries about the future. It was one thing not to get a letter of recommendation from Vachon, but if he complained to the College, her chances of reinstatement were sunk.

That night she walked up the path by her house, reflecting on what she needed to do. She took a long drag on her cigarette. The dog was a reassuring presence against the possibility of bears. A few stars illuminated the black hills, undimmed by light pollution. She hummed the song that had been bugging her for days. Where was it from? She closed her eyes, trying to place it. Something about wanting him to know. She sang a bit more and found herself murmuring "fire at the warehouse." She laughed aloud. It was "Little Star," a song from *Romeo + Juliet*, that nineties movie. As a moody teen, Cate listened to the soundtrack a thousand times. She'd heard the tune quite recently. Was that before or after Vivienne had mentioned the film when she was cutting her hair? She couldn't remember.

———————

HER MONDAY MORNING SHIFT AT THE CLINIC WAS BUSIER THAN NORMAL. Based on the questions they asked and their mild symptoms, she suspected some of her patients had caught wind of her presence at Bethany Farnham's murder scene and wanted to get the gossip. She maintained a strict silence on the subject, and they left disappointed.

Her phone rang. "Dr. Spencer? It's Madge Taylor." The older woman hardly needed to identify herself; her voice was easily recognizable. "I'd like to talk with you. Are you free?"

"My shift is over," Cate said. "What's the issue?"

"I need to speak to you in person. Something has happened."

Timmy met her in the inn's lobby and ushered her to a small library off the main entrance. This room was cozy and chic with a couple of leather armchairs, a black bearskin rug, and two walls of hardcover books. A large fireplace took up the rest of the space.

Timmy noticed her admiration. "This was the cheapest room to outfit. I bought the chairs from a junk shop in Lennoxville, and I got all these books for free. Some old guy over the border in Derby died, and his widow wanted to get rid of them. She said she would have paid me to take them away. They look great, but they're mostly about stamps."

"What about the rug?" Cate asked, stepping on it gingerly.

"That's a legit family heirloom. My grandfather, Madge's husband, killed him. Bam, shot square between the eyes."

"Did your grandfather shoot that too?" Cate asked, pointing to the huge moose head over the fireplace.

"Yup. We're a family of crack shots."

"Bullshit." Madge teetered into the room with the help of a cane. "You couldn't hit the side of a barn. Your daddy is a decent shot, but your mother is better. Sit," she said to Cate, gesturing to a chair by the fire.

Timmy hovered as Madge got settled, and then he handed her a bright afghan. She took it without thanks and turned to him. "Scram. Go and tend to your fancy frogs. I saw a couple of them parking their bikes."

Timmy bowed his head and hurried out the door. Madge watched him go and shook her head. "Those Frenchy cyclists are a bunch of clowns. Have you seen their outfits? With the helmets, wraparound sunglasses, and the skintight suits? They look like walking sperm."

Cate laughed.

"Where's your little friend?" Madge asked.

"I didn't think it would be appropriate to include Kevin."

Madge grunted. "Makes sense if he shot that wife of his. Heard she was Marc's mysterious girlfriend."

"Yes. You really had no idea it was her?"

"None," Madge said. "I should have guessed. Marc was desperate to leave town, and a woman like Bethany would be anxious to ditch the Eastern Townships."

"Bethany told me Marc had no plans to leave. In fact, she broke up with him on Thursday because of that."

Madge frowned. "The Thursday before his death? I saw him Friday. He was still as keen as ever to find the gold. He was almost panicked about it. Maybe he hoped to dig it up and win her back."

Cate recalled Bethany's lack of sentiment about Marc's death and her conviction that their relationship was merely a fling. "Bethany said she wasn't going to run away with him."

"She was lying," Madge said flatly. "Marc was heading for the hills."

Cate wavered. Her impression that Bethany was done with Marc might be wrong. After all, the dead woman had reason to lie about her plans: A messy breakup gave her motive to murder Marc. She returned to her new theory. "Could Marc have had another girlfriend?"

Madge shrugged. "Who knows. He might have been sticking his pecker into a dozen women. All I can say for certain is that he wanted to leave town with one of them, double-quick."

Cate took heart. Her theory about a second girlfriend might be right. If Vivienne didn't know any gossip, she'd return to the feedstore and question more of Marc's colleagues. Renata, the store manager, had been good friends with Marc. She was in rehab, but maybe Cate could find a way to speak with her. "This is very interesting," she said to Madge, "but I don't think it's why you called me."

Madge clasped her hands. "Early this morning we had a distur-bance." She glanced at the door. "I haven't told Timmy about it, be-cause that numbskull will worry."

Cate nodded.

"My bedroom is one of the front rooms here, overlooking the church. It's a big one, with my bed at one end, a couple of armchairs in a little sitting area, and my dresser and closet by the second door, which leads out to the veranda that runs along the whole second story. You can get up to that second-floor balcony by a set of stairs off the parking lot."

Cate had noted the building-long balcony the first time they'd visited.

"Now, we usually keep the veranda door at the top locked, but it's broken, and Timmy's been too busy to fix it." She paused to take a breath before continuing. "Anyway, it was about seven this morning. I'm nor-mally down in the kitchen by then, making sure those greasy bastards get the chow out. When we're really overrun, I've been known to wait a table or two. I tell you something, if you want to get a good tip, send out the tottering ninety-year-old grandma—the guilt opens wallets."

Madge had wandered away from the point. "Something happened this morning," Cate prompted.

"Right. I was feeling a little woozy, so I decided to have a lie-in. I was curled up in bed, with the curtains drawn. It was quite dim be-cause the sun rises late these days. That's when I saw the outside door open, and a figure in dark clothes and tuque pulled low over his eyes crept in. I sat up real quiet and didn't say a word."

"Weren't you startled?" Cate broke in. "Terrified?"

Madge shot her a pitying look. "I spent my childhood in deer blinds. I know how to stay calm, move slow, and wait." She took a sip of water and continued. "There I was, sitting as quiet as the grave, watching him. He didn't even look over at me."

"Who was it?" Cate asked. "Did you recognize him?"

Madge looked rueful. "My eyes aren't what they used to be. I can't see much in dim lighting. It was a man, though . . . or a largish woman."

She paused and shook her head, obviously annoyed she couldn't identify the person. "Anyway, the bastard was absorbed in the other side of the room, by my closet and drawers. I've also got a big wooden chest there. It's filled with quilts and old keepsakes. He started with that, pulling out every item. Real slow."

"What did you do?" Cate asked.

"I knew exactly what he was looking for, and I knew he wasn't going to find it in the chest. Still, while his head was buried there, I leaned over and pulled out my short pistol from under the bed."

"Oh my God," Cate said.

"Now, I can't say that I did all that smoothly or without making any noise, but that mouth-breathing numbskull was too focused on the chest to pay much attention to me."

She took another sip of water, obviously enjoying Cate's undivided attention. "Once the gun was in my hand, I felt pretty good. I stood up to get a clear shot around the armchairs in the sitting area."

"What do you mean 'clear shot'? Didn't you say you don't see well?"

Madge ignored the question. "I took aim and cocked the pistol. The little turd caught that noise, because his head reared up like a groundhog spotting a hawk. I said in a clear voice, 'I don't know who the fuck you are, but you have three seconds to get out of my god-damn room or I will blow your goddamn head off.'"

Cate laughed aloud.

"That cowardly so-and-so didn't even hesitate. He dove for the outside door and was running down the stairs before I could even see who it was."

"Damn, Mrs. Taylor, you chased off a burglar. That's impressive."

Madge smiled. "Mangy little turd. I gave him a good scare."

"You said you knew what he was after. Is it connected with what we talked about? The Megantic Outlaw's gold?"

"It's what I showed Marc. It's what convinced him the gold was worth looking for." She fumbled in her large purse and pulled an object out with some difficulty. "I've slept with this under my pillow for seventy years. My grandpa gave it to me on my wedding night."

She held a thin metallic rectangle up to the light.

Only when Madge handed it to her, and Cate startled at its weight, did she understand what it was. "This is a gold bar."

"Yup," Madge confirmed. "Granddad said his father gave it to him. It was part of Donald Morrison's treasure."

Cate turned the bar over in her hand. It was about the size of a deck of cards but thinner and heavier than it looked. Here was tangible evidence of the existence of the gold and a solid motive for Marc's murder. "You have to tell the police what happened and about the connection to Marc."

"I suppose you're right," Madge sighed. "Timmy will get all hot and bothered."

"You did fend off a home invasion from your bed." The intruder was after the gold and likely murdered both Marc and Bethany. Madge was lucky to have escaped with her life.

Once again, Madge ignored her. "I'd like them to catch the bastard who killed Marc. He was a good boy. He didn't deserve that. That girl probably didn't either."

"Go to the police," Cate said. Madge needed protection, and this news would force Vachon to acknowledge there might be more to the case than simply a jealousy-crazed husband.

"I'll tell Timmy about it," Madge promised. "He can make the call."

"Good. You need to protect yourself. This person is dangerous. They've killed twice before."

Madge scoffed. "I'm not afraid of him, because I'm not afraid of death."

Cate hoped to have even a quarter of Madge's sangfroid when she reached her nineties. "Did your grandfather say anything else about the gold bar?"

"He said at least thirty more like it were buried on the MacGregor property, but we could never find them."

"Why didn't your grandfather know their location?"

"Donald Morrison never got the chance to tell anyone where he hid them because he was arrested right after he buried them. People knew the rumors, so the prison guards read all his letters and monitored his visits. They only let him out when he was dying, and he was taken straight to the hospital. He couldn't explain the location then, for fear that someone would overhear. That's why he recited the last lines of that poem. They were his dying words to his brother, my great-grandfather."

"Did you tell Marc about the poem?"

"Yep. As soon as he accepted the treasure was real, he wanted clues. The poem mentions a river, so he was convinced the Outlaw buried the gold on the banks of the Pekeda."

"We found the poem in Marc's notes at the archives."

"'My Mary's asleep by thy murmuring stream, / Flow gently, sweet Afton, disturb not her dream.' I've read those lines a thousand times, and we dug up half of MacGregor's riverbank looking for it. We stopped when Thomas MacGregor took over the orchard from his father. He'd come at us with his shotgun, crazy bugger. That fool never believed there was any gold."

"If you couldn't find the gold, maybe it was never there." She saw Madge's face redden and amended. "Maybe someone got to it first, I mean. Morrison was arrested more than one hundred and thirty years ago. It could have been unearthed in that time."

"Do you think if someone dug up a fortune in gold bars, they'd keep that quiet?"

Discovering an illicit treasure might be great motivation to keep your mouth shut, especially if you didn't want to split the find with the property owner.

Madge must have read the doubt in her face. "People have been after this gold for more than a hundred years. Hell, the Montaignes and the Renauds have been mad as hell at each other for a century over it. It's real. It's only a question of finding it."

"Did Marc know the story behind his family's feud with the Montaignes? Did he know it started with the gold?"

"Not until I told him, but he paid attention. Said it was his destiny to get the gold. When he bought a fancy metal detector from the internet, I knew he'd find it."

"What made you so sure?"

"I could see it in his eyes. I used to search because it was a lark. Marc was motivated by something else, something urgent. He was desperate to get some money, and desperate men accomplish great things . . . . Look at Donald Morrison. He brought law enforcement to its knees for months. Marc was made of that same stuff. He was going to find that gold or die trying."

CHAPTER 31

Madge's news. The police officer had already heard from Timmy and had sent a constable to get the old woman's statement. He wasn't overly interested in the development, and Cate hung up the phone hastily to avoid venting her frustration at him.

Cate was brushing her teeth when the flash of headlights appeared on the road in front of her house. It was ten o'clock, and she'd already seen MacGregor drive home. She went out to the porch, and the dog emerged from the shed, silent and alert.

The car swung into her driveway. She didn't recognize the vehicle and couldn't make out the driver. Her heart rate increased. A murderer was stalking the countryside. She walked down her steps, and the dog moved to her side. The car door opened. Cate gaped. Matthew Tomkins—ex-husband, ex-lover, ex-everything—emerged.

What the actual fuck was he doing here?

The dog approached, hackles raised. His growl was a deep rumble.

"Whoa," Matthew said when he spotted the animal. He backed toward his car.

Cate wasn't sure she could control the dog if he decided to attack. "Shh, it's OK." She hurried forward and grabbed his collar. The dog's entire body was tense, and his eyes were trained on the visitor. Matthew stood by the car, looking nervous.

"It's OK," she said, unsure if she was reassuring herself or the dog. "He's a friend." She recalled all the voice mails Matthew had left. She hadn't checked again to see if more had accumulated. "Or at least he's friendly."

To her relief, the dog relaxed, though he continued to eye Matthew warily. Cate released his collar but left her hand on his broad back. It was reassuring to have the dog by her side. For once she wasn't outmatched by Matthew. "What are you doing here?"

Matthew glanced at the dog and then at her. "I'm doing what you asked."

"What I asked?"

"The other night. You left me a message, saying that we should talk. Clear the air once and for all."

The night of the funeral. She'd been so sad about Jason's death. Consumed with self-pity and too much wine, she'd drunk-dialed Matthew and left him a voice mail. Her stomach clenched. How could she have been so stupid? "And you came all this way? It's almost a five-hour drive."

"I wanted to make a grand gesture. Literally show you how far I am willing to come." He smiled at her, but she wasn't softened by his charm. "I would have been here sooner, but I was in court, wrapping up a case."

Cate glared at him. Matthew always had trouble respecting her boundaries, and this was a prime example. "I made one phone call when I was obviously vulnerable"—who knows what garbled nonsense she'd said to him—"and you thought it was an invitation to start everything back up again?"

Matthew stepped toward her, and the dog tensed. "Not to start back up again, to start fresh. Like we talked about in the summer. I'm a different man from the one you married. I've worked on my issues. The one thing that hasn't changed is how I feel about you. Please, Cate. We were good together, at least at the beginning. I want to get back to that."

His voice held real pain. The early years of their relationship had been wonderful. Matthew challenged her, made her laugh, and made her a better person—at least until everything soured.

"I only want to talk, then I promise I'll leave. I've booked a room at the Blakeney Inn."

The news that he didn't expect to stay with her—wasn't completely invading her space—softened her a little. A chilly wind blew from the west, and Matthew shivered. He wasn't wearing a coat. He looked older than when she'd seen him in July, back when they'd fought and had sex and fought some more. His hair held a touch more gray, and new lines had appeared around his mouth. Matthew was always the one in control during their relationship. Now he needed her so desperately he'd driven hours to see her. There was something intoxicating in that. "Fine, you can come in." Cate waved him up the steps.

She patted the dog's head. "It's OK, boy," she soothed as her ex edged past. Matthew paused at the front door, holding it open for the dog.

"It's no use," she said. "I've been trying to coax him inside, but he's not ready. He sleeps in the shed. He's a little bit wild."

They went into the house, leaving the dog guarding the steps. "You took in a stray?" Matthew asked. "You don't even like dogs."

Cate shrugged, irritated that he presumed to know her. "People change." She gestured to the sofa. "Have a seat."

She was glad they weren't at her home in Ottawa. She wouldn't want Matthew in her personal space, looking at her furniture and knickknacks, making assumptions about her postdivorce life. The farmhouse was a neutral safe zone.

"Do you want something to drink? I've got wine, coffee, or water."

"A glass of wine would be great." He sat on the couch.

She opened a fresh bottle of red. It was a Californian merlot, like he preferred. She hadn't realized she'd continued to buy his favorite after the divorce. Was it a way to keep a reminder of him? A taste? What else were "Matthew things" she adopted subconsciously?

She poured two generous glasses and returned to the living room. She'd hear Matthew out, put his hopes to bed, and ask him to leave.

She handed him his glass and took the armchair. The coffee table was a nice, solid mass between them.

Matthew looked around with interest. Cate's shoulders straightened. Was there anything revealing lying in sight? Her medical bag was on the dining room table, the dog food she'd bought at Lachance Feed by the door. Her laptop was closed on the table in front of them. Nothing too personal. She relaxed. While the farmhouse didn't have the aesthetic glamour of Bethany Farnham's home, it was cozy, clean, and comfortable.

"Nice place," Matthew said, echoing her thoughts.

She glowered. She didn't like to be reminded of how in sync they used to be. She recalled this summer's impetuous night of sex under the stars. "Thanks."

He pointed to a framed photo of her and Jason by the door to the kitchen. It was the only personal item she'd put up since renting the place. "That's a great picture." Matthew loved and admired Jason almost as much as she did.

"Yeah," she said. "It's from a couple of years back. It was the first warm day of an Ottawa spring, and we ate on a patio. Of course, it wasn't actually hot, and we froze our asses off." She laughed at the memory. Jason insisted they stay, despite the strong wind, because the sun was shining and they needed their vitamin D.

Matthew smiled and took a sip of his wine. "I was so happy when you called."

"You left a lot of messages."

He flushed, discomfited.

Cate shifted in her chair. It was strange to be in the driver's seat.

"I'm sorry. I know all those calls were out of line." He ran his hand through his hair, a familiar gesture. "This summer was hard. Reconnecting with you unmoored me."

He'd already told her this, right before they had sex.

"I've separated from Tansy, and I've started divorce proceedings."

"I'm sorry," she said, but she wasn't.

He nodded, taking her words at face value. "I feel bad for her. I was never really committed. I shouldn't have married her, not when I was still—"

"Matthew," she said with a warning note in her voice.

He ignored her cue. "Cate, do you think we could try again? That you and I—"

"No," she said firmly. "This summer was a mistake. We shouldn't have slept together. You might have gone to therapy and worked on yourself, but whatever you think this is"—and she gestured from him to herself—"is not good. You left me those voice mails and drove all the way out here. It's too much, Matthew. I don't trust you." She was proud of the assurance in her voice.

He remained calm in the face of her words. "I get that. I do. Only, I love you, and I'm convinced you have feelings for me."

"I might," she surprised herself by admitting. His eyes lit up, and she put out a hand to stop his excitement. "I'm trying to be honest with you and with myself. I might still have feelings for you, but I'm also trying to figure things out. This summer was insane. I lost Jason, I was attacked, nearly killed. We had that thing. My career stalled. I came here, back to Pekeda Township, to Canterbury—the only place I've ever felt safe. I'm finding my feet. A relationship with you would jeopardize all that."

Matthew stared at her, his eyes searching her face. She reddened slightly under his intense gaze. "That's bullshit, Cate. If you have feelings for me, we should get back together. It's only logical."

Matthew worshipped at the altar of the logical, the practical, the efficient. Problem was, the things he deigned "logical" always happened to coincide with the things he wanted. When she disagreed with him, she was "irrational."

"We're not getting back together, Matthew, because I don't want to. You can't railroad me into a relationship."

She crossed her arms and stared at him. His mouth turned down, and she braced herself for an argument, undoubtedly ending in him yelling at her.

Instead, he took a deep breath and said, "OK."

Cate blinked. Surprised. And if she were honest, a tiny bit disappointed that he wasn't willing to fight for her.

The air pulsed for a moment with the unsaid, but then Matthew cleared his throat and asked about her father. A safe topic.

"Dad's doing OK. I've got him a live-in nurse. He terrorizes her, and she ignores it while masterfully bossing him around. They're a match made in heaven."

Matthew smiled.

They sipped their wine and talked about their respective families. Cate got up and refilled their glasses before opening a new bottle and bringing it to the living room. She told him stories about her time in the Townships, giving him the highlights of the investigation and talking about her work at the Canterbury Clinic.

"Wait, Anya Patel is the headmistress?" he asked. "Was she at our table at Dr. K's wedding?"

"That's her," Cate confirmed.

"The one Jason slept with?"

"What?!" Cate exclaimed. "No. Anya and Jason didn't sleep together."

Matthew crooked an eyebrow at her. "Pretty Indian woman? Super intense? A-type personality?"

Cate's mouth fell open, but she managed to nod.

"That's the one." Matthew sounded confident.

"How do you know that?"

He shrugged. "Jason let it slip that they'd had an affair."

Cate tried to compute what she was hearing. "When? Where?"

"I don't really know." He looked at her face. "Hey, this is upsetting you." He frowned, concentrating. "That wedding was ten years ago, right?"

"Yeah, I think so." Cate barely heard the question, too busy processing what she had learned.

"OK, well, Jason said their dalliance happened a few years before that. She was working somewhere in Africa."

"Central African Republic." Now that she thought about it, Jason had been posted there about a dozen years earlier. He never mentioned running into Anya, though; Cate would have remembered.

"Yeah, that's right," Matthew said. "CAR. Jason said he'd bumped into her, and one thing led to another."

"Anya was married," Cate said, putting her wineglass down. Anya and Wylie had been together for at least fifteen years.

Matthew chuckled. "I don't think that ever bothered Jason."

"Jason wouldn't do that. He was so morally righteous." Cate's wine buzz deserted her. Her mouth tasted sour.

Matthew shook his head. "He wasn't righteous. He was a regular person, just like you and me."

Just like her. Hadn't she slept with another woman's husband, or at least boyfriend, only two nights ago? Why was she holding Jason up to some high standard she didn't even meet? Still, the idea of Jason and Anya was too weird, too upsetting. "But to have an affair, and with Anya? You can't tell me that that's not strange. I mean, for a while we thought he might be gay!"

Matthew laughed. "That was your theory. I never bought it. Women loved Jason." He paused. "And Jason loved women."

She didn't like Matthew's tone. "What do you mean by that?"

"Jason was kind of a player."

"He was?" None of this computed with what she knew of her brother.

"Sure. He was a good-looking guy, and it must have been lonely on those missions. He always had a girl on the go in Ottawa. Sometimes one in Montreal too."

"I never knew that." How did her brother keep such an essential part of himself a secret? How did she not notice? Was she so wrapped up in her own life?

"You're his little sister. He wouldn't have discussed his love life with you."

She stood. She didn't like learning about this side of Jason. "I guess." She paced the living room as she recalled her recent interactions with Anya. At tea with Dr. K, the headmistress had cried talking about Jason. At the time Cate thought those tears were manufactured, but now she realized the other woman was mourning a much more personal loss. "Don't you think it's odd neither of them ever mentioned it?"

Matthew shrugged. "Not really. I mean, Jason did talk about it to me, and Anya probably kept her mouth shut because she's married."

It was unthinkable that Anya would do something as messy and inappropriate as cheat on Wylie.

"Jason didn't even like Anya," Cate said, recalling his assessment of her friend after Dr. K's wedding. "He said she was high-strung and high-maintenance."

Matthew laughed. "You can find someone annoying and still sleep with them."

She disliked Matthew's knowing laugh. Her cozy sense of well-being evaporated. What was she doing getting so friendly with her ex-husband? She stopped pacing and sat down on the edge of the sofa.

Her anger and shock was ebbing, leaving only a destabilizing sense of bewilderment. Her voice shook. "Did I even know Jason?" Was she grieving a mirage?

"Hey," Matthew said, meeting her gaze. "Jason was a good guy, and he loved you. I know that." Once again, he seemed to read her thoughts and know what she needed to hear.

As if sensing her change in mood, Matthew widened his arms. "Come here."

She hesitated. This was dangerous territory. She and Matthew shared a wild attraction. She had been on a similar couch only two nights ago with Reggie. This was different. Matthew wasn't some attractive stranger. He was the man she had loved, might still love. He was right here, solid and in front of her now.

It was a relief to scoot herself under his outstretched arm, so that they were cuddled together. She pulled the blanket over both their laps and leaned back. His familiar scent filled her nose. It was like five years ago, when they were still married. OK, maybe seven years ago, when their marriage was still good.

She closed her eyes and relaxed. When Matthew's hand began absentmindedly stroking her arm, she didn't object. Instead, she turned her face up toward his, and his mouth met hers. The kiss was long and sweet.

She leaned in deeper and twisted her body so she was facing him. His hands gripped her shoulders.

She kissed him harder, and he groaned. His hand traveled down her body. "I've missed you so much," he murmured into her hair.

"I've missed you too." She'd been so devastated and angry after the divorce. So much of that was sadness that she wouldn't get to spend time with this man anymore. Yes, they were toxic, and yes, a new relationship wouldn't work. That didn't mean that sex couldn't be restorative. Cate needed something reassuring. She slid her hand up his shirt, her fingers trailing across his warm chest.

"Are you sure?" he asked.

She looked into his familiar eyes and nodded.

"Bedroom?" he asked.

Her heart rose in her throat, and her stomach tightened in anticipation. "No," she said sternly. "You'll stay here." She pointed to the couch. "Lie back."

Matthew obeyed, a slow, lazy smile spreading across his face. They had played this game often enough in their marriage. Normally Matthew was in control, issuing the orders she hurried to obey. This time, however, she was in charge. She thrilled at her sense of authority.

"Good." She straddled him. "Undo your shirt."

Fingers fumbling, he obeyed.

CHAPTER 32

CATE WOKE THE NEXT MORNING FEELING GOOD. LAST NIGHT'S SEX WITH Matthew had been incredible. Better than the lovemaking was the fact that he had left without a murmur of protest at three in the morning when she asked him to go. Boundaries respected.

As she was getting into her car, MacGregor rumbled past in his truck, giving a friendly honk. At least Cate assumed it was friendly. He was undoubtedly headed for his morning coffee at the Dépanneur Jaune. She pulled onto the dirt road and had almost reached the Boisvert dairy farm when she noticed a car approaching. Her house and MacGregor's were the only two down the road. For a moment she worried it was Matthew returning to pressure her, but the vehicle was the wrong color. She slowed as they pulled alongside one another and was surprised to see Reggie in his Audi. Thank God Matthew had left already. She would not have enjoyed managing morning introductions between the two men.

Reggie rolled down his window, and Cate did the same. He smiled. "I was coming to see you."

"What's up?" She peered down at him in his low-slung vehicle. She hadn't noticed last time she was in the car, but it was quite messy. Cate glimpsed old coffee cups discarded in the seat well, fast-food wrappers on the passenger side. A quiver with arrows spilling out lay on the floor. A bunch of dirt-covered gardening tools littered the back seat.

"Can we talk? I texted, but you never responded." His curly hair was brushed back from his forehead, and he looked very handsome and very young. Suddenly their eight-year age difference seemed enormous.

"I've been busy."

"I wanted to make sure we're cool."

"We're cool," Cate said a tiny bit impatiently. She regretted sleeping with Reggie. It was wrong to compare him to Matthew, but sex with her ex was like a strong, cleansing swig of scotch; sex with Reggie, while not quite a glass of milk, wasn't a shot of tequila, either.

"I mean, it was a wonderful night, really special for me," Reggie continued. "You're an amazing woman." Did he practice getting that perfect note of frustrated longing? Enough to keep the women he slept with interested, without promising them anything.

Reggie continued, his voice full of sympathy and disappointment. "Only, it's like I explained on Friday, things are complicated for me."

He waited, obviously counting on her feminine curiosity to ask the question.

When she didn't, he carried on. "Fiona and I have been together for years. She's finishing her PhD in Montreal. She comes down most weekends. It's long-distance, and it works because she knows that sometimes I get lonely. She understands me."

Cate recalled what Rose said about Reggie hooking up with a student when he was a teaching assistant. Did he regularly pick up the college students—and other women—who came to the archives? Did he give them all this pathetic explanation? Cate was embarrassed she had fallen for Reggie's special brand of corny. He was so immature, so unformed. Matthew didn't need to explain himself. Sure, his arrogance was maddening, but it also demonstrated a very attractive self-confidence.

"Reggie," Cate said firmly, "I have no desire to ever sleep with you again."

His head drew back as if she'd hit him. "No need to be so harsh, Cate. I was letting you know the lay of the land."

"Consider me informed," she said. "Is that everything?"

He looked disconcerted. When he didn't reply right away, Cate said goodbye and sped away. She glanced in the rearview mirror. His car was still sitting there. Reggie was obviously taking a moment to recover from the shock of having his brush-off brushed off.

CATE WAS HEADED TO THE CANTERBURY CLINIC WHEN SHE SPOTTED ANYA walking her two kids to the school's elementary drop-off. Cate's hands balled into fists. This woman who purported to be her friend, had lied to her for years. She'd been to enough therapy to know she was actually angry at Jason for never confessing the affair, but her brother was conveniently dead, so Anya was going to feel the brunt of her betrayal.

Cate waited until after Anya had said goodbye to her kids, and then marched over. "I need to talk to you," she called.

"Can you make an appointment?" Anya asked. "I'm swamped today, doing some crisis management." Indeed, her skin was ashen, and her hair was in a muddled bun rather than under its usual sleek control.

"A problem with the school?" Cate asked, her voice holding the right note of concern.

"Something like that."

"This won't take long."

Anya's eyes flashed with irritation, but she held out her hands. "What's up?"

Cate spoke quietly. "I figured some things out."

"Oh?"

Did Cate catch a hint of wariness in her eyes? "Things about you and Jason."

Anya stiffened, bracing for bad news.

"You two had an affair," Cate said quietly.

"Jesus, Cate," Anya hissed, staring back at the playground where she'd left her kids. She began to walk briskly away from the school, far from listening ears. Cate hurried to follow her. Once distanced from the school, Anya's voice was matter-of-fact. "You put the pieces together. What was it? A hotel receipt among Jason's things? A note I left him?"

"It doesn't matter." Cate's anger unfurled in her chest. Anya's re-laxed admission was more maddening than a denial. "I can't believe you lied to me. I can't believe Jason did this." She immediately wished she hadn't blurted out that part, the part that really hurt.

Anya seized upon her admission. "You have always hero-worshipped your brother." Her tone held a slight lecturing note that made Cate bristle. "He wasn't the golden boy you thought he was."

"I never thought he was a saint."

"Please. You adored him and couldn't see him for who he was."

This was Cate's greatest fear: that her Jason, the one who was dead and gone forever, never really existed. If Cate didn't even have the memory of her brother, what was left to mourn? "Oh, and you knew him so well?"

"As a matter of fact, I did." Anya's eyes flashed with anger, or was it hurt? For a split second, Cate glimpsed how much emotion the head-mistress kept bottled up. "Jason and I had an on-and-off thing for years. Even after I married Wylie. I'm not proud, but we both enjoyed the thrill of possible discovery. The risk."

This was too much, and childishly Cate wanted to press her hands over her ears.

They were walking away from the school, Anya unconsciously leading them back to her house. Now that the truth was out, the headmistress seemed eager to unburden herself. "When Wylie and I moved here, Jason would come down. Usually he stayed at the Blak-eney Inn."

"If Jason was making trips back to Pekeda Township, he would have told me." Cate then recalled Dr. K saying that her brother came to Old Home Week. He'd kept that visit a secret, so why not others?

The condescension returned to Anya's voice. "You have an impression that Jason led this quiet existence—the noble doctor flying to the developing world to do good and coming home to Ottawa to hang out with you. He was much more than that. He had a whole messy, vibrant life. He wasn't robotic and emotionally stunted like—"

"Like me?" Cate burst in. Did Jason and Anya talk about her? Her stomach dropped. Did her big brother laugh at her with his married lover?

Anya looked flustered by her interjection. "No, not like you. I was going to say like your father. Cate, this affair had nothing to do with you. I said that you hero-worshipped Jason, but I know he loved you more than anyone, and your good opinion was important to him. He kept our affair secret because he didn't want to disappoint you."

"Did he think so little of me that I would reject him over this?" She blurted out the terrible fear that was squeezing her heart, not even worried that she was exposing her vulnerability to Anya. "I don't care about this affair. I care that he lied to me."

Anya seemed surprised to find herself in front of her own house. She lowered her voice. "Of course, you're upset," she soothed, glancing at her front door. "Don't you see, Jason held misconceptions about you too. He saw you as his little sister, the one he needed to protect, even when the thing he was protecting you from was seeing who he really was."

Cate shook her head, rejecting Anya's empathy. "Is that why you offered me this job? A pity gesture?" Her voice rose. "A final gift to your lover? Maybe Jason told you that I was some lonely, pathetic loser and you felt sorry for me."

Anya blinked and hesitated.

It was the only answer Cate needed. She flushed red. Anya's email had arrived just when Sylvester Williams told her that her suspension was extended. She'd been flailing and ready to drink herself into oblivion. Now she realized she was only here out of Anya's sense of obligation to Jason. "I can't believe this!" Cate shouted.

The door to the house opened, and Wylie emerged carrying a briefcase. "Everything OK?"

Anya flushed. "It's fine, darling. I dropped the kids off and forgot something."

He smiled at her. "That's not like you. You have been so preoccupied these last few weeks." He bobbed his head at Cate. "Good morning, nice to see you." He was the bemused professor oblivious to the drama in front of him.

Anya stared at her imploringly, which irritated Cate. She wasn't going to ruin a marriage because she was mad at her brother and pissed with Anya. Instead, she said good morning to Wylie and waved as he drove away. As soon as he was gone, Anya turned to her. "Cate, I didn't hire you out of pity. We needed a doctor, and I thought it would be nice to have you nearby. I hoped we could both grieve, together."

It almost sounded reasonable, but there had been too many lies. "Enough," Cate said, suddenly exhausted. She needed to put some distance between herself and Anya. She turned and hurried back across the grounds. She was so preoccupied, she collided with some-one outside the school's main doors.

Yannick Poitou, though short and thin, was surprisingly mus-cular. "Dr. Spencer," he said with his usual indecipherable twinkle. "How are you this morning?"

"Fine, fine."

He stared at her with his sharp, assessing gaze, and she knew he saw that she was upset. "Do you need to sit? A cold drink, perhaps."

"No." She needed to pull herself together and get to the clinic. Patients were waiting. Poitou looked across the lawn to Anya's house. Uncharacteristically, the headmistress was still standing where Cate had left her, her arms hanging by her side, as if in defeat. "Is every-thing all right? Have you had distressing news?" His nose practically quivered in his search for information.

"Everything is fine," she said firmly.

"Good, good." He cleared his throat. "I was meaning to make an appointment with you, Doctor."

"Oh, yes? You can talk to the receptionist. I'm sure she can squeeze you in." Cate edged away from him.

"It is my neck, you see. I have terrible pains."

Her stint as a family physician had reminded her that many people could not bump into a doctor without oversharing about their health issues. This hadn't been a problem when she was a coroner. As a spe-cialist in death, she found that people were much more likely to avoid her than pump her for medical advice. "Make an appointment, and we can discuss it." She was more brusque than she intended.

"I'm sure the issue is quickly resolved. My doctor in Gatineau prescribed me a wonderful pain reliever. Very effective. I simply need you to renew the prescription."

This stopped Cate. She recalled Logan Pierce, the student exhibiting drug-seeking behavior. Poitou's pushiness might be more than the simple neediness of a hypochondriac. "I'm wary of prescribing any type of pain killer without a full medical workup and very close supervision. As a first step, make an appointment with the receptionist. After we meet, I'll request your complete medical history from your physician and assign some tests. Then I'll decide about a course of treatment. The process will likely take a couple of weeks."

She watched his reaction. A patient looking to score opioids would be unhappy with her reply.

Poitou's face was unreadable. "Very well, Doctor. I will make that appointment."

It almost sounded like a threat.

CHAPTER 33

CATE WAS WALKING THE DOG, OR, MORE ACCURATELY, WALKING WITH the dog. She'd tried to leash him a couple of times, but as soon as she'd approached, he'd dropped his hindquarters and refused to budge. Instead, she learned that if she strolled down the dirt road, he would stay beside her. She usually ventured toward MacGregor's farm because there was little traffic in that direction.

Thanks to a busy shift at the clinic, she hadn't spent the day dwelling on Jason and Anya's affair. While she was still hurt by their lies, having it out with Anya had actually helped. She knew the truth now and she could see that their love lives were none of her business. Though it was painful to learn she hadn't been as close to Jason as she'd thought, she understood why he'd kept this from her. She breathed deeply. Was this growth?

Cate usually turned around when she saw the roof of MacGregor's house, but the walk was clearing her head, so she carried on to the base of his driveway. Peering up, she saw a police cruiser parked next to the old man's truck. It must have driven past her house before she got home from work or while she was in the shower.

Calling the dog closer, she walked up the driveway. She knocked on the front door, but no one answered. Following a hunch, she turned to the orchards. Most of the apples were gone now, either picked or deadfall underfoot. As she got closer to the river, Cate noticed that the police tape was removed. She spotted Constable St. Onge and MacGregor talking by the water.

St. Onge looked up as she approached. "What are you doing here?"

"Saw your car and wanted to see what was going on."

"You're very nosy."

Cate almost smiled. The joy of Constable St. Onge was that you always knew where you stood with her. "You're very rude. What are you guys doing?"

St. Onge scowled, but MacGregor spoke up, "The officer wanted to have a look at Bartlett's Crossing."

This was interesting. St. Onge had all of Marc's notes. Perhaps they confirmed what she and Reggie had conjectured: that Marc thought the gold was buried at Bartlett's Crossing. It seemed St. Onge was taking a connection between the gold and the murder seriously. "Do you think the Outlaw's gold is buried here?"

"This is about the gold?" MacGregor asked St. Onge, annoyance lacing his voice. "You told me you wanted to look for evidence of trespassing since the murder."

"That was classified," St. Onge hissed at him.

"Trespassing since Marc's death?" Cate asked.

St. Onge glowered at her.

"You think someone is still trying to find the gold," Cate said. She recalled how quickly the officer gathered up Marc Renaud's notes back at the archives. "You saw something in Marc's records, something that revealed who was after the treasure—who might have killed him."

St. Onge looked away, and Cate knew her guess was correct. She tried to recall what was in the notes. What had she missed?

"Hogwash. No one would try such foolishness on my property," MacGregor interjected. "I have my shotgun, and I'm always on the lookout."

"That's not entirely true," Cate couldn't help saying. "You have a standing nine o'clock date at the Dépanneur Jaune. You're reliably gone every morning. I even saw you leave today."

Cate saw St. Onge jot down a note and felt a jolt of satisfaction. She turned to the officer. "Did you talk to Madge? Did you see what she has?"

St. Onge attempted a poker face, but Cate noticed the slightest flicker in her left eye. She was figuring out how to read the younger officer.

"If you think the gold plays a role in the murder, then you're working a different angle from Vachon," Cate said excitedly. "You don't think Kevin is guilty any more than I do."

"There you are wrong," St. Onge said sternly. "Kevin Farnham has been arrested for the murder of Bethany Farnham. Charges are pending for Marc Renaud's death."

"What?" Cate's heart sank. "When did that happen?"

"The Sûreté picked him up this afternoon."

"That was so fast," Cate said. "They couldn't have any forensic results back."

"Indeed," St. Onge said. "They found the murder weapon."

"What?" Cate asked again.

"The gun that killed Bethany. The Sûreté got a tip. It was retrieved from the back of Kevin's pickup."

"A tip," Cate repeated. She wondered how Kevin was coping. He was still in a state of shock over Bethany's death; jail might destroy him.

"Forensics will confirm, but it was Mr. Douglass's antique firearm. Initial tests found a match."

"I knew Bartholomew Douglass was a fool to make such a palaver about that stupid pistol of his," MacGregor interjected. "Claiming it was the Megantic Outlaw's and bringing it out for every wedding and baptism. Ridiculous."

"Who called in the tip?" Cate asked, ignoring the farmer.

"An anonymous Good Samaritan," St. Onge said.

"Or the murderer."

"Eh?" Macgregor said.

"Think about it, Constable," Cate addressed St. Onge, her voice pleading. "It would be a simple matter for the murderer to slip the gun into Kevin's truck."

"Doc has a point."

Cate carried on, uncertain whether MacGregor's support was helping or hindering her argument. "Kevin's the perfect patsy because he's got the best motive."

"Exactly," St. Onge said firmly. "He's got the perfect motive. His wife was cheating with Renaud. Kills the boyfriend, kills the wife. We see it all the time."

"Do you?" Cate snapped. "How many homicides have you investigated, Constable? I seem to remember it's zero."

Two bright spots appeared in St. Onge's cheeks, and Cate regretted her outburst. She wouldn't win over the officer by insulting her. It was too late, however, because now St. Onge was stone-faced. "You may not have a high opinion of me, Doctor, but I can assure you I am committed to bringing the murderer to justice." The constable nodded curtly to them both and then marched back to her car. Damn it. She could have handled that better. She should head home. She looked around for the dog and realized he was missing.

She scanned the countryside. "My dog," she turned to MacGregor. "Have you seen him?"

The farmer jutted out his chin toward a hill. "He wandered off in that northerly direction."

"Here, boy!" Cate called, walking to the hill. "Here, boy!" Where was he? Usually he came at the sound of her voice. Could he have taken this opportunity to make a break for it? Leave her company, as so many had before him? Her throat tightened. A movement farther up the hill, and Cate's worry turned to relief. The dog emerged from the remnants of a stone fence. His ears were up, and his tail wagged. She raced to him, giving him a good scratch around the neck.

Calmer now that the dog was by her side, she turned to examine the old fence. She soon realized it was actually the foundations of a house. Walking the perimeter, she scrutinized the lumps in the grass, detecting where the walls would have been. The space was not much larger than her woodshed. She was puzzling over a fallen pile of stones when MacGregor strolled up the hill behind her. She was surprised to see him climb the rise. The old farmer was tougher than he looked.

"Glad you found him," MacGregor said. "I know how special a dog can be."

"He's not mine," Cate said quickly. "Just a stray I'm looking after until I have time to get him to the vet and then the shelter."

MacGregor looked at the animal standing by Cate's side, her hand resting on his head. "Money can buy you a fine dog, but only love can make him wag his tail."

Cate grinned. "That's beautiful," she said. "Who said that, John Wayne?"

MacGregor barked out a laugh. "Nah, I think it was Kinky Friedman."

It was Cate's turn to laugh. "What was this building?" Her gesture encompassed the rough square of fallen rocks and the grassy lumps surrounding them.

"This is the original MacGregor homestead, one of the first dwellings built by the Hebridean immigrants. My great-grandfather was born here. He lived to be one hundred. He'd tell me stories about what it was like when he was little. All the children slept on the floor around the warm hearth." He pointed to a pile of rocks in the center. "That would have been the fireplace. It couldn't have been fun to sleep on a dirt floor in a Canadian winter. It's hard to believe I knew someone who lived through that."

Cate recalled the maps that Reggie had shown her. "Could Donald Morrison have sheltered here, do you think?"

"No. This house dates to the 1840s. By 1888, my family had built a more substantial home closer to the current house. They would have stripped this tiny house of its usable parts. It would have been a roofless ruin by the time Morrison came along. There were other, better hiding places for the Outlaw."

They turned and walked down the hill. "You really don't believe there's any gold?" she asked.

"No. My father got caught up in the nonsense. He let people traipse around our property for years. I always hated the sight of the grinning fools, wandering around, shouting to one another. Acted like they owned the place. I was happy to tell them to pack it in when I inherited."

Cate thought of a young Dr. K with his metal detector. Madge and her husband were out here too. She recalled Dr. K mentioning a ton of local names—the Montaignes, the Farnhams, and the Pattersons among them. Funny to think their children were now embroiled in a mystery with ties to the treasure.

"I wasn't hoodwinked like my father. I knew there was nothing out here."

"What made you so sure?" Cate asked.

MacGregor shrugged. "People can't keep secrets. Morrison would have needed help moving it and burying it. He would have told his loved ones where he stashed it. He would have whispered the story to a fellow prisoner. Nothing stays hidden forever."

Cate thought about what she'd learned about her brother. Maybe MacGregor was right. "The truth will out," she said.

MacGregor stopped. "That's Shakespeare. *The Merchant of Venice*. Amazing what the old brain retains."

Cate smiled. "I think you're right." She was reminded of Dr. K, with his endless quotations. What was the full line? "Murder cannot be hid long; a man's son may, but at the length, the truth will out."

She shivered. Sometimes the bard was too spot-on.

Cate's walk home was interrupted by a phone call from Rose. They chatted for a bit, and Rose asked when she was due back in Ottawa.

"My contract at the clinic is over in December." That's also when Cate was supposed to have the decision from the College. If it wasn't in her favor, could she stand being back in the city? Her stomach twisted, and she regretted her rudeness to St. Onge all over again. Her father was in Ottawa, and he was increasingly needy. Matthew was in the city too, of course. She wasn't sure if that was a good thing or not. Last night was wonderful, but it was a step backward.

"I can't wait for you to get back," Rose interrupted her thoughts. "I've been spending a lot of time with Jess—you know, my new boss? You're going to absolutely love her."

The mention of Jess irritated Cate. "We'll have to do brunch when I get back," she said sarcastically.

Rose was too excited to notice her tone. "That's exactly what I was thinking. Jess knows a great place—it has bottomless mimosas!"

If she didn't get reinstated as a coroner, would she be condemned to a life of brunching with friend-stealing, overeager archivists? She needed to get her job back, and to do that she needed to solve these murders.

CHAPTER 34

CATE WAS JUST MOUNTING THE PORCH STEPS WHEN HER PHONE RANG again. It was Brilliant Aduba, apologizing for his delay in returning her call.

While the questions around Jason's involvement with the adoption charity had faded from the forefront of her mind, she still wanted answers, so she got right to the point. "I've seen a few news items about this Rescue the Children scandal."

"These revelations are a huge blow to us," Brilliant said in his Nigerian accent.

"Why?" Cate asked. She turned and headed up the path along the hill, taking in the sunset spreading over the dark-green forest. "Medical Aid International doesn't have anything to do with adoptions."

"No, but any time impropriety is exposed, the public gets suspicious of all humanitarian endeavors."

"You're saying people will lose trust in what you're doing due to this?" The dog was walking a little ahead of her, tail wagging as he sniffed at groundhog holes.

"Absolutely. It will harm the whole ecosystem. It was bad when the UN peacekeepers spread cholera in Haiti, but this is infinitely more damaging. People are passionate when children are involved."

"Jason was working at their biggest orphanage right before he died. Do you know what he was doing there?"

"I'm not sure. Your brother was an incredibly giving man. He could have simply been trying to help."

Cate was struck by his choice of words. *"Could have?* Do you think something else was going on?"

Brilliant paused and then spoke slowly. "Cate, I know this summer you thought there was some sort of conspiracy around Jason's death, but that was proven wrong. I don't want to add to your confusion by making a conjecture."

Cate practically spat the words. "My confusion? Jason is dead. If you know or suspect something, tell me."

Despite the force of her words, Brilliant just reiterated his refusal to speculate. Cate hung up the phone, shaking with frustration. She did not need to be shielded from the truth. She wasn't some irrational fool who was going to fly off the handle. She had a right to know the circumstances around her brother's death, and she was more convinced than ever that something was amiss. All her worries and fears from this summer came swirling back. Her trip to Kinshasa had lulled her into a false sense of security.

Without giving herself time to think, she dialed Matthew's number. He answered on the first ring. She was startled at how relieved she felt to hear his voice.

"Cate, I was just about to head back to Ottawa. Unless—"

"No," she said more harshly than she intended. The dog looked at her inquiringly. "I'm sorry, Matthew, I shouldn't have called you, only . . . I need to talk to someone who knew Jason."

There was a pause, and she could picture his mouth tightening in disappointment. "What's up?" he asked with a trace of weariness.

She told him about her brother's unexplained work with Rescue the Children and her increasing suspicions.

At the end of Cate's speech, Matthew was quiet. Her grip on the phone tightened. She couldn't handle it if he dismissed her concerns.

"You might be on to something, Cate."

Her heart lifted. Matthew could be a bastard, but he was always in her corner. "What do you mean?"

"I can't see your brother volunteering to work at an orphanage. Kids were not very interesting to him, you know?"

Cate knew exactly what he meant. Pediatrics was never a possibility for Jason. Indeed, she wasn't even sure how many kids he came across in his nonprofessional life. Most of his friends were child-free doctors in demanding careers or globe-trotting aide workers who had no time for children. His choice to volunteer at an orphanage was out of character.

"So, what do you think?" she asked. Matthew had a sharp legal mind, which, when it wasn't trained on tripping her up or getting her to do what he wanted, she admired.

"I wonder if things are more complicated than a simple volunteer stint."

"You're saying—"

"In light of the revelations, I wouldn't be surprised to learn Jason was working for the United Nations to expose the charity's abuses."

Cate nodded. That's exactly where her mind had gone. That kind of high-minded work would be right up Jason's alley. If her brother had been working against the charity, that had big implications. How far would Rescue the Children's leadership go to protect its secrets? Could they have learned of Jason's investigation? Perceived him as a threat? Her breath caught in her throat. "Do you think his death was deliberate? Could Rescue the Children have engineered that plane crash?" There had been overwhelming evidence that it was accidental, but maybe she'd missed something.

Matthew's laugh was incredulous. "Come on, they're a charity, not a terrorist organization."

Cate wasn't so sure. The scope of Rescue the Children's corruption demonstrated its reach. They had been stealing African children and selling them to Westerners for years. They had a huge stake in keeping that from becoming public. "Someone driving a car with a Congolese bumper sticker attacked me this summer," she said to Matthew. "You saw the aftermath. That's the night we . . ." She remembered the fear she had felt after the attack and the way Matthew had appeared out of the darkness to comfort her.

He might have been recalling the same scene, because his voice cracked. "That was terrifying, Cate. You were so shaken up."

His voice held such tenderness and worry that Cate took courage. "I assumed from that clue that it meant the Congolese government was responsible for the attack, but what if it was Rescue all along? They are based in the DRC."

"Maybe," Matthew said, though she could tell she hadn't convinced him.

"If Rescue the Children was involved in Jason's death, my trip to Kinshasa must have panicked them."

"You didn't encounter any intimidation while you were there, did you?"

"No, nothing like that. Everyone was very helpful. It seemed clear that it was an airplane accident."

"Listen, Cate. I don't have to return to Ottawa right away. I can push a couple of meetings. I'll stay here, help you figure this out."

Cate hesitated. It would be so comforting to have Matthew on hand. He was smart, and he cared about what had happened to Jason. "Well—" she began.

"Excellent," he interrupted. "I'll come over now. If I remember correctly, Rescue's Canadian arm is based in Ottawa and has a lot of ties to the current government. Undoubtedly, we've got some clients who can give me some insight. I'll make some inquiries. Meanwhile, you should call that Brilliant guy back and get Jason's timeline absolutely clear."

For a moment she couldn't speak. This was the classic Matthew takeover. He was high-handed and controlling. He stopped listening to her. He insisted on his own way. This is why their marriage had disintegrated. This is why even contemplating a reunion was insanity. "No," she interjected. "I don't want you to stay, Matthew."

"Cate, you're making a mistake." His voice was rough with anger, and she heard him draw a deep breath, mastering himself. He said more calmly, "You need my help."

"No, I don't," she said crisply. "I will untangle this myself." She was in a hurry to get off the phone. She needed to think.

She hung up and walked back down the hill. Had she made a mistake sending him away? He was an obvious asset in any investigation. As he said, his law firm was tied to all sorts of political movers and shakers, and Rescue the Children was apparently quite connected. It was actually kind of surprising she didn't know anyone who worked at the charity, since creating leaders for that kind of big, high-profile aid organization was exactly Canterbury Day and Boarding School's mission. She frowned. Anya probably knew someone from the charity.

Anya had admitted this morning that she'd offered Cate the job as a chance to grieve. Indeed, returning to Canterbury had helped Cate stop obsessing about Jason's death. Her nightmares had eased, she'd softened her attitude, she'd even befriended a goddamn dog. Only, being tucked away in the countryside, distracted by new duties, she'd also stopped asking questions about her brother's death.

The Rescue leadership must have been relieved when she took a job out here, safely buried in the boonies. Her position at Canterbury Clinic was very convenient for them. What if it wasn't a coincidence that she had ended up in Pekeda Township? She replayed her conversation with Anya. Several things didn't add up, but others slid into place. She pictured Anya this morning, walking her two children across the lawn. Her eyes widened.

Anya was lying to her about a lot more than her affair with Jason.

CHAPTER 35

looked even more haggard than earlier.

"I can't rehash this morning's conversation," Anya said when she saw Cate in her doorway. "I have to deal with some major issues."

"This can't wait," Cate said firmly.

Anya stared at her, about to argue, but instead she chuckled. "You know, when you glare at me like that, you look like your brother." Anya went to the filing cabinet, where she surprised Cate by yanking out a bottle of scotch. "Dr. K left this here. I hardly touch the stuff, but I need it to get through round two."

She grabbed two teacups from the decorative set by the window and poured generously. She thrust a cup at Cate and sat down, taking a small sip and grimacing at the taste.

Cate could smell the sharp, peaty scent. She swirled the amber liquid in the teacup. She hadn't drunk scotch in months. "I'm not here to talk about the affair."

Anya stiffened, and if Cate held any doubts about her suspicions, they evaporated. "I was wrong this morning. You didn't hire me out of pity, but in a deliberate attempt to get me away from Ottawa and my investigation into Jason's death."

"What?" Anya put down the teacup. She took a moment to speak but then said forcefully, "Don't be absurd. I offered you this job out of concern. You were falling apart. Jason would have wanted me to help you."

Cate asked a question that had occurred to her when she revisited the morning's conversation. "But how did you know I was falling apart?"

Anya shrugged. "The media said that you were embroiled in a nasty murder case. That you'd acted erratically. Put yourself in danger."

"No, they didn't," Cate said. "They reported that I helped solve a double homicide. If anything, they portrayed me as a competent hero. There was nothing in the coverage that would have led you to assume something was wrong." She could speak with such assurance because she'd googled it herself before driving over.

"You flew off to the Congo. You can't deny that the trip was related to Jason's death. To your inability to accept it." Anya's chin jutted out.

"Of course it was related to his death," Cate said. "That's not the issue. The question is how you knew that I went to the Congo. I didn't announce it on social media. I never posted anything about it online."

Anya shrugged. "I don't know, the grapevine." She took another tiny sip of whisky, her face screwing up in an adorable, feminine way at the taste.

Cate shook her head. "That might make sense if I lived here, in this small, gossipy town, but I don't have any friends in Ottawa. You know, I'm robotic and closed off, like my father." At one point not so long ago, it would have been embarrassing to admit this to Anya, but not now. "There was no way you could have known I went to the Congo."

Anya's eyes shifted. "That's right. I talked to your father. I called him to offer my condolences, and he mentioned your trip."

If Cate wasn't so upset, she would have been grimly pleased. "My father?" she repeated, allowing Anya to dig her own grave.

"Yes," she said with more assurance. "I talked to Dr. Spencer Senior. He told me all about your trip."

"That's odd," Cate said. "He is cognitively impaired and has difficulty remembering that Jason is dead, let alone where I am."

Anya was a fighter, however, and she didn't give up. "I must have caught him on a good day."

"Anya, cut the bullshit."

The headmistress's nostrils flared. She was not used to being cursed at, even when caught flagrantly lying.

Cate continued, laying out the accusation she had mulled over on her drive to the school. "You were keeping track of my movements out here, not in a friendly, interested way, but out of worry that I might uncover the truth. You even hired someone to follow me this past summer, didn't you? You must have been delighted when I assumed it was an operative from the Congolese embassy."

Anya's posture slumped, and her face suddenly deflated. "That was a freelancer they hired. He's Congolese but has no affiliation with the government. You jumping to the wrong conclusion about him was a bonus. It meant you weren't looking at the real culprit."

"And who is 'they'?" Cate asked, her tone quiet. "Who is the 'real culprit'?"

"Rescue the Children, of course."

Cate almost laughed. Her suspicions of a conspiracy around Jason's death were right all along, only it wasn't the Congolese government out to stop her, but an international charity.

Anya had obviously decided the game was up. She swallowed more scotch and adopted the brisk condescending tones of a teacher. "The charity's been doing incredible work for decades, making a difference in sub-Saharan Africa. They have literally saved thousands of children. This damning, biased, inaccurate United Nations' report would kill it. I couldn't let that happen."

Anya's admission soured Cate's stomach, and she couldn't yet bring herself to throw out her biggest accusation. Instead, she took her first sip of the scotch. The burning liquid almost made her gasp, but the discomfort was overshadowed by its sweet relief. She asked a less urgent question, but one that was bothering her. "Why go to all that trouble for some charity?"

Anya looked annoyed. "Don't you get it? The head of Rescue the Children Canada is a Canterbury alum, and I recruited him to chair our fundraising committee. We've established scholarships for Rescue adoptees, and we've featured their orphanages in our brochures. I've been nurturing this relationship since I became headmistress. Goodness, I've sent a dozen of our students to work in Rescue the Children orphanages."

"The scandal won't affect the school. You guys were hoodwinked like the rest of the world."

Anya stood and began pacing. "You're so naive, Cate. How do you think a school like ours survives? Tuition covers only a fraction of the costs. We can't maintain these old buildings, staff the dormitories, and fund expensive field trips from that alone. Our endowment is key to our survival. I don't broadcast this, because I know how beloved Dr. K is, but the school was on the verge of bankruptcy when I took over. I turned it around. I forged strong relationships with influential people. Our fundraising has been massively successful. I saved Canterbury." She paused and took another swig of the scotch.

"Now our close affiliation with this charity threatens everything. Two of the kids I sent to volunteer with Rescue last year were the daughters of cabinet ministers." Anya laughed incredulously. "We used our connections to get photo ops of the prime minister with Rescue when he visited the Congo. His wife is an alumna here, and she's one of their most prominent fundraisers. We've put the country's political elite in bed with this scandal, and they are furious. This is exactly the type of juicy story that the opposition and the media will grab. It could affect our enrollment. It could affect political careers. This charity's downfall is Canterbury's downfall. Maybe even the government's downfall."

Anya was exaggerating, possibly to distract from the true issue. "At the end of the day, it's not going to look good for you," Cate said quietly.

Anya frowned.

"I wouldn't be surprised if this finishes your career as headmistress. The perfect Anya Patel exposed as a colossal failure."

Anya's face twisted.

"There's more than that, though," Cate said, revealing the part that convinced her of Anya's involvement. "This is personal for you."

Anya flushed and resumed pacing.

Cate recalled Anya walking Sophia and Emmerson to school. "You adopted your kids through Rescue the Children."

"We followed all the rules," Anya flared. "We used an honest orphanage, we vetted everything. Rescue the Children assured us that it was aboveboard. My kids are happy. They have every advantage. They're attending Canterbury, for God's sake. Average Canadians can't even afford that." Anya's voice rose. "You're telling me that they would have been better off in some African slum?"

Cate stared at her friend. "You worried the children might have been kidnapped. Stolen from their parents. That's why you've been so keen to help the charity cover this up. That's why you had to stop me from uncovering the truth." Cate's hand flew to her throat. "That's why that man assaulted me this summer."

"I was furious when I found out about the attack on you," Anya said defensively. "I told them they'd taken things too far. He was only meant to keep an eye on you."

Cate scoffed, thinking of the terror of that moment in July. "I guess he didn't get the memo. You and your pals must have panicked when he failed to scare me off and I went to Kinshasa."

"We were worried that your presence would do further damage. We knew the report was coming, but we still thought we could contain it. Your questions were making everything more volatile."

It was painfully satisfying to hear Anya admit to everything. "You wanted me out of the way. That's why you offered me this job. And after I got here, you encouraged me to investigate Marc Renaud's death. Anything to keep me from asking questions about Jason." Cate took a shaky breath. This was the part she was dreading, the poisoned part that was making her feel ill. "You underestimated me, Anya, because I am going to expose you and everyone else. You and this charity murdered Jason, and you will pay."

Anya gasped. "What?" she whispered, stumbling to her desk chair and sinking into it. "Cate, do you really think I could have murdered Jason, or protected those who did?" Her voice was low. "I would never have hurt Jason. I loved him."

Cate shook her head. "No more bullshit, Anya. Why would I believe you? Everything you've told me is a lie."

"I did," she said. "I loved him."

"Then how could you let them kill him?"

Anya looked at her sorrowfully. "Cate, listen to me. No one murdered Jason. He died in an unfortunate accident on a shoddy plane. It
happens all the time."

"You honestly expect me to believe that? You're trying to tell me
he wasn't at the Rescue the Children orphanage, gathering evidence?"

"Oh, Cate," Anya said, and she looked genuinely sorry. "Jason
wasn't there to expose Rescue the Children." She bit her lip, and
looked like she was wrestling with a decision. At last she spoke. "He
was there for me. I knew about the UN report. It was going to rock
Canterbury. But more than that, I was worried about my family. I
couldn't risk my children." She paused and stared at Cate, as if willing
her to put the pieces together, but Cate said nothing, still processing
what Anya was revealing.

She continued, "I asked him to go to the orphanage and find Sophia's and Emmerson's records. It was easy. He did a couple of days
of free clinics for them. Then one evening he snuck into their records
room and took the dossiers. All the administration is still on paper.
I don't even know if the records revealed that the children were ille-
gally adopted or not. The paperwork was destroyed when Jason's plane
went down."

"You're saying that Jason—"

"Wasn't trying to expose Rescue the Children for child trafficking.
He was helping to cover up their crimes."

CHAPTER 36

"JASON WOULD NEVER DO THAT," CATE SHOUTED AT ANYA. "HE WOULD never support a corrupt charity." Her mind was a kaleidoscope of thoughts and images. Jason sitting on her couch, listening to her troubles. Jason chatting with her in the sunshine at Vimy brewery. Jason and Anya at Dr. K's wedding, laughing at their shared table. Jason had devoted his life to helping others. He wouldn't support corruption. He wouldn't.

Cate stood. "You're lying."

Anya shrugged, her controlled demeanor slipping back on like a mask. "You can think that if you want, but the truth is the truth. I asked Jason to cover up my children's adoption, and he did. I could tell he didn't like doing it, but he was a loyal friend."

That sounded like Jason. Cate's stomach cramped.

"I can see the disgust in your face," Anya continued. "You're judging me, and I guess I deserve it. But that's your problem, don't you see? You're too hard on people. You have these high expectations that no one can meet. Jason certainly couldn't. You might not see it the way I do, but Jason was a hero. He fought for his friends, and he protected us, even when it went against his own values."

"I can't . . . I can't hear this." Cate took a step back and stared around her. The walls of this homey, cozy study were closing in on her. She shook her head and ran out of Anya's office. Cate drove into town without seeing the scenery or noticing other cars. She could still taste Anya's scotch, and she wanted more. She went to the liquor store, but it was already closed. She hit the steering wheel in frustration. All she had at home was wine, and merlot wasn't going to cut it. Jason had broken the law, helped a corrupt charity, and perhaps aided and abetted in the removal of two children from their biological parents. What hurt more than any of that was that he had lied to her over and over.

She pulled into a parking spot down the street from Fowler's Diner, the only restaurant open at this hour. They had a liquor license. Fowlers didn't have scotch, but a vodka shot started a nice numbing process.

Cate sipped the second one and waited for her shoulders to relax and her mind to lose its sharp edges. Her relationship with Jason and his status as a good man were the rocks upon which she had built her whole foundation. Even in his death, she had his memory to hold her steady and keep her upright. Now she doubted all her decisions. Her investigation of Marc Renaud's death was a desperate bid to keep a job that was lost forever. Sleeping with Reggie was a foolish mistake. Hell, even her empowering night with Matthew was a terrible error in judgment, sucking her back into a toxic relationship. Her foundation had been swept away under the tidal wave of Anya's revelations.

She flagged the waitress, a tired-looking older woman with hair dyed an unnatural shade of red. "Can I have two more, please?"

The waitress raised an eyebrow. "I can get you a ginger ale," she said in a gravelly voice betraying years of smoking.

"I don't want a soft drink," Cate snapped. The two shots weren't enough. She needed more, and she needed them quickly. "Get me two more vodkas."

"No. We aren't a bar, and we don't get people wasted, Doctor."

Cate's cheeks burned. The rebuke was bad enough, but the waitress's recognition was humiliating. "Bring me my drink," she hissed.

The waitress, whose name tag read "Francine," stood up straighter. "I can't serve you." She placed the emphasis on *you*. Cate's blush deepened. "If you want more booze," she said, increasing her volume, "you'll have to find it elsewhere."

A family of four looked up from their hot dogs, staring at Cate curiously.

"I ordered a drink," Cate said quietly. "Is my money not good enough for this fine establishment?" She waved her hand, taking in the vinyl booths and dingy counters.

"Nope." Francine glanced over at the cook, who was watching events unfold through the order window. He scowled at Cate and jerked his head toward the door.

"That's fine," she said, trying to regain her dignity. "I'll leave. I only needed something to unwind."

"Rough day at the private school?" Francine asked snidely.

Cate didn't need this on top of everything else. "What do you care?"

"That damn school stole our medical clinic." The waitress thrust her bosom out, looking affronted.

"I know," Cate said sourly. "You have to walk farther from the parking lot."

"It's not the parking lot. My grandson's addicted to fentanyl he bought at that damn place."

That caught Cate's attention. "You think someone at the school is selling drugs?"

Francine's mouth was a thin line. "I know it. For the past couple of years, there's been more bad drugs floating around this village and more good people getting hooked. It's all from Canterbury."

"Come on, there's a literal opioid epidemic. It's everywhere. What makes you so sure it's the school?" Somewhere, however, an alarm bell was dinging for Cate.

The waitress shrugged. "Those rich pricks get the illegal drugs, and they serve it up to our good citizens."

Cate threw a twenty on the table and stood. She swayed for a moment. It had been months since she had imbibed anything harder than merlot. The waitress noticed her wooziness and smirked, apparently confirming her opinion that the new doctor at the elitist clinic was a drunk.

Cate glared at the woman and stalked to the front of the restaurant. The Thirsty Bucket was a ten-minute drive out of town. They'd have scotch and no judgment. She could obliterate herself and what she had learned about Jason, about everything she once believed in.

She yanked open the diner door but paused at a huge sign proudly stating that this establishment served Egg Man Eggs. A photo of Kevin and Bethany appeared beneath the lettering. Kevin, round and beaming, had his arm around his wife, who looked immaculate and invulnerable. Bethany didn't deserve to die the way she did. Vachon wasn't going to find her real murderer. Bethany needed someone to speak for her, to ensure she had justice. Cate might have been wrong about Anya. She might have been wrong about Jason. But she wasn't wrong about Kevin. He didn't kill his wife. She turned back to Francine and asked her in the sweetest way possible to pour her an extra-large cup of coffee. She was going to need her wits to solve this murder.

Once she felt sober, Cate got in her car and headed for home. She was going to sit on her porch and think through everything she knew. Maybe she'd make one of those red-threaded "serial killer boards" like in the movies.

She drove past the turnoff to Dr. K's house. Someone had stolen his metal detector. That was meaningful. The locals were convinced that Canterbury was linked to the drug trade. Could that be another of Anya's cover-ups? Cate came to the turnoff to the Thirsty Bucket and wavered. Gripping the wheel tightly, she turned right, away from the bar. Vivienne had met Guy Montaigne at the Bucket. Jean-Michel Renaud had beaten up Thierry Montaigne's father there, and the two cousins had fought Marc Renaud in the same spot. The bar was a flashpoint for Renaud-Montaigne animosity.

She turned onto her road, driving past the Boisvert farm. She'd bumped into Reggie here this morning. He'd driven out to apologize to her. But why brush her off in person? When she thought about it, their whole exchange was odd. Unless he wasn't coming to see her. The only other house along the road was MacGregor's, but he wasn't home when she'd chatted with Reggie. As she herself had pointed out, everyone knew the farmer had a nine a.m. standing date at the Dépanneur Jaune. What was Reggie up to?

Cate recalled his car. It was surprisingly messy, with arrows scattered on the floor. The back seat was loaded with gardening equipment: a shovel, a sturdy waste disposable bag, and a Weedwacker . . . only it wasn't a Weedwacker. She could see it in her mind's eye: a big, battered rusty thing. It was a metal detector. It didn't have a digital readout like Marc's. It was analogue and old—probably like the one Dr. K used back in the day.

Dr. K had said that Reggie's mother was one of the treasure seekers, but Reggie never mentioned her when talking about his interest in the Megantic Outlaw. Surely his mother would have told him those stories; why pretend he'd only learned about them in school? Reggie also knew about gold bullion. He'd explained to her how easy it was to sell on the black market. He'd joked about her "coroner mojo" in an attempt, she now realized, to learn more about the case.

She turned into her driveway. The dog came out of the shed, tail wagging, but she didn't get out of the car. Earlier today, St. Onge was looking for evidence of trespassing on MacGregor's land. Cate recalled the way the constable had gathered up Marc's notes at the archives. She had thought it was because St. Onge saw something in them connecting the gold and the murder. Now Cate tried to recall the scene exactly. St. Onge wasn't even looking at the papers when she announced she was confiscating Marc's notes. She'd reacted to Reggie. He said that in his research he'd identified the Robert Burns poem that Marc's notes referred to. Cate groaned aloud. Reggie claimed he'd never looked at Marc's notes, but with one slip of the tongue, he revealed his lie. He knew about the poem before they discovered it in Marc's notes, because despite his claims to the contrary, he'd already examined them. Constable St. Onge had caught his slip, but Cate had been oblivious.

Recalling her first visit to the archives, Cate realized that Reggie hadn't even mentioned the research notes. Ilyana was the one to reveal them. Reggie was trying to keep them a secret because he was using Marc's research to track the gold for himself.

She turned the car around and drove back into town. She needed to have this out with Reggie. She wasn't going to let anyone lie to her. Not anymore.

CHAPTER 37

FOR THE THIRD TIME THAT DAY, CATE DROVE THROUGH CANTERBURY'S high gates. Now instead of going up the main drive to the school, she turned left on the lane that led to the archives and, beyond that, Reggie's home. The lights were on. Good. She pulled into his driveway. But before approaching his door, she called St. Onge. The constable didn't answer, so Cate left her a voice mail. "I think Reggie Patterson is the murderer. He's after the Outlaw's gold. He tried to keep Marc's notes to himself and stole Dr. K's metal detector. I'm at his house now. Meet me here." The sensible thing was to wait for the cops, but she was too angry.

Reggie answered the door in jeans and a "St. Barths Bucket Regatta" T-shirt.

"Cate," he said, glancing behind him. "This isn't a good time."

He had a girl in there. That, or his actual girlfriend was visiting from Montreal. "I don't care who you're entertaining, Reggie. I'm coming in."

"What?" He took a step back in surprise, and Cate used the moment to her advantage, pushing past him. She glanced around, but the room was empty.

Reggie moved to stand between her and the kitchen. He was hiding something.

"Cate, I know you're upset, but in time you'll see that you and I are not meant—"

"I couldn't care less about that, Reggie," she said. "I'm here about the Outlaw's gold. I think you're after it. And in case you get any funny ideas, I've told the police my suspicions. They're on their way here." Maybe . . . if St. Onge took her message seriously.

Reggie blanched. "Cate, what have you done?"

She hesitated for a moment, seeing real fear in his eyes, but the idea that Reggie lied to her—just like Anya, just like Jason—made her push forward. She darted around him, dashing into the kitchen. His table was covered in papers: copies of all of Marc's research, including his hand-drawn maps, which Reggie had blown up and annotated. She felt a surge of vindication: she had caught him in his lies. Then she realised that he hadn't tried to stop her. She went to the living room in time to see him end a phone call.

"Who were you calling?"

"No one." He tried for calm but was clearly rattled. He pushed past her and began stacking the pages of notes and maps that were spread out on the table. "Seriously, Cate, you're blowing this out of proportion. Yes, as you see, I've got a hobbyist's interest in the gold. It's a fascinating story that captured my imagination. I couldn't resist photocopying Marc's notes before showing them to you and Constable St. Onge." He forced a laugh. "I don't think that's a crime."

Cate wavered. She'd been drinking tonight, and she was so upset and confused about Jason's news she wasn't sure where her mind was. Maybe this wasn't such a big deal.

He saw her hesitation. "Why don't you call the cops and tell them you were mistaken."

His tone was wheedling. She didn't like being manipulated. "I might if you answer my questions first. Did you steal Dr. K's metal detector?"

He bit his lip and shrugged. "I didn't steal it. My mother mentioned he had one and I borrowed it. It's a forty-year-old piece of junk. I don't think that warrants a police visit, do you?"

"You broke into Madge Taylor's room?"

"No, I didn't."

"If you want me to call off the cops, you've got to tell me the truth."

"Fine, I did that too."

"Why?" Cate asked, although she knew the answer.

"You mentioned that she said something that convinced Marc the gold was real, and I wanted to find out what that was. I didn't think the old girl would be there. She scared the hell out of me. I should file a police complaint against her!" He chuckled.

Cate ignored his attempted joke. "Why are you obsessed with finding the gold?"

"I wouldn't say 'obsessed'—more like 'mildly curious.' Can you call off the cops now?"

"The mildly curious don't break and enter. They don't do what you did. When you realized Marc might be on to something, you followed him to MacGregor's land."

"What?" Reggie said. "No!"

His denial angered her. More lies. "Cut the crap. You're not a hunter, but you've spent a lot of time at the archery range. You got the town league organized. You know how to aim. You focused your shot and brought Marc down before he could find the gold you wanted for yourself."

Reggie tried to chuckle but didn't quite manage it. "That's preposterous. I'm not a murderer."

Cate had hoped Constable St. Onge would have arrived by now. She edged around the counter to the sink, where she spotted a large knife. "You killed Bethany too."

"No! I'm not like that."

She was so sick of being lied to. She picked up the knife. "Admit the truth, Reggie. You went to Geneviève's house, maybe to search for information Marc might have left. You stumbled across Bethany and killed her in a panic."

Reggie stared at the knife and took a step back. Cate took satisfaction from his fear. She was in control. "Admit your lies, Reggie. Admit them."

Reggie gaped at her, unable to form words.

"I'd ask you to put that knife down, Mademoiselle Spencer," a voice said behind her.

Cate whirled around. Yannick Poitou, Canterbury's assistant gym teacher, stood in the living room doorway pointing a gun at her.

"What the hell?" Cate laughed in shock.

"Miss Spencer, please put down the knife and step away from the counter," Yannick said in a calm voice.

"It's 'Dr. Spencer,' actually," Cate replied, hanging on to the knife. She didn't like having guns pointed at her. "Who the fuck do you think you are?"

Yannick stepped into the kitchen. "I'm Detective Daniel Lemieux with the Guns and Gangs Squad of the Sûreté du Québec." He flashed a piece of identification that looked, from Cate's quick glance, legitimate. "We don't have much time before the local force shows up or, worse, the Sherbrooke Sûreté. I need you to tell constables Douglass and St. Onge that you've made a terrible mistake."

"Why would I do that? Reggie's a prime murder suspect. In two murders, actually."

Yannick Poitou or, if he was to be believed, Daniel Lemieux, sighed and lowered his gun. "Listen, Dr. Spencer," he laid emphasis on her title. "You are interfering in a highly costly and important investigation of a sophisticated drug and money laundering operation. I'm happy to provide you with the name and contact information of my superior officer, Xavier Turcotte, to confirm that what I am saying is legitimate. Your friend Mr. Patterson is a key actor in this ongoing police operation."

"What are you talking about?" Cate demanded.

"A few weeks ago, we were approached by an informant willing to hand over vital information related to one of the area's largest and most violent criminal organizations. This low-level dealer in the Diderot crime syndicate was desperate and willing to snitch. He would help us gather evidence that could bring down a substantial portion of the organization, in exchange for protection and immunity from prosecution. It was a golden opportunity."

"I wouldn't call myself low-level," Reggie protested. "My connect is the number two in charge of this whole region."

Even as Cate struggled to comprehend what Lemieux was saying, she could appreciate that Reggie was as eager to name-drop as ever. She put the knife down. "You're a drug dealer?" she asked, incredulous. "But you're an archivist."

Lemieux snorted. "You'd be surprised with what they get up to . . . Years ago, I dealt with quite a slippery one from the Dominion Archives."

Cate didn't have time to follow up on that aside. She turned to Reggie. "Why would you take such risks?"

He shook his head. "I needed the money. My salary here is a pittance, and I can't keep up."

Keep up with what? Cate almost asked, but she knew the answer. If your best friends owned polo ponies and vineyards, an archivist's paycheck wouldn't cut it.

Lemieux seemed anxious to move things along. He spoke briskly. "With Mr. Patterson's intel, we established that Canterbury School was a site for community-wide distribution of illegal opiates. What's more, at least one student was supplying the larger and more lucrative Montreal market. Since an officer was required to monitor the operation and maintain contact with Mr. Patterson, I was seconded from my home base in Gatineau to work undercover in the school community."

Reggie was distributing during the town archery lessons. That's why he set up the program. She turned to him. "How could you? Children attend Canterbury." She thought of that drug-seeking student, Logan. Was he one of the distributors or simply a poor kid who'd gotten hooked?

"I didn't sell to the students," Reggie said haughtily.

Cate wondered how he could be so delusional. She asked a more pressing question, however. "What made you go to the police?"

Reggie shifted his weight. "I came to realize how destructive my actions were."

Lemieux coughed.

Reggie cast him a quick glance. "Also, my supplier thinks I've been skimming off the top. He threatened to kill me if I didn't come up with the shortfall, which is almost a quarter of a mil. I don't have that kind of money."

Cate stared at him. "Were you? Skimming off the top?"

Reggie blustered. "Finn had an investment opportunity that would have changed the game for me. I merely borrowed some money to buy in."

How could anyone be so stupid as to steal from organized crime? Hadn't Reggie watched any prestige drama in the last decade?

"Anyway, my connection told me I needed to pay back the cash or he'd kill me. That's when I latched onto Marc's idea. He was so certain he'd find the gold. I figured if I could locate it before him, I could clear my debt and get out of the drug game altogether."

"And when Marc caught on, you killed him?" Cate asked.

"I didn't kill him, I swear it."

Lemieux made an impatient gesture. "Of course, he didn't kill anyone. Patterson's been under surveillance for weeks."

"He broke into Madge Taylor's room, and he stole a metal detector. He did that while he was under surveillance."

"He was debriefing with me the afternoon of Marc's murder, and we were driving him back from Sherbrooke when Bethany Farnham was killed. He is fully in the clear."

"Shouldn't he be charged with breaking and entering? Theft?"

Lemieux shrugged. "We don't interfere in petty crime when our eye is on a bigger prize. Mr. Patterson will put some very bad men in jail. That is why you must be quiet about what you've discovered. I need you to call your police officer friends and tell them you made a mistake. The locals and Sherbrooke homicide aren't involved in our case. It's strictly Guns and Gangs, and we don't want this murder investigation derailing our hard work."

"But I didn't make a mistake. Reggie was looking for the gold, and he's a drug dealer."

"Of course, of course," Lemieux agreed impatiently. "But if Mr. Patterson is arrested now, our case is trashed. I am appealing to your sense of right and wrong."

She could understand his reasoning. They heard a car door closing. Lemieux glanced through the window. "Go out there and deal with St. Onge. Tell her you were wrong and apologize. Make it go away."

Cate reddened. She had figured out Reggie's involvement and exposed his lies, but she was going to have to pretend she hadn't. "I'll do it," she said reluctantly.

"Good girl," Lemieux said.

Cate stiffened and almost changed her mind.

She stared at the door. If St. Onge was annoyed with her before, she'd be disgusted now. Cate's chances of getting Vachon's recommendation or even avoiding a complaint seemed nonexistent. She wasn't completely defeated, however. She turned to Lemieux. "I'll do all this on one condition . . ."

CHAPTER 38

THE NEXT DAY DAWNED CLOUDY AND OVERCAST. THE AIR WAS THICK with a storm. Cate's head ached from the previous night's booze. She called work and told the receptionist to cancel her appointments because she wouldn't be returning to the Canterbury Clinic. She could not handle talking to patients, listening to their problems. And she certainly couldn't handle running into Anya. She was quitting, running away, giving up. She drank two cups of coffee and contacted Kevin's sister to find out how he was doing but got no new information.

Splashing water on her face, Cate stewed over her failures. Last night had been humiliating. She'd had to apologize to St. Onge and Douglass. Her excuses for calling them were weak; the disappointment and pity in St. Onge's eyes cut her to the quick. Behind that moment was her greater sense of betrayal: Jason had lied to her; Anya had lied to her; Reggie had lied to her. Hell, even Canterbury's assistant gym teacher had lied to her.

Cate looked at her haggard face in the bathroom mirror. She'd undone months of willpower by drinking hard liquor. She was a pathetic, weak failure. A loser. She thought she'd been making progress here in Pekeda Township—moving on from Jason's death, softening. Yet when things got tough, she had abandoned all that effort and found relief at the bottom of a bottle.

She paused. Except, she hadn't continued drinking after she had come home from Reggie's. True, she'd spent the rest of the night chain-smoking and muttering to the dog, but the fact that she didn't take another sip of alcohol was something. She'd slipped, but she hadn't plummeted straight back to her old depths. She stood a little taller. She'd always defined herself in relation to Jason. She'd been the inferior sibling: not nearly as smart, not nearly as charismatic, not nearly as good. Turned out neither was he. She laughed, which turned into a smoker's hacking cough. When the paroxysm subsided, she straightened her shoulders. Maybe she could live with this new vision of Jason and this new vision of herself in comparison.

Now she needed to sort out her next chapter. Quitting Canterbury Clinic meant leaving Pekeda Township. Her attempts at solving the murder and exonerating Kevin were obviously fruitless. Given the low regard the cops held her in, her involvement would harm his case more than help. She'd return to Ottawa. Fight for her job. Sort out the messiness with Matthew. Take care of her father. She pushed away her shame at quitting. This was the right thing to do. She needed to walk away.

She made an appointment for the vet to examine the dog that afternoon. Over the phone, they gave her the name of a reputable animal shelter. Apparently the facility was staffed by fierce pet lovers who would work hard to find the dog his "forever home." Her heart clenched when she contemplated leaving him, but she had no choice. Despite what Rose and Mr. MacGregor might think, she couldn't bring him to Ottawa.

Luring the dog into the car was less difficult than she'd feared. He'd developed a taste for the liver treats she'd bought at Lachance. Once he was settled in the back, she drove into town. Every time she looked in the rearview mirror, she saw his big, liquid eyes. "I have to do this," she told him sternly. "I have a small backyard, and I work crazy hours. You would hate it."

He gave a little whimper but didn't protest when she led him into the vet's office. They were backed up, and the receptionist told her to leave the dog with them and come back in a couple of hours. Cate hesitated but smiled when the vet tech fed him a treat and his tail wagged.

Next stop was the Dépanneur Jaune. She was out of smokes. Cate was paying for her cigarettes when Diane Doucette and Joseph Ngoma walked in and headed to the back of the store. She didn't need to engage with the Olympians; her time investigating the murders was over. She had failed. They strode right past Cate without noticing her.

Cate was in the clear. But instead of being relieved at escaping an interaction, she found herself hurrying after them. Apparently she wasn't quite ready to give up.

"Excuse me, Ms. Doucette, Mr. Ngoma. Can I talk to you?"

They turned, and Joseph asked, "Dr. Spencer, right?"

"Yes. We spoke at Marc's funeral."

Diane nodded.

"I wondered if anyone has heard from Geneviève yet. You're friends, right? Is she back?" The police must have located her by now, and Cate was curious despite herself. Marc's sister might have additional insight into his death or Bethany's.

Diane bit her lip. "No, she's not home." She glanced at Joseph. "She's still hiking. Unreachable."

Cate stepped closer. "I know she's not hiking. I know where she really is."

Joseph crossed his arms, and Diane scowled. Her voice was cold. "What do you know about Geneviève?"

Cate spoke quietly. "I know she's in rehab for an opioid addiction."

"That's private information," Diane bit out. "Not to be shared."

Cate put up her hands. "I'm not gossiping. I learned about it while assisting Kevin in his investigation."

"Kevin Farnham's been arrested. He murdered Marc Renaud. He killed his own wife." Diane's voice shook with outrage.

"He didn't," Cate argued, getting drawn in despite herself. "He couldn't have. He doesn't have the shooting skills."

"He was faking incompetence, obviously," Diane snapped.

Cate turned to Joseph, recalling something Kevin had once mentioned. "The Farnhams were members of the archery club. You're the coach. Do you think Kevin could have made those shots? Was he able to aim like that? To focus?"

Joseph considered. "He wasn't very good." He turned almost apologetically to his wife. "He really has no athletic ability. I don't think he was faking."

"Someone's framing Kevin," Cate said. "Which means that the murderer is still out there."

Diane's face fell, and the anger of a moment ago deserted her. "The killer is still on the loose?" She shivered. "I want him caught. Locked up."

"It means that Geneviève might be in danger. It's possible that Bethany was killed accidentally, and Geneviève was the target. After all, Bethany was killed in her home."

"Oh God," Diane whispered. "I hadn't thought of that." She reached for her husband's hand and squeezed.

Cate could see she'd brought the couple to her point of view. She lowered her voice and moved to a quieter part of the store. "It's terrible that the police haven't located her. She needs to be informed."

Diane nodded her head. "I know. I was just talking to Mireille and Jacques. The police have contacted every facility in Québec and haven't found her. She must be in some small, privately run center. I mean, that makes sense, because Gen is a shy, quiet person. A homebody. She wouldn't like being in a big institution like the one in Sherbrooke. Problem is that Marc didn't tell anyone where he was taking her."

"If Geneviève's not at a treatment center in Québec, maybe she's out of province. Are the police looking at facilities in Ontario or the rest of Canada?"

"Mireille told them not to bother. Gen doesn't speak much English."

"No English?" Cate said in surprise. Most people in Pekeda Township were bilingual.

"Her English is decent but she's shy about it. She avoids speaking it if she can."

"Marc was the same way," Joseph chimed in. "He was bilingual and his English was better than Gen's, but he was self-conscious about it."

Cate recalled Madge's stories about Marc's travel plans. It was odd that he, a true country boy who never evinced a desire to live anywhere but Manasoka, suddenly longed to move to a big city like Toronto or Vancouver. His desire was especially odd if he wasn't comfortable in English. The clerk at Lachance even speculated that Marc was a separatist. Why would Marc Renaud want to leave his beloved Québec? It seemed as if his sudden interest in travel was less about finding a new life and more about running from an old one. That begged the question, who was Marc Renaud hiding from?

Diane twisted her hands together. "I wish the police would find Geneviève. It is so upsetting to think she still doesn't know Marc is dead. She's going to be devastated. They might have fought, but they had a close relationship. She relied on him. She broke her collarbone this past winter, and Marc couldn't have been a better older brother. He brought her home and made sure she was comfortable. He took care of her."

Marc protected his sister. He rescued her from an abuser, looked after her when she was hurt, brought her to treatment when she was addicted. Two murders had just rocked this peaceful township, and thanks to Marc, Geneviève was stashed away in safety. Was that good fortune, or the work of a protective brother who knew violence was coming?

"I know this is obvious, but have you tried to call her? Sometimes treatment facilities do allow limited contact."

Diane shook her head. "Geneviève gave Mireille her phone on the day Marc took her to the facility. She said she wouldn't be allowed to make calls and it was better to remove the temptation."

"Mireille saw them on that Saturday before they went to rehab?" Cate confirmed.

"Yeah, Marc took their car to drive Geneviève."

"It's odd that Marc borrowed their car, isn't it?"

Joseph shrugged. "He had a big truck and Gen's car was old. Theirs was better on gas."

As Cate knew from personal experience, it was shockingly easy to put tracking devices on cars or a telephone. By leaving Geneviève's car and phone at home, Marc had made her much more difficult to surveil. Was Marc worried about someone following them?

"Poor Mireille is devastated that she didn't get details about the facility from Marc," Diane continued. "At the time she was just so bowled over by news of Gen's addiction, she wasn't thinking straight. It still astounds me that Geneviève was taking drugs."

The clerk at the feedstore had said something similar. As had Vivienne.

"Very out of character," Joseph agreed. He glanced at his watch. "Chérie, we have to go. We need to pick up something for dinner."

Cate said goodbye and walked to her vehicle. Where was Geneviève Renaud? Cate was certain the missing woman was key to these murders. Diane had called the younger woman a homebody. That jogged Cate's memory and she stood very still, the door of her car opened, as she concentrated. In their final conversation, Bethany told her that she and Marc met at Geneviève's house because his sister was never home. That begged the question: where was Geneviève all those nights that Marc and Bethany were hooking up? The wind gusted, bending the limbs of a nearby tree and foreshadowing the impending storm. Cate climbed into the car, slamming the door shut. Maybe Marc wasn't the only Renaud sibling with a secret relationship.

Cate didn't start the vehicle right away, instead letting images and thoughts wash over her: Marc's body lying in the orchard. Geneviève's disappearance. The perfect shots, executed by a master marksman. Cate closed her eyes. The recurring tune, "Little Star," came back to her. She hummed it for a moment. It was from the soundtrack to *Romeo + Juliet*, but she'd heard it recently. Shakespeare kept popping up in this case. MacGregor had quoted the poet, as had Dr. K. Someone else had as well. Was it Anya? Cate's eyes flew open. She recalled who had said the other quote. She also remembered where she first heard the tune. The information slotted into place and she began to form a theory.

An accident the previous winter sent Geneviève to the local hospital. That might be the key to understanding everything. She knew where she needed to go to confirm her suspicions. Cate put the key in the ignition. The sky was dark now, obscuring the late-afternoon sun. The storm was about to arrive. She glanced at her phone to check the weather, but cell reception had evaporated. She had an hour before she was due to pick up the dog at the vet.

Canterbury Day and Boarding School was quiet on this windy, cloud-laden night. The students were all in the meal hall or hanging out in their dormitories; the teaching staff was gone. Cate looked down the echoing hall. A light was on in the small side office Dr. K used for his historical research project. She rushed past the doorway. She didn't want to talk to her old headmaster right now. Outside, the storm arrived with a crash of thunder.

She slipped into the clinic and grabbed the keys to the record office.

It was musty down there, and she could hear a pipe dripping somewhere above. Her footsteps echoed as she hurried to the locked back rooms. She opened the one containing the medical files. The fluorescent bulbs took a second to warm up and the light was an unhealthy green.

Ignoring Marc Renaud's medical file, Cate pulled out his sister's. Anya would undoubtedly disapprove of her unsanctioned examination of files. To hell with her. There were the details of Geneviève's medical history. Cate flipped past the terrible injuries she had sustained escaping her abusive boyfriend years ago and stopped at last winter's slip on the ice. Geneviève was admitted to the hospital for two nights while her fracture was dealt with, and she was monitored for concussion.

As Cate remembered, the notes showed no suspicion the accident was anything other than a winter mishap. Maybe Cate's theory was wrong. She slowed down, reading more closely. A nurse's note caught her eye, and one name stood out. If she'd been a different kind of person, she would have fist pumped. There it was, proof of a connection six months before Marc's murder. Pieces slotted into place. Cate stowed the file and locked the records room, hurrying back to the stairs. She needed to talk to Dr. K. Hopefully he was still in his office. Her thoughts were interrupted on the bottom stair when, with a flicker, the lights went out. Power outage, thanks to the storm.

The stairs were dark, but Cate used her phone's flashlight function and hurried up. She didn't have any time to waste. Her former headmaster was locking his office, and holding a large, heavy flashlight, which cast a warm glow around him.

"Hi, Dr. K," she called, slightly breathlessly.

"Catherine," he beamed. "What a delightful surprise. This is some storm. Hope we haven't lost power at home. Frederick was cooking a boeuf bourguignon." He pointed the flashlight toward her face, temporarily blinding her. "Is everything all right?"

She wanted to laugh. Nothing was all right. "I'm fine."

He lowered the flashlight and continued, "I heard a rumor today."

"Oh?"

"You might be leaving us prematurely?"

Obviously, the clinic receptionist wasted no time spreading the news. "That's right. I need to get back to Ottawa."

Dr. K took a step toward her. "Is everything all right?" he asked again.

She was tempted to throw her arms around him and blurt out her problems, but she was no longer a lost little girl, and he was no longer her unimpeachable, stalwart headmaster. "I've learned some things that make it impossible to stay here. Anya is not who I thought she was." She paused and met his eyes. "Canterbury is not what I thought it was."

Dr. K exhaled. "We tried our best, but sometimes I do wonder if our approach was the right one. I look at an organization like Rescue the Children—"

Cate tensed. She could not cope if it turned out that Dr. K was abetting the charity's cover-up.

"And I wonder if good intentions were enough. Perhaps our approach was unhelpful or problematic in its own way. I worry about that, but ultimately I do think we did the right thing. We helped a lot of people. It's like Jason's death. He died for a noble cause."

Cate stifled a bitter laugh. She loved Dr. K and respected his intelligence and kindness, but his brand of patronizing benevolence was rotten; Rescue the Children's crimes made that clear. Here was another foundational stone upon which she'd built her life: a belief in those childhood values. That was gone now too. Cate didn't want to talk to Dr. K about her existential crisis, however. "What did you say the other day with Frederick, when we were talking about the murders? About the gunshot wound. What was the quote?"

"It was Shakespeare—'Eyes, look your last! Arms, take your last embrace!'"

"Right, which play?"

"What play do you think it was?" Asking students questions until they worked out the problem for themselves was Dr. K's preferred method of instruction. Socratic. At their cozy tea tête-à-têtes, she found this old habit endearing; now she wanted to scream at him to spit it out. "I don't know."

"If I recall our syllabus correctly, you would have studied it in tenth-grade English. In fact, I remember there was quite a mania for the play back in the day—a film came out reinventing the bard for the youngsters. I personally don't think he needs to be gussied up like that, but I know it was very popular with your set."

"The play, Dr. K," she said more urgently. "What was it?"

"*Romeo and Juliet*, of course. It's in Romeo's final speech as he embraces Juliet for the last time."

She recalled the other quote she'd heard in the past weeks. "What about 'Violent delights have violent ends'?"

"*Romeo and Juliet* as well," Dr. K said with the pleasure of a proud teacher. "Friar Lawrence warning Romeo of the dangers of forbidden love."

It wasn't just Shakespeare that kept coming up in this case, but specifically *Romeo and Juliet*. "Their love was forbidden because two families hated each other," Cate said slowly. "The feud."

"Yes, indeed. The whole star-crossed-lovers thing. People have been swooning over the story for centuries. Excites the imagination. Completely unhealthy."

"What do you mean?"

Dr. K shrugged. "Keeping something like a relationship hidden closes the couple off to everyone else—friends and family no longer matter. Even the individual's sense of self disappears. Shakespeare understood that. By act two, scene six, our young heroes are obsessed with one another and isolated from the rest of the world. Tragedy is inevitable."

Cate frowned. That sounded a lot like what happened in abusive relationships. It was clear to her now that Geneviève was in a secret relationship, one that was likely abusive, or at least controlling. One her brother rescued her from. What's more, thanks to the song, Cate knew who Geneviève's "Romeo" was.

She left Dr. K and rushed through the driving rain to her vehicle. She needed to pick up the dog before the vet closed. She slammed the car door and listened to the water drumming against the roof. All this precipitation would be good for the water table. People's wells would get a top-up. She recalled what Joseph Ngoma had said: "Find that gun, and you'll find your killer." She'd fallen to her knees in Guy Montaigne's yard and Thierry had taken pleasure in hurting her as he pulled her to her feet. She started her engine. She knew exactly where the killer had hidden the gun that shot Marc Renaud and she was going to retrieve it.

CHAPTER 39

THE DOG WAS THRILLED TO SEE HER, EXCITEDLY LICKING CATE'S EAR AS she drove. The smart thing to do would be to head straight to the police station to explain her theory. Only she'd shredded her credibility with them last night and couldn't tolerate St. Onge's pity or Vachon's bombast. At this point, she doubted they'd even listen to her. Better to hand them irrefutable proof.

She pulled the car over to the side of the road by the wood near his house and peered through the rain. His truck wasn't in the driveway. He must be out somewhere. Perfect. If she did this right, she would retrieve the gun that killed Marc Renaud and have the evidence she needed to exonerate Kevin before the killer returned. She unrolled the window a bit to give the dog fresh air and then scratched his head. "I won't be long."

Hurrying across the yard, she took care not to stumble on the wet ground. She skirted the side of the house, which was in darkness. With no friendly porch light casting a welcoming glow, she navigated murky terrain. She hadn't paid much attention to the woods that stood at the edge of the property on her last visit, but now, in the slashing rain, her anxiety transformed the trees into sentinels, watching her every move—menacing and dangerous. It was risky to use her flashlight, the killer could come home at any moment and she didn't want to attract his attention. Nevertheless, she turned on her weighty metal flashlight and stared intently at the illuminated patch in front of her. There it was, just as she remembered: the well, with its lid still misaligned. She'd tripped over it when she and Kevin had interviewed the Montaigne cousins. She'd been so focused on Thierry's aggressive response to her fall, she hadn't wondered why the cover was askew in an otherwise neat and orderly yard. Now she knew why.

She dropped to her knees and tugged at the heavy covering. It was hard to get purchase on the slippery material in the rain, but she pulled it clear at last. Thunder rumbled overhead, and lightning streaked the sky. She aimed the flashlight into the hole and peered anxiously into the blackness. She couldn't see a thing. She swung the light back and forth, turning the beam to its highest power level. She stopped at one point, and waited for a lightning flash, hoping the illumination would allow her to see into the well. After a couple of attempts she had to concede the obvious: the well was too deep and too dark. She couldn't see anything.

She sat back on her haunches, contemplating her next steps. Her flashlight couldn't pierce the blackness, and even if it did, the gun might be submerged. She realized with resignation that she'd need to convince the cops of her theory and get them to do a proper search. Her fait accompli wasn't going to happen.

It was in that moment of acceptance that the hairs on the back of her neck rose. Some primitive part of her brain had alerted her: she was being watched. Her mouth dried up and her heart rate accelerated. Keeping low, she turned slowly. Her body buzzed with adrenaline. It was raining hard. A shadow unpeeled itself from the side of the house. The person was between her and the car. She recognized him through the rain. How long had he been there, watching? Waiting? Blood pounded in her ears. He meant to hurt her. She turned and sprinted toward the woods.

Something whistled past her ear: Guy Montaigne had fired an arrow. He was shooting at her. Trying to kill her. Terror gripped her and she gave in to instinct. She sprinted in a zigzag, desperate for the cover of the wood.

She needed thick tree trunks between herself and the next arrow. At the edge of the wood, she tripped on an exposed root and crashed to earth. The flashlight fell from her hands. Scrambling, she grabbed it and switched it off. It was all darkness now in the pounding rain.

At every moment she expected the bite of an arrowhead to pierce her back, stab her calf, or thrust into her neck. She couldn't stay where she was, so she forced herself to move quietly. Thick brush turned the small wood into a jungle. Thunder smashed overhead. The car wasn't far, just beyond the trees. Almost there. Blood hammered in her ears. Her breath came in jagged pants.

She turned back and lightning flashed, illuminating Guy. He stood by a tall elm, about fifty yards away. He loaded another arrow in his bow and aimed at her. She dove out of the way; the arrow whistled past her head. Once again, she scrambled amid wet, slimy dead leaves. Twigs and rocks cut into her palms. She kept low, not daring to stand.

She could hear him behind her, not bothering to be stealthy. "It is no use, Doctor. I know these woods as I know my own hand. Give up, little doe. The hunter has found you."

His words, calmly spoken, froze her for a moment. But she wasn't ready to die like an animal. She crawled through the brush, ignoring the sting in her hands and the bruising in her knees. A break in the trees, and she nearly gasped aloud. The road was ahead. She saw the outline of her car. Guy's truck was parked beside it. She paused, listening. He was silent again. She didn't dare look back. She would have to make a dash for it. She reached into her pocket to check she had the keys. They jingled ever so slightly. She froze. The forest listened.

A raucous laugh came from behind her and to her left. "Your car offers no escape. I will kill you before you reach the door."

Cate stifled a cry of rage. What was she going to do? She tried to muffle her breathing, sinking to the forest floor. She could feel his eyes on her, imagined him notching the arrow. She waited for one heartbeat and rolled from her spot. She heard the thunk of an arrow hitting the ground behind her.

The exceptional hunter was not finding her an easy target. She could reach the car while he was notching another arrow. She'd take her chances on escape. She stood tall and bolted through the woods.

It was about one hundred yards to the car. She beelined to it, not bothering to zigzag.

She heard a curse behind her and footsteps. He was chasing her. She increased her speed, her lungs bursting. She had almost reached the car when her shoulder detonated with pain. He'd hit her with an arrow. Her vision blurred, and she fell to her knees. She touched the wound, and her fingers returned sticky with blood.

Yet the pain was already easing. The arrow had only grazed her. She looked down. She was kneeling on it. With her unhurt hand, she yanked the dented shaft toward her. It snapped, and she shoved the broken-off arrowhead up her sleeve.

Guy jogged toward her, chuckling. "Romeo said, 'She'll not be hit with Cupid's arrow,' but Cupid wasn't as good a shot as me."

He was almost upon her. Her shoulder ached, but she ignored it. She turned and saw him brandishing a large hunting knife with a serrated edge. "You see," he continued, "I always get my quarry."

Cate fought back dizziness and turned to the car. A long snout pressed up against the window. Two large ears were on the alert. She punched her key fob; the car beeped and unlocked.

"Don't you get it, bitch. It's over. Stop." Guy's voice was angry.

Cate ignored him and rose to her feet, stumbling the final few steps to the car.

"Arrêt, espèce de salope." He grabbed her left arm, yanking her around.

Her shoulder exploded in pain. Her vision blurred. She reached out with her right hand, her fingers slipping on the door handle. Her last act before passing out was to heave the car door open.

CHAPTER 40

CATE CAME TO A MOMENT LATER, HER HEAD PRESSING PAINFULLY against the wet road. She heard grunts and shrieks of pain. She pushed herself into a sitting position.

The dog was out of the car. It must have tripped Guy and now had his leg in its powerful jaws. Guy kicked savagely, but the dog evaded the blows and tore into his jeans, biting his calf. Heartened by the dog's defense, Cate leaped up, grabbing her heavy flashlight. Guy raised his knife to plunge it into the animal. She lunged toward him, smashing his hand with the flashlight. He shrieked in pain and dropped the knife but kept kicking at the dog. The index finger on his left hand bent at an odd angle from where she'd brought the flashlight down.

Cate smashed the flashlight down again, targeting his temple, a blow she hoped would knock him out. Her aim was off, and it landed on the side of his head. He grunted in shock, and his thrashing subsided.

Cate picked up the knife and kicked the arrows away. The dog's front paws were on Guy's chest, and the animal snarled as it bit at the hunter's neck and arms. Cate saw the white flash of bone and crimson blood when Guy brought his injured hand up to protect his face. The dog's bites deepened as Guy weakened.

She hesitated. She'd broken the man's finger and hopefully concussed him, but he was big and strong. If she pulled the dog off, could Guy resume his attack? Could he run away? But if she did nothing, the dog might kill him. "It's OK, boy," she said in a shaky voice. "Easy." The dog continued to snarl and bite. "Stop, now," she said in a louder, more commanding voice.

The dog eased up, his growls continuing. Cate grabbed his collar. Guy lay unmoving in the dirt, low moans the only evidence he was still alive. Her shoulder ached but the adrenaline must have been dulling the pain. In the relative quiet, Cate realized the rain had stopped. The storm eased. Maybe her cell reception was back. She checked her phone but had no bars.

She patted the dog's enormous head. "Good boy." Guy's arm and chest were bleeding heavily. His right hand was covered in deep wounds. The skin was torn away from his wrist, and she could see tendons. His jeans were ripped, and an angry bite marked the tender flesh of his upper thigh. He moved his torso stiffly, and she wondered if there were more injuries there. He looked pale and was breathing rapidly. Tears of pain trickled from his eyes. Cate stifled her compassion, remembering this man had been hunting her only moments earlier.

Guy groaned softly and sat up with an effort. He looked at her with venom. "You fucking, fucking bitch," he said. "I'm going to kill you."

She backed away. He tried to stand but collapsed into a slumped position. She should get into her car and drive to the police station, but she couldn't leave an injured man alone. Her shoulder ached, and she drew a shaky breath. That's when she heard a deep voice behind her, speaking in French.

"What the hell is happening here?"

She whipped around, confronted by Thierry Montaigne pointing a shotgun at her chest.

She saw the scene through his eyes: Cate covered in scratches, hemorrhaging from her shoulder, the dog poised at her side. Guy slumped in the mud, bleeding and weak.

"Thierry, thank Christ," Guy said in a frail voice. "Shoot the bitch."

Thierry hesitated.

"No," Cate shouted back in French. "Your cousin tried to kill me."

"Guy? Is this true?"

"Bullshit," Guy muttered.

"I swear it's true," Cate said, making eye contact with Thierry. She could see his dark eyes struggling to understand the scene.

"Don't listen to her," Guy snapped at Thierry. "Shoot her, and shoot that motherfucking dog. I'll explain everything."

Thierry pointed the gun at Cate. "Drop the knife."

She'd forgotten she was holding it; she threw the weapon toward the wood, far away from both men. "He murdered Marc Renaud and Bethany Farnham."

Guy laughed. "Aren't you glad I killed that fucker, T? You hated him. Remember what the Renauds have done to us?"

Thierry's eyes darkened at the mention of Marc's last name.

"Bethany Farnham didn't deserve to die," Cate said.

"She was a stuck-up bitch," Guy snarled. He groaned and shifted position. He was alarmingly pale, and sweat gleamed on his brow. He might be going into shock.

The dog growled, and her hand tightened on his collar. She didn't dare set him loose; Thierry would shoot him.

Guy cleared his throat. "You've got to get rid of the doc, T. She knows too much. I'll help you. We can throw her body into the Delvaigne Ravine. They'll never find it."

Thierry hesitated.

"It's me or this bitch, T," Guy continued, his voice rising. "Go on. She's got no family, no friends. No one will miss her."

Thierry raised the gun and aimed at Cate.

"Wait," she shouted. "Do you know why he shot Marc? It wasn't because of your family feud. It wasn't to avenge your father or for the Montaignes' honor. He did it because he was having an affair with Marc's sister."

Thierry laughed. "Now I know you're lying. Guy wouldn't fuck one of those cockroaches."

"It's true," she insisted. "He was in love with a Renaud. He betrayed you."

"What?" Thierry asked, turning to Guy.

"She's a liar," Guy snapped. "Shoot her."

"It's true," Cate said again. If Thierry let his guard down, she could urge the dog to attack and then grab the gun. They'd have a fighting chance. She revealed what she had learned: "He thought he was Romeo, and she was Juliet."

"Jesus, Guy. Are you still hung up on that bullshit?" Thierry turned to Cate, more aggrieved family member than vengeful killer. "He's been obsessed with that tapette movie ever since he got mono in grade ten. He was stuck in bed for weeks, and that was his only DVD. *Romeo + Juliet*—a fucking Shakespeare romance." Thierry's voice dripped with scorn. "That's where he learned his English, for fuck's sake."

Guy raised his head, the most energized he'd been since receiving the blow to the skull. "You never understood. It's not a sappy love story. It's warfare. Guns. Fighting. It's hard-core."

That was not Cate's recollection, but teenage Guy focused on the film's gangland violence rather than the sweep of Paul Rudd's bangs.

Thierry was also dubious of the film's street cred. "Yeah, it was such a metal movie you bought a doorbell off Amazon that played that gay song."

Thierry was more focused on teasing his cousin than murdering her. Cate decided to capitalize on that. "That's how I figured it out," she said. The words came easily, adrenaline sharpening her French skills. "He quoted the play and used the word *villain* to describe Marc. He flirted with Vivienne at the Bucket by calling her "Juliet." It was only when I finally identified that doorbell tune—"Little Star" from the movie soundtrack—that I realized how much Guy loved *Romeo + Juliet*. He was primed to fall for Geneviève—a gorgeous blonde, the daughter of the rival, forbidden family. They were star-crossed lovers."

"What the fuck?" Theirry glared at his cousin.

She had his attention, so she continued. "It started last winter at the hospital when he was the orderly assigned to assist with Geneviève's concussion."

"I told them I didn't want to work with her," Guy protested. "I said no."

"But the hospital wouldn't let your feud interfere with the provision of medical care, would they? You had to talk to her and then you fell for her."

"That's not true," Guy said, but his voice carried less conviction.

"I saw her patient records. You were her orderly."

"She's not like the other Renauds." Guy turned to Thierry. "You should have seen her lying in that hospital bed. She was a perfect, golden-haired angel."

"Goddamn it!" Thierry was now facing Guy.

Cate's grip tightened on the dog's collar. This was an opportunity, but the big man kept his finger on the shotgun's trigger. She didn't want to make her move yet.

"An angel? What the hell are you talking about?"

Guy's head drooped, and his breathing quickened. He spoke in a low mumble. "She leaned on me as I walked her up the hallway. She smelled so good. 'My only love sprung from my only hate.'" Guy's face softened, and he looked almost gentle.

"You were fucking Geneviève Renaud?" Thierry's voice held anger and bewilderment.

The shotgun lowered farther. Thierry was fixated on his cousin. Cate wanted to keep it that way. "It must have been exciting when you two started dating."

"It was perfect." Guy's face lost the bemused look, and his eyes darkened. "Most of the time." He looked around wildly, as if plagued by memories. Agitation and anxiety could be symptoms of shock. "Sure, I got frustrated when she didn't listen to me, jealous when other men talked to her, but that's just love," he scowled. "She knew what she needed to do to keep me calm, but sometimes she'd bug me on purpose. It wasn't my fault when I hit her."

There it was. Cate recalled Guy's expression when he'd caught her rubbing her arm after Thierry had grabbed her. At the time she took it for sympathy, but now she understood it as a man taking pleasure in a woman's pain.

Guy shifted again, wincing. "We couldn't tell anyone because of our families. It was perfect. I had Gen all to myself. She was my little secret. Mine alone."

Cate recoiled. It was just as Dr. K had said, Shakespeare's tale of forbidden love as romantic cover for abuse.

"You dumb shit," Thierry said. "You've wrecked your life over some Renaud whore."

"I had to kill Marc," Guy protested. "He moved into Gen's house, and we couldn't stay there anymore. Marc figured out we were dating. He told Gen I was dangerous. The villain convinced Geneviève to break up with me, but I went there one night with my gun. Told Gen I'd kill her if she tried to leave, and promised Marc a bullet if he interfered. I told them that no matter where she hid, I would hunt her down. That smartened her up. For a few weeks, she was nice to me. Very nice."

Guy smiled at the memory, and Cate's stomach curdled. That must have been when Marc talked to Madge and started desperately looking for the gold. Given how the authorities had failed his mother, she could understand why Marc felt Geneviève had to run and why they needed money to fund a foolproof escape.

"Then Geneviève disappeared. Marc, that cocksucker, stole her away. Her car was in her driveway and her phone was at her mother's. I couldn't track her. She'd vanished."

"So you killed Marc," Thierry said, as if that was the next logical step.

The matter-of-factness of his statement made Cate realize that the bigger man saw nothing wrong with killing a Renaud, only disagreeing with Guy's motive.

Guy smiled. "You know it. We've talked about putting a bullet in Marc since the fight at the Thirsty Bucket. Cocky asshole. It was good to end him. A perfect shot."

"You chose the eye on purpose," Cate interjected. She wanted to remind Thierry of the reason for the killing. " 'Eyes, look your last! Arms, take your last embrace!' "

Guy smiled smugly, but Thierry looked annoyed. "Jesus Christ, you are a fucking idiot. You've killed two people because of some stupid movie and a hard-on for a goddamn Renaud."

Guy clenched his fist. "That Farnham bitch was an honest mistake. I saw her car in Geneviève's driveway and was sure it belonged to some new boyfriend. The cops confiscated my rifles, but Old Man Douglass was always bragging about his revolver. I took it and walked into Gen's kitchen. She was standing with her back to me. I aimed, and when Bethany turned, it was too late. I had to fire."

"You murdered Bethany Farnham by accident," Cate said. Her phone vibrated in her pocket, and her heart leapt. It was a text message, which meant cell reception was back.

Guy shrugged. "Bitch shouldn't have been in Gen's house."

"You fucking, fucking moron," Thierry spoke with such scorn that Cate almost felt sorry for Guy.

"Did you see my shot, though?" Guy said eagerly. "Another perfect one. Straight through the eye."

Cate's brief pity evaporated. "After you killed Bethany, you framed Kevin by planting Mr. Douglass's firearm in his truck."

Guy waved his hand in assent.

"Did you wear gloves when you handled the weapon?" his cousin asked.

Cate's heart sank. Thierry was checking to see if Guy could really get away with the murders. If that was the case, it meant silencing her. She needed to do something fast.

Guy nodded and looked queasy at the movement. "Course I did," he said weakly. "I'm not an idiot."

Cate's mouth dried at Thierry's next question to his cousin.

"Are you strong enough to move the body? I can't lug her and the dog to the ravine without help."

Thierry was going to kill her. It was now or never. Summoning her strength and her nerve, she launched herself at the upright man, piling into his side. He fell to the ground with a surprised "oof." She fell with him. Instantly, he grabbed her head, pulling an arm back to punch her. With a terrifying growl the dog was upon them, biting at Thierry's hands and arm; Thierry howled in pain. His grip on Cate slackened and he was distracted by the animal, who was worrying his forearm. With an oath, he released Cate completely and scrambled for the shotgun. Before she could react, Thierry smashed the butt down on the dog's head. The animal whimpered and went still.

A red blur of rage and fear colored Cate's vision, and she leapt up, throwing herself again at Thierry and grabbing him by the arm the dog had attacked. He grunted and dropped the gun. She picked it up and drove the butt into his temple, this time meeting her target with a resounding crack. Thierry fell back to the earth and didn't move. Cate turned to the dog, but before she could see how badly he was wounded, she was tackled.

Guy had lumbered over and thrown himself at her. His two hands wrapped around her throat. She couldn't breathe. She clawed at his face. He grunted as her nails dug into his cheek but tightened his grip. For a moment she was back at that attack from July. Everything went black but she fought off the panic. Something sharp poked her wrist. The arrowhead she'd stuck up her sleeve. She shook it loose. It felt hard and lethal in her hand. Without hesitation she drove it into Guy's eye. He cursed, clawed at his skull, and fell to the ground. Cate didn't think she had thrust the arrow deep enough to kill him. He was unmoving and she hoped he was only in shock. She picked up the shotgun and pointed it at Thierry, who was on his hands and knees, throwing up. "Sit the fuck down," she barked. He wobbled back on his haunches and keeled over. She punched 911 into her phone. After summoning the police, she rushed to the dog.

Still holding the gun, she sank to her knees and stroked his head. "Hey, hey, are you OK?"

His ears twitched, and his eyes fluttered closed.

CHAPTER 41

CATE STEPPED OUTSIDE THE EMERGENCY VET SERVICE IN SHERBROOKE and lit up a smoke. The rain had stopped, but the air was damp and cold. The leashed dog leaned against her. He was still woozy from the head injury but was "tiguidou" according to the cheery doctor, which took the stressed Cate a moment to realize meant "all good."

"Hey, Dr. Spencer."

Cate looked up, surprised to see Constable St. Onge emerge from a squad car. "What are you doing here?"

"I figured you were coming to this one. It's the only twenty-four-hour vet in the region. How's the dog?"

"He's going to be all right," Cate said and surprised herself and St. Onge by bursting into tears.

"It's OK." The officer pulled her into a hug. Cate relaxed into the embrace, crying for what had happened that night and for the relief she had felt when the vet had said that the dog was fine.

Only minutes after Cate made her call, Constables St. Onge and Douglass raced up to Guy Montaigne's house, looking stunned by the scene before them. Cate handed over the shotgun, gave a statement, and then insisted on getting the dog to a vet.

"Did you get Guy and Thierry to the hospital?" Cate asked when her tears subsided.

"Yup. Thierry's got a bad concussion, a broken finger, and major lacerations on both hands. Guy's got some damage from the dog but the doctors were mostly concerned about the arrow a goddamn avenging Amazon jammed into his eye." She met Cate's eye and grinned.

Cate smiled in return. "It was kind of badass, wasn't it?"

"As Dougie said, those are two of the toughest sons of bitches in Pekeda Township, and you took them both down. Pretty impressive."

Cate stood a little straighter. She was proud of herself. When she'd been attacked this past summer, she wasn't able to fight back. Now she knew what she was capable of. "I assume they're both under arrest?"

"Double homicide and attempted murder for Guy. We fished the gun out of his well, no problem. Dougie's making sure he's also charged with stealing his grandpa's pistol."

Cate's shoulders unknotted. "What about Thierry?"

"We're still figuring out what to charge him with, but definitely assault and attempted kidnapping."

The dog tugged at his leash, and Cate winced at the pain in her shoulder.

"Hey, you should get that looked at," St. Onge said with concern.

"It's only a flesh wound. I'll clean it when I get home."

St. Onge shook her head. "You might be *the* toughest son of a bitch in Pekeda Township."

Cate laughed. "Thanks."

"I don't think Detective Inspector Vachon will be pleased at how this rolled out, though."

Cate's heart sank. She may have cracked the case, but she'd destroyed his pet theory. That wouldn't help her reinstatement.

"I know it doesn't have the same weight, but Dougie and I will write you letters."

Two recommendations from junior officers at a local force probably wouldn't mean much, but Cate was touched by the offer. "That would be great." She paused. "Only, can you make sure to proofread Constable Douglass's? I'm not confident about his spelling skills."

St. Onge smiled. "You're telling me."

Cate and the dog got into the car, and she unrolled the window, calling out to St. Onge, "You know, we were both wrong. These murders were never about the gold."

The officer smiled. "I guess 'My Mary' will stay asleep wherever she's lying."

Cate grinned and started the engine. She didn't drive away, however; instead, she pulled out her phone and googled the poem, lingering on those last two lines: "My Mary's asleep by thy murmuring stream, / Flow gently, sweet Afton, disturb not her dream." Dreams. Sleep. Madge Taylor slept with a gold bar under her pillow for seventy years. Cate recalled the map Reggie copied of the MacGregor property. Mary and her dream.

She knew where the gold was buried.

CATE PLUNGED THE SHOVEL INTO THE GROUND ONCE AGAIN, LIFTING THE dirt, heavy with the previous night's rain, and placing it behind her. Her wounded shoulder ached, but the pain meds were keeping it manageable. Despite the pain, there was something cathartic about the digging. The hole was about a foot wide and almost two feet deep already.

She was tired, but the morning air was fresh after the storm and the sunshine was bright but not too warm. At first the dog was fascinated by her actions, sniffing around the hole, excitedly smelling each shovelful. He'd lost interest about twenty minutes in, and now he looked at her with his big, liquid brown eyes, obviously dismayed by her folly.

MacGregor shared that opinion. Initially he'd narrated the quality and depth of her foolishness, but now, sitting in his camp chair, he quietly whiled away the minutes by scratching the dog's ears.

Sweat streamed down her forehead. She wished she had brought water. A few more inches, she decided, and she'd concede that her hunch was wrong. She had believed she'd cracked the secret of the poem. Despite what everyone thought, references to the "murmuring stream" were not relevant.

Instead, it was the poem's final words that offered the clue: "disturb not her dream." Donald buried the gold where one would dream.

The original homestead cabin was a ruin even during the Outlaw's lifetime. It had a dirt floor that the whole family had slept on. Based on the position of the fireplace and MacGregor's reluctant help, Cate made an educated guess about where those original settlers would have slept and started digging at the spot where their heads would have lain. Now it appeared she was wrong.

She wiped the sweat from her brow and turned to MacGregor. "You were right. This was a fail—"

She stopped. The farmer was staring behind her, his hand clenched around the dog's collar. Cate turned.

A black bear, the biggest she had ever seen, was sitting on its haunches at the edge of the orchard. He was about ten meters away. Cate kept her breathing steady.

The animal watched them for a moment and then stood and stretched to its full height. The bear met her gaze. Something in its eyes—a hint of sadness—made her breath catch in her throat. He held her stare for another moment and then turned and ambled away.

"Holy cow," she breathed a few seconds later.

MacGregor grinned and kept a firm hand on the dog's collar. "Told you there were black bears in these parts."

Cate returned to the hole. The bear had reenergized her, and she plunged the shovel into the ground. A tiny clink, metal scraping metal. She shoveled carefully in order not to damage whatever was down there. MacGregor leaned forward. She uncovered the corner of a metal box. Quickly relocating the center of her hole, she dug with vigor. After a little more effort, she uncovered a strongbox, rusty but still in good shape. It was very heavy, and she and MacGregor worked together to pull it out. They hauled it onto the grass beside the dog. He sniffed it once and wandered away.

The lock was rusted closed, and it took some serious bashing before they were able to open it. They were greeted by thirty bars, identical to the one Madge owned, lined up like the golden treasure from a fairy tale.

CHAPTER 42

CATE DROVE WEST. THE EASTERN TOWNSHIPS WAS FAR BEHIND HER, AND ahead lay her future. She squinted through the glare of the setting sun. She was driving toward Ottawa's downtown core now, and though it was impossible, she thought she could spot, just to the north, the Gothic outline of the parliament buildings.

Geneviève Renaud had been found. Her supposed addiction had been a cover, allowing her brother to hide her away at the family's isolated fishing camp in the Gaspé. Marc had concocted the plan after his friend Renata at the feedstore had had to go to rehab and was suddenly incommunicado. His idea was for Geneviève to lie low while he got some money together and then he'd return to fetch her. She had no TV, no phone, and no way to communicate with the outside world. When Marc didn't turn up after two weeks, she'd walked into town and learned the truth. Her testimony sealed Guy Montaigne's fate.

The gold was genuine. Cate thought of all the angst and strife that had swirled around this mythic treasure. It had sparked the Montaigne–Renaud feud that a century later resulted in two deaths. MacGregor had tried to insist she take the gold, but she refused. Instead, she told him to donate her half to the Eastern Townships Women's Shelter. In a strange way, Marc Renaud would continue to protect women, even in death.

Cate thought of Jason. He had been trying to help a friend. He'd made choices she wouldn't have made and done things she wished she could yell at him over, but she could forgive him. Whether the board of governors at Canterbury Day and Boarding School would be as forgiving of Anya Patel and her ill-advised alignment with a discredited charity was less certain.

Beside Cate on the passenger seat were three glowing letters of recommendation to the Ontario College of Coroners. Constable Douglass wrote a paragraph about how great the "doc" had been. St. Onge penned three pages, single-spaced, documenting precisely where Cate was of assistance in resolving the murders of Marc Renaud and Bethany Farnham.

The third, and the one that would carry the most weight with the College, indicated that Dr. Cate Spencer was instrumental in assisting with a complex drug investigation. It was signed Daniel Lemieux—a.k.a. assistant gym teacher Yannick Poitou—Sûreté du Québec Guns and Gangs Provincial Team. It had been her one condition for covering up Reggie's lies.

Cate glanced in the rearview mirror and saw the dog's enormous face, panting from the back seat.

"Almost home, boy."

He cocked his head.

"Now, what are we going to name you?"

THE END

AUTHOR'S NOTE

PEKEDA TOWNSHIP IS AN INVENTION, BUT ITS ETHOS—THE RURAL JOY of Québec's Eastern Townships—is real, as is the Megantic Outlaw. I grew up hearing stories of the Outlaw, and Bernard Epps's book *The Outlaw of Megantic* was both a childhood staple and an invaluable research tool for this novel.

While Donald Morrison, aka the Megantic Outlaw, was indeed a real person and the facts of his life as I represent them here are truthful, his "lost gold" is entirely my own creation.

ACKNOWLEDGMENTS

THANK YOU TO THE TEAM AT TURNER PUBLISHING FOR THEIR SUPPORT. Thanks especially to Ryan Smernoff, Makala Marsee, and Cindy Cavato for all their help sustaining my writing and championing my books. Thanks to Kathy Haake for her editing.

As always, I want to acknowledge the world's best critique group—Alette Willis, Chris Crowder, and Wayne Ng—who knocked *Honor the Dead* into shape.

Thank you to my wonderful and generous beta readers, Phoebe Rowe and Megan Butcher. You offered excellent insights, and this book is stronger because of you. Thanks to Courtney, who provided some beachside insight into hunting, guns, and bullets.

Thanks to the community of supportive people and bookstores out there who encourage and promote writers. Thanks especially to Danny and Lucy at Brome Lake Books, Michael at Perfect Books, and Cole and Stephen at The Spaniel's Tale.

Thanks to Élizabeth Mongrain for her help with the French cursing—*merci, tabarnak!* Thanks to the rest of the ladies—Lisa, Christine, Johanna, Laura, and Dara—for some wonderful evenings on my porch. Huge thanks to Amy, Meghan, Serena, and Christa for your humor, support, and hospitality. Thanks to Kathryn and Sara for your friendship, help, and the endless text chain.

Thanks to my family: my mother, who is so proud; Tina, who is my biggest cheerleader; Susie, who has all that medical know-how; Mark, who is always supportive; and Emily, whose enthusiasm and brilliant insights make her my favorite reader. Thanks, as well, to my wider family of Horralls and their partners for all the encouragement—especially Cait, who buys so many copies of my books!

Thanks to Daffodil, who though not the "strong, silent type" like the dog in this book, was still the inspiration for a true and loyal puppy.

Finally, thanks to Andrew and Vi for literally everything.

ABOUT THE AUTHOR

AMY TECTOR WAS BORN AND RAISED IN THE ROLLING HILLS OF QUEBEC'S Eastern Townships. She has worked in archives for the past twenty years and has found some pretty amazing things, including lost letters, mysterious notes, and even a whale's ear. Amy spent many years as an expat, living in Brussels and in The Hague, where she worked for the International Criminal Tribunal for War Crimes in Yugoslavia. She lives in Ottawa, Canada, with her daughter, dog, and husband.

CREDIT: MEGHAN HALL